THE
SECRET
PHOTOGRAPH

BOOKS BY SIOBHAN CURHAM

An American in Paris

Beyond This Broken Sky

The Paris Network

The Secret Keeper

The Storyteller of Auschwitz

The Scene Stealers

Frankie Says Relapse

Sweet FA

NON-FICTION

Something More: A Spiritual Misfit's Search for Meaning

Dare to Write a Novel

Dare to Dream

Antenatal & Postnatal Depression

SIOBHAN CURHAM

THE
SECRET
PHOTOGRAPH

bookouture

Published by Bookouture in 2023

An imprint of Storyfire Ltd.
Carmelite House
50 Victoria Embankment
London EC4Y 0DZ

www.bookouture.com

ISBN: 978-1-83790-771-7
eBook ISBN: 978-1-83790-770-0

PROLOGUE

Some people say that, when faced with their death, their whole life flashes before their eyes. All of their highs and lows, achievements and regrets, compressed into a mental kaleidoscope of tumbling images. But as I face the threat of imminent death I only see one memory – myself at the age of ten, vowing that I should never, under any circumstances become a parent. As the man's footsteps pound across the floor above, I glance at Joseph's tiny form on the makeshift bed in the corner of the cellar. Mercifully he is asleep and oblivious to the horror unfolding upstairs, although who knows what nightmares could be plaguing his dreams. How wrong I had been to not want children. Since saving him that day on the street the Gestapo tore him from his mother, he has inspired in me a kind of love I didn't know existed. And it's that love I feel coursing through me now, hot and fierce as lava, as I slowly, carefully, take the pistol from my bag and release the safety catch.

Joseph sighs and the blankets rustle as he stirs, causing me to freeze. *Please don't wake up!* I silently implore. If he calls out for me now he could have us both killed. Thankfully, his breathing settles and I tiptoe over to the stone steps leading up to the kitchen. Leading up to the man who could be there to kill me.

All has gone quiet in the kitchen above and for a fleeting moment I dare to hope that he's gone. But I can't risk Joseph's life on a hope, especially now we've come so far, and his safety is within touching distance. I need to know for sure. I reach the top of the steps and take a breath before nudging the kitchen door. It opens with a deafening creak. Please, please, let the man be gone. I push the door open further and step into the moonlit room. My heart plummets. I'm staring straight into the barrel of a gun.

1

JULY 1942, PARIS

I once heard it said that there comes a point in every relationship when the thing that most attracted you to your significant other, the thing that had your heart aflutter and your knees weak, becomes the very thing that most repels you. It's a fascinating phenomenon really, when you stop to think about it. And even more fascinating in the case of my husband and I was that we both appeared to reach that point at exactly the same time. It was shortly after seven in the morning on Thursday 16 July 1942 – an oppressively humid day that would go on to change the course of my life forever. Of course, I didn't know that at the time. All I knew right then was that I hated my pig of a husband with a vengeance.

'Why do you always have to be so damned headstrong?' he yelled at me from the bedroom doorway.

'Why do you always have to be so controlling,' I spat back through a mouthful of hairpins, scowling at his reflection in the dressing-table mirror.

Of course, I hadn't seen his behaviour as controlling when I'd first fallen for him. I'd seen his need to manoeuvre the people in his life like chess pieces on a board as masterful, all part of the complex package that made up the celebrated French portrait artist Pierre Lavigne. Back then I'd enjoyed the way we sparked off each other and I'd gladly risen to the challenge of loving him. But the sparks between us had been snuffed out long ago by a creeping blend of regret and disappointment.

I pinned my hair into a chignon and fanned my flushed face with a copy of *Vogue Paris*. It was the last edition to have been published before the Germans began their occupation and stripped the city of its joy and panache. Maybe the Nazi noose tightening around the neck of Paris had hastened the demise of our marriage. Or maybe Pierre had always been an infernal skunk and it had taken six years for the scales to fall from my eyes.

'You can mock all you like, but I'm doing this job,' I repeated for the third time in as many minutes. 'Being asked to shoot for a cosmetics company the size of Elizabeth Arden is an amazing opportunity, and Lord knows there's few of those around these days.'

I went over to the closet and took my trusty Kodak Six-20 and some rolls of film from the shelf.

Pierre leaned against the door frame and a stark flash of his pale belly appeared through a gap in his robe. Unlike the majority of Parisians, the punitive rationing imposed by the Germans hadn't affected his waistline. But when you were Pierre Lavigne you had the best black-market contacts, naturally.

'I don't understand why you have to fool around at being a photographer,' he said with a laboured sigh. 'You're much more suited to being a model.' His gaze flitted to the huge portrait of me on the wall opposite the bed. He'd painted it the week after we first met, when I was fresh off the boat from New York and giddy with excitement at being free to start over again.

I used to think it symbolic that I'd met Pierre within hours of reinventing myself as Clarisse Alarie. I saw it as a sign that he was going to be a key figure in my new life, so when he'd invited me to sit for him, I'd jumped at the opportunity. I figured that sitting for an artist as revered as Pierre Lavigne would be the perfect introduction to French society. And besides, I'd already done a fair amount of modelling in the States; I was used to men looking at my body as if it were a piece of clay to be moulded to fit their gaze. When Pierre had asked me to unbutton my dress, and then lose it altogether, I'd ignored the way my stomach clenched. Being painted naked wasn't salacious, I'd told myself. It was art. And anyway, hadn't I chosen Alarie as my new surname because it meant 'all powerful'? What could be more powerful than a woman confident with her body, at ease in her own skin?

'I'm not fooling around, I've been taking photographs since I was thirteen,' I replied through gritted teeth.

'Ah yes, your little street photographs,' Pierre sneered. 'But that's just a hobby. Photography isn't your calling the way painting is mine. It isn't your raison d'être.'

I tried to ignore the way his putdowns stung, but self-doubt began nipping at the corners of my mind. Was he right? Was my photography no more than a frivolous hobby? Was I more suited to being a human mannequin, pulled and coaxed into various poses, than depicting the world through my lens? Pierre was wrong about photography not being my reason to live, though. He knew precious little about my former life. No one in France did. As soon as I'd got there I'd hidden that life away, like a dress that no longer fits, stuffed into the back of a closet. Pierre didn't know how photography had saved me, how that first humble viewfinder of mine had brought me back from the brink and helped me make sense of the world again.

'I need to go,' I said, hoisting my bag over my shoulder and approaching the door.

For a moment, I thought he wasn't going to let me pass. The

bald patch on his head that he tried and failed to cover with wisps of his grey hair glimmered with sweat and the whites of his eyes were stained pink from last night's wine. A wave of revulsion passed through me.

'Don't forget your papers,' he said, breathing hot fumes of stale garlic into my face. 'Rumour is, more round-ups are coming. I heard that several American women were arrested yesterday.'

My pulse quickened. 'Heard from whom?'

'One of my gendarme friends.'

How he could still be friends with any of our traitorous police was beyond me and did nothing to ease my growing contempt.

'Yes, but according to my papers I'm French,' I replied.

'Hmm, let's just hope no one realises they're forged.' He finally stepped aside, a smug smile on his thin lips.

Was he threatening me? Surely his obsessive need for control wouldn't lead him to denounce his own wife. I felt sick at the thought but was determined not to show that he'd rattled me.

'I'll see you later,' I said, heading for the door.

Outside on the street, the heat was even more oppressive and the air as thick as gruel. I wasn't sure if it was my altercation with Pierre, but I felt a real sense of foreboding as I headed for the Metro. Trying to allay my fears, I focused on the job ahead.

To help address the severe shortage of silk stockings in Paris, which now cost 300 francs apiece on the black market, Elizabeth Arden had created an iodine-based dye for women to paint on their legs instead. The dye came in three shades – flesh, gilded flesh and tanned flesh – and they'd asked me to do the shoot for their advertising campaign.

And they wouldn't have asked you if they didn't think you were a talented photographer, I reassured myself to try to counteract Pierre's jibes.

As I approached the station, I saw a queue snaking down the road. A group of Gestapo in plain clothes were gathered at the entrance, checking people's papers. My heart skipped a beat. I'd had my papers checked many times in the two years since the Germans had occupied France and they'd never aroused any suspicion. Pierre wasn't the only one with great contacts in the city; I happened to know one of the best counterfeiters on the Left Bank. I'd also been fluent in French long before moving to Paris and since living here I'd honed my accent to a T, removing all trace of my native New York twang, but Pierre's parting shot had unnerved me.

Deciding to walk to the Arden salon instead, I cut down a side street. What happened next seemed to take place in slow motion.

The first thing I noticed was a bus parked midway down the road and a group of police officers huddled deep in conversation beside it. One of them pointed to a house and they marched en masse to the door. Our police had long since become puppets for the Germans and, as such, they were now a sight to be wary of, so I hung back, pretending to look for something in my bag. A loud bang caused me to jump, and I looked up to see one of the officers hammering on the door.

'Open up!' he yelled. 'Open up now!'

My throat tightened. Had Pierre been right? Was another round-up taking place?

Since spring, round-ups of foreign Jews living in France had become increasingly frequent.

A window slid open on the second floor of the building next door to the house and an elderly man leaned out.

'Who are you looking for?' he called down to the police.

'The Kramer family,' one of them shouted back, while the others continued hammering away. 'We understand they are Jewish.'

'They are indeed,' the man replied with such obvious glee I

instantly felt my hackles rise. To my mind, people like him, so weak-willed and quick to hate for hate's sake, were the lowest of the low.

'Open up!' the policeman called again.

I prayed that the Kramer family weren't home, but to my horror the door creaked open and a girl of about twelve poked her head out.

The policeman asked her something and she nodded and he grabbed her arm and pulled her out onto the street.

'No!' someone screamed from inside the house. The cry was so piercing, it seemed to slice right through me.

The next-door neighbour leaned further from his window, trying to get a better view.

A woman came flying out of the house and flung herself at the policeman, kneeling on the ground beside him and throwing her arms round his legs. 'Please don't take her, she's just a child,' she cried. 'Take me. I beg of you. Just take me.'

I held my breath. So far, government policy regarding the round-ups had been to leave any children behind, but the policeman kicked out his leg, trying to shake the woman off as if she was something unsavoury he'd trodden in.

'You both have to come with us,' he snapped.

Another head appeared beside that of the gawking neighbour. A woman, his wife probably, come to watch the show.

Instinctively, my hand felt for the hard leather body of the camera in my bag. When I'd first arrived in Paris, I'd spent countless hours roaming the streets with my trusty Six-20, capturing candid moments that might otherwise go unnoticed. Snapshots of life in all its messy glory, moments of wonder and beauty. But ever since the Germans had arrived, it had become increasingly hard to find moments of wonder and beauty on the streets of Paris. All there seemed to be these days were moments of horror and I'd never felt inclined to photograph them – until now. There was something so poignant about this scene and how it encapsulated both the best and worst of humanity, our capacity to love and to hate, I felt the strongest urge to capture it.

I took the camera from my bag, but in my haste to open it, my fingers kept slipping on the catch.

The policeman was still shaking his leg, but the woman clung on. Another couple of officers took the girl from him and started frogmarching her towards the bus. She had short hair and large brown eyes, and one of those hideous yellow stars with the word JUIF emblazoned upon it was pinned to her chest. The stars had been introduced last month and every Jewish person over the age of six had been ordered to wear one. It sickened me to my stomach that people should be labelled in this way, and I'd made a point of offering a smile of solidarity to everyone I'd seen wearing one.

'Lillie!' the woman screamed after the girl. 'Lillie!'

'Maman!' the girl cried, looking back at her mother over her shoulder.

One of the officers standing by the mother raised his truncheon and brought it swinging into her head with a sickening crack. She collapsed onto the pavement, blood trickling from her temple.

'No!' I gasped, but fear kept me rooted to the spot. If I tried to intervene I'd only be arrested. But there was something I could do. I fumbled again with the catch on the camera and this time it accordioned open. I quickly raised the viewfinder, lined up the shot and pressed the shutter release. At exactly that moment, the girl turned and our eyes locked. I shoved the still open camera back in my bag, but it was too late, I saw the flicker of shock on her face. Then she glanced up at the neighbours hanging out of the window.

I'm not like them, I wanted to cry. *I'm not getting a morbid pleasure from your pain.* I felt as if I was witnessing a crime and needed to record the evidence.

'Maman!' the girl cried, her voice as shrill as a wounded animal, then she looked back at me. Her face was pale and her eyes gleaming with tears. I wanted to run to her, wrench her from the policemen's grasp. But there were too many of them, and, as an American in Paris with false papers, I couldn't risk being captured. So I stood there, completely impotent, as she was hauled onto the bus. Then, to my horror, it pulled away. The remaining policemen picked up the mother and slung her into the back of their van. I watched, stunned, as they drove off.

The neighbours' window slammed shut as they disappeared back inside. Show over.

I looked back at the pavement where the mother had lain. A thin trail of blood was all that remained, the only evidence of the horror that had just occurred there. I was about to look away when I noticed something glimmer in the sun.

After checking the coast was clear, I hurried over. A silver oval locket lay on the ground, its chain broken. Had it been the mother's, torn off in the struggle? I picked it up and opened it. On one side there was the tiny photograph of a man and woman on their wedding day, and on the other, a photo of a girl – the girl I'd just seen being dragged onto the bus, I was sure of it. She was younger in the picture but had the same wide eyes.

I shut the locket and slipped it into my pocket.

Sweat pooled at the nape of my neck as I strode off along the street. All the excitement I'd been feeling about the Arden shoot had gone. All I could think about was the girl, and her haunted expression that had resonated so deeply within me, now captured on a spool of film inside my camera.

Somewhere in the distance, I heard another pounding sound, followed by a yell, and I pictured more innocent people being dragged from their homes. How could this be happening here? It didn't make any sense. How had the 'City of Light' that I'd loved for so long been plunged into such utter darkness?

2

It's safe to say that I did not have a conventional upbringing. Being the only daughter of a widower, who also happened to be a small-time mobster, meant that was pretty much guaranteed, but if there was one conventional thing about Frankie Esposito, it was the way he prioritised education – of all kinds. Not only did he send me to a fancy upstate school where I learned all about the anatomy of flowers and the history of art and how to become fluent in French, but he also schooled me in what he termed 'wiseguy wisdom'. Never ratting on your friends was rule number one, but he put equal importance on always having a 'getaway fund' – a secret stash to be squirrelled away in case of emergencies. For mobsters, this meant having enough money to escape the cops or a rival gang, if need be. But Frankie drilled it into me that, as a female, it was imperative to have a getaway fund so I would never become dependent on a man. 'I know how men's minds work,' he used to tell me. 'I know how they think about dames. And I don't ever want no good-for-nothing bozo treating my daughter like his personal slave.'

As I let myself into my studio apartment tucked into the

eaves of a four-storey building in the heart of Montmartre, I said a silent prayer of thanks to my pops for teaching me how to take care of myself. I'd bought the studio back in 1939 with money I'd squirrelled away from my modelling jobs and Pierre still knew nothing about it. One bonus of being married to a self-involved pig was that it didn't seem to occur to him that I could have any kind of existence outside of him.

I'd initially bought the apartment as somewhere to develop my photographs in peace. I had a darkroom in Pierre's apartment in Montparnasse, but he always got so grouchy if I spent too much time in there and had developed an infuriating habit of barging in unannounced and exposing my developing pictures to the light. My apartment in Montmartre only consisted of two rooms plus a cupboard-sized bathroom, but I was increasingly coming to see it as home.

I'd turned the bedroom into my darkroom and bought a daybed for the living room for the occasional nights I stayed over – the nights Pierre was 'away on business' – his code for seeing his latest mistress. I never let on that I knew what he was doing when he slunk out with his hair shiny with Brilliantine and reeking of his leathery cologne. This was another trick Frankie had taught me: 'Never show your hand until the time is right, babycakes, always maintain a poker face.' Truthfully, I was grateful that Pierre had turned his attention to his latest young models, thankful that his sausage-like fingers no longer reached for me in the middle of the night.

I headed straight for my darkroom and turned on the red light. The shoot for Arden had passed by in a blur. All I could think about was the girl, Lillie, and developing my photograph of her. I filled the three trays lined up on the desk with the correct solutions, then took the film from my camera and carefully immersed it in a large bowl of water to remove the stiffness. Then, still holding the film in a U shape by the ends, I placed the bottom in the tray containing the developing solution and slowly seesawed it back and forth until every inch of the film had been submerged.

As always, I felt a shiver of excitement as the pictures started to appear, but this time my excitement was tinged with worry. I really hoped I hadn't fluffed the shot. It felt too important. I'd taken so many photographs by now it was as if my camera had become an extension of my eye, but you never knew for sure until you saw the finished image.

Once I'd seesawed the film through the developing solution, I repeated the process in the stop tray and finally in the tray containing the fixer. I rolled a cigarette while I waited the required ten minutes before I could turn the white lights on for the moment of truth.

Once the time was up I turned on the lights and studied the photo. There'd been a slight light leak in the bottom corner, but the girl, with her haunted expression and her short, jagged dark hair, had come out crystal clear. The fear in her eyes caused my breath to catch in my throat. It was a feeling I knew only too well.

The image blurred as my eyes filled with tears and I was cast back in time, a picture developing in my mind. Me and my pops, sitting on our front stoop in the sunshine. Jumping at the squeal of car tyres. Frankie getting to his feet, hitching up his suit trousers – 'Always dress to impress, babycakes.' A car slowing, someone leaning out, the sharp crack of a pistol shot. My tall, strong pops collapsing like a rag doll to the ground. Me crying out, just as the girl had done today for her mother. Then kneeling over his dying body.

I snapped back to the present, and hung the image on the wire to dry, attaching another clothes peg to the bottom to stop it from curling. I looked the girl in the photograph straight in the eyes, and I vowed right there and then that I would do every-

thing in my power to help her, to help all who were being persecuted by the Germans and the Vichy government. I didn't know
how or what I could do, but I knew with absolute certainty that
it was no longer good enough to do nothing.

I went through to the living room and placed the kettle on
the tiny stove. There were still another couple of hours before
the curfew. The sun was setting and sending a shaft of golden
light through a crack in the blackout blinds. Dust motes danced
in the beam. I'd gotten really good at blocking Frankie's death
from my mind in recent years. And having lost my mother
before I was even a year old meant that I was practised in the art
of avoiding painful thoughts. Moving to Paris and recreating
myself as Clarisse Alarie had certainly helped but now I felt
like that teen girl from New York all over again, raw and
vulnerable.

I lit my cigarette on the flame of the stove. Up until this
point, smoking had been one of my few acts of defiance against
the Vichy government as they'd banned women from having
tobacco rations last summer. But my small rebellion suddenly
seemed pathetic. I needed to do more, but what? I could take
photographs of what was happening, of what the Germans, and
indeed our own police, were doing, but where could I send
them? Who could publish them? If only I had a way of reaching
the contacts I had at US Vogue from my modelling days, but, of
course, overseas mail had been banned long ago. Perhaps I
should focus on trying to help the girl. But how, and where
would I begin? I could try to find out where the detainees had
been taken and see if I could get her mother's locket to her. I
took it from my pocket and held it tightly. Yes, that would be a
good starting point.

Once I'd had a cup of tea, I set off back for Pierre's place,
with the photograph of the girl safely tucked inside my purse.
Despite having lived with him for five years, I still thought of
the Montparnasse apartment as his home, not ours. It was

almost curfew and the streets that had once bustled with life late into the night felt stripped to the bone. The only people out and about were all scurrying home like frightened mice. Sadly, there was still no let-up to the heat. If anything, it felt even worse, and the back of my dress clung to my skin.

I arrived at the apartment to find Pierre reclining on his chaise longue, a bottle of wine and a plate of cheese and crackers on the low table beside him. There was something about this vignette that felt deeply offensive to me. Perhaps it was the sharp contrast between such obvious comfort and the pain of the girl in the photograph. I wondered how he'd got the cheese. Was it through a black-market contact or could it be down to something more sinister? The wry joke doing the rounds in Parisian cafes and bars that summer was that the only people who didn't now need a belt to hold up their clothes were those collaborating with the Germans. And didn't Pierre say only that morning that he'd been talking to a friend in the police? After what I'd witnessed the police do that morning, I prickled with indignation at the thought.

'You're late,' Pierre said, resting his hand on the mound of his stomach. The ring on his pinky finger, a chunky gold affair housing a large rectangular ruby, glistened in the lamplight.

'I've been working. At the Arden shoot.'

'Hmm.'

God, how I wanted to wipe the smug smirk from his face. Thanks to Frankie teaching me martial arts from the age of five, I knew I could if I wanted to, so I took comfort in imagining delivering a deft kick to the side of Pierre's head.

'Did you hear about the round-up?' he asked, topping up his wine from the bottle on the table.

'Yes, someone mentioned it at the shoot,' I said casually, perching on one of the armchairs by the fireplace.

'Biggest one yet,' he remarked, as if talking about a prize-winning vegetable rather than the persecution of innocent people.

'Really?'

'Yes. They've arrested so many they've had to send most of them to the Vel d'Hiv.'

'The velodrome?' I stared at him in shock. How could they be using a sports stadium, a venue popular for its six-day cycle races, as some kind of prison? I felt sick to my stomach at the thought.

'Yes, the camp in Drancy is overflowing already,' Pierre said matter-of-factly, before helping himself to a chunk of cheese.

I couldn't help shivering in spite of the heat. I'd heard about the internment camp in the Parisian suburb of Drancy a while ago. The site was initially intended to be a complex of high-rise apartment buildings to rival those in America – the perfect model for modern living – but the government had requisitioned it before construction had even finished. Who could have imagined it would end up being used as a prison camp for French citizens? I thought of the girl Lillie being sent there, or to the velodrome, and my heart broke for her.

'Why don't you come here,' Pierre said through a mouthful of cheese, patting the space on the chaise beside him.

My stomach churned, but I did as I was told. I couldn't show my hand yet, especially now I wasn't sure he could even be trusted.

'You're sweating,' he said, tracing his finger down the side of my face. 'Perhaps you ought to take off that dress.'

My feeling of nausea grew. How had I ever found this man attractive?

'I think I might take a bath.'

His smile faded.

'To freshen up for you.'

He nodded. 'Very well.' He picked up his wine and took a large gulp.

I went into the bathroom and shut the door behind me, then pressed my burning face to the cool tiled wall. 'You have to get out of here,' I whispered to my flushed reflection in the mirror. 'You have to leave him, even if he ends up denouncing you.'

And I swear I could hear the ghost of my pops whispering, *Attagirl!*

3

APRIL 1985, PARIS

Last night, I had the nightmare again. It had been a while since the previous time, six weeks at least, so when I woke in a cold sweat trembling from head to toe, I was filled with gloom. *I'm never going to be free from what happened. I'm never going to escape what they did to me,* I kept thinking on a loop as I stared up at the ceiling. I did a lot of staring at my bedroom ceiling, so I knew every crack and blemish in the paintwork intimately. I even knew that if you squinted at the damp stain by the window just as the sun was setting it bore an uncanny resemblance to the *Mona Lisa*, complete with enigmatic grin.

It was only four in the morning, but I knew I'd never get back to sleep, so I hoisted my weary body out of bed, trudged into the living room and put Jane Fonda's latest aerobics tape into the video recorder. The best way I knew to exorcise the demons that plagued me was to shake them out of my body – or 'feel the burn', as Fonda would say. I didn't even bother putting on my leotard and leg warmers. I just jumped and jogged and lunged about in my pyjamas.

By the end of the workout, I felt vaguely human again. My stomach was also growling with hunger, so after a quick wash, I pulled on a skirt and blouse and headed out in the direction of my favourite boulangerie.

Think how lucky you are to be able to eat whatever and whenever you please, I told myself. *Think how lucky you are to see the sky and the sun and hear the birds in the trees.* But the residue of my dream clung to the insides of my mind, like the dregs of a cup of coffee. I knew that no amount of good fortune could ever erase what had happened. No amount of sky and sunshine and freshly baked pastries.

As I opened the boulangerie door, my nostrils were flooded with the sweet smell of bread baking.

'*Bonjour!*' Jacob, the baker's son, greeted me cheerily.

'*Bonjour,*' I replied, forcing a smile.

'The usual?' he enquired, tongs poised above a tray of freshly baked croissants.

'Yes— No, actually could I have a pain au chocolat today please?'

'But of course.' His eyes sparkled with fun and I felt a wistful pang. He was the type of guy I would have loved when I was younger. Exuberant as a puppy with a generous pinch of mischief.

I caught a glimpse of my reflection in the glass-fronted cabinet housing the macaroons and felt another pang. It was hard to reconcile the greying hair and drooping eyes with the much younger woman I still imagined myself to be. As I took my wallet from my bag, I noticed the veins protruding slightly on the backs of my hands. It was almost impossible to imagine that there might have been a time when someone like Jacob would have looked at me with lust rather than the gentle affection a young man might have for his grandmother.

I gave him the money and he handed me the pastry in a brown paper bag. It was still warm and smelled delicious, but as I stepped outside, I felt the strangest urge to cry. Perhaps it was a hangover from the dream, or perhaps it was the realisation that

I had reached the autumn – or possibly even early winter – of my life and there was no way to roll back the seasons.

I decided to walk along the rue des Martyrs into Montmartre. Perhaps the sight of the sun shimmering on the white domes of Sacré-Coeur would cheer me up. And perhaps a coffee with my pastry would reinvigorate me. But my knees were aching from too many squats and as I spied the basilica on top of the hill, I was accosted by another unwelcome memory. Walking around Paris now, in the mid-1980s, there was no obvious sign of what had happened some forty years before, but I could see the ghosts of those days everywhere. Oh, how I envied the young, who could gaze along the boulevards and sip wine outside the bistros and only see the beauty. Oh, what I wouldn't give to not be constantly reminded of the evil that had once haunted these streets.

4

JULY 1942, PARIS

The next day, Pierre was busy in his studio painting his new muse, or latest victim as I preferred to think of her, so I set off into the city, under the guise of going to queue for food. Most of our time these days seemed to be spent queuing for rations, especially if you didn't qualify for the priority queue, which, as a woman with no children in Marshal Pétain's France, I certainly did not. It was the perfect cover story, though, if I wanted to stay out all day. So instead of heading for the nearest market, I set off for the velodrome. I hoped against hope that Pierre had been mistaken and his sources had been wrong and it wasn't being used as some kind of prison.

But as I looked up at the Eiffel Tower, I felt a shiver run down my spine. Of course the velodrome could now be used for sinister means; after all, hadn't the Germans already stamped their hate over so many Parisian landmarks? The day they'd displayed their huge V for victory on the Eiffel Tower along with a sign proclaiming *DEUTSCHLAND SIEGT AUF ALLEN FRONTEN – Germany is victorious on all fronts –* it made me cry with sorrow and frustration.

Ever since I was a kid and had first laid eyes on a picture of the Eiffel Tower in a book, I'd had the certain conviction that one day I'd see it for real. My fascination with Paris was further encouraged by my French teacher, the glamorous Mademoiselle Hermet, who made me fall in love with her home city long before I ever set foot there. 'There is nowhere on earth like Paris,' she would say in her rich, velvety accent, a dreamy expression upon her face. 'It is the most romantic city in the world. It makes you fall in love with life itself.' When I was about thirteen, I'd cut a picture of the Eiffel Tower out of a magazine and pinned it to my bedroom wall. My friends all had pictures of Hollywood heart-throbs on their walls; I had a wrought-iron lattice tower.

Pops wasn't remotely concerned about my fixation with Paris, though; in fact, he encouraged it. I guess he found it a whole lot easier to have his daughter swoon over a city rather than some deadbeat guy. 'Some day you're gonna take Paris by storm,' he used to say to me. 'You're destined for great things, babycakes, I just know it.'

When I finally did set foot in my beloved Paris six years ago, I spent hours wandering the streets, completely wonderstruck at the elegance of the architecture and the beauty on display. Mademoiselle Hermet had been right – there was a magical quality to Paris, a sense that a serendipitous meeting or adventure could be waiting around every corner, that made you fall in love with life itself. Never in a million years would I have imagined that this magic would one day be stripped away by the Nazis.

As I got closer to the velodrome, a bus drove past, rows of anxious faces pressed to the windows. My heart sank. Surely the police weren't still rounding people up. I turned the corner onto boulevard de Grenelle and I saw the bus pulling up outside the velodrome. Another two buses were parked there already.

I stopped walking and felt in my purse for my camera,

pressing the button to open it and pulling on the catch so it would be at the ready. The door of the bus opened and people began spilling off, onto the pavement. A group of grim-faced police officers were there to greet them, shepherding them into the stadium through the nearest entrance. I watched as parents and children, young adults and the elderly, some barely able to walk unaided, shuffled inside. They were all dressed smartly, many of them carrying small suitcases, as if they were going on holiday for a few days. The confusion on their faces was palpable. I wondered if they too had spent fun evenings watching cycle races at the velodrome before the occupation. How must it feel to be brought back here now, as prisoners?

My hackles began to rise. What possible threat did any of these people pose? How could the French authorities do this to them? I skulked behind a lamp post and took a quick shot of the people being marched into the stadium. How different it was to the days when crowds used to swarm in there of their own free will, to watch the races. I thought of the girl in my photograph and gazed up at the arena, wondering if she was somewhere inside. The glass domed roof was shut, the sun beating down upon it. It had to be unbearably hot in there.

A truck pulled up beside me and for a horrible moment I thought it might contain German soldiers, but to my relief I saw a sign for the Red Cross on the side. A couple of women got out of the truck in nurses' uniforms. One of them caught my eye, so I went over to her.

'Excuse me, are you going into the velodrome?'

She nodded.

'I think someone I know has been taken there. A girl named Lillie Kramer. Is there any way I might get something to her?'

The woman looked at me as if I was mad. 'Do you know how many people are in there?'

I shrugged.

'Thousands,' she replied. 'Seven thousand at least.'

'Oh... I... I see,' was all I was able to stammer in response.

'Come,' the other nurse said officiously, and they set off for the stadium.

I stood there staring after them in shock. As I tried to imagine what it must be like for so many people to be crammed inside, another bus pulled up, bringing me to my senses. I couldn't hang around for too long or I might arouse suspicion. I felt so helpless as I walked away, so useless, and so stupid for imagining that I could waltz down there and deliver the locket to the girl. Life as we had known it in Paris had changed beyond all recognition and it was completely disorientating.

Feeling dazed from the shock and the heat, I walked aimlessly until I found myself in the Latin Quarter. I couldn't get the faces of those people out of my mind, and I didn't want to. I desperately wanted to help them, but how and what could I do? For the past two years, I'd tried to continue with life as normal in spite of the occupation, telling myself that surely one day soon it would all be over. When America joined the war back in December, I'd been convinced that victory was within the Allies' grasp, but now it seemed that things were getting much, much worse. And, as Pierre so thoughtfully liked to remind me, as an American in Paris, albeit with a false French woman's identity, my own freedom was looking increasingly precarious.

I was wrenched from my gloom by a bright splash of colour further up the street. A young man was walking towards me wearing an oversized emerald-green jacket that almost came down to his knees. His dark wavy hair reached his collar and an inch of canary-yellow sock was visible between the bottom of his narrow trousers and the top of his thick-soled shoes. In spite of the scorching sunshine, he was carrying an umbrella, one of the long British types the size of a walking cane. The overall effect was so joyful and unexpected it reminded me of the days before the occupation, when moments of wonder were abundant. Then I noticed one of those wretched yellow stars pinned to his chest and felt a stab of concern. Surely it wasn't safe for him to be walking around Paris with the round-ups going on, especially dressed as gaily as a peacock.

Once again, I felt the instinct to reach for my camera. The urge to capture this strange creature was overwhelming and I took it from my bag, opened it fully, and stepped back into a darkened shop doorway.

He drew closer, singing 'Minnie the Moocher' as he twirled his umbrella. I raised my camera and took a shot but knew I could do better. I needed to get one with his umbrella in the air. I wound the film on and waited till he raised it again and pressed the shutter.

'La-la-la-la, la-la-lee,' he sang. 'Who is that that I can see?'

I frowned. Those weren't the lyrics.

He stopped twirling his umbrella and looked straight at me. Damn. I used to be so good at taking street photos unseen, so good at blending into the background. Clearly my lack of recent practice meant I was losing my touch. Or maybe the people of Paris had more reason to be alert and on their guard these days.

I stepped out of the doorway. '*Bonjour*,' I said with what I hoped was a winning smile. 'I hope you don't mind, but I just had to take a photograph of your outfit.' Now he was up close, I saw that the yellow star he was wearing didn't say JUIF in the centre; it said ZAZOU, which was a new one on me.

'What for?' He took a step closer, looking at me warily. In spite of his neatly groomed Clark Gable-style moustache, he looked to be barely older than twenty.

'For myself,' I replied. 'You look so colourful, and so interesting. I couldn't resist.'

'Hmm, well you certainly know how to charm a fellow,' he said in English with a comically exaggerated British accent.

My heart skipped a beat. Had he seen through my own accent? Could he tell I was American?

I stared at him blankly, pretending I couldn't understand.

'Pardon?' I asked, eyes wide.

'I am very flattered that you should think me interesting,' he replied in French. 'Personally, I think that being seen as interesting is the highest compliment a person can be paid.'

'I agree!' I exclaimed. Ever since I was a little girl, people had told me I was pretty, but it always left me feeling flat. I didn't want others to notice me for the shape of my legs or my breasts or my face, like Pierre did; I longed for people to be curious about what lay beneath.

'Well, you are certainly interesting to me,' he continued. 'I mean to say, what is a woman like you doing loitering in a doorway, secretly taking photographs of people.'

There was something about the way he said this, a suspicion in his voice, that made my heart sink. Paris was now crawling with collaborators and denouncers. I really hoped he didn't think I was working for the police or the Germans.

'I'm a photographer,' I said.

'So I see.' He looked at my Six-20.

'No, I mean professionally. I'm a fashion photographer. That's why I couldn't resist taking a picture of you – I love what you're wearing.'

'Hmm.' He stroked his moustache and looked me up and down. 'And what is it exactly that you love about my clothes?'

'The fact that you look so different.'

'So different to what?' He frowned.

'To everyone else. I also love that you haven't followed our government's decree to have your hair cut off so that it can be made into slippers.' I held my breath, hoping this would be enough to convince him that I wasn't a traitor.

He stared at me for a moment, then laughed. 'That was indeed a ridiculous decree.'

'Hmm, not as ridiculous as the one banning women from tobacco and trousers.'

'So, you are a fan of tobacco and trousers?' He raised his thin dark eyebrows.

'I'm a fan of being able to do whatever I damn well please.' I stared straight back at him.

Much to my relief, his face broke into a smile. 'What is your name?' Then he held up his hand as if to stop me. 'No, don't say it, I would like to guess.'

'Good luck!' I laughed.

He tilted his head to one side and frowned as if deep in thought. 'I feel like it must be something that exudes passion and strength. Something like Cleopatra.'

I laughed. 'No, but now I wish it was!'

He looked me up and down, but not in the lascivious way Pierre did, more in the way someone might study a book cover when deciding whether or not to read it.

'Is your name...' He paused for effect. 'Fire?'

'Fire?' I stared at him.

'Yes.'

'No.' I grinned. 'But, again, I kind of wish that it was.'

'In that case, I shall call you Fire,' he said, planting the tip of his umbrella on the ground, as if staking his claim to that part of the pavement.

'Very well, and what should I call you?' I asked, beginning to warm to this verbal game.

'What would you like to call me?'

I looked him up and down. 'The peacock.'

'The peacock?' He pursed his lips as if contemplating whether or not to accept this.

'Yes, because you remind me of a peacock, the way you brighten up the place.'

He laughed and his mask of debonair detachment fell away. His green eyes sparkled and dimples appeared in the centre of each cheek.

He held his hand out for me to shake. 'Very nice to make

your acquaintance, Mademoiselle Fire.'

'Likewise, Monsieur Peacock.'

But just as I took his hand, I heard a yell from the far end of the street. A group of young men in blue shirts were striding towards us.

'Uh-oh,' the peacock muttered.

'Scalp him!' one of the men cried and they broke into a run.

'Quick!' the peacock said, pulling me down an alleyway beside the shop.

'Zazou scum!' I heard another of the men yell. They were clearly French.

'Who are they?' I gasped as we sprinted to the end of the alleyway.

'This way,' he said, tugging me to the left. 'They're *Jeunesse Populaire Française.*'

A mixture of hatred and fear began coursing through my veins. I knew all about the French Popular Youth created by the fascist politician Jacques Doriot. I'd heard him wax lyrical about his dreams of turning France into a twin of Nazi Germany on Radio Paris. The young men recruited to the movement were encouraged to attack Jews and anyone else not toeing the line of the Vichy government.

The peacock and I raced on deeper into the Latin Quarter. It had been a while since I'd run anywhere, but thankfully I was able to match his pace.

'Not much further now,' he gasped as we turned onto a narrow, cobbled street.

Not much further till what? I wondered. *Being scalped and beaten to a pulp by a pack of bloodthirsty fascists?*

'Kill the zazous!' I heard one of the men scream.

Scalped, beaten and *killed*. I started mentally replaying some of the key self-defence moves Frankie had taught me. *Fist to the throat, babycakes, knee to* le palle!

The peacock pulled me down a passageway halfway along

the cobbled street. It was full of overflowing bins which stank in the heat and was without a doubt the ugliest place I'd ever seen in all of Paris. He stopped by a nondescript door.

There is no way I'm taking my last breath here, I thought to myself. If I was going to die in Paris, it was going to be somewhere spectacular, goddammit, like plunging to my doom from the top of Notre-Dame. I was not going to be murdered by fascist scum in an alleyway. *Adopt the stance, babycakes!* I imagined Frankie yelling at me and I set my feet apart.

The peacock rapped on the door twice fast, then twice slow, in what sounded like some kind of code. The door opened a crack.

'Quick,' he hissed at whoever was inside and the door opened fully. He pulled me in and the door slammed shut behind us, plunging us into total darkness. We stood there for a moment, listening for our pursuers. My heart was pounding and sweat was pouring down my face. Mercifully, all remained quiet outside.

'I think we gave them the slip,' the peacock whispered.

'Who was it?' a deep man's voice reverberated in the dark.

'*Jeunesse Populaire Française,*' he replied.

I had no idea where I was or what I'd gotten myself into but as I fought to regain my breath, I experienced the most unexpected feeling. A feeling not unlike elation.

'And who the hell is this?' the man growled.

I heard the sound of a match being struck and he raised the flame to my face.

5

'This is Fire; she's a photographer,' the peacock said, as if that made my unexpected appearance completely understandable.

The man lit a lamp with his match and scowled at me. He was short and stocky with bristly dark hair and eyebrows. His chin was dark with stubble.

'A photographer?' the man said, staring at me suspiciously.

As my eyes adjusted to the gloom, I saw that we were standing in a narrow corridor. The air smelled of cigarettes and I could hear the faint sound of music coming from somewhere below.

'Yes, that's how we met. She was taking a photograph of me.' The peacock grinned at me. 'Until we were so rudely interrupted.'

'How long have you known each other?'

'Oh, about five minutes.' He laughed quietly. 'Come, we should go downstairs.'

'You've known her for five minutes?' The man's scowl deepened.

'Yes, but if it's any consolation, they were the longest five minutes of my life.' The peacock gave me an apologetic grin.

'Due to the pack of animals chasing us, obviously – not your company.'

'Glad to hear it.' I followed the peacock as he headed along the passageway and the sound of music grew louder. *Any enemy of the* Jeunesse Populaire Française *is a friend of mine*, I tried reassuring myself. I could feel the stocky man right behind me, breathing down my neck.

'Are you sure she can be trusted?' he said over my shoulder.

I came to a standstill and spun on my heels, almost causing him to crash straight into me. 'For your information, I did not just risk life and limb running all over the Quarter because I'm a fascist in disguise.'

'Ha! You tell him, Fire,' the peacock said with a chuckle. He opened a door at the end of the passageway and the swinging rhythm of jazz music boomed out to greet us.

I felt momentarily disorientated as we descended a spiral staircase into some kind of basement club. A basement club that was packed to the rafters with people dancing, chatting and drinking. It was the strangest sight after the heat and bright sunlight outside, like going straight from day to night.

'Let me buy you a drink,' the peacock said, leading me over to the bar. 'It's the least I can do after all the hullabaloo.'

The bartender greeted him like an old friend, pouring him a beer without needing to be asked, and adding a shot of syrupy grenadine, causing the head on the beer to turn pink.

Seeing as everyone else seemed to be drinking alcohol, I ordered a red wine. I needed something to steady my nerves.

We took our drinks and went and sat at a small table in the corner. Thankfully, the goon who let us in had disappeared.

'I'm sorry for making you come with me,' the peacock said as he sat down. 'But I didn't think it would be safe to leave you there once they'd seen you with me.'

'Of course,' I replied, taking a sip of my drink. In spite of the early hour and the fact that most wine was watered down now, it tasted surprisingly good. 'What is this place?' I asked, gazing around the low-ceilinged, wood-panelled room.

'Café Capoulade,' he replied. 'Favoured hangout of the zazous and a Nazi-free zone.'

'I didn't know places like this still existed.'

'You obviously haven't been mixing with the right people.'

Ain't that the truth, I thought to myself, taking another sip of my drink.

Ever since the occupation began, Pierre had used it as a way of curtailing my movements, constantly drip-feeding me fear-inducing warnings about my safety and advising me to stay home rather than go to the cafes and bars I used to frequent. Ending up in this basement club with the peacock was the most exciting thing to have happened to me in two years. As I looked around at the people chatting and nodding along to the music, I felt my old self spark back to life.

'So, tell me, what does it mean to be a zazou?' I asked.

'It means loving swing music and being free to dress and do as we please,' he replied with a grin. 'Especially if it annoys our occupiers and traitorous government. Hence the long hair and the oversized jackets.'

'Cheers to that!' I exclaimed, raising my glass.

'Cheers.' He clinked his beer glass against mine. 'It's good to meet you, Fire.'

'And you,' I replied. 'Although, I have to admit, I'm finding your pink beer concoction a little disturbing.'

'You've never had grenadine in beer?' He pulled an expression of utter bewilderment.

'I can't say that I have.'

'Well, then you must try it immediately.' He offered his glass to me.

I took a sip of the bizarre beer cocktail expecting it to taste foul, but the sharp floral taste of the grenadine did add a certain *je ne sais quoi.* I nodded my approval and handed back the drink.

'Why do you wear that?' I asked, pointing to the yellow star on his chest.

'In solidarity with the Jewish people.' He took a battered silver tobacco tin from his jacket pocket. 'I wish everyone in France would wear one. To show our government that we still believe in liberty, equality and fraternity.'

'Yes!' I exclaimed. 'Instead of Pétain's pathetic new slogan, *"travail, famille, patrie".'* I thought of the Jewish girl I'd photographed the day before, and wished I'd been wearing a yellow star in solidarity when she'd seen me. 'I admire your bravery.'

'Oh, I'm not brave,' he replied straight away. 'I just can't sit around and do nothing when the country I love is being destroyed.'

'I wish I could do something,' I said, partly thinking out loud. 'I witnessed something yesterday – a young girl being rounded up while her mother was beaten senseless by the police – and it made me feel so powerless.' I felt in my pocket for the photograph and took it out. 'I took this picture of her, and ever since, I can't stop thinking about her.'

He took the photograph from me and studied it. 'Wow, this is very powerful. Her expression, it is so full of pain and fear.'

'I know, but I'm not sure if I should have taken it. At the time, I wanted to record what was happening, but now I worry that I was being some kind of morbid voyeur.'

'I think you were right to take it,' he said, and I felt a surge of relief. 'People need to know what is happening here and this photograph says so much. What is that saying? A picture paints a thousand words.'

I nodded. 'Did you know that the people who've been rounded up are being taken to the Vel d'Hiv?'

'The velodrome?' His eyes widened with shock.

'Yes. They've run out of room at the other camps, like Drancy.' I sighed. 'What is happening to our country?'

'Don't despair, Fire, there are plenty of people who want to save France from this insanity. This place is full of them for a start.' He gestured around the bar, at the people deep in conversation at the tables. 'If you want to do something too, then maybe you could use your photography to help make people aware of what is happening.'

'But what can I do with my photographs? How can I get people to see them? The Germans control all the papers and magazines.'

'Not all of them.' He looked at me for a moment. 'Are you serious about wanting to help?'

'Yes!' After so long feeling helpless, I'd never been more sure of anything in my life.

'I could make a few enquiries, introduce you to some people maybe.'

'People who could help distribute my photographs?' I looked back at the picture of Lillie. 'I want to do something to help her,' I said softly.

'Yes, and you will if you keep taking photos like this.' He leaned forward and lowered his voice. 'Leave it with me. I can connect you with someone in the Resistance.'

A shiver ran up my spine. The thought of using my photography to resist the German occupation was simultaneously nerve-wracking and thrilling.

I smiled at him gratefully. 'Thank you.'

The peacock nodded. 'I'm glad our paths crossed today.'

'Me too!' If only he knew how glad.

'It's good to think that even in these dark days we can still experience a moment of magical serendipity.'

'Absolutely.'

'So, tell me, where is your husband?' He stared pointedly at my wedding ring.

'With his new lover,' I couldn't help blurting out.

'What?' The peacock, who'd been about to take a drink, put down his glass.

'It's OK, I don't care,' I replied, wondering why on earth I'd revealed so much so quickly. But there was something about the peacock and his boyish charm that had disarmed me.

'But why would he have a lover when he is married to you?' he said, instantly blushing. 'Sorry. I didn't mean to be forward, it's just that I don't understand.'

'Thank you. I'm flattered by your response.' I laughed, although privately I couldn't help feeling depressed. When I'd come to Paris and reinvented myself as Clarisse Alarie, I'd had such high expectations of how my life was going to be. Of *who* I was going to be. All powerful, by name and by nature. So how had my life come to this? How had my situation become so tragic that a complete stranger was looking at me as if I was the most pitiful creature he'd ever encountered? 'It's the war,' I said by way of explanation. 'I would have left him long ago, but since the occupation...' I trailed off, hoping this would be enough of an explanation, but the peacock was still looking at me expectantly. 'It felt too dangerous to leave.'

'Dangerous in what way?'

I frowned, unsure how to respond. Even though I was certain I could trust him, I didn't dare tell anyone that I was in fact an American citizen. 'To be a woman on my own in Paris while it is crawling with Nazis.'

'You don't seem like the type of woman who would be scared to be on her own,' he responded.

I'm not! I wanted to cry. So why had I been living like a coward for so long?

'I'm not,' I said quietly. 'It's just that my husband...'

'Yes?'

'He's a powerful man and I'm afraid that if I leave...'

He looked at me expectantly.

'I'm afraid he'll denounce me.'

The peacock stared at me incredulously. 'Why would he denounce you?'

'He'd make something up,' I said, hoping this would be enough to convince him.

'Your husband sounds like a piece of shit,' he said matter-of-factly.

I burst out laughing. 'You are uncannily perceptive.'

'Why, thank you. I consider it one of my greatest gifts.' He smiled at me. 'Perhaps that's why fate made our paths cross today.'

'Why?'

'So that I can help you escape your piece-of-shit husband.'

'I don't need anyone's help,' I said, my pride instantly bruised.

'Oh no, I'm sorry, I didn't mean you need me to save you. I just meant you might like someone to remind you.'

'Remind me of what?'

'Of who you really are.'

I frowned at him. 'How old are you?'

'What's that got to do with anything?'

'I just don't understand how you look so young yet speak with the timeless wisdom of a sage.'

'So I was right then?' He looked jubilant, but not in the arrogant way that Pierre did whenever I had to concede that he was correct about something. His elation was more like that of a kid who'd got a question right in class and really wanted to impress his teacher.

'Yes,' I muttered. 'You were right.'

He nodded and smiled. 'Well, then I feel very honoured to be the one to remind you of your true, fearless self. And I'm twenty-one,' he added. 'How old are you?'

'Did no one ever tell you that it's rude to ask a lady her age?'

I quipped, although personally I'd never seen what the big deal was.

'Why is it rude to be interested in someone?'

I laughed. 'You have an answer for everything, don't you? I'm twenty-six.'

'Excellent.'

'Why is that excellent?'

'Because twenty-six is my favourite number.'

'Hmm, now why do I think you would have said that no matter what age I was?'

He grinned. 'Well, you'll never know, will you?'

'I guess not.' I felt a sense of fun bubbling up inside of me that I hadn't experienced in years. It felt good to be reunited with the sparky woman I used to be, before the slow drip-drip of fear had corroded my spirit.

'So...' He looked at me expectantly.

'So?'

'When are you going to leave your husband?'

I met his gaze across the table. 'Today.'

Of course, it was one thing being full of bravado when my veins were pumping with adrenaline and alcohol in a basement bar. By the time I returned to Pierre's apartment that evening, after hours of queuing for a paltry ration of a couple of slices of ham and some stale bread, I felt a growing apprehension about my bold declaration.

I had been hoping that Pierre would still be in his studio on the other side of Montparnasse Cemetery, seducing his latest victim, but, to my disappointment, I found him pacing up and down the living room. Over the years we'd been together, I'd developed the uncanny knack of being able to read Pierre's alcohol consumption with pinpoint accuracy and one look at his flushed face and untucked shirt told me that at least two bottles of wine had been consumed, which always spelled trouble.

'Where have you been?' he snapped, looking me up and down.

I wondered if he was able to read me just as well and could see the adrenaline still coursing through my veins. 'Queuing for food. I told you.'

'All day?'

'Yes. You know how long the queues get.' Actually, he didn't have a clue as I was always the one sent to get our rations, while he miraculously produced luxuries like cheese and fresh bread from his black-market contacts without breaking a sweat. 'And as we don't have any children, I'm not allowed to join the priority queue, so I have to wait for the scraps.'

'Hmm, maybe we should fix that.' In a split second, his gaze changed from anger to lust, and I had to suppress a grimace.

'I really don't think that now is the right time to be bringing a child into the world.'

'Why not?'

'Are you serious? With the Nazis crawling all over France.' I tried to suppress my growing panic. The way in which I'd lost my mother had left me vowing I'd never become a parent, and the thought of having children with Pierre and being tied to him for life was a complete anathema to me.

He shrugged as if there were a lot worse things that could be happening. 'I think we should have a child and I think we should start trying right now.' His voice was thick and garbled.

I'm not sure if it was the fact that I'd just spent hours opposite the peacock with his flamboyant look and irrepressible spirit, but in that moment, Pierre had never appeared more repulsive to me. The contrast was like a jolt to my nervous system.

What are you doing here with him? You need to leave, a voice urged from deep inside of me.

'And it's better to have the Germans in charge rather than the communists,' he slurred, beginning to unbutton his shirt.

I stared at him, hoping that this was some misguided attempt at humour, but he continued undoing his buttons and staring at my breasts.

'Take off your dress.'

'I need to go to the bathroom.'

He frowned.

'And slip into something more comfortable,' I continued, feeling sick.

He licked his wine-stained lips. 'Hurry up then.'

'I will.' I picked up my bag and raced into the bedroom, glancing around in panic. This was the strongest indication yet that Pierre's sympathies now lay with the Germans. I thought of Lillie and the promise I'd made to her photograph. I had to leave; if I didn't go now, I would have to have sex with a drunken, slobbery Pierre – a prospect so hideous it didn't bear thinking about. But how would I get away without him seeing or hearing me leave? The fire escape!

I heard a loud belch from the living room. I had no time to lose. I grabbed my Leica 35mm and all of the cassettes and rolls of film from the cupboard and a change of clothes from the wardrobe and shoved them all, along with my bag, into a small case. Then I hurried through to the spare bedroom and slowly opened the windows and shutters, being careful not to make a sound. Thankfully no one was in the courtyard below.

I clambered over the windowsill and out onto the wrought-iron fire escape. I had no idea if what I was doing was an inspired stroke of genius or the dumbest thing ever. All I knew was that I couldn't tolerate another second in my husband's presence. My true self had woken up and was refusing to go back to sleep.

6

APRIL 1985, PARIS

I washed down the last flakes of my pastry with a mouthful of coffee. Normally, I liked a café crème, but for some reason it tasted far too creamy today and I wished I'd taken it black instead.

I paid my bill and headed across the road to the wide stone steps leading to Sacré-Coeur. High above me, fluffy white clouds scudded by on the breeze and the first of the blossom was bursting into life on the trees in great puffs of lilac and pink. It was shaping up to be a beautiful spring day, the kind where you can smell the sunshine on the air.

As I reached the top of the steps, I turned to take in the panoramic view of Paris spread out beneath me. The white of the buildings set against the bright blue sky would have made for a stunning photograph, but the ghosts of my nightmare still haunted me. How could I photograph such beauty when I knew of the ugliness that had existed here? Any picture I took would feel like a lie.

A busker was setting up a few steps below me, tuning his guitar. Trying to catch people on their way to work, I guessed. As he strummed a few chords, I sat down. He started singing

'Imagine' by John Lennon and my breath caught in my throat. I wished I could imagine that there was no hell below us, but I knew it wasn't true. I knew that the potential for evil existed inside every one of us. But the busker's voice was so beautiful, and the song so hopeful, I couldn't fail to be moved.

Midway through the song, a little bird flew down onto the step beside me. It looked at me and tweeted, as if it was asking me a question.

'What is it, little one?' I asked softly. 'What do you want?'

The bird chirped again and cocked its head to one side, as if waiting for me to answer.

The singer crooned about living life in peace and I wished more than anything that this could be the case, but Iran and Iraq had been at war for four years now, and the Russians were fighting in Afghanistan, despite losing over twenty million of their citizens in World War Two. It was impossible for me to imagine a time when humans would stop fighting, and this had weighed heavy on me for years.

I was about to get up and head off to work when the strangest thing happened. The little bird hopped along the step and up onto my lap. I sat, motionless, not wanting to scare it off. I'd heard it said that the spirits of our deceased loved ones sometimes visit us as birds and always dismissed it as wishful thinking, but there was something so magical and unexpected about this, I couldn't help feeling that it was a visitation of sorts.

'Who are you?' I whispered.

The bird raised its beak and began chirping a beautiful chorus.

'Is it you?' I whispered, my eyes filling with tears.

The bird trilled again, then puffed its tiny chest, opened its wings, and fluttered off.

Below me, the busker was singing about being a dreamer. I watched the bird soar and swirl up into the sky and I thought back to a time, long ago, when I too had dreamed of a better, brighter future. It was like looking back on a totally different person. But I *had* been that person, once upon a time. She was still somewhere inside of me, surely?

The song came to an end and I got to my feet. It was the strangest thing, but I felt lighter somehow, like a weight I didn't know I'd been carrying had fallen from me. I took a couple of francs from my wallet and dropped them into the busker's guitar case.

'Thank you so much,' he said with a warm smile.

'No, thank *you*,' I replied before heading down the steps and into the city. He and the little bird had given me the sweetest gift. I wasn't exactly sure what it was yet, but it felt a lot like hope.

7

JULY 1942, PARIS

I took the backstreets to Montmartre with the stealth of a cat, clinging to all the darkest places. When I finally reached the safety of my apartment, I locked the door behind me and slid onto the floor, my heart thumping. I'd left Pierre. The enormity of the realisation hit me like a freight train. For so long I'd dreamed of leaving, but now the dream had come true I couldn't help feeling a creeping sense of alarm.

He must have realised I'd left by now, unless he'd fallen into a drunken stupor while waiting for me to get changed. Whatever the case, one way or another he'd soon know and then what would he do? Would he think I'd been mysteriously abducted and ask the police to try to find me? Or would he realise that I'd left him and call the police to denounce me? Either way, there was a high chance the police would be on the lookout for me soon.

What if Pierre came looking for me? Or what if our paths happened to cross? My apartment was about five miles away from his and he never deigned to visit Montmartre anymore, believing it to be yesterday's news for artists as successful as him, but still. Had I acted too rashly? Should I have formulated more of a plan before leaving? I tried to suppress my growing doubt, but my life suddenly felt dangerously rudderless. The only things I had to ground me were the peacock, who I'd arranged to meet again tomorrow, to talk more about his contact in the Resistance, and the girl in the photograph, who was fast becoming my raison d'être.

I took the picture from my bag and held it up to the dying light. 'I promise I'll help you,' I whispered. And just uttering those words filled me with strength. I might have left the security of my life with Pierre, but if I was able to use my photography to help the Resistance, I would at least now have a purpose and my life would have some sort of meaning. I wouldn't look back anymore, only forward. I'd done the right thing, of that I was sure, and besides, there were things I could do to stop myself from being recognised.

I fetched a pair of scissors from the kitchenette and went through to the bathroom. Standing in front of the mirror, I let my hair down and shook the long waves loose. I'd always longed to have shorter hair, but this was another thing I'd acquiesced to Pierre over. Well, not anymore. I hacked off a chunk and let it fall to the floor. Then another and another until I had one of those shoulder-length, Flapper-style bobs. It was a little uneven, but there was no denying that it made me look different. And perhaps I could dye it tomorrow...

I returned to the kitchenette feeling emboldened. Thankfully, I still had the rations in my bag, so I had something to eat, which was a very good thing as I was suddenly ravenous. I took out the sliver of ham and the dry baguette and placed them on a plate, filled the kettle and set it on the stove. I didn't have to go back to Pierre's apartment to be pawed at and undermined. I'd left. I was free. I took a bite of the rock-hard baguette. Stale bread had never tasted so good.

. . .

I woke the next morning with a stiff neck. The little daybed was definitely not as comfortable as Pierre's huge four-poster, but it was a price well worth paying, that was certain.

I went over to the window and peered through a crack in the blackout blind. A group of German soldiers were patrolling down below and I instantly felt a jolt of fear. Leaving Pierre had definitely increased my risk of being arrested, but I was able to bat the fear away. The sad truth was, I'd rather take my chances and risk being captured by the Germans than spend another minute with my pig of a husband.

I turned my back on the scene and headed to the kitchen table, picking up the photograph of Lillie. 'Today I'm going to figure out a way to get your mother's locket to you,' I whispered, and for the first time in what felt like forever, I allowed myself to think about my own mother. Not that I had any real memories of her as she'd died when I was just nine months old. I'd spent my first ten years believing that my mom had passed due to 'heart problems', but then, when he got drunk one Christmas, Pops let it slip that she'd taken her own life. At the age of ten I was old enough to know what suicide was but not nearly old enough to understand why my mom could have done such a thing. I wasn't sure if I'd ever be old enough to truly understand. Seeing Lillie torn from her mother had pierced me deep inside, triggering a longing for my own mom I'd tried to suppress for years. It sickened me that I hadn't been able to do anything to help them stay together. Reuniting Lillie with her mother's locket was something I could try to do though.

After I'd breakfasted on the remains of last night's baguette, which had become so hard I almost broke my teeth biting into it, I freshened up and prepared to set off for the velodrome. The day before I'd been unprepared for what I'd witnessed, but today I had more of a plan. I was going to try to find a way to get inside the stadium and see if I could locate the girl. I'd take my Leica this time too – as a non-folding camera, it would be easier and quicker to use and I figured that the peacock's contact in the Resistance would want to see what was happening in the Vel d'Hiv.

When I reached the stadium, I saw a couple more Red Cross workers, this time leaving the velodrome. They looked ashen-faced as they walked past the armed police guarding the entrance. As they drew closer to me, I heard one mutter the word, 'Inhuman...'

I came to a halt in front of them. 'Excuse me, but do you know how long the people are going to be held inside the velodrome?'

One of them, a slight young woman with mousy brown hair, shook her head. 'I don't know, but if it's for much longer there are going to be many deaths.'

My skin prickled with goosebumps.

'The conditions are appalling,' she went on. 'Animals would be treated better than that. They're keeping all of the windows and the roof closed to stop people from escaping, so there's no ventilation. And the toilets are all blocked.' I shuddered as I thought of the implications.

'Come,' her colleague said, tugging on her sleeve and they hurried on their way.

I carried on walking and saw some men filling buckets with water from a street hydrant. I watched as they hurried inside the stadium. The water from the hydrants came straight from the Seine. Surely it wasn't being used as drinking water for those inside.

I looked up at the velodrome and could hear announcements being barked over the tannoy, the way the races used to be announced. There had to be some way to get inside, not only to find Lillie, but to take photographs of what was happening so that I could show them to the peacock's contact in the Resistance. I needed to prove that I could be of use to him.

I spun on my heel and chased after the Red Cross women.

'Excuse me!' I called and they came to a halt. 'I was just wondering if you needed any help? Volunteers I mean, for in there.' I nodded towards the stadium.

'Are you any good at making soup?' the mousy-haired woman asked.

I shook my head. 'No, sadly I wasn't blessed with the gift of cooking, but I'd be happy to help serve soup.'

'Have you volunteered for us before?' the other woman, who was older and more stern-faced, asked.

I shook my head.

'Well, you'd need to go and register at our office first.'

A sense of urgency began building inside of me. 'Are you sure there's nothing I can do right now?'

The older woman frowned at me. 'Why are you so eager to get inside?'

There's two kinds of lies, I heard Pops' voice echo back through time at me, *good lies and bad lies. Good lies are the kind that help somebody.*

'I... I think someone I know might be in there,' I stammered. 'My friend's daughter. She's only twelve and she's all alone. I have something of her mother's I want to give to her, to bring her some comfort.'

The mousy-haired woman sighed. 'There are thousands of people in there. Finding your friend's daughter would be like trying to find a needle in a haystack.'

I felt so dejected at this, it was as if Lillie and her mother truly were my friends. The urge to do something to help was becoming overwhelming. If I didn't, what was the point in risking everything by leaving Pierre?

A truck pulled up beside us and I saw the Red Cross insignia on the side.

The younger woman must have taken pity on me because she gave her companion an enquiring look. 'Perhaps she could help us carry the soup pots inside? Save you having to do it as your arm is hurting.'

To my huge relief, the older woman nodded. 'But you must be careful and stay with us,' she said. 'Trust me, you don't want to end up getting trapped in there.'

My heart began to thud. As an American in France with false papers, I really did not want to get trapped inside the velodrome. 'I promise, I won't leave your side.'

'What's your name?' the younger woman asked.

'Clarisse.'

She shook my hand. 'Please to meet you, Clarisse. I'm Audrey.'

She led me round to the back of the truck. The driver had got out and opened the doors. He looked so flustered, he didn't give me a second glance.

Audrey reached inside and pulled out a Red Cross armband and handed it to me. 'Put this on.'

I did as instructed, then helped her heave one of the pots out of the truck. We carried it between us to the nearest entrance to the velodrome. A group of gendarmes were standing there on duty, another sinister reminder of how different things were now. Thankfully, they took one look at us and waved us through.

The second I set foot in the corridor leading into the stadium, I was hit by the stench. A terrible mixture of urine, excrement and sweat. The heat, which had been bad enough outside, intensified to a level where I could barely breathe.

Audrey and I carried our huge pot of soup through the corridor leading to the racetrack on the ground floor of the stadium. As we drew closer to the heart of the arena, the noise grew louder and louder, but unlike the expectant chatter and cheers of a race day, all I could hear were anguished cries and screams above the incessant announcements. Now I was inside, I realised that it was the police broadcasting over the tannoy system, telling people to be quiet and urging them to stay calm and in their place.

As we reached the track, I had a flashback to the first time I'd come to the velodrome to see a race and the excitement I'd felt. Now it was like a completely different place. People were everywhere, not just in the stands, but all over the track and in the central island, where row upon row of makeshift beds had been assembled. Or rather blankets arranged in rows on the floor. The glass ceiling had long ago been painted dark blue for the blackouts and formed an oppressive lid, amplifying the noise and the heat. The looks of confusion I'd witnessed the day before as people filed into the stadium had been replaced with expressions of pure anguish. Their faces were flushed and shiny with sweat.

'I did warn you,' Audrey called to me, obviously noting my horrified expression.

As soon as people saw us with the soup, they came surging forwards. A policeman with a gun yelled at them to stay back. The whole place was in utter chaos. It felt like descending into hell itself. I thought of Lillie being brought here after seeing her mother so brutally beaten and I felt completely helpless. As I gazed around the sea of anguished faces, I realised that Audrey was right, there was no way on earth I was going to find her. It all seemed so futile. But then I remembered the vow I'd made the night before, about using my photography to help the Resistance. If I was able to take some pictures in here, to show people on the outside what was happening, to capture the pain and the suffering, it might encourage more people to fight back. But how on earth would I manage to take any photographs unnoticed?

We deposited our soup on a table where more Red Cross staff were trying to do the impossible job of serving the clamouring masses. The pot, which I'd thought huge when carrying it in, now seemed woefully inadequate compared to the number of mouths needing to be fed.

'Let's go and fetch another pot,' Audrey said, and we began making our way back towards the exit.

Hands grabbed at my arms, pulling me back from Audrey, and I was greeted by imploring faces.

'Please,' a young woman begged me. 'Please help us get out of here.' Traces of her black mascara were smeared beneath her eyes and the armpits of her silk blouse were dark with sweat. I could tell that before she was brought here, she would have looked beautifully put together, but her now ravaged appearance seemed symbolic of the horrors being inflicted inside the velodrome.

'I will,' I said. I felt in my purse for my Leica and leaned closer so I could speak in her ear. 'Can I take your picture?' I opened my bag wider to show her the camera. 'To show people what's happening in here? I'm a professional photographer.'

I was scared she'd be offended by my suggestion, but to my relief, she nodded.

I glanced around to make sure there were no police lurking and quickly aligned the image in the viewfinder to make the woman's face come into focus and took the photo, my heart pounding. I slipped the camera back in my bag and grasped her arm. 'Please stay strong,' I urged. 'There are people outside who are trying to bring an end to this insanity.'

She nodded and her eyes filled with tears.

I hurried to catch up with Audrey and as we reached the corridor leading to the exit, I turned back, hoping to take a shot of the arena. But just as I was winding the film on, with the camera still in my bag, I saw a policeman staring at me and it felt as if my heart had leapt up into my throat. I took a handkerchief from my bag and pretended to blow my nose. The policeman slowly turned away and I grabbed the camera, swiftly raised it to shoulder height and pressed the shutter-release button, my hand trembling. The policeman began turning back, but I managed to stuff the camera into my bag just in time and followed Audrey to the exit. I was worried my trembling hand had caused the picture to blur, but it was the best I could do given the circumstances.

Back outside, the humid air felt positively fresh, but as I heard yet another instruction being barked over the tannoy I felt a wave of guilt that those inside weren't lucky enough to be able to leave.

Another Red Cross truck had pulled up behind the first.

Audrey instantly looked alarmed. 'My boss is here. You'd better go.'

'Of course.' I took off my armband and handed it to her.

She gave me a sad smile. 'I'm sorry you weren't able to find your friend's daughter.'

'It's OK. You were right, there were too many people,' I replied numbly.

We said goodbye and I set off along the street, trying to process what I'd just witnessed. How could this be happening? How could it be allowed to happen? The anguished faces I'd seen inside the stadium kept reappearing in my mind, especially that of the young woman I'd photographed. Who was she, I wondered, and what would happen to her? What would happen to all of the women, men and children who'd been rounded up and treated with such cruelty?

Anger began to burn through the fog of my shock. This barbarity had to be stopped and I had to do whatever I could to help. I marched off to meet the peacock, my indignation growing with every step.

8

I arrived on the steps of the Sacré-Coeur feeling hot and fraught. My dress was sticky with sweat and the cloying stench of the velodrome still seemed to be clinging to my nostrils. I hoped with every fibre of my being that the peacock had been able to meet with his contact in the Resistance, and that they'd find some use for my photographs. I desperately needed an outlet for my growing outrage at what was happening and a way of fighting back.

I gazed up at the white domes of the basilica at the top of the hill. What if he didn't show up? Then what would I do? Panic began swelling inside of me.

I heard the sharp clip of boots on the pavement and turned to see two German soldiers on patrol. *Get out of our country!* I wanted to yell.

But it's not your country and if you get caught you'll end up in the Vel d'Hiv too, my inner voice cautioned, doing nothing to help my anxiety.

You need to go. Get back your apartment, I told myself. *It's not safe to hang around like this.*

But just as my fears were reaching a crescendo, I felt a tap on my shoulder.

'It is you!' the peacock exclaimed as I turned to face him. He was wearing another oversized jacket, purple this time, with a pink shirt and thin black tie and narrow black trousers. 'I wasn't sure because of the hair.'

In everything that had happened, I'd completely forgotten my new haircut. 'Oh... yes, I... I cut it myself.'

'So I see.' He gave me a sympathetic smile. 'Don't worry, I will be able to fix it.'

'What do you mean, fix it?' I frowned at him.

'Make it look less like you put a pudding bowl on your head and cut around it – while you were drunk, and possibly temporarily blinded. Make it look more like an actual style and—'

'OK, OK, I get the picture,' I cut in.

'So, did you do it?' he asked, his eyes wide. 'Did you leave your shit of a husband?'

'I did.'

'Yes!' he cried and kissed me on both cheeks.

Just like our encounter the day before, I felt his zest for life begin working its way inside of me like some kind of emotional osmosis and the tension I'd been feeling began to ease.

'Were you able to talk to your contact?' I asked eagerly. 'About my photography?'

'Let's get out of here first,' he said, nodding at a couple of police officers coming down the steps towards us.

'Where to?'

'My place, so I can work my magic on you.'

I stopped walking and frowned again.

'I'm talking about your hair!' he exclaimed with a chuckle. 'Don't worry, I never make love to a woman I've only met twice. It's a rule of mine that I will never break, no matter how hard you might beg.'

'Oh really?' I couldn't help laughing at his cheek. 'Well, I'll have you know, I never make love to a man who criticises my hair, ever.'

He looked momentarily crestfallen before the smile returned to his face. 'I won't be critical of your hair once I've fixed it. I shall do nothing but lavish it with praise.'

Again, I couldn't help laughing.

'Where do you live anyway?' I asked as we walked up the steps.

'The other side of Sacré-Coeur. I have an attic room above a hat shop.'

'Sounds a bit like my place,' I replied. 'Only mine is this side of the church.'

He stopped and stared at me. 'You live here in Montmartre?'

'Yes.'

'But I thought you had left your husband?'

'I have. He lives in Montparnasse.'

'Wow, you are a fast worker, already finding a new place of your own.'

'No, I've had my place for years. I got it as a studio to develop my photographs – and somewhere to escape to,' I added.

'Your husband, does he know about this place?'

'No.'

He looked at me and smiled. 'Fire, you are just like an onion.'

'Excuse me?' I stared at him.

'It's a compliment,' he said. 'You have many layers to you, just as an onion does – and each one is more interesting than the last.'

I chuckled. 'Well, I've never been likened to an onion before, but I think I like it.'

'Good.'

We carried on in companionable silence until we reached the other side of Sacré-Coeur. The peacock led me down a side street containing a row of shops. He stopped by a milliner's and unlocked a door beside the shop, gesturing at me to go inside. The door opened straight onto a steep flight of stairs.

'How long have you lived here?' I asked as we made our way up.

'Three years,' he replied. 'Since I ran away to Paris to make my fortune as a jazz musician.'

'You're a musician?' Clearly I wasn't the only one with many layers.

'I am – or at least, I was trying to be, until the Germans arrived and thwarted my plans.' We reached the top of the stairs, and he unlocked another door. 'Welcome to my humble abode.' He stood back and ushered me in with a flourish.

'Thank you.'

The room was steeped in darkness thanks to the blackout blinds, but I could just make out the outline of a small table and a couple of chairs. The pine scent of cologne hung in the air. After the stench of the velodrome, I inhaled it eagerly.

The peacock took a book of matches from his pocket and lit a candle that had been stuck into the neck of an empty wine bottle on the table. As more of the room appeared, I saw a guitar propped against the wall next to a record player and a teetering pile of records. A mattress lay along the opposite wall, covered with a blanket woven in vibrant shades of yellow, red and orange and topped with an equally colourful array of cushions. A poster from the surrealist movie *L'Age d'Or* was pinned to the wall above the table and a pair of maracas were lying randomly on the floor. It was so different to Pierre's apartment, where everything was in muted shades and had to be in its rightful place. I loved it instantly.

'This is great,' I said, turning to see a kitchenette even smaller than mine in the corner of the room. A set of bongo drums had been placed on top of the tiny stove. 'Very bohemian.'

He looked suddenly shy. 'Can I get you a drink? I have wine or tea. I refuse to drink that travesty they now call coffee.'

I laughed. I was no fan of the ersatz coffee either. 'Could I have some wine please? I feel in need of some alcohol.'

'Of course.' He looked at me, concerned. 'Are you OK? I imagine it must be quite a big deal, leaving your husband.'

'No, it's not that.'

'Please, sit.' He pulled out one of the chairs.

'Thank you.' I sat down and gave a heavy sigh. 'I went to the Vel d'Hiv today,' I said as he went over to the kitchenette. 'I wanted to do something to help the girl in the photograph I took. I found her mother's locket on the floor after she was beaten and taken away by the police, I wanted to get it to her, I thought it might bring her some comfort, and I managed to get in.'

'How?' He turned and stared at me.

'I saw some Red Cross volunteers taking soup inside. I offered to help them carry one of the pots.' I gazed down at the table and traced my finger along a crack in the wood. 'It was horrific,' I murmured. 'The people inside, they're being treated worse than animals.'

The peacock came and joined me at the table, placing half a bottle of wine and two glasses in front of me.

'There's so many of them. And it's so hot in there. They've closed the windows and roof so people can't escape. And the smell is unbearable. The toilets are all blocked, so I guess they're having to go in the stands, with no privacy.'

'My God!' He shook his head. 'And did you find her, the girl?'

I felt a stab of pain at the thought of Lillie trapped inside that hell on earth all by herself. I really hoped she'd found someone to take care of her. 'No. There were way too many people. It was mayhem.'

'I'm sorry.' He sighed. 'How is this happening, here in Paris?'

'That's what I keep asking myself and I can't find the answer.' I leaned back in my chair. 'For so many years, I dreamed of moving here. I thought it would be the most magical place on earth.'

'Me too. And it was.' He took the cork from the wine bottle and poured me a drink. 'Where are you from originally?'

I felt a jolt of shock. What was I thinking blabbing away about not being from Paris? For a moment, I'd totally forgotten about the need to hide my true identity. 'Brittany,' I replied, thinking of my cover story.

'I don't believe it!' he exclaimed. 'That is where I am from too. Whereabouts in Brittany?'

Damn! I'd never set foot in Brittany before. 'Oh, um, the central part,' I said. 'So, did you see your contact in the Resistance?' I asked quickly, eager to change the subject. 'Could they make use of my photographs?' I crossed my fingers under the table, hoping he'd say yes.

'I did,' he replied. 'Are you free tomorrow? He wants to meet with you.'

I felt a surge of relief. 'I have a photo shoot tomorrow morning, but it should be done by early afternoon.'

'Excellent! My band are playing at Café Capoulade tomorrow afternoon. I would love it if you'd come as my guest, and then you can meet my contact. We are playing down in the cellar and we start at three.'

'That sounds great.' I gave him a grateful smile. 'So, you're a guitarist?' I asked, eager to keep the conversation from straying back to Brittany.

He smiled. 'Yes, jazz guitar.'

'You'll have to play something for me.'

'Yes, yes I will. Once I've fixed your hair.' He poured himself a drink.

'Hmm, but will you really be able to fix it, or will you make it worse?' I teased.

'Oh, I'll fix it all right.' He grinned and stood up. 'Let me fetch my scissors. I ought to do it now before I drink any wine.'

'Yes, that does sound sensible.' I breathed a sigh of relief that he seemed to have forgotten all about my fictional place of origin.

He returned with a pair of scissors, comb and a hand mirror. 'So you'll be able to check my handiwork,' he said, passing me the mirror.

'Thank you.'

'Do you trust me?' he asked, looking me right in the eyes.

'What? Yes... yes of course.' My pulse quickened.

'I think you would really suit a crop.'

'A crop? What, like a man's haircut?'

'Yes. You have the kind of face to carry it off for sure... I think,' he added with a frown of uncertainty.

'Hmm, you're not exactly filling me with confidence,' I quipped. But in spite of his uncertainty, there was something about this suggestion that actually appealed to me. I was quite a fan of the androgynous look, and besides it would make it even harder for Pierre to recognise me if we were to pass each other in the street. 'OK, go ahead,' I replied, taking a gulp of wine for Dutch courage.

'Are you serious?' Judging by his look of glee, he hadn't been expecting me to be quite so agreeable.

'Yes, quick, before I change my mind.'

I took another drink and he set to work snipping at my hair whilst singing away to himself under his breath. He was certainly the most exuberant hairdresser I'd encountered. As long as his talent matched his enthusiasm, I was in safe hands.

Finally, he put the scissors down. '*Et voilà!*' he exclaimed, holding the mirror up in front of me.

I couldn't help gasping. I looked radically different, but he was right, the crop really did suit my face. I put my hand up to my head and stroked what was left of my hair, and the now bare nape of my neck. No doubt it would feel a lot cooler in the oppressive heat too. 'I love it,' I said.

'Me too!' he exclaimed. 'Now you look even more interesting. It is as if I have added another layer to the onion!' he exclaimed theatrically.

'OK, OK, no need to get carried away.'

As he sat down opposite me, I smiled at him in the flickering candlelight.

'You are like an onion too,' I said. 'A sharp-dressing zazou, a jazz musician, *and* a hairdresser. So many layers, so many talents.'

'And there are many more for you to discover, believe me,' he said, raising an eyebrow suggestively.

I couldn't help but laugh at his audacity. 'You are very confident.'

'It's not about being confident,' he said seriously. 'I just like to focus on the positive – and think thoughts that make me happy.'

I nodded. It certainly seemed like a great ethos to live by, if a little difficult given the current state of affairs.

He took a sip of his wine. 'Trust me, I'm not confident in everything. There are certain things that make my nerves rattle like those maracas.' He pointed to the maracas on the floor.

'Such as?'

'Such as the thought of kissing you.'

I let out another laugh, trying to ignore the unexpected flutter in my stomach at the thought. 'You're very presumptuous.'

'But obviously I don't have to worry about that yet, due to

my rule.' He sprang up out of his seat again. 'Would you like to listen to some music? I have a fairly impressive record collection if I say so myself.'

'Sure.' Being with the peacock felt like being whisked up inside a whirlwind and after so long feeling suppressed and subdued it was wonderful to be jolted awake again.

I joined him sitting on the floor by the stack of records. And as we riffled through albums by the likes of Cab Calloway and Johnny Hess, I said a silent prayer of thanks that, somewhat miraculously, we should have met. The peacock was a like a ray of sunshine in human form, and a welcome contrast to the darkness I could feel gathering all around.

I stayed with the peacock until just before curfew, talking and playing records and sipping wine – we had to sip very slowly due to the rations. It was the perfect way to decompress after the horrors of the Vel d'Hiv. He insisted on walking me home and when we reached the door to my apartment, a mere five-minute walk away, he laughed and shook his head.

'We are practically neighbours!' he exclaimed before kissing the back of my hand. 'I very much look forward to seeing you again.'

'You too. And thank you so much for organising a meeting with your contact tomorrow,' I whispered. 'I can't tell you how grateful I am.'

'I feel certain you're going to make a really important contribution to the fight,' he whispered back, and I felt a nervous fluttering in my stomach. I really hoped I'd live up to his expectations.

Once inside my apartment, I went straight to the bathroom and studied my reflection in the mirror. The peacock was right, my short hair did make me look like a different person, but somehow I felt that I looked a lot more like me – the me I was supposed to be.

I took the locket from my pocket and carefully placed it in the new hiding place I'd created for my Resistance photographs and their negatives under the floorboard beneath the sink. 'One day, I'll get it to you,' I whispered to Lillie, as I wedged the floorboard back in place.

The following day, I had a job booked for *Marie Claire*, photographing hats. Ordinarily, a job like this wouldn't have filled me with excitement, but ever since the occupation and the shortage of material for new clothes, French women had become increasingly enterprising when it came to their hats, fashioning them into all kinds of weird and wonderful confections. *Marie Claire* wanted me to shoot a selection of the most outlandish designs they'd come across on the streets of Paris.

I turned up at the studio to find it a hive of activity and it was instantly comforting to be surrounded by people. The models were brought over to me one by one. Normally, on fashion shoots, I liked to do things a little differently, whether that meant using unusual props or getting the model to strike an unexpected pose. But I realised straight away that this shoot required no extra gimmicks; the hats were so outlandish, they needed to be distraction-free. One hat had a pack of playing cards arranged like a garland around the brim; another had a fringe of brightly coloured ribbons cascading down around the model's head. The pièce de résistance was a black top hat with a stuffed magpie perched on top.

'Isn't it wonderful,' the photo editor from the magazine said, as I took a close-up of the bird. 'French women will never be beaten. We will use our inimitable style as an act of resistance.'

'But of course!' I replied with a grin. It was occurring to me that, with a bit of imagination and a lot of grit, one could find many different ways to resist.

As was the norm, the shoot ran over the allotted time and I didn't get to Café Capoulade until past four, jittery with nerves. It was so long since I'd gone to something unaccompanied and even though I was going as a guest of the peacock, he'd be at work and with his crowd, and I couldn't help worrying I'd feel out of place. And I was even more anxious about meeting his contact in the Resistance.

I'd been up half the night developing my pictures from the velodrome and creating larger prints to show him. The compact 35mm camera might be wonderfully discreet, but the photographs it produced were tiny. Thankfully, the pictures I'd taken in the velodrome had come out well, but would they be enough to make a good impression?

Get a grip, you're an Esposito! I imagined Pops saying and I smoothed down my newly cropped hair, adjusted the collar on my dress and stepped inside. I'd loved going out on the town on my own when I first arrived in Paris. I needed to rekindle some of my old adventurous spirit.

The upstairs of the cafe was full of people clustered around tables deep in conversation. Judging by their earnest expressions and the plethora of books on the tables, they seemed to be an intellectual crowd. When I noticed a man reading a novel by Ernest Hemingway, it filled my heart with joy, as books by US authors had been banned by the Nazis as soon as America entered the war. It was wonderful to see a pocket of Paris untouched by the Germans. The fact that they'd taken over so many of our restaurants and bars was another thing that had put me off going out.

I wove through the tables to the back of the room and a sign pointing to the basement club. As soon as I opened the door onto the stairs, I heard swing jazz playing and my nerves intensified.

You used to love going to these kinds of places, I reassured myself, *you're just out of practice, is all.*

I emerged into the cellar club to quite a scene. The round dance floor in the centre of the room was crowded with young people dancing. The men were all in the zazou uniform of over-sized jackets, drainpipe trousers and narrow ties, their long hair gleaming with Brilliantine. As for the women, they took my breath away, they looked so happy and free. Almost all of them were wearing short, flared skirts, tight tops and wooden plat-form shoes. Many of them had dyed their hair blonde and their lips were painted bright red. They looked like bohemian Holly-wood sirens and I felt as drab as the German women who now worked in Paris in comparison. 'Grey mice' we called them, due to their dreary, unimaginative uniforms. I took my lipstick from my purse and applied a quick coat.

Once again, I was struck by the way Pierre had worn me down over the years, so slowly and subtly, I didn't even realise he was doing it. How he'd look me up and down critically if I was wearing a particularly flamboyant outfit, saying things like, 'You're not wearing that out, surely?' Or, 'Is it wise for an Amer-ican in France to draw attention to herself by dressing so provocatively?' It was as if he'd taken an eraser and slowly rubbed all the colour from me – and not just from my appear-ance, but my personality too.

I peered through the crowd to the small stage at the far side of the room where the band were playing. From what I could make out there were five of them. The singer – an African American man in a sharply cut zoot suit – was hollering into a microphone at the front. The drummer was behind him and there were a trumpet player and saxophonist to his left. Finally,

I spied the peacock to the right, deeply immersed in playing his guitar. They all sounded incredible, and the music was instantly uplifting. It was so long since I'd gone dancing, but I could feel the instinct stirring inside of me, pulsing from my heart to the soles of my feet. But I couldn't dance on my own surely.

Why not? I imagined my pops yelling. *You're an Esposito, you can do whatever you damn well please!*

The band began playing 'Cotton Tail' and I could no longer resist. The rhythm seemed to rush inside of me and carry me onto the dance floor. The other dancers instantly parted like waves in the sea to make room, and although I felt a little awkward and out of practice at first, it wasn't long before I'd relaxed into the melody. The heat in the basement helped too, as if softening my limbs.

About midway through the song, the rest of the band quietened down and the peacock began playing a guitar solo. It reminded me of a guitarist I'd seen once before the war, named Django Reinhardt. The peacock's playing was so mesmerising and magical I stopped dancing and made my way closer to the band to watch. At one point, his fingers were moving so fast across the strings that my vision blurred.

One by one, my fellow dancers stopped to watch, awestruck too, and when the solo finally came to an end and the rest of the band resumed playing, everyone burst into spontaneous applause. The peacock looked up, an expression of surprise and delight upon his face. Our eyes met and his smile grew.

The song ended and the singer announced that it was the end of their set. I felt terrible that I'd got there late, especially as they were so good. For a moment it had felt as if the music had swooped me up like a magic carpet and transported me to another world. A world where everyone had joy in their hearts, and the Nazis didn't exist.

The peacock put down his guitar and hurried over.

'You came!' he exclaimed. 'I was worried you might have changed your mind when I didn't see you earlier.'

I gave him an apologetic smile. 'I'm really sorry, my shoot took longer than expected. I only got to see the last song, but what a song! It was incredible. *You* were incredible.'

His face lit up. 'Thank you so much, and please don't be sorry. You're here now. And me thinking you weren't going to turn up has made your surprise appearance all the sweeter.'

'Well, that's a very positive way of looking at it.' I couldn't help privately chuckling. Pierre was such a stickler for time-keeping – other people's anyway. If I'd been this late for something of his, I'd never have heard the end of it. Once again I felt a surge of relief that I'd no longer have to tolerate his endless hectoring. 'I hope I haven't missed being able to meet with your contact.' I looked at him anxiously.

'No, it's fine. Come with me.' The peacock lightly placed his hand on the small of my back, but it didn't feel possessive; if anything it felt comforting. 'Let me buy you a drink.'

'I think I should be the one buying you a drink after that performance,' I replied.

'No, no, no, I insist,' he said, guiding me through the crowd.

When we got to the bar, I ordered one of the strange grenadine beer cocktails. We sat down at a table in the corner and I clinked my glass to his. 'Your performance was incredible. You remind me of Django Reinhardt.'

His green eyes widened in surprise. 'You have no idea how much that means to me. That man is my hero. It's an honour to even be mentioned in the same sentence as him. He's such an inspiration, achieving what he has after everything he went through.'

'What did he go through?'

'Years ago, there was a fire in the caravan where he lived and he suffered serious burns. They were so bad he lost the use of two fingers.'

I thought back to the night I'd seen Reinhardt play. There'd been no sign of any physical disability, quite the opposite. 'But how is he still able to play the guitar so brilliantly?'

The peacock took his silver tobacco tin from his jacket pocket. 'It took him over a year to recover and he had to develop his own unique way of playing to overcome his disability. In fact, it's what makes him sound so different to anyone else. Cigarette?'

'Yes please. So, he turned a disaster into an advantage?'

'Exactly.' The peacock took two cigarette papers from the tin and laid them on the table.

'I love that. It's so inspiring.'

The peacock placed a pinch of tobacco on each of the papers and nodded. 'Yes, he is my greatest inspiration. Any time I feel like giving up, I think about what Reinhardt went through and how he kept going.'

I couldn't imagine the irrepressible peacock coming close to giving up on something and he must have read the disbelief on my face because he looked at me questioningly.

'Why do you look so puzzled?'

'I can't imagine you ever giving up. You always seem so positive.'

'Yes, well, maybe you bring that side out in me.'

As I contemplated his words, I couldn't help smiling. It hadn't occurred to me that he might be getting something from our new friendship too. It was a notion that made me feel warm inside.

'Aha!' he cried, waving at someone behind me. 'Raymond, come here.' He leaned forward and lowered his voice. 'Raymond is the contact in the Resistance I was telling you about.'

My skin prickled with excitement, but then I looked round and my heart sank. It was the burly guy who'd let us into the club the day we'd been chased by the fascist thugs. He'd hardly been pleased to see me then; hopefully his social graces had improved since.

'Raymond, this is Fire,' the peacock said. 'I know you met briefly before, but it wasn't under the best of circumstances. Please join us.' He gestured to the empty chair beside me.

Raymond grunted something unintelligible and plonked himself down, placing his meaty hands on the table.

'As I was telling you, Fire would really like to help us through her photography.'

Raymond shifted sideways to look at me. 'So, what kind of photos do you take?'

'I'm a fashion photographer by profession, but—'

'Great,' he cut in, his voice laden with sarcasm. 'I don't really see how pictures of dresses are going to help us beat the Germans.'

There was something about his derisive tone that reminded me of Pierre and caused my hackles to rise.

'If you'd let me finish, I could explain exactly how I can help,' I replied tartly.

'Go on then.' Raymond's dark eyes bored into me.

'I'm also a street photographer, with many years' experience.'

He raised his bushy eyebrows. 'And?'

'*And* that means I'm skilled at taking spontaneous photographs of everyday life without being seen.'

'I still don't see how this—'

'Photographs like this,' I interrupted, taking my pictures of Lillie and the velodrome from my purse. The picture of the arena had turned out better than I'd expected, perfectly capturing the cramped and chaotic conditions, and the devastation on the face of the young woman I'd photographed was powerfully apparent. 'Photographs that show what is happening to our great city.'

'Where is this?' Raymond asked, pointing to the picture of the velodrome.

'I took it inside Vel d'Hiv, after the recent round-ups.'

'How did you get inside?' He looked back at me, but this time his expression was one of curiosity rather than derision.

'I saw some Red Cross workers about to go in and I offered to help them carry their soup.'

'Very enterprising,' he said, every trace of sarcasm gone. He looked back at the pictures.

'I told you she was good,' the peacock said, passing me a freshly rolled cigarette.

'Hmm.' Raymond nodded thoughtfully. 'Can I have this one?' he asked, pointing to the picture of the inside of the arena.

'Of course.'

'Thank you.' He put the photo in his inside jacket pocket and stood up. 'I'll let Louis know when I need you again.'

'Louis?' I looked up at him blankly.

'That's me,' the peacock said, smiling at me. 'But I prefer you calling me the peacock.'

Raymond gave a laboured sigh and pushed his chair back under the table.

'So, you want me to take more photos for you?' I asked, eager to confirm that I hadn't misheard, and he really had said *when* he needed me, rather than if.

'I'll let Louis, or rather, *the peacock*, know,' he repeated drily.

'It's OK, I'd prefer it if you didn't call me that,' the peacock said to him.

'Good!' Raymond retorted, and with that he stalked off through the bar.

'Phew!' I exclaimed before taking a large gulp of my beer. 'He seems very hard to please.'

'His bark is definitely a lot worse than his bite,' the peacock replied. 'He's been through a lot since the start of the war. He experienced a terrible personal loss a few months ago. It might not seem like it, but there's a very big heart beneath that grizzly bear of an exterior.'

'I'll take your word for it.' I settled back in my chair and exhaled happily. Raymond might not have given me the warmest of receptions, but he wanted one of my pictures so that had to mean something. Hopefully it would mark the start of my work for the Resistance.

For the next half an hour or so, people kept coming over to our table to congratulate the peacock on his performance. It was lovely to be amongst happy and enthusiastic people and great to see the peacock get the recognition he deserved, but I also couldn't help feeling a little shy. It had been so long since I'd mingled with a new crowd, my conversational skills felt rusty, to say the least. I contemplated making my excuses and leaving, but then I'd have to go back to my apartment and spend the rest of the night on my own, which was even less appealing. So I kept drinking and another of the beer cocktails appeared, and then another. And before long everything had a rosy tinge, not unlike the grenadine-stained head on my beer, I mused poetically, or at least I thought I was being poetic.

'Are you all right?' the peacock asked during a brief respite in visits from his fans.

'Oh yes, I'm wonderful!' I exclaimed. 'This place is wonderful. This drink is wonderful!' I raised my glass to my lips.

He tilted his head to one side and looked at me. 'Hmm, perhaps we should go and get something to eat.'

'Ha!' I laughed, more loudly than I'd intended, but everything seemed louder all of a sudden. And the colours seemed brighter too. The women's dyed blonde hair and generously applied make-up seemed increasingly garish. 'And what do you suggest we dine on?' I asked. 'Two-day-old bread, or three?'

He stood up and offered me his hand. 'Come, let's get out of here. I have a tin of sardines and bread that's only a day old.'

'Aha! Don't think I can't see through your cunning plan,' I cried. As I got to my feet, the room seemed to tilt.

'What cunning plan?' He looked at me, clearly amused.

'Trying to seduce me with your tin of sardines.' As soon as the sentence left my mouth, it seemed like the funniest thing I'd ever said, and I let out a loud snort of laughter.

'Hmm, that's if you don't seduce me with your pig-like snorts first.' He grinned and took my hand and I didn't protest. Frankly, by that point I needed him to keep me upright.

Outside, dusk was falling and the air was a little cooler. I took a couple of deep breaths to try to sober up a little.

'I'm very sorry,' I said, my voice sounding fuzzy. 'I appear to have accidentally become drunk.' And it truly was an accident. I always tried to avoid getting intoxicated as I hated feeling out of control.

'Don't worry, it happens to the best of us,' he replied with a grin. 'Once you have some food inside of you, you'll feel better...' He paused. 'That's if you'll allow me to seduce you with a tin of sardines?'

'I'll allow you to feed me,' I replied, my voice now weirdly shrill, 'but there will be no sardine seduction tonight!' Once again, as soon as the words left my mouth, I found them hilariously funny and let out another snort of laughter.

'It's OK, you're perfectly safe,' he replied. 'I never make love to an inebriated woman.'

'Really. I thought that most men would jump at the opportunity to take advantage.'

He shook his head. 'Firstly, I'm not most men. And secondly, if we were ever to make love, I'd want us both to be completely sober, so that we could truly appreciate it.'

I nodded, dumbstruck. Once again, the peacock was proving himself to be the polar opposite of Pierre.

We made the rest of the journey back to Montmartre in silence, and with every step, my drunkenness slowly faded, replaced by a growing feeling of embarrassment. By the time we reached the little door beside the hat shop, I was mortified.

'I'm really sorry,' I said as he unlocked the door. 'I never normally get like this.'

We stepped into the tiny hallway and he shut the door behind me, plunging us into almost total darkness.

'Fire, I will never judge you,' he said softly.

There was something so warm and genuine about his tone, it made me want to weep. It had been so long since I'd been on the receiving end of such obvious and heartfelt affection.

'Thank you,' I whispered.

'You're welcome,' he replied. 'Now let's eat and then I have something important to tell you.'

I followed him upstairs, my curiosity growing.

Since the rationing had been introduced, I'd become accustomed to nibbling at my meagre portions to try to make them last longer, but that night I wolfed down my sardines and bread as soon as the peacock placed the plate in front of me.

'It's great to see such appreciation for my cooking,' he joked.

I opened my mouth to reply and a huge burp came out. 'My God!' I clamped my hand to my mouth and started to laugh.

'Can you please stop being so damned seductive,' he said drily, causing me to laugh even harder. 'Do you have any more wind you wish to expel, or can I tell you my news?' He raised his eyebrows and I stifled another giggle.

'It was the gas in the beer, and then eating so quickly,' I mumbled.

'It's OK. I like a woman who is uninhibited when it comes to expelling wind; it shows a great freeness of spirit.'

This made me laugh even harder.

'I'm sorry,' I gasped. 'What was it that you wanted to tell me?'

He leaned in towards me. 'When you were using the bathroom at the club, Raymond came back over to see me and he has an assignment for you.'

'He does?' He instantly had my full attention. 'What is it?'

'Next week there is to be a protest led by women.'

'Where?'

'At a market.'

A shiver ran up my spine. 'Like the Mother's Day protest on the rue de Buci?'

He nodded. 'It would be great if you were able to capture some photographs of what happens, so that word can be spread, and we can encourage people to have more protests.'

My nervous excitement grew. Back in May, a group of women who'd reached the end of their tether over the incessant queuing for paltry rations stormed a grocery store. Madeleine Marzin, the teacher who had organised the protest, urged the other women present to help themselves to jam and sugar. The grocer and one of his staff had attempted to capture the women and hold them in the shop, which resulted in the crowd storming the place. When the police arrived to try to regain order, control shots were fired from the protestors and two officers were shot. What at first seemed like a huge victory for the Resistance resulted in a massive retaliation from the authorities and a wave of arrests and deaths. As the organiser of the protest, Marzin was sentenced to death, although Pétain intervened and commuted her sentence to a lifetime of hard labour. As I remembered this, it was as if all the alcohol left my body and I suddenly felt completely and utterly sober.

'Where will it be?' I asked.

'At the market on rue Daguerre,' he replied.

I knew the market well but prayed I'd misheard. 'In Montparnasse?'

He nodded and my stomach clenched.

It was in Pierre's neighbourhood and where I used to go to get most of our rations. I'd really been hoping to avoid going back there so soon.

'So, what do you think?'

'I'll do it – of course.' My desire to help the Resistance by far outweighed any fear I had of being spotted by Pierre.

'Are you sure?' The peacock stared at me intently through the flickering candlelight.

'Yes, yes of course.'

'You don't have to do it if you don't want to. You—'

'I want to,' I interrupted. There was no way I'd bump into Pierre at the market, or at any other market for that matter. He'd be getting one of his minions or mistresses to fetch his rations now I'd gone, of that I was certain. And besides, he'd be the least of my worries. If there was any kind of protest, there was bound to be a huge police presence. After what had happened at rue de Buci, the authorities were keeping a close eye on all the markets. A nightmare scenario began playing in my mind, of me being arrested and the police discovering that my papers were forged. But then I thought of the girl in the photograph tucked inside my pocket. She needed me to be strong – all the people currently crammed inside the velodrome and the intern-ment camp at Drancy did.

'Excellent,' the peacock said. 'You can pretend to be queuing for rations and then, when the time comes, you can produce your camera and snap, snap, snap.' He mimed taking photographs. 'I think it's wonderful that women are leading the way with the protests,' he continued. 'It must be driving Pétain crazy.'

I laughed. 'Yes, especially as he's so obsessed with turning women into baby-makers and keeping us chained to the kitchen. It makes me mad!'

He raised his eyebrows. 'You don't want to have children?'

My face flushed. Much as I liked the peacock, there was no way I could tell him how my mother had taken her own life just months after having me, and the residual fear this had left me with that I might have inherited this trait and find parenthood equally impossible. Although Pops had tried to reassure me that my mom's suicide had nothing to do with me, I couldn't help finding the timing depressingly telling. 'I don't want to be told when to have children,' I said quickly, hoping he hadn't noticed my awkwardness 'And besides, I have a lot more life to live yet.' As soon as the words left my mouth, I realised the irony of my statement given that during the past two years of the occupation with Pierre I'd allowed my life to shrink down to the size of a postage stamp. But that was all the more reason for living life on my terms now that I was finally free of him. Or as free as I could be in Occupied France.

'I understand what you're saying. And who would want to bring a child into the world now, with everything that's going on?'

The sadness in his tone felt so poignant. The peacock with all his exuberance for life would surely make an excellent father.

'Enough of this sadness,' he said, springing to his feet and taking off his jacket. 'I have an idea.'

'Oh yes?'

'Yes, I'm going to teach you to dance.' He hung his jacket on the back of his chair.

'I can dance perfectly well, thank you very much.' I squirmed as I thought back to my earlier awkward moment on the dance floor. Had he seen me?

'I don't doubt that for a moment. But can you do the zazou dance?'

'Er, no.'

'I thought so.' He went over to the pile of records and put one on the record player. I recognised the track immediately; it was 'Je Suis Swing' by Johnny Hess. 'Come.' He beckoned at me to join him.

'First you have to hop on the spot,' he said.

I did as instructed, trying not to laugh.

'Then you shout, "Zazou, hey, hey, hey, za zazou!"' he called over the music. 'And slap your hips three times, shrug your shoulders twice, like so...'

I stopped hopping and watched as he shrugged.

'And then you turn your head to the side,' he said.

I giggled as I tried to copy him, slapping my hips. 'Hey zazou!'

'Not *hey zazou*,' he corrected. 'Zazou, hey, hey, hey.'

After about three attempts, I had it down and we were doing the bizarre zazou dance in perfect synchronicity. Just as before when I'd been dancing in the club, it felt so good to move and release some of the tension of the past two years from my body.

'It is fun, no?' he said as the song came to an end.

'It is!' I exclaimed.

'And it's even more fun when we do it in front of swastikas on buildings.'

'What?' I stared at him in shock.

'Yes, sometimes we will arrange to gather outside a town hall or a monument where the Nazis have draped their flag and do the dance on the spot. What better way to protest than to bring joy to their hate.' He grinned.

'I think that's wonderful!' I exclaimed, trying to imagine the vibrant scene as the zazous fought back against German hostility with a display of pleasure and unity.

'I think you're wonderful,' he replied, before looking down at the floor.

'Thank you.' I smiled, then glanced at the clock on the mantelpiece. 'Damn, it's almost curfew.'

'I'll walk you home,' he said, fetching his jacket from the

back of the chair. As I watched him put it on, I felt awash with gratitude. It was so nice to be in the company of a man who didn't try to control or coerce me, who gave me the space to simply be. And I was even more grateful that he'd introduced me to the Resistance. My work to help overthrow our occupiers was about to officially begin.

10

APRIL 1985, PARIS

My new-found feeling of hope, instilled in me by the busker and the little bird, lasted all the way back along the rue des Martyrs, and as I passed my local *boucher* and *fromager* setting up their signs outside their shops, I greeted them cheerily.

Frederic, the *fromager*, must have noticed a difference in me because he gave me a beaming smile and grabbed my arm.

'I have more of your favourite goat cheese in stock,' he said, instantly causing me to drool.

'Can you save me some?' I replied. 'I can't stop now, I'm late for work.'

'But of course!' he exclaimed. 'And I'll throw in a jar of *figue et noix confiture* as a special gift. They go so well together.'

'Thank you so much,' I said, touched by his generosity.

'No, thank *you*,' he replied with a twinkle in his eye. 'Your smile it is like a ray of sunshine.'

'Thank you again!' I laughed. Flirting came as naturally as breathing to French men and I knew better than to take it seriously, but still, it felt nice to simply accept the compliment rather than brush it off as I normally would.

I arrived at the library ten minutes late, which was unheard of as I was always early. As I hurried through the huge wooden doors, my boss, Max, who was standing behind the desk, raised one of his thin grey eyebrows. Max's eyebrows were so expressive, I felt certain that if he should ever tragically lose the power of speech he'd still find it perfectly easy to communicate.

'I'm sorry, I got distracted, listening to a busker,' I said, deciding that honesty was the best policy, especially as I was never late, so surely I could be excused just this once.

Max raised both eyebrows at this, clearly demonstrating his complete shock that his most mundane and reliable colleague should have gone rogue in this way.

Rather enjoying my unprecedented air of unpredictability, I decided to see if I could get his eyebrows to reach his hairline. 'He was singing the most beautiful rendition of "Imagine" by John Lennon and then a little bird hopped down onto my lap and started singing too,' I said, joining him behind the desk. 'It really was the most magical experience.' I watched his face, trying not to grin.

His eyebrows drooped, knotting together in an expression of utter confusion. 'Well, how very Snow White of you,' he remarked, drolly. He twirled the pen on a string that he always wore around his neck. 'I hate to bring you crashing back down to earth, but we have some new stock that needs labelling.' He nodded to a box of books under the counter.

'Of course,' I replied. 'I'll get right to it.'

It would be an exaggeration to say that I'd loved my lengthy career as a librarian, but I'd certainly gained a great deal of contentment from my thirty-five years of book lending. After the turmoil and trauma of the war, I found the tranquillity and order of the library hugely soothing. The war had given me enough chaos to last a lifetime and I drew comfort from the fact that in the world of the Dewey Decimal System, everything had its rightful place. I liked that the most chaotic thing to happen in the library would be finding a detective novel wrongly shelved in the cookery section – a problem that was so easily fixed.

The sense of order in my work life had filtered into my home life too. I always kept my apartment neat and tidy with minimal clutter, and what constituted my social life also fell into a structured routine. I had still life art classes on a Monday night, took myself out for dinner every Wednesday and Sunday, and I'd visit an exhibition or go and see a movie on my Saturdays off. Now, as I made a start on the box of new stock, I wondered what my younger, pre-war self would have made of this woman I'd become. She'd certainly never dreamed of being a librarian, that was for sure. She'd probably be horrified by the way I dressed too, I thought, as I glanced down at my cream blouse, tweed skirt, and sensible, loafer-style shoes.

I took one of the books from the box. It was called *Absolutely Free* and the front cover featured a headshot of a woman with cropped grey hair and a piercing stare. Just as I'd experienced on the steps by Sacré-Coeur, I felt a strange stirring deep inside of me. There was something so appealing about these words and yet the concept of being 'absolutely free' felt completely foreign to me. The life I'd created for myself after the war might have brought comfort and security, but it most certainly didn't feel free. It was rigid with routine.

I turned to the inside sleeve to read about the author. Her name was Madeleine Bernier and she'd had a long and successful career as a documentary film-maker. Her book was part-memoir, part commentary on what it was to be a woman in the 1980s, or rather, how it should be.

'I decided long ago that I was going to live my life on my own terms and pursue my passions with gusto,' she was quoted as saying. I'd always been a fan of the word 'gusto', loving how the zestful sound perfectly mirrored the meaning. But as I thought of my own life, I couldn't help feeling wistful. My younger self had been full of gusto and she'd hated routine.

As I stuck a library label inside the book, I was struck by the craziest notion. What if the little bird that had come to visit me that morning hadn't been the spirit of a deceased loved one, but the spirit of my younger self, come to remind me of who I used to be? And what if this book could help me?

I took it over to the issuing desk and booked it out on my ticket.

11

AUGUST 1942, PARIS

Over the next couple of weeks, I felt like a tightly budded peony finally coming into bloom. Every day without Pierre there to hector and chastise me, an aspect of myself I'd had to stifle began to unfurl, like a petal revealing itself to the light. Upon waking, I'd tune the radio to a station playing music, rather than the hate-spewing, German-controlled Radio Paris that Pierre so loved to listen to, and I'd dance my way into the new day. I acquired some clothes from a fashion shoot and took great pleasure in adding my own personal flourishes, shortening a skirt and stitching beads to the hem and adding lace trims to the collars of blouses like I used to. I spent most of my spare time during the day wandering the streets of Paris with my camera, just as I did before the war. Now that I felt there was some purpose to capturing shots of the occupation, it didn't seem quite so depressing; in fact it felt as if I was compiling evidence. And on the odd occasion I felt my resolve weaken, I thought of the girl, Lillie Kramer, and my vow to one day reunite her with her mother's necklace and it was all the motivation I needed. Most evenings I spent with the peacock, listening to records at his place or going to the club and I felt the real me dance further into the light.

The protest on rue Daguerre was due to take place on a Saturday. I got up early on the day, feeling the need to properly prepare. I wanted to dress in a way that would draw the least attention – to adopt the look of the humble housewife Pétain so badly wanted us women to aspire to be. I chose my longest dress, which was made from a muted mustard fabric. I combined it with my flat, cork-heeled shoes, just in case I needed to make a swift exit, and completed the look with a wicker shopping basket the peacock had procured for me. I hid my camera at the bottom beneath a shawl. I decided not to apply any make-up, but when I looked in the mirror, I couldn't help frowning. My new, short hairstyle might have been a great disguise if it came to bumping into Pierre, but I was worried it might draw unwanted attention from elsewhere – specifically, the police. Thankfully, I had a scarf, so I wrapped it around my head like a turban – a look that was fast becoming all the rage due to the shampoo shortage. Finally satisfied that I looked sufficiently nondescript, I prepared to leave.

It was another scorching hot day, which didn't do anything to ease my nerves.

There's no way you're going to bump into Pierre, I reassured myself as I set off for the Metro. *He won't be up this early for a start; he'll still be sleeping off the night before.*

Fortunately, no one was checking papers outside the station, so I was able to go straight inside, where I bought two tickets from the clerk. The peacock had told me to keep a spare ticket in my pocket in case I lost my bag in any fracas and needed to make a hasty exit. My dress didn't have any pockets, so I quickly tucked the spare ticket into my bra.

When I reached the platform, I saw a group of people wearing those cursed yellow stars all huddled together at the end. Another recent *statut* from the Vichy government ruled that Jewish people were now only allowed to travel in the last carriage of trains. I was about to walk on by, then stopped. If I rode the last carriage too, they'd hopefully see it as an act of solidarity.

The train rattled out of the tunnel and into the station. I boarded the last carriage with the others and saw a couple of them look at my chest, perhaps wondering where my yellow star was. I settled back into my seat and tried not to breathe too deeply. As was commonplace these days, the train stank. Soap was in just as short supply as shampoo and in the hot weather the smell of sweat clung to Paris like an acrid fog. But it seemed somehow appropriate that Paris should no longer smell of the perfume and cologne, coffee and freshly baked bread. To me, the stench seemed symbolic of the evil that had invaded us.

As the train pulled into the next station, a policeman boarded our carriage, causing the people sitting opposite me to flinch and shrink back into their seats. The officer walked down the aisle, pausing every so often to ask to see people's papers. When he reached me, he stopped and frowned.

'Where is your star?' he said in a whiny voice that instantly set my teeth on edge. He had a look of utter disdain upon his face.

'I don't have one,' I replied, trying not to feel nervous.

'You do realise that it's illegal to not wear a star now,' he said officiously.

I felt all eyes in the carriage focus up on us.

'I'm not Jewish.'

'You're not?' He stared at me, clearly surprised. 'Papers please.'

I took my papers from my purse, my heart thudding. I thought I'd been doing the right thing riding the last carriage in solidarity with the Jewish passengers, but what if it led to my arrest before I even got to the protest? Had I just been incredibly stupid?

As the policeman studied my papers, I looked down into my lap and tried to remain calm. After what felt like an eternity, he handed them back to me.

'You do realise that you don't have to travel in this carriage.' He leaned closer and lowered his voice. 'This carriage is for the Jewish pigs.'

'Well, I'm happy to travel in it,' I said loudly, whilst thinking, *The only pig present is you.*

He was silent for a moment, then shrugged. 'Suit yourself.'

As he moved on, I breathed a sigh of relief.

The woman sitting opposite gave me a small, grateful smile and it made all the fear I'd just experienced more than worth it. I was no longer standing by in the face of cruelty and evil; I was doing whatever I could to help.

When I reached Montparnasse, I was careful to avoid going anywhere near Pierre's apartment. It had only been a couple of weeks since I'd left, but it already felt like a lifetime ago.

I reached rue Daguerre to find the pavement crowded with women, queuing outside one of the grocery stores. I wondered how many of them were members of the Communist Party, who had organised the protest. The organisers must have surely been there already. Could the woman in the red hat be one of them? Or perhaps the tall, thin-faced woman ahead of me who kept glancing around anxiously. Whoever they were, I was even more impressed with the organisers' bravery now I was there.

A couple of police officers walked by on the other side of the street and my stomach churned. Whatever happened today, there were sure to be some arrests. And if the organisers were captured, they would likely face the same fate as Marzin, a lifetime of labour at least. It was so inspiring to think that the women of France were taking the lead in this way, that they weren't going to be beaten down by Pétain's obsession with stealing our liberty.

More time passed and I started to wonder if the peacock had been misinformed or maybe the protest had been called off. A woman walked past and joined a friend in the queue in front of me, causing a flurry of protest to break out behind.

'Get to the back of the line,' another woman yelled. 'We've been queuing for hours. No pushing in.'

'My friend was saving my place,' the queue-jumper called back. 'So why don't you go to hell.'

Bickering like this had become commonplace when it came to getting our rations. Queuing for hours on end only to receive next to nothing took its toll on the nerves as well as the feet.

'Women, don't be divided by quarrelling,' a voice boomed and I turned to see a woman walking up the road towards us, handing out leaflets to everyone she passed.

The hairs on the back of my neck stood on end. Was this one of the organisers? Was the protest about to begin? I felt beneath the shawl at the bottom of my basket and wrapped my fingers around my camera.

'Your anger is justified,' the woman continued as she drew level with me, 'but don't turn it upon each other; turn it upon the real culprits.' She was short and wiry with dark, almond-shaped eyes and an intense stare.

'Yes!' another woman cried. 'We must stand together.'

'Turn your anger on Vichy, the protector of the hoarders, the protector of those who starve our people!' the woman with the leaflets shouted.

A murmur of agreement rippled along the crowded pavement.

'If we unite in our struggle, we will save our children and our homes,' the woman called as she marched on towards the grocery store.

'The women of the Communist Party are with you!'

another cried. 'Together we will demand more food for our starving families.'

'Let us storm the shop,' the first woman yelled.

A cheer rang out and the anxiety I'd been feeling turned to excitement. I took the camera from my basket and focused it on the woman, who was now giving out her leaflets at the front of the queue.

'Let us take what is rightfully ours!' she yelled, raising her fist in the air.

I pressed the shutter release and the crowd surged forwards. I quickly sidestepped into the road to avoid the stampede and to be in a better position to take pictures. As the women began surging into the store, I took another picture, my pulse racing. If I could get these photographs to Raymond, hopefully he'd be able to distribute them to other parts of France and encourage the women there to have their own protests.

Some men in flat caps appeared in front of a butcher's shop on the other side of the street. As they yelled words of encouragement to the woman, my heart began to sing. The Germans and the Vichy government had tried starving us into submission, but the French spirit was clearly still alive and kicking and it was a wonderful sight to see.

But, sadly, my joy was short-lived. I heard the pounding of footsteps and turned to see about ten police officers charging towards me, batons raised. I leapt to the side just in time but felt the whistle of air rushing by my head as a baton swiped past it. I hurried onto the opposite pavement, where the men in caps had congregated, and took cover in the doorway of an apartment building. The smell of sawdust and raw meat from the butcher's next door flooded my nostrils, instantly making me nauseous.

The police reached the grocery store and began yanking women out, some by their hair. Screams of pain and anger filled the air. I raised my camera and took a quick shot of an officer pulling a woman back, his arm around her neck in a chokehold.

The men beside me started shouting in anger and then I saw a sight that turned my blood to ice. One of them was taking a pistol from the inside pocket of his jacket. Was there going to be a repeat of what had happened on rue de Buci? Was he about to start shooting at the police? Part of me wanted to run for cover while I still could, but another part urged me to stay. If I didn't capture what actually happened, the story would no doubt be twisted into untruths in the German-controlled press.

Outside the store, one of the women collapsed to the ground. As a police officer started dragging her away by her foot, the man with the gun took aim. I quickly took a photo of the police officer pulling the woman, her head bumping on the cobbled ground. Then a shot rang out, and for a second or two, everything seemed to freeze and fall silent, apart from the ringing in my ears.

The policeman collapsed to the ground, blood pooling from the side of his head. And then pandemonium broke out.

I stuffed the Leica back in my basket and began walking off along the street, fighting the overwhelming instinct to run, for if I ran, then I would surely look guilty and be more likely to be apprehended by the police. *Just walk, just walk, just walk*, I repeated over and over in my head, trying to calm my nerves. Too late, I realised I was heading in the direction of Pierre's street, but I had no choice. I had to get away and it dawned on me that if I could just make it to Montparnasse Cemetery, I could take cover there until the furore had blown over.

More police officers came racing past me, running in the direction of the store – this time with guns drawn rather than batons. I noticed my camera sticking out from beneath the shawl and whipped off my headscarf and placed it on top, all the time keeping what I hoped was a calm expression on my face. But inside I was anything but calm. I'd just witnessed the vicious beating of women queuing for groceries and the shooting of a police officer right in front of me, on the streets of my beloved city. It was like being trapped in a nightmare there was no waking from.

Finally, the stone wall of the cemetery came into view. I hurried across the street, studiously avoiding looking at the white Art Nouveau-style apartment buildings on Pierre's road, heading in the opposite direction towards the cemetery entrance. I'd whiled away many an hour in the cemetery over the last couple of years whenever I felt stir-crazy, cooped up in Pierre's apartment.

I heard another gunshot and another coming from the direction of rue Daguerre and I quickened my pace, my spirits sinking. The protest had descended into chaos before it had even begun. And if the police officer had been killed, it would be used as yet more propaganda against the Resistance, not to mention an excuse for brutal reprisals.

But you have the photographs of what actually happened, of what led up to the shooting, I reminded myself, trying not to think of what would happen to me if I were apprehended and the police or the Germans found the camera on me.

Just as I reached the entrance to the cemetery, I heard a man calling from behind, 'Excuse me.'

Pretending I hadn't heard, I practically ran into the cemetery. I usually liked the rows of stone tombs and the way they looked like a town of small houses for the dead, but now, as I heard the man's footsteps gaining on me, they seemed sinister and full of foreboding. The iron door on one of the tombs had somehow come open and I contemplated slipping into its dark and dusty interior.

'Excuse me, you with the short hair,' the man called.

Realising that any attempt at escape was now futile, I came to a halt, feeling sick to my stomach, and slowly turned to see a police officer approaching.

'Pardon me, officer,' I said, hoping he couldn't detect the tremor in my voice. 'How can I help you?'

'Where are you going?' he asked. He was about forty, with closely set eyes and a thin, straight line of a mouth.

'Home,' I replied. 'I was going to go to the market, but then I heard gunshots and thought better of it.'

'I see.' He looked me up and down. 'And where exactly is home?'

'Rue Victor Schoelcher,' I replied. Perhaps the protest being in Pierre's back yard could be to my advantage after all.

'Can I see your papers please?'

'Of course.' I took my papers from my bag and handed them to him, cursing my fingers for trembling.

'Clarisse Alarie,' he muttered as he read and then a look of surprise came over his face. 'I know this name. And this address.'

My heart began to thud. Had Pierre denounced me? Had this officer been told to be on the lookout for me?

'This is where the artist Pierre Lavigne lives, no?'

I fought the urge to retch. 'Yes, he... he's my husband.'

The officer frowned for a moment, then handed me back my papers.

I breathed a sigh of relief. But my relief was fleeting.

'Right, Madam Alarie,' he said firmly. 'I need you to come with me.'

12

'Where are we going?' I asked anxiously as the policeman took my arm and led me back out of the cemetery. His grip was firm but not too firm; I knew I'd be able to slip free if I wanted to. I contemplated hotfooting it down the street, but Montparnasse was now crawling with police – one yell from him and more could come running. I thought of the camera in my basket and what they would find if they developed the film. The reel didn't only contain photos from the protest; it also contained a couple of pictures I'd taken during the week: a shot of an SS man yelling at a Jewish boy, a close-up of some silver Shabbat candlesticks I'd seen bravely displayed in a window. These were no Kodak Girl snapshots of happy family moments as portrayed in the camera advertisements. It would be obvious as soon as the images were developed that I was on the side of the Resistance.

'We're going to see your husband,' the policeman replied.

'What?' I stopped in my tracks, my palms clammy. 'Why?'

'Because he has reported you missing.'

Shit! My blood turned to ice.

The policeman tugged on my arm, and we carried on walking down the street.

'That was all a misunderstanding,' I said, trying desperately to come up with a believable story. 'I'd gone to see my cousin in the country and had difficulties getting back to Paris. I returned home yesterday.'

'Hmm, I think I should take you back home anyway, just to be on the safe side.' He gave me a sideways glance. 'You don't match the description your husband gave us.'

'My cousin gave me a haircut,' I said, trying not to let my panic show. *Why oh why did I remove my scarf?* 'She's a hairdresser.'

'I'd say she was more of a barber.' He looked pointedly at my crop and tightened his grip on my arm.

My mind whirred as we walked down the street. On the positive side, it didn't appear that Pierre had denounced me for being American – at least not yet. But what would he do or say when the police officer deposited me back at his apartment? And what was I going to do or say? How would I explain myself? Where would I tell him I'd been in the two weeks since? *Think, think, think*, I urged myself as we drew closer to the apartment building. It was still relatively early; hopefully he'd still be sound asleep.

When we arrived at the main door to the building, the policeman looked at me expectantly.

'Presumably you have a key,' he said drily.

'Oh, yes!' I confirmed. But did I? As I opened my bag, I tried to remember if the key to Pierre's apartment would still be in there, or if I'd taken it out when I'd moved into my studio in Montmartre. 'Aha!' I exclaimed as I felt the keys in the bottom of the bag. I took them out and brandished them triumphantly, as if this was all I needed to make him go away. I opened the glass door and gave the policeman a beaming smile. 'Thank you so much for accompanying me home, officer. I'll be fine now.' I went to shut the door, but he put his foot over the stoop to block me.

'I'll see you right up to your apartment, just to be on the safe side,' he said again. Never had the word 'safe' sounded so menacing.

'There really isn't any need, I can—'

'I insist,' he interrupted firmly.

'Very well.'

We walked past the row of gleaming mailboxes on the foyer wall. I wanted to take the stairs to buy myself some more thinking time. I needed to come up with something to tell Pierre, especially as I'd told the police officer that I'd returned home yesterday. But to my horror the policeman reached out and pressed the button for the lift. As it whirred into life, I became consumed with panic. How on earth was I going to wriggle out of this?

The lift arrived and the policeman slid open the iron lattice door. The interior was small at the best of times but being crammed in beside the man who could potentially be moments away from arresting me felt so claustrophobic, I could barely breathe. My only hope was that Pierre was out, which was highly unlikely this early in the day, or that he was in a deep sleep from the previous night's alcohol consumption.

By the time we reached the apartment door, I felt like a condemned prisoner about to meet her executioner. The irony that I also happened to be married to my executioner was not lost on me.

I unlocked the door and as we stepped inside, I was hit by the smell of stale cigar smoke. Instantly, I felt myself shrink a little.

'Pierre, my dear,' I called gaily, realising that my best course of action would be to try to brazen it out. 'I think he's still asleep,' I whispered to the policeman, 'and he hates being woken, especially on a Saturday, so it's probably best if you go.'

'Clarisse!'

I jumped at the sound of Pierre's voice and turned to see

him standing at the far end of the hallway in the bedroom doorway, clad in a pair of navy satin pyjama bottoms, his pale stomach spilling over the top. 'Where the hell have you been? And what the hell have you done to your hair?'

'I thought you said you returned from your cousin's yesterday,' the policeman remarked. I wanted to yank his baton from his belt and stuff it in his mouth to shut him up.

'I did, but my husband was out when I got back,' I muttered. 'You've brought me home to him, so shouldn't you go?'

'What's going on?' Pierre said, making his way down the hall towards us.

My heart sank. From the way he was ricocheting from wall to wall, he was clearly still intoxicated from the night before.

'I found your wife in the cemetery, Monsieur Lavigne,' the policeman said, with an irritating smugness. 'There have been some disturbances on rue Daguerre today and I wanted to make sure she wasn't involved in them. Then, when I checked her papers, I recognised her name and your address.'

'Tremblay, is that you?' Pierre asked, squinting up the dimly lit hallway.

My heart sank. They knew each other. Was this one of Pierre's gendarme friends? The one who'd told him about the round-ups?

'Yes, Monsieur. I just wanted to confirm that she is your wife?'

Finally, Pierre reached us and he stared at my hair. 'It's her all right, but she appears to have been scalped. Where the hell have you been?' he barked at me. I could smell stale whisky on his breath.

'I went to see my cousin,' I said, waiting for all hell to break loose. Pierre knew there was no cousin, but would he reveal this?

'Your cousin?' Pierre swayed slightly.

'Yes, in Brittany,' I muttered.

The policeman looked from me to Pierre and back again.

'I see,' Pierre finally replied. 'Well, thank you, officer, for being so diligent and bringing her home.'

'She told me she came back yesterday,' the policeman said. He reminded me of one of those annoying classroom snitches who so love getting the other kids into trouble.

Take his baton and shove it where the sun don't shine, I imagined Pops yelling.

'Very well,' Pierre said, lurching for the door and ushering him out.

I stared at my husband, unsure if I should be relieved at this development. Although it was great that Pierre didn't seem to want to rat on me to the police, I felt certain that it was because he was intent upon meting out his own particular brand of justice.

He closed the door on the policeman and turned back to face me. 'Where the hell have you been?' he yelled, causing a drop of his saliva to land on my lip.

'I... I just needed to get away for a while.'

'Get away where? And why?'

'All your talk of having a baby – it scared me,' I said. It was the only thing I could think of.

'What talk of having a baby?'

I internally groaned. He'd clearly been so drunk, he couldn't even remember saying it. 'You told me you wanted us to start a family,' I replied, trying desperately to think of how I could make another escape. After two weeks of freedom there was no way on God's green earth I could go back to my former life with Pierre. It would be like a living death.

'I did?' He looked genuinely baffled at this. 'I don't remember... But was the thought so hideous that you had to run away?'

'No... yes... I panicked. It's just that with the entire world being at war and with barely enough food to feed ourselves, I couldn't see how on earth we'd be able to take care of a baby.'

'We don't need to worry about that,' he said breezily. 'I have friends. We'll be well taken care of.'

'What do you mean? What friends?'

'In the police. Like Tremblay who was just here. Nothing bad is going to happen to us, trust me.'

I felt sick to my stomach at what he was saying: that he could be friends with the people committing such inhumane atrocities in Paris, the very people I was now working against.

'But I don't understand why you've cut your hair. You look like a man.'

'I... I wanted to donate my hair to the government, to make sweaters and slippers,' I added quickly, remembering the ridiculous government directive.

He stared at me, still swaying slightly. 'You've been with another man, haven't you?'

'What? No!'

'Liar! We both know that you don't have a cousin in Brittany. You don't have any family here in France.'

'I was staying with a friend,' I murmured.

'Which friend?'

'A model I met on a photo shoot.'

'I don't believe you.' He lurched towards me and grabbed my neck.

Knee him in le palle! I imagined Pops yelling.

'I think you've been with another man, and I think I need to teach you a lesson.'

The hypocrisy of his outrage after he'd constantly cheated on me made me burn with indignation. But before I could react he caught me by surprise, tightening his grip on my throat and forcing me to the floor.

'Get off me!' I gasped.

'You're my wife. I can do whatever the hell I like with you,' he rasped as I choked for air. 'It's time I taught you a lesson.' He shoved his other hand up my dress.

I tried to struggle free, but he was so much bigger than me and so heavy, he had me pinned to the floor.

'You're my wife,' he gasped, tearing at my underwear.

I turned my head from side to side trying to shake his hand free, but it only made him grip my neck tighter. I could feel my vision narrow; I was starting to black out.

Knee him in le palle! I imagined Pops crying, but his voice was becoming fainter.

I felt Pierre thrust himself between my thighs and then everything went black.

13

I came round to find Pierre lying beside me on the hallway floor, his chest heaving as he panted. The space between my legs felt as if it were on fire and my neck ached. I tried to summon the energy to sit up, but tiny stars spiralled before my eyes, making me feel dizzy.

'Why do you have to be so damned obstinate?' Pierre gasped.

I slowly propped myself onto my elbow. His eyes were shut and I saw the shiny trail of what looked like a tear coming from the corner of one of them. Was he crying? I sat up and stared at him in horror and disgust.

'Why can't you just be a good obedient wife?' he said with a sob.

He *was* crying! He, who had just attacked me, was crying like a giant baby.

I stumbled to my feet, and looked at him lying naked on the floor, his satin pyjama bottoms rucked around his ankles. I saw my basket on the floor by the door, took my camera from it and quickly took a picture.

On hearing the click of the shutter, his eyes opened. 'What are you doing?'

'Gathering evidence,' I replied.

'Evidence of what?' He attempted to roll onto his side to get up, but I was there like a shot, delivering a swift kick to the side of his ribcage.

'Ow!' he cried, clutching his side.

'Evidence of your attack on me,' I replied as calmly as I could muster.

'I didn't attack you.'

I stared at him, incredulous. 'You choked me until I blacked out. You raped me.'

'You're my wife!' he exclaimed.

'You're an animal!' I spat.

Again, he tried to get up, but his size was working against him now, and another kick from me sent him rolling onto his back like a beached whale.

'This marriage is over and if you do anything to try to find me, or denounce me to the police, I shall make sure that all of Paris knows the truth about you.'

He gave a derisory snort. 'And how would you do that?'

'I'm going to share my photographs and story with one of my contacts in the magazine industry, with the instruction to publish them should anything happen to me.'

'What photographs? What story?'

'The story of how you attacked me. The photographs of my injuries.' I could tell from the way my throat was aching that there was bound to be bruising. And, sure enough, as he looked up at me, I saw him visibly recoil. 'I can't imagine too many women wanting to sit for you after that story comes out – or do anything else with you for that matter.' Again, I noticed him flinch. I came and stood right by him, placed my foot on his genitals and pressed down slightly. 'I'm going now and if you know what's good for you, you'll leave me the hell alone, do you understand?' I pressed down a little more. Part of me – the Esposito in me, I guess – wanted to stamp right down until I caused him the kind of pain he'd caused me.

'Ow! Yes!' he cried.

'Good.' I removed my foot and headed for the door.

'I'm better off without you anyway,' he muttered and I had to fight the urge to march back over and kick him in the head.

It was only when I was back out in broad daylight that the reality of what had just happened hit me. Every step I took sent a sharp dagger of pain shooting up inside of me. But even worse was the pain I was feeling emotionally. It was as if all the strength I'd regained since leaving Pierre had been forced from my body, leaving me feeling as flimsy and breakable as a paper doll.

The peacock had told me to come straight back to his place after the protest, but how could I face him now after what that monster had done to me? How could I not tell him though? How would I explain any bruising?

When I finally got back to my street, my legs almost buckled from the sheer relief. But then I saw a flash of colour. The peacock, clad in a sea-green suit, was pacing up and down by my door. I was about to turn on my heel and beat a hasty retreat, but it was too late. He'd seen me and was running up the road towards me.

'Fire!' he cried. 'Are you OK?'

Hearing his name for me made me want to weep. He thought I was so fearless, so powerful. What would he think if he knew how easily I'd been overpowered by Pierre?

'Are you OK?' he asked again as he reached me. 'I heard that a police officer was shot. I was worried that you might have been arrested.' He gasped in shock. 'What happened to you?' He gently touched the side of my neck. 'Did the police do this to you?'

I wanted to nod, but I couldn't bring myself to. He was always so honest and open with me; how could I not be the same?

'Can we go inside?' I murmured.

'Of course! Come.' He took my hand. 'You're trembling.'

'I'm sorry.'

'Don't be sorry!'

I somehow managed to unlock the door and we stepped into the tiny hallway. As soon as I closed and locked the door behind us, I burst into tears.

'What happened?' he asked softly, holding me tight.

'The police... my husband...' I sobbed.

'Your husband.' The shock in his voice filled me with dread. How could I tell him what had happened? How could I bring myself to relive it?

He guided me upstairs and we sat at the kitchen table.

'A... a police officer apprehended me – after the shooting,' I stammered. 'He asked to see my papers and realised that my husband had reported me missing.'

'No!' The peacock looked horrified.

'So he took me back to my husband's apartment and...'

'And?' His eyes widened in horror. 'Did your husband do that to you, to your neck?'

I nodded, my mouth so dry, I could barely swallow.

'Oh, Fire!'

I tried to look calm, but I couldn't stop shaking.

The peacock pulled his chair closer and took both my hands in his.

'What did he do to you?' he said softly.

'He... he pushed me to the floor and choked me till I blacked out,' I replied, looking down into my lap, unable to meet his gaze. 'I feel so pathetic,' I sobbed.

'Why?' He stared at me, clearly shocked.

'I wasn't able to fight him off. He... he...' I couldn't bring myself to say the words.

'What?' All the colour seemed to drain from the peacock's face. 'Did he do something else?'

I was shaking so hard now, it was as if my entire body was convulsing. 'Yes, while I'd blacked out.'

'He attacked you?'

'Yes.' My voice was barely more than a squeak.

'I'm so sorry.' He let go of my hands and started stroking my hair.

'I feel so disgusting,' I sobbed.

'You're not disgusting. He's the one who's disgusting.' There was a tightness in his voice I'd never heard before. He looked around the room as if searching for inspiration. 'I have an idea.'

I watched as he stood up and went and filled the kettle and set it on the stove.

'Coffee?' I asked, bemused.

'No – that ersatz rubbish won't make you feel better. Here.' He reached into his jacket pocket and pulled out a small, square package wrapped in brown paper. 'I was given this yesterday and I was planning on giving it to you on a special occasion, like your birthday.' He handed me the package. 'But I think you should have it now. Go on, open it.'

As I undid the paper, the most beautiful smell of rose petals wafted up through the air. 'Soap!' I gasped.

'Yes.'

I put the bar to my nose and inhaled the delicate floral scent.

'Maybe you could use it to wash him from you?' he said softly.

I stared at him through my tears, once again astounded at how he always seemed to know exactly the right thing to say or do.

'Thank you,' I whispered, clutching the soap to my chest.

As I caught another waft of the fragrant scent, I made a silent vow that I was going to scrub every trace of Pierre from my mind as well as my body. I couldn't let what had happened defeat me. Not now, when so much was at stake. I had to choose to think empowering thoughts, just as the peacock chose to think himself happy.

14

APRIL 1985, PARIS

For the rest of my shift in the library, I was filled with a strange restlessness. Even when Max asked me to reorder some of the archives down in the basement – normally one of my most absorbing work tasks – I was unable to concentrate. I couldn't shake the feeling that my younger self had somehow come back from the dead for a reason. But what was it? And why now? I'd done such a good job of burying her once the war ended. I'd lost so much, and was so fearful of losing more.

I still felt too distracted to be able to focus on my walk home from work, so I decided to give my still life class a miss and spend the evening in the company of the indomitable Madeleine Bernier and her new book, *Absolutely Free*, instead. But first I stopped off at Frederic's *fromagerie* en route to collect my cheese.

'Twice in one day!' he exclaimed as soon as I walked through the door. 'I must be the luckiest man in all of Paris!'

'Or the smoothest-talking,' I quipped. It was most unlike me to make a joke like this and he looked at me in surprise.

'There is something different about you today,' he said, eyeing me curiously. 'Did you make love last night?'

'What? No!' I exclaimed, my cheeks flushing.

'Good,' he replied.

'Why is that good?'

Now it was his turn to blush. 'No reason. Let... let me get your cheese,' he stammered. 'I kept it out back so it wouldn't accidentally be sold to anyone else.'

As he disappeared into the back of the shop, I gazed at the vast array of cheeses on display in the glass-fronted cabinets. Huge wheels of Camembert, slabs of snowy white Brie. Cheeses marbled with blue, and others encased in brown and red rind. It was hard to imagine that there'd once been a time when we'd had to queue for hours for the crumbs our rations allowed us. Having spent so much of the war aching with hunger, I still had a morbid fear of running out of food and kept a cupboard in my kitchen crammed with tinned goods just in case.

'Here you are,' Frederic said, plonking a huge slab of goat cheese on top of the glass counter.

'Thank you.'

'And here is your complimentary confiture.' He produced a glass jar of the dark brown preserve.

'Thank you very much.'

'You are very welcome.' He put them in a paper bag and rang up the price on the cash register. 'So, do you have any plans for this evening?' he asked but without looking at me.

'No, I'm staying in with my cheese and a new book.'

He nodded and for a moment I thought he might say something else, but he gave me my change instead. 'Have a nice time.'

As I walked out onto the street, it occurred to me that I probably seemed like the saddest woman on the planet to Frederic, spending the night with cheese and a book, but I felt excited as I contemplated my evening in. I couldn't shake the feeling that I'd come across *Absolute Freedom* for a reason, and I was itching to discover what it might be.

As soon as I got home, I changed into my pyjamas, opened a bottle of cabernet and fixed myself a platter of bread and cheese. Then I curled up on the sofa with my book.

Madeleine Bernier had structured it so that each section focused on a different way in which she'd achieved 'absolute freedom'. After the breakdown of her marriage in her early thirties, she'd vowed to herself that she'd never again 'lose herself for the sake of a relationship' and had decided that it was infinitely preferable to 'take lovers' instead. The notion of 'taking a lover' felt so surreal to me, it made me want to laugh. I wasn't even capable of flirting with the man in the cheese shop! But I was happy in my life of celibacy – wasn't I? After what happened during the war, life felt infinitely simpler and, more importantly, safer without the risk of falling in love with anyone. But as I read about the lovers Bernier had taken in San Francisco, Rome and the Caribbean, and the fun she'd had with them, I felt another wistful pang for what might have been.

I glanced up at the row of old black-and-white photographs on the mantelpiece. The trouble with love was that it came hand in hand with loss, and I'd experienced enough loss to last several lifetimes. Much as I was enjoying reading her tales, I knew that I could never fall in love as often or as freely as her.

Refilling my glass of wine, I moved on to the section in the book about Bernier's travels, which she credited with bringing her the most amount of freedom. As I read about her escapades on safari in Africa and horseback riding in Argentina, where she'd 'taken' another lover, I found myself sighing with every page. The after-effects of the war had left me craving stability, so I hadn't felt the desire to travel much at all. Other than the occasional holiday in Provence or the Loire Valley, my world had shrunk to fit inside the city limits. Reading Bernier wax lyrical about stunning African vistas and Nepalese mountainscapes made me think of my younger self again. As a child, I'd longed to travel. What had become of that adventurous spirit?

I stood up and began pacing the room. I'd been so immersed in the book, I hadn't realised how much wine I'd consumed and felt a little light-headed. It wasn't an unpleasant feeling, though – in fact, it felt good to feel a little looser than normal. I never usually allowed myself more than one glass.

Feeling emboldened, I put the radio on and turned the dial away from my usual news station until I found some music. An old jazz number filled the room and I closed my eyes and began to dance. As I swayed to the rhythm, I felt the presence of my younger self again. She'd so loved to dance. I stretched out my arms and pictured taking her by the hands. It was probably the wine, but I was sure I could hear her laugh as I imagined us twirling around. And then suddenly, my eyes were swimming with tears. What had I done, smothering this young and vibrant part of me out of existence?

'I'm so sorry,' I whispered as I sank back down onto the sofa. 'It was all just too painful. I had to try to forget.'

As I blinked my tears away, I swear I saw my younger self perch down on the other end of the sofa.

'*But now you must remember,*' she whispered.

15

SEPTEMBER 1942, PARIS

I took the silver locket from its hiding place under the floorboard and undid the tiny clasp.

'Hopefully today you will be reunited,' I whispered to the picture of Lillie as a little girl before snapping the locket shut again and going into the living room. I sat down at the table, tore a page from my notebook and began to write.

Dear Lillie,

I thought you would like to be reunited with your maman's necklace.

Warmest regards,

Your friend, Clarisse

I kept the letter deliberately brief because I was certain the guards at Drancy would read all of the incoming mail before distributing it to the prisoners and I didn't want to write anything that might arouse suspicion. Hopefully this sounded like a simple note from a family friend, which I suppose it was – in my mind at least. I thought about the girl so often it was as if she'd become a friend to me.

I knew that, as an American in Paris with false papers, I'd be taking a huge risk going to Drancy, but I still felt the desperate desire to help Lillie and I'd heard via the peacock that the people who'd been rounded up and sent to the velodrome had now been moved there.

I folded the page and put it into an envelope along with the locket, writing *To Lillie Kramer* on the front.

Going to the internment camp at Drancy was also part of my bid to remain emboldened after Pierre's attack, which was proving to be a lot harder to achieve than I'd hoped. No matter what I did to try to distract myself, I couldn't stop flashbacks from that day intruding upon my mind. The sight of him bearing down on me. His fingers tightening around my throat. Everything going black... And even on those days when I was able to shut him out, he ended up haunting my subconscious, looming large in my nightmares instead.

My friendship with the peacock continued to be a source of joy, but what happened with Pierre had caused a subtle shift between us. I instinctively shied away from any displays of physical affection and, responding to my cue, he no longer joked about seducing me and kept a respectful distance.

I tucked the letter inside my bag, along with my camera wrapped in a headscarf. Rumour had it that the internment camp at Drancy was now overflowing with prisoners and I hoped to get some photos for Raymond while I was there. He'd been pleased with the pictures I'd taken at the food riot, telling me that they'd 'come in very useful indeed'. I still wasn't entirely sure how he was using the pictures I'd given him, but at least he was using them.

I set off for the station with that thought firmly at the fore-front of my mind. I was now part of the fightback against the occupation; I had far more important things to focus on than Pierre and what he'd done to me.

Thankfully, the train ride to Drancy passed without incident, and when we arrived at the Paris suburb, I was relieved to see several other people alighting from the train, most of them holding parcels. Hopefully they were delivering them to people at the camp too and I wouldn't stand out.

Sure enough, my fellow passengers and I formed a raggle-taggle procession of sorts all the way to the housing development. As the square-shaped, five-storey structure, complete with armed watchtowers, came into view, I couldn't help shuddering. What must the architects have thought seeing their vision for comfortable living turned into a prison camp? It struck me in that moment that Drancy was the perfect symbol for what Hitler was doing to the world – stamping out imagination and hope and replacing them with cruelty and despair.

As we drew closer, I noticed that the windows in the building were still just holes in the walls. The Germans and their Vichy puppets had been so eager to create their prison camps, they'd commandeered the development while it was still a construction site. I wondered what would happen to the poor people inside once the bitter winter winds arrived.

I stopped for a moment, pretending to look for something in my bag until the people behind me had passed by, then I took out my camera and took a quick shot of the site, complete with one of the watchtowers. Or at least that's what I hoped I'd captured. I didn't dare lift my camera above waist-level to check the viewfinder for fear of being seen. I put the camera back in my bag and hurried after the others.

As I rounded the corner to the entrance of the complex, I saw that it was actually three-sided, like a square-shaped horse-shoe, and through the fence, I caught a glimpse of a courtyard. People were milling about, heads bowed, expressions grave, all wearing those cursed yellow stars.

I felt certain that Raymond would want a picture of the inside of the camp, but how would I be able to take it, right under the eagle eyes of the guards in the watchtower?

A sudden breeze whipped up and it gave me an idea. I took the headscarf from my bag and waited for another gust of wind before letting it slip from my fingers. Just as I'd hoped, it drifted over to the fence.

'Oh dear!' I exclaimed, hurrying after it, one hand inside my bag, holding my camera at the ready.

'What are you doing?' a man's voice bellowed from the watchtower above.

I stopped and looked up at him, my heart thudding.

'I'm sorry, officer, my scarf blew away.' I pointed at the scarf, which had now attached itself to the fence. 'I'll just quickly get it,' I called in what I hoped was a breezy tone.

'Stay where you are!' he bellowed.

Damn! I hesitated for a split second. Should I do as he said, or risk everything to try to get a picture?

Pretending not to have heard him, I hurried over to the fence, grabbed the scarf, and with my other hand, and my back to the tower, I raised the camera to the top of the bag and pressed the shutter. Again, I had no idea how the picture would come out, but that soon turned out to be the least of my worries. As I headed back to the pavement, I saw the guard coming down from his post.

No, no, no! my inner voice wailed. What had I been thinking, taking such a risk?

I slipped one hand back inside my bag, trying in vain to wrap the scarf around the camera again.

'Did you hear what I said?' the guard yelled, marching over.

'I'm so sorry, officer, did you tell me not to get my scarf?'

He glowered at me, his eyes as dark and beady as a crow's. 'What are you doing here?'

'I have a letter for someone I think has been brought here.'

He tilted his head to one side, looking even more crow-like. 'Is that so?'

'Yes, the young daughter of a family friend.' I hoped that if I mentioned I was here for a child, it might soften his mood, but, if anything, he looked more irate.

'Jew, is she?' he snapped and instantly my hackles rose.

She's a child, I wanted to yell, *an innocent child*.

'Yes,' I muttered.

'And you're a *friend*.' He spat out the word with such disdain, it was as if I'd confessed to being friends with an axe murderer.

I nodded.

'Papers please,' he barked.

I fumbled in my bag for my papers, trying to hide the camera beneath the scarf. 'Here you are.' I handed them to him, my fingers trembling.

He studied them, a scowl etched deep into his face. After what felt like forever, he looked back to me. 'Right, come with me.'

My heart was beating so hard by this point, I thought it might burst from my chest.

'Come with you where?' I asked, my voice wavering.

'I want to show your papers to one of my colleagues,' he replied, causing dread to sweep through me. He grabbed my arm and started marching me towards the main entrance of the camp. This couldn't be happening. I had to do something. But what?

The other people from the train were all gathered around the entrance, waiting to be seen by the military police on duty. The guard marched me to the front of the queue, his grip on my arm tightening, and it triggered a memory from one of my child-hood self-defence classes with Frankie. He'd taught me how to get out of just such a hold, but sadly he hadn't taught me what to do if my aggressor had two armed buddies standing right by us.

'I need you to check some papers,' the guard called to one of the policemen.

I heard the rumble of an engine and turned to see a truck pulling up beside us on the street. My heart sank as two more armed guards got out and marched round to the back. They opened the rear door and pulled out a couple of young men. One of them looked instantly familiar, but I wasn't able to place him. Our eyes met and I saw a flicker of recognition on his face, and with a jolt, I remembered. His name was Leo and he worked behind the bar at Café Capoulade.

'We've got two more Jews for you,' one of the guards called.

I frowned. I'd never seen Leo wearing a yellow star.

'This one thought he could outsmart us by not wearing a star,' the guard continued, giving Leo a shove.

Leo muttered something, then he tilted his head back before sending it crashing full force into the guard's forehead. There was a sickening crack and the guard collapsed to the floor, blood gushing from his head. Leo raced off down the street and pandemonium ensued as all the other guards apart from the one holding me set off in hot pursuit.

I held my breath, praying he wouldn't be caught. *Run, Leo, run!* I silently urged.

He was fast as a gazelle and it looked as if he was going to outpace them, but then one of the guards drew his pistol.

No! I watched, horrified as a shot rang out and Leo fell to the ground.

My fellow passengers from the train, who'd been waiting and watching in silence, let out gasps of horror.

'Animals!' one of the men yelled at the guard holding me. 'You should be ashamed.'

'Be quiet!' the guard yelled back, loosening his grip on my arm.

'No, I won't,' the man said, marching over and squaring up to him. 'How can you do this to your own people?'

'Those aren't my people!' the guard spat back and he let go of my arm, just as the man gave him a back-handed slap across the face. As the guard staggered backwards, my papers fell from his hand. I dropped to the floor and grabbed them. Thankfully, the guard was too busy looking at the man who'd hit him to notice. I took a step back, and another.

'You'll pay for this!' the guard yelled, advancing on the man.

Seizing my chance, I turned and started running down the road.

Please, please, please, don't let him see me, I silently chanted as adrenaline coursed through my body.

'Come back!' I heard the guard yell and my stomach lurched.

What if he pulls his gun and shoots me just like the other guard shot Leo?

But if I stopped and went back, I'd be arrested for sure. I had to take my chance. I had to keep running, even if it meant getting a bullet in the back.

It was the strangest feeling, racing down that road knowing that I could be about to be killed at any moment. But I kept going until I reached the corner. *I've reached the corner!* As I turned it, I felt awash with relief. I was out of firing range, but for how long?

I kept running faster and faster until my lungs felt as if they were on fire. *Please, please, please, don't let me be killed,* I prayed as I ran.

I noticed a passageway between a couple of buildings to my left and decided to take it, hoping against hope it wouldn't be a dead end. Thankfully, it led to a narrow backstreet lined with small houses. I slowed my pace to a rapid stride, not wanting to arouse suspicion. I knew I was headed in the general direction of the station, but I'd deviated from the way I'd come, so I was at risk of getting lost. But would it be wise to go to the station now in any case? If the guard was trying to find me, then surely he'd go there too.

I heard the hiss of a train and as I reached the end of the road, I saw the station right in front of me. I glanced all around for any sign of the guard, but it seemed as if the coast was clear. Deciding to take my chances, I hurried across the road and into the station.

A station guard stood on the platform beside the train, about to blow his whistle.

'Excuse me,' I called, running over. 'Is this the Paris train?'

'It is indeed,' he replied, 'but you'd better hurry.' He opened one of the doors and ushered me onboard, then gave a loud blast on his whistle.

The train slowly lurched into motion. Painfully slowly.

I stood back from the door, peering through the window anxiously. *Go faster! Go faster!* I silently begged the driver as the train jerked and lurched like an arthritic wildebeest along the track. Just as we were mercifully pulling out of the station, I heard the sound of footsteps pounding along the platform and a man's voice yelling, 'Stop!'

I leaned back out of view, my skin sticky with sweat. *Don't stop! Don't stop!* I chanted in time with the chugging of the train.

To my huge relief, instead of stopping, it picked up speed. I let out a gasp and leant against the swaying wall. I'd made it to safety. Or I'd made it out of Drancy at least. But if that had been the guard yelling at the train to stop, would he call the next stations, warning them to be on the lookout for me? *It might not have been the guard, it might have been a passenger*, I tried reassuring myself, but it did little to soothe my nerves.

When the train finally arrived in Paris, I joined the queue of people waiting to have their papers checked like a Death Row prisoner about to meet my maker. Had the guard called the station? Would the men manning the checkpoint be keeping an eye out for me? As I shuffled closer and closer, my nausea grew to the point where I could barely swallow.

Finally, it was my turn, and I handed my papers over. I was so convinced that my number was up, I stood motionless for a moment when the guard handed them back.

'Go on,' he said, nodding to the exit.

'Oh, yes, thank you,' I stammered before hurrying outside.

It wasn't until I'd got back to my apartment that I was able to properly breathe again. I collapsed onto a chair and put my bag on the table. I'd made it. I was safe. But I hadn't been able to deliver the locket to Lillie, and now I'd never be able to go back to Drancy.

I took the envelope from my bag, opened it and removed the locket.

'I'm sorry,' I whispered, clasping it tightly.

I was about to put it back beneath the floorboards when I felt the sudden urge to put it on instead. Perhaps if I wore the necklace, it would act as a lucky talisman and lead me back to Lillie in the end. I wasn't normally one for such superstitious thinking, but I was desperate by that point. Seeing Leo shot down right in front of me and then having to flee had shaken me to the core.

You have to keep going, you can't give up, I told myself as I put on the necklace. Not just for Lillie but for Leo too.

I took my camera from my bag and headed through to the darkroom to develop my latest photographs.

16

FEBRUARY 1943, PARIS

Autumn withered into winter and just like the previous year, the weather became brutally cold. I spent my days alternating between working on fashion shoots and taking photos for the Resistance and I wore my lucky talisman, the locket, at all times. Lord knows, I needed the inspiration of thinking of Lillie to help combat the persistent gnawing hunger and biting cold. And however hard it was for me, it was bound to be so much worse for her and her fellow prisoners. Then, in February 1943, the Germans banned the distribution of fashion photography in France, so I was officially out of a job. I once more felt a debt of gratitude to my pops for instilling in me the need to squirrel away an emergency fund – although I wasn't sure how long I'd be able to stretch it out for.

I trudged home from collecting my final fashion shoot payment feeling increasingly dejected. I'd worked so hard to become a professional photographer, and as one of the few women in the industry, it felt like a huge achievement to be respected for my work. I knew there were far worse things that could happen, especially at that moment, but it angered me that my hard-won career could be taken away just like that. Then, as I made my way along the rue des Martyrs, the most wonderful thing happened. A middle-aged woman wearing a headscarf and a long, frayed overcoat approached me. She looked around furtively before stuffing a piece of paper into my hand, then turned on her heel and scuttled off.

I unfolded the paper and saw that it was a flyer with the words *VIVE LA RÉSISTANCE* printed across the top. There was a black-and-white photo beneath the words and as I looked at it, I felt a jolt of recognition. The picture was of the internment camp at Drancy, but that wasn't why it looked familiar; it was because I was the one who had taken it!

The text beneath the photograph referenced the increasing numbers of trains leaving Drancy headed east and how they were rumoured to be taking people to camps in Germany and Poland.

We have to stop the mass internment and deportment of our people, the text concluded. *Join the resistance and help defeat our oppressors.*

I quickly stuffed the flyer into my bag and carried on walking, all of my earlier dejection gone. This was the first time I'd seen how Raymond was using my photographs and it filled me with joy and pride. It didn't matter a jot that I was no longer able to work on fashion shoots; what mattered was that my photography was being used to encourage people to fight back against the Germans. I couldn't think of a more worthwhile career.

One Saturday morning in mid-February, I set off for the peacock's place. He'd told me to meet him there as he had a photography assignment for me. He wasn't any more forthcoming other than to say we'd be going to a 'protest with a twist'. I'd dressed in a sartorial act of resistance – a 'divided skirt', or culottes as they were referred to in Britain and America. They'd become all the rage in Paris in recent months, mainly as a way for women to wear the now banned trousers in disguise and allowing them to cycle with more elegance and ease. I'd teamed mine with a tight sweater and box jacket, and my flat, cork-soled shoes. As always when going on a Resistance assignment, I was dressed for a quick getaway, although there was no need to tuck a spare Metro ticket into my bra this time as apparently whatever we were doing was taking place there, in Montmartre.

As I let myself into the peacock's building and climbed the stairs to his apartment, I wondered what it could be, and if it was really wise to do something right on our doorstep. I did our special coded knock on his door and he opened it in a trice, clad only in his underpants and vest.

'You might be a little cold outside in that get-up,' I remarked drily, whilst trying not to look too closely at his half-naked body. His lithe physique was so different to Pierre's it was hard to tear my gaze away, and to my surprise I felt a tingling deep in the pit of my stomach. It wasn't an unpleasant feeling. In fact, after the numbness I'd experienced since Pierre's attack, it was wonderful to sense my body coming back to life again.

'I'm having a crisis.' He ushered me inside and shut and locked the door behind me. Items of clothing in just about every colour of the rainbow were strewn all across the room.

'What happened?' I asked, sitting down on the only chair that hadn't been swamped with garments. 'It looks as if you've been raided!'

'I can't decide what to wear.' He began pacing up and down the room, clearly anxious.

'Well, if you tell me exactly what you have planned, I might be able to help.' I'd never seen the peacock in such an anxious state and it was infectious. 'What *do* you have planned?'

'I want it to be a surprise, and you'll soon see. But in the meantime, I need you to help me. I need an outfit that yells defiance, but with a sprinkling of joy.'

'Geez, I thought my days of working with fashion divas

were over,' I said, shaking my head. I picked up a bright red jacket from the table. 'How about this for the defiance? It's nice and bold.'

'Yes, but it's the same colour as the Nazi flags.'

'Good point.' I looked around the room and spied a canary-yellow jacket. 'How about this for the joy?'

He nodded.

'And perhaps if you teamed it with that purple shirt, you'd give off an air of defiance.'

'How do you mean?'

'Well, you'd be defiantly declaring to the world that you have no regard whatsoever for colours that go well together.'

He burst out laughing. 'Oh Fire, I really do...' He broke off and looked away as if embarrassed.

'You really do what?' As I looked at the peacock I felt the tingling sensation inside me again, stronger this time. Had he been about to tell me how he felt about me? My heart lifted at the thought, and I wanted to cheer out loud. Not only was I suddenly able to feel again, but to my surprise and delight, I was feeling something suspiciously like love.

'Nothing.' The peacock picked up the purple shirt and hurriedly put it on. 'OK, so we have the shirt and jacket, now for the trousers and tie.'

We finally set off about half an hour later, the peacock a defiant and joyful – if somewhat clashing – vison in yellow and purple. To my surprise, he brought his guitar.

'Are you sure it's wise to have a protest so close to home?' I whispered as we made our way down the stairs to the front door. 'And shouldn't you leave your guitar here?' I wasn't sure if it was his earlier anxiety, but I couldn't shake a strange sense of foreboding, made all the worse by my growing suspicion that I might have fallen in love with him.

'Don't worry, we're not doing anything that will get us arrested,' he said. 'At least I hope not. And I need Sylvia.' He patted his guitar lovingly.

Normally, I laughed at his pet name for his guitar, but this time it did precious little to ease my fear. It was as if someone had picked me up and shaken me like a snow globe, causing my emotions to tumble all about. There was no need to panic, I tried reassuring myself. I just had to let my feelings settle. After all, it wasn't every day you got to see your closest friend in his underpants. It was bound to stir things up, but it didn't necessarily mean I was in love with him. Did it?

The pale winter sun was doing its best to break through the thick bank of white cloud filling the sky and the queue outside the butcher's shop snaked all the way down the hill. The people queuing bore the scars of the long cold winter, grim-faced and thin and not speaking at all. The constant cold and hunger seemed to have even killed the gallows humour that had sustained us for so long.

The peacock and I wound our way round to the front of Sacré-Coeur. There were clusters of people gathered at the top of the steps, taking in the view of Paris spread out beneath them.

'Yes! They are here!' the peacock exclaimed.

'Who are?' I looked at the people more closely and saw from their clothes that they were zazous. Then I noticed the peacock's band members heading our way, also holding their instruments.

The men greeted each other warmly.

'Let's set up here,' the peacock said, pointing to a row of German propaganda posters pasted to a nearby wall. They showed a cartoon-style picture of a cheery young man with a shock of blond hair and a beaming smile, carrying a pick over one shoulder. *FRENCH! Go to work in Germany, the German worker invites you!* the text read. The Vichy scheme urging

French men to volunteer to work in Germany made my skin crawl. Everyone knew that going to work there was like accepting a death sentence as the German factories would be a prime target for Allied bombs.

As the band set up in front of the posters, the peacock turned to me. 'Get your camera ready, Fire, the show is about to begin.'

'You're doing a show? I thought you said it was a protest.'

'It's a zazou-style protest,' he replied with a grin as I took my camera from my bag. 'I think you should go down there.' He pointed to the bottom of the first flight of steps. 'That way you'll be able to get all of us in the shot.'

'All of you?' I frowned. There were only four of them. I hardly needed to go that far away.

'Quick,' he urged, so I did as I was told.

When I reached the spot, I instantly saw what he meant. The zazous who'd been loitering around admiring the view were now arranging themselves into some kind of formation on the steps in front of the band.

'Ready?' the singer called.

'Ready!' they all called back.

'Swing!' the peacock yelled and the band began to play and the others started to dance. At exactly that moment, the sun burst through the clouds, shining upon them like a spotlight from the heavens above. I looked through the camera viewfinder and lined up the shot.

'Zazou, hey, hey, hey, za zazou!' the dancers cried, slapping their thighs in a perfectly choreographed routine and I quickly took a couple of pictures.

As the song continued, I heard a giggle and turned to see a woman with a little girl coming up the steps behind me. The girl's face was a picture as she gazed at the dancers.

'What's happening?' the woman asked, clearly awestruck as she took in the spectacle. And it was quite a sight to see so many zazous all dancing for joy in their brightly coloured clothes.

'I think they're trying to bring some joy back to Paris,' I replied.

The woman looked at her daughter, who was now dancing along in time, waving her arms in the air and grinning from ear to ear. 'Well, they've certainly succeeded!'

We both laughed as we watched the girl mimic the dancers and shrug her shoulders.

'Can I take a picture of her?' I asked.

'Of course!' the woman replied. 'It's so nice to see her looking so happy. There hasn't been much to smile about lately.'

'I know.' I crouched down so that I was level with the girl and took a picture of her slapping her thighs, a radiant smile lighting up her face.

Before long, a crowd had gathered, everyone singing along and clapping at the impromptu show. I looked up at the peacock, playing his guitar in that irrepressible style of his and my heart practically burst. I was so proud of the way he brought joy wherever he went, and so grateful that he chose to shine that joy upon me. And in that moment, I knew without a shadow of a doubt that I had fallen in love with him.

I went up a few steps to get a close-up of the band in front of the posters. Their act of defiance would make for a striking image. But just as I pressed the shutter, I heard a yell from the direction of the basilica. I looked over to see a sight that made my blood run cold. A group of about ten young men clad in the blue shirts of the *Jeunesse Populaire Française* had gathered outside Sacré-Coeur and were staring down at the band.

'Scalp the zazous!' their cry rang out. But, to my horror, the peacock and the rest of the band didn't appear to hear above the music and they and the dancers were all facing me with their backs to the thugs.

'Run!' I yelled, waving my arms frantically. 'Run!'

'It's time to go,' the woman said to her little girl, bustling her away to safety.

The young men in their blue shirts started making their way down the steps towards the band. I shoved my camera in my bag and began running up.

'Run!' I yelled, waving my arms again. This time, some of the dancers noticed me and stopped and turned.

'Shit!' one of them cried. 'Let's go!'

As the dancers started fleeing, the band finally realised that something was wrong and stopped playing.

'Run!' I screamed at the top of my lungs.

The peacock met my gaze and looked at me, clearly bewildered. Then finally he turned and saw the thugs descending upon them. He and his band members started to leave, but it was too late, the *Jeunesse Populaire Française* had formed a ring around them.

'No!' I gasped, clapping my hand to my mouth.

The band all but disappeared in a frenzy of flying fists and kicking feet.

I looked around frantically for someone, anyone, who might be able to help, and I saw two police officers making their way up the hill.

'Help, please, you have to stop them!' I cried.

The officers glanced up at the melee. One of them, the younger of the two, had the decency to look slightly concerned.

'Please, someone is going to get killed,' I cried.

'Who are they attacking?' he asked.

'Just a group of musicians. They weren't doing any harm.'

'Scalp him! Scalp him!' one of the fascists cried and I saw a glint of silver in his hand catch the sunlight – a razor blade.

'Are they zazous?' the older policeman asked.

'They're ordinary French men just like you. Please, I'm begging you, do something.'

The younger policeman made to go up the steps, but the older one stopped him.

'We have something else to attend to,' he said to me, and they turned and went back down, the younger one shooting me an apologetic look over his shoulder.

Oh, how I wished I had a pistol in my bag. I couldn't stand there a moment longer though; I had to do something. I ran up the steps, my heart racing. And then I saw a procession of nuns in blue habits were making their way down the steps from the church.

'Stop it!' one of them commanded as they reached the young men.

'Stop it!' I echoed from the other side.

One of the thugs in blue shirts stopped punching and glanced at me over his shoulder. To my horror, I saw flecks of blood splattered across his face. Was it the peacock's? What had they done to him?

The nun grabbed the arm of one of the men. He turned, snarling, then did a double take when he saw who was apprehending him.

'Stop it!' she said again, and to my surprise he did as he was told, telling his cronies to stop too.

'Come on, we've done what we needed to,' he said to the others.

As the circle of blue shirts parted, I caught a glimpse of the band members sprawled upon the stone steps. *Please, please, please don't let them be dead*, I prayed as I rushed over. *Please let the peacock be OK.* As the fascist thugs swaggered past, I felt a rage inside of me the like of which I hadn't felt since my father was killed.

The nuns formed a new ring of blue around the band and I made my way through and saw the peacock. His eyes were closed, but he was moaning and moving slightly.

'Oh no!' I cried as I took in the scene. Locks of his dark hair lay on the floor around his almost bald head and his beloved guitar, Sylvia, had been smashed to smithereens. I knelt on the floor beside him and cradled his head in my hands. 'Are you all right? Say something, please.'

His eyes fluttered open and he stared up at me plaintively. 'They... they killed Sylvia.'

17

In the days following the attack, the peacock fell into a sharp decline. Just like Samson in the Bible, being shorn of his hair seemed to sap him of his strength and zest for life. I longed to make him happy again, the way he'd made me so happy in the months since we'd met, but everything I suggested was answered with a shrug of the shoulders and a noncommittal 'we'll see' or 'maybe'. He didn't even want to go to his beloved Café Capoulade. He'd simply look at Sylvia's battered carcass propped against the wall with her broken strings springing out at all angles and sigh and shake his head.

On the third day after the attack, I stood half frozen to death in a queue for food wondering if I'd ever get my beloved, fun-loving peacock back again. It was hard to believe that in the moments before the thugs had arrived the band had brought so much joy back to Montmartre. I thought of the little girl dancing and the look of pure elation upon her face. In all of the subsequent commotion, I'd completely forgotten about the girl and her mother and the photo I'd taken. Suddenly, an idea occurred to me. I wasn't entirely sure if it would help the peacock, but I was getting desperate.

I peered along the queue. I was still no nearer the front. Should I risk leaving and the prospect of coming back to find there was no more food? Some things were more important than food, I decided, even when you were starving, and the peacock's happiness was definitely one of them. I slipped from the queue and down the hill in the direction of my studio.

I hadn't been back to my apartment since the attack, not wanting to leave the peacock for a moment longer than necessary. As soon as I let myself into the darkroom, I felt the tensions of the past few days dissipate, as if I'd shrugged off a heavy coat at the door. As I prepared the trays of solutions and carefully took the film from the camera, I felt myself slipping into that magical world where my problems no longer seemed to exist. All that existed here were my pictures and my feelings of excitement as they began to appear. Watching photographs develop always felt like some kind of birth to me. You never knew quite how your 'babies' would turn out, but that was all part of the wonder and the mystery.

After rinsing the film in water, I seesawed it through the developer and waited, hardly daring to breathe. I don't think I'd ever been so concerned about a picture – it felt as if so much was riding on it. Gradually, the young girl appeared and even in the red glow of the darkroom the joy on her face was luminous, and hopefully infectious.

Once I'd fixed the photo, I hung it in front of my heat lamp to speed up the process. As soon as it was dry, I put it in an envelope and slipped it into my bag and set off back to the peacock's apartment. I found him standing in front of the fireplace, clad in his dreariest clothes, a dark red shirt and black trousers.

'I was waiting for you to get back,' he said. His previous lethargy had gone, replaced by a strange, agitated energy.

'Why?' I asked apprehensively.

'So I could light the fire,' he said.

'The fire? But we don't have any coal.' No one had any coal, apart from the Germans – another thing that had made the cold, harsh winter almost intolerable.

'No, but we have some wood,' he announced.

'Wood?' I peered around him into the small hearth and gasped as I saw the remains of his guitar. 'Oh no! You can't burn Sylvia!'

'Why not? I can't play her anymore.' He struck a match and threw it into the hearth on top of some crumpled-up paper he'd put there for kindling. 'It's what she would have wanted,' he added with a sad smile.

'Oh, Peacock.' I went over and flung my arms around him.

'I don't feel much like a peacock anymore,' he muttered. 'More like a scrawny old hen.'

I cupped his face in my hands. 'That's enough of that kind of talk. You're still the most beautiful man I've ever known, and I'm not just talking about how you look. Besides, your hair will grow back.'

'It's not about the hair,' he murmured.

'I'll get you another guitar, I promise, even if I have to scour all of Paris to find one.'

'It's not about that either.' He looked down at the floor.

'What is it then?'

'Those men who attacked us, they didn't even know us and yet they were so full of hate. Just like the police and the Vichy government who so willingly sided with the Germans. What hope is there for the world if so many people find it so easy to hate?' It was horrible to hear the peacock sound so defeated. If an eternal optimist like him gave up, what hope was there for the rest of us? I had to help him rediscover his joie de vivre.

'The *Jeunesse Populaire Française* have been whipped into a frenzy by that idiot Jacques Doriot with all of his talk of rediscovering the French Imperial spirit,' I replied, taking hold of his hand. 'It's exactly what Hitler did in Germany. Promising the poor and the disempowered the earth. Lying to them.'

'But why don't people see through the lies?' He looked at me imploringly and I saw that his eyes were glassy with tears.

'Some people are like sheep, they're so easily led. We have to keep believing that love is stronger than hate.' I wasn't entirely sure that I believed what I was saying, but I had to do something to bring the old peacock back to life.

He frowned and shook his head. 'I used to think that, but now I'm not so sure. I think that hate might be stronger.'

I took the envelope from my bag. It was time to reveal my trump card. I only hoped that it would work. 'That's not true. Love is our natural state, I'm sure of it. And here's the proof,' I declared, passing him the envelope.

'What is it?'

'Look inside and you'll see.' I waited with bated breath as he took out the photograph and studied it. To my huge relief, I saw the flicker of a smile playing on his lips, a sight more beautiful to me than any sunrise.

'She's very cute. Who is she?'

'One of your many admirers.'

He frowned. 'What do you mean?'

'She was on the steps that day. She's dancing to your music.' I pointed to the beaming smile on the girl's face. 'This is what you do to people. You make them feel joy deep inside. You make them feel glad to be alive. And that's why you mustn't give up.'

The peacock shrugged. 'She's a kid; all kids love to play.'

'But I'm not!' I exclaimed. 'I'm a grown woman and you make me feel like this every single day.'

'I do?' His eyes widened in surprise.

'Of course. I... I love you.' Telling him how I felt was simultaneously thrilling and terrifying.

'Oh, Fire.' He clasped my hand in his. 'You're not just saying that to make me feel better?'

'Of course not! I know I've kept you at arm's length ever since my husband—' I broke off and looked down at the floor. 'I'm so sorry.'

'It's OK. I understand.' He clasped my hand tighter.

'It was like a part of me shut down. But when I saw you on the steps after those thugs did what they did... when I thought I might have lost you. It was terrifying. I don't want to lose you.' I looked back up and met his gaze. 'I want to... I want to love you.'

'Oh, Fire. I think you just made me the happiest man on earth.' He smiled, really smiled, and the sight made my heart sing. 'I had no idea you loved me too. Ever since we met, I've had the fear that one day you'll grow bored of me.'

I stared at him in shock. 'Are you crazy?'

'You tend to keep your cards very close to your chest, my dear,' he said in his comical British voice.

'What can I say, my daddy was a master poker player, he taught me well.'

His mouth fell open in shock. 'You... you speak English!'

'Shit! I mean *merde*!' I'd been so relieved to hear the peacock speak in his jokey British voice, I'd completely forgotten to respond in French.

'You speak English with an American accent!' He continued staring at me in shock.

'It was a line I once heard in a Hollywood movie,' I replied lamely in French.

'No, you understood what I said. You replied perfectly. Are you—'

'Shh!' I said instinctively. Even though we were alone in his apartment, in these days of collaborators and denouncers it felt as if even the walls had ears.

'Are you American?' he whispered theatrically.

There seemed to be little point in lying to him, and after confessing my love for him, I didn't want to keep anything from him. 'Yes, but nobody knows. Nobody can know, for obvious reasons.'

'Your French accent, it is so convincing.'

'I've had a lot of practice.'

He smiled and shook his head. 'There is so much I want to ask you, I don't know where to begin.'

I was so relieved to see the old peacock come back to life, it felt worth the risk to my own safety. 'Well, how about you ask me if I'd like you to kiss me.'

He laughed. 'Would you like me to kiss you?'

'Yes! Yes! Yes!' I cried in English.

Making love to the peacock was unlike any other intimate encounter I'd had with a man before. It was as if our bodies already knew exactly what to do to perfectly express the love we had for each other.

'Wow!' he exclaimed afterwards, stroking my hair. 'That was incredible.'

'You are incredible.' I looked at his face; his angular cheekbones appeared even more prominent in the candlelight. 'In fact, I have an idea.'

'What is it?' he asked as I got out of bed.

I went over to my bag and took out my camera. 'I want to take a picture of you.'

'What, now?' He instantly looked bashful.

'Yes.'

'But...' He touched his shaven head.

'I want to capture the way you're glowing in this moment, after what we've just done.'

At first, I was worried that he might slip back into his gloom, but thankfully he got out of bed.

'Should I put some clothes on?'

'No. I'll just take a headshot.'

He smiled at me shyly. 'OK, where do you want me?'

I pointed to the wall by the table so he'd be bathed in the lamplight. 'I can't wait for you to see this, so you will see what I see,' I said softly as I peered through the lens.

'What do you see?' he whispered.

'Such bravery and beauty.' My vision blurred with tears. I blinked them away and pressed the shutter.

The following day, I shaved off the remaining clumps of the peacock's hair and he dressed in his bright lavender suit, complete with Chamberlain umbrella and bowler hat, and we set off for the Latin Quarter.

'Thank you for bringing me back to life,' he said as we made our way along the boulevard Saint-Michel.

'We've brought each other back to life,' I replied, squeezing his hand. Ever since seeing my father killed right in front of me, I'd thought that not allowing myself to truly love another would keep me safe from hurt, but admitting my love for the peacock had made me feel invincible.

As we made our way down the stairs to the cellar bar at the Capoulade, I could tell that something was up right away. For the first time ever, there was no music playing and we found the people there huddled around the tables talking in hushed tones.

Raymond came hurrying over. 'I heard about the attack, how are you?' he said to the peacock, greeting him with a kiss on both cheeks.

'I'm a lot better, thanks,' the peacock replied. 'Thanks to Fire.' He kissed me on the lips.

Raymond raised his bristly eyebrows and gave us a nod of acknowledgement, which I guess was as close as we'd get to his seal of approval. His attitude towards me hadn't warmed all that much since our first meeting. Whenever I delivered my photographs to him, he'd give me a brusque thank you and I knew from the peacock that he was happy with my work, but still, would it really be so hard for him to crack a smile in my direction from time to time?

'Have you heard the news?' he asked.

I could tell from his grim expression that it wasn't the longed-for news of the Allied landing or Hitler's demise.

'No, we haven't been anywhere for the last few days,' the peacock replied. 'What's happened?'

'The government has brought in a new law, forcing young men to go and work in Germany.'

'Forcing them?' I stared at him, horrified.

'Yes.' He nodded. 'After the failure of the voluntary scheme, they've changed the *Service du travail obligatoire* so that all men born between 1920 and 1922 have to go and work in Germany.'

I looked at the peacock, my heart thudding. 'What year were you born?'

'1921,' he replied glumly.

'Same as most of the men in here.' Raymond glanced around the bar.

'But being sent to work in the German factories is a death sentence,' I said, echoing the sentiments of many of the young wives I'd encountered queuing for rations. 'They're bound to be the target of the Allied bombers.' I looked at the men sitting at the bar and the tables and shivered as I pictured them all fading from the scene like a photograph developing in reverse.

'Yes, and they wouldn't even die fighting,' Raymond agreed. 'They'd die helping the Germans make munitions for their war effort.'

I took the peacock's hand and gripped it tightly. 'You can't go. You mustn't.'

'But will I have any choice?' he replied.

'There is a choice,' Raymond said quietly, and he steered us over to a table in the corner. 'You can leave Paris. My cousin has gone to the mountains in Brittany. He tells me that many young men are going there. They're being joined by Spanish fighters, veterans of their civil war, and being trained in preparation for the fight to win back our country.'

The thought of my gentle, fun-loving peacock going to the mountains to become some kind of guerrilla fighter hardly filled me with joy, but at least he would still be in France, at least we'd still be in the same country. Maybe I could even go with him?

'Are women going there to fight too?' I asked.

Raymond looked at me as if I was being ridiculous. 'Women aren't good for fighting. You need to stay here and work for the Resistance above ground.'

I bit my lip, grateful yet again that I hadn't been raised by such a chauvinist pig. 'How?'

'Keep taking your photographs and collect food and clothing vouchers for men on the run.'

'Is that it?' I frowned at him. 'I think we women have a lot more to offer than that.'

He gave a sigh of exasperation and placed his chunky hand on the peacock's arm. 'So, what do you say? Do you want me to arrange your passage to Brittany? Are you ready to join the fight to free our country?'

'I'm ready,' the peacock said, giving me a nervous smile.

I returned the smile, my heart thudding. Everything was about to change, and something told me it was definitely not for the better.

18

APRIL 1985, PARIS

The morning after my night with Madeleine Bernier's book, I woke feeling strangely chipper. Perhaps it was all the cheese I'd eaten, but my dreams had been rather enjoyable for once. I was only able to remember random fragments, but I know that at one point I was riding a horse up a mountain – with Frederic, the *fromager*, of all people. I couldn't help laughing as I got out of bed. I even enjoyed the fact that my head was heavy from the wine.

Feeling the urge to listen to music, I took my transistor radio into the tiny bathroom and sang along to Abba's 'Dancing Queen' as I washed my hair over the bath.

Buoyed up by the music, I decided to wear something a little brighter than usual to work. I stood in front of my open wardrobe, staring at the sea of beige and navy blue on display. It seemed like the perfect analogy for my life, all so neutral and bland, designed to blend in rather than stand out. I felt the younger me twitch back into life again, shaking her head and pooh-poohing my sensible sartorial choices. I thought of the clothing store I passed every day on the way to work. Its windows were always full of fabulous creations – perhaps I'd pay it a visit at lunchtime, buy myself a colourful scarf at least.

When I arrived at work at my normal time, ten minutes early, Max raised both eyebrows and looked at his wristwatch. 'What, no Snow White escapades today?'

'Very funny,' I replied. 'I've actually given my seven dwarves the day off.'

This prompted another eyebrow raise.

'Speaking of fairy tales, don't forget you're doing story-time this morning,' Max said, heading over to the trolley of books that needed to be shelved.

'Of course. I'll go and set things up.'

Story-time was a highlight of the week for me and I headed to the children's section with a spring in my step. I loved watching the kids' faces light up as I drew them into the world of the books. It was nice to be able to give their mothers a break for half an hour too.

I took a copy of *The Very Hungry Caterpillar* down from the shelf. It was always a favourite, as much with me as with the kids. I added a picture book about a bad baby and another about a runaway elephant. I was in the mood for some humour today and there was no sweeter sound to me than that of children's laughter.

One by one, the children arrived, plonking themselves down on the cushions I'd arranged in a circle on the floor. The mothers of the older kids took the opportunity to have a browse for some books of their own, while the mothers of the youngest sat right behind their kids. They were all regulars and we greeted each other warmly.

I was about to read the first book when a little boy of about four came racing over.

'I'm here for story-time!' he declared at the top of his voice.

'Excellent. Have you come on your own?' I asked, looking around for any sign of a parent.

The other mums laughed.

'No, my maman is coming, but she's really slow.'

This prompted more giggles from the other mums.

Finally, a flustered-looking heavily pregnant woman waddled into view.

'She's not fat,' the boy informed us all earnestly. 'There's a baby in her stomach. It's going to be my brother or sister. I hope it's a brother,' he added quietly.

We all laughed as the mother shook her head. 'Honestly, Jon!' she sighed.

'Welcome to story-time,' I said, bringing her over a chair.

'Thank you,' she said, wiping the sweat from her brow.

Jon joined the circle of children, and I began to read. But as I did so, I saw the ghost of my younger self sitting down on one of the cushions too. I tried to focus on the very hungry caterpillar and his feast, but my thoughts kept wandering. Having children of my own was another choice I'd deprived myself of, a choice that had seemed logical at the time, but had it been a terrible mistake? The mothers sitting beside me might look tired, but they were also in possession of one of life's greatest gifts. And they'd never face a lonely old age with no family members to take care of them. I felt a lump building in the back of my throat and my mind whirred as I continued reading the story. What was happening to me? Was I having some kind of breakdown? I needed to get a grip. Experience had shown me in no uncertain terms that having children involved terrible risk. They might be one of life's greatest gifts, but, my God, if you were to lose them...

From somewhere in the darkest depths of my mind, I heard a piercing scream, and when I looked back at the circle of children, my younger self was nowhere to be seen.

19

MARCH 1943, PARIS

'OK, my love, smile for the camera please.' The peacock looked at me through the lens, then peered over the camera with a frown. 'Why won't you smile?'

'Because I have nothing to smile about,' I replied melodramatically. 'You're going away and all I want to do is cry.' I winced as the words left my lips, flinching at my weakness. But ever since I'd been honest with the peacock about how I felt about him, it seemed impossible to lie about anything.

'It won't be for long,' he said, putting the camera down and coming over to give me a hug. 'The STO is going to completely backfire on the Germans and the Vichy government. Instead of forcing young Frenchmen to go and work in Germany, it's encouraging them to join the Resistance. Raymond says that the British are now sending regular weapons drops to the Maquis in the mountains. And with us attacking from the inside and the Allies from the outside, there's no way the occupation can survive.' Keeping one arm around my waist, he took my hand and started waltzing me around the room. 'And then France will be free. We will be free! Can you imagine what that will be like, to live in a free France together? To be able to do as we please, dress as we please.' He grabbed his bowler hat from the table and plonked it on top of my head.

I imagined the peacock and me strolling through the streets of Paris, clean and well dressed and well fed, on our way to a jazz night or a show, no need to worry about the click-click of German boots on the pavement, being able to trust the police again and never having to worry about who might be a collaborator. I couldn't help smiling.

'That's it!' he exclaimed, picking up the camera. 'That's the image of you I want to take with me.' He pressed the shutter button. 'Imagine us dancing through the streets of a free Paris,' he cried. 'Imagine being able to yell at the top of your voice, "I'm American, goddammit!"'

It was impossible not to giggle at his American accent, which was even more ridiculous than the British one, and he pressed the shutter again and again.

'You look so beautiful when you laugh. So young and carefree,' he said.

'If I hadn't met you, I bet I'd look like an old hag by now, all hunched and etched with worry,' I replied. 'You've made me feel the happiest I've ever been – and that's some achievement, given that we're living in hell on earth!'

He put the camera down and placed his hands on my shoulders. 'Promise me you won't lose your happiness after I've gone. Promise me you won't let the Germans win and break your spirit.'

'I'll try.'

'No!' he said firmly. 'You must promise me.'

'OK, I promise.' But, in truth, I wasn't sure how I was going to cope. The thought of him being so far away and risking his life every day made me ache with sorrow and fear.

He whipped the hat from my head. 'And now, my darling, I am going to make love to you as if our lives depend upon it.'

'Don't say that!' I cried.

'Why?' He instantly looked crestfallen. 'I was trying to be passionate and romantic.'

'Can you try being romantic and passionate without implying that we might be about to die?'

'I'm sorry.' He kissed my ear. 'Now I am going to make love to you as if you are more precious than all the tea in China and all the umbrellas in Britain.'

'Hmm, maybe you should just stop talking.'

'If you insist.' He slipped the straps of my bra from my shoulders and backed me gently towards the bed.

The peacock left first thing the following morning and although if felt as if my heart was being wrenched from my body, I managed to keep a brave face. The last thing I wanted to do was make our parting more difficult for him than it had to be. Raymond had organised for the peacock and a couple of others to be smuggled out of Paris on the back of a dairy truck. They'd promised they'd send word to the Café Capoulade once they'd made it to the safety of the Brittany mountains – or the relative safety, at least.

After a tense week, with the peacock and his safety occupying virtually all of my thoughts, I returned to the Capoulade with my latest photographs – some surreptitious shots of potential collaborators visiting the Prefecture of Police – and found Raymond attending to some paperwork down in the cellar bar.

'They're safe,' Raymond said brusquely upon seeing me and I was so elated at this news I had to fight the urge to hug him. Something told me that a hug from me would be about as welcome as bowl of cold, lumpy gruel.

'Are you sure there's nothing else I can do to help?'

He looked back at his paperwork. 'I told you what you can do. Keep taking your photographs and collect vouchers for the men.'

There was something about his dismissive tone that reminded me of Pierre and a red mist descended.

'I don't know who you think you are, but you need to be taught a lesson in respect,' I said, glowering down at him. As soon as the words left my mouth, I was reminded of my pops. This was exactly the kind of thing he would say. I imagined him slapping me on the back and hollering, *You tell him, babycakes!*

'Oh really?' Raymond put his pen down and glared up at me. 'And who, exactly, is going to teach me?'

I wasn't entirely sure how to respond to this, which irritated me even more. 'I don't know, but someone needs to.'

He smirked and looked back at his paperwork.

'You are truly insufferable,' I muttered before stalking to the door.

It was only when I was back outside and marching, red-faced, along the boulevard that I realised I'd just insulted my one and only link to the peacock. If I wanted to keep receiving updates from Raymond, I was going to have to eat some crow for sure, a thought that made my blood boil even more.

The only way I was able to make it through the first month without the peacock was by putting on a pair of emotional blinkers. If I thought about him risking his life in the mountains, I got eaten up with worry. If I thought about the fact that, thanks to the Germans, I could no longer work as a fashion photographer, I became enraged. So I focused all of my attention on my Resistance photography, trying to capture moments that summed up the travesty of what was happening to my beloved Paris.

The German charm offensive of the first two years of their occupation was now well and truly over and scenes of their barbarity were on display for all to see. I clung to what the peacock had said about needing to document the horrors so that one day the world would see what had happened here. And all the while, I kept the photograph of Lillie with me, and her maman's locket around my neck, as a constant reminder of why I was doing this. Each night before I went to sleep, I would place the photograph on my pillow and whisper a prayer of sorts: 'Please still be alive. Please let me find you again.'

Then, one day, when I was on my way back from yet another interminable queue for food, I heard a young child scream. I turned to see two members of the Gestapo engaged in a macabre version of tug of war, one pulling on a young boy, the other pulling on a woman I assumed to be the boy's mother, trying to separate them. The woman was wearing a star, but the boy wasn't, which meant he had to be under six years old.

I wanted to yell 'no', and run to their assistance, but if I did that, it would mean certain arrest. And after what had happened at Drancy, I was wary of acting rashly. If I was detained I'd be of no help to anybody. So I stepped back into a darkened doorway and reached for my camera instead. Families being wrenched apart was becoming an all too common sight on Parisian streets and I felt certain that Raymond would be able to use a couple of photos of the horror unfolding before me.

As I focused the image in the viewfinder and took a picture, the anguish on the boy's face was heartbreaking, and once again I was cast back in time to that terrible morning my father was killed. Is that how I had looked as I'd crouched over his body? I know that I screamed. I remember hearing the sound and not realising at first that it was coming from me. I pushed the unsettling memory from my mind and slipped the camera back into my bag.

Finally, the Germans tugged the pair apart and they bundled the mother into the back of their black Mercedes. The boy stood crying on the pavement. Surely they weren't going to leave him there on his own? I watched in dismay as they got into the car and sped off. The woman's face was pressed to the rear window, her cries silenced by the glass. Meanwhile, the boy's sobs grew louder. I started running towards him when an older woman wearing a yellow star appeared from a nearby building and gathered him in her arms.

'It's all right, it's all right,' she kept saying over and over as she rocked him.

But it wasn't all right. Nothing was all right. We were living in the middle of a nightmare there was no waking from.

'They... they took his mother,' I stammered as I reached them. 'The Germans. They took her from him, took her away in their car.'

'They are animals,' she said, her eyes shiny with tears.

'Maman!' the boy cried, looking down the street after the car.

'Do you know him? Does he live here?' I asked.

The woman shook her head. 'It's all right,' she soothed, still hugging the boy tight. 'Do you live near here?' she asked him. 'Do you have any other family? A dad, brothers, sisters?'

The boy's bottom lip quivered. 'No. Papa had to go away. The police took him,' he whimpered, causing my heart to ache.

'Do you live near here?' I asked, crouching down in front of him. He had a shock of dark curly hair, and a sprinkling of freckles across his nose. His eyes were a striking shade of golden brown.

He shook his head. 'I live on the other side of the river.'

'Do you know your address?' I asked before looking up at the woman. 'If we find out where he lives, we might be able to find some friends or neighbours he could stay with.'

'Good idea,' she agreed, but once again the boy shook his head.

'Do you know anyone who lives near here? Had you been visiting someone?'

'No.' The boy's lip trembled even more. 'We were trying to

run away from the bad men. But the bad men found us and they took Maman.'

My heart sank. 'What should we do?' I whispered to the woman.

'The *Oeuvre de Secours aux Enfants* might be able to help him,' she replied, glancing anxiously up and down the street.

'Who are they?' I asked.

'They're a society that help Jewish families in need. They provide safe homes for Jewish children.'

'Would you be able to get him to one of them?'

She looked at the star on her chest and gave a sarcastic laugh. 'Oh yes, of course. I'm free to go wherever I please.'

I felt a stab of guilt at my stupidity. 'I'm sorry. I didn't mean to be insensitive. I just thought you might know someone in the organisation.'

She shook her head. 'I only know of their existence. And it would be too dangerous for me to take him in – for him, I mean.' She looked down the street in the direction the car had gone. 'They could be coming for me any day.'

'I'm so sorry,' I said, but my words felt meaningless. 'I'll take him,' I said quickly. I had to do something. 'I know some people who might be able to help.'

'Oh, that's wonderful.' The woman crouched down in front of the boy. 'What is your name, my dear?'

'Joseph David Lieberman,' he replied formally with a sniff.

'OK, Joseph, this nice lady is going to take you somewhere safe.'

He looked up at me and blinked away his tears. 'Is my maman going to be there?'

'No, I... I'm afraid not.'

His eyes filled with tears again.

'Not yet,' I said hastily. 'But I'm going to help you and hope-fully someday soon you'll be able to see her again.'

The woman nodded to me over his head.

I took the boy's hand and shook it. 'It's very nice to meet you, Joseph David Lieberman. My name's Clarisse.'

He stared at me for a moment. 'Why do you have such short hair? You look like a boy.'

I laughed. 'Well, someone told me that boys have the most fun, am I right?' To my relief, he gave me a weak smile. 'So, shall we go and have some fun?'

'Will Maman be there?'

'You'll see her again, I promise.'

'OK, then, Clarisse, I'll come with you,' he said in a serious voice, once again sounding a lot older than his years.

'I'll take him to my place tonight, then tomorrow I'll see about getting him to a safe house,' I said to the woman.

'Yes, yes, go before more of those monsters turn up. Good-bye, Joseph.' She patted him on the head and hurried back inside.

'Is it all right if I hold your hand?' I asked the boy. I'd hardly spent any time in the company of children so I didn't have the first clue about how to interact with one so young.

'I suppose so,' he replied resignedly.

I took his hand. It was icy cold. 'All right then, let's go.'

'Where are we going?'

'To my apartment.'

'Will the bad men be there?' His voice wavered.

'No, they definitely won't be there. That's why I'm taking you there, so you'll be safe.' I felt his grip on my hand tighten and I gave it a reassuring squeeze.

'Are you friends with my maman?'

I thought for a moment before answering. If I said no, it would undoubtedly make him feel anxious, so perhaps it would be better to lie. 'Yes, I know your maman.' Sure enough, he gave me a relieved smile, so I decided to expand a little. 'That's why I turned up when I did, so I could take care of you and take you someplace safe.'

He squeezed my hand again, and I squeezed it back, happy to have found this simple but seemingly effective way of communicating with him.

Thankfully, we didn't encounter any police or German soldiers on the way to my studio and Joseph seemed to relax slightly. 'I live at the top of those stairs,' I said as I unlocked the front door and let him in.

'That's a lot of stairs!' He gave a weary sigh.

'You want a piggyback?' I asked, remembering how Frankie used to hoist me onto his back and pretend to be a racehorse whenever I got tired as a kid. It was so much fun, I used to feign being tired just to get a ride.

'Yes please,' he replied, so I crouched down in front of him and he scrambled on, wrapping his arms around my neck.

And here's Nan Esposito riding the thoroughbred Jersey Boy, I imagined Frankie saying in his race commentator's voice.

'That's better,' Joseph said as I started climbing the stairs. 'My legs are very tired.'

'Well, that's because they're still very short,' I replied. 'So everything is a whole lot further for you.'

'You're right!' he exclaimed, like I'd just revealed the law of gravity.

I unlocked the door to my apartment and lit the lamp before setting him down by the table. 'So, this is my place,' I said as my tiny guest began walking around the living room, examining everything like he was some kind of government inspector.

I took my meagre rations from my bag and placed them on the table.

'I like it,' Joseph replied, staring pointedly at the baguette and piece of cheese.

'Are you hungry?'

'Yes.' He came and hoisted himself up onto one of the chairs. 'I might be little, but I have a very big appetite. That's what my maman always says.'

'Does she?' I chuckled.

For so long I'd felt a bubbling envy towards French mothers and the way they were prioritised when it came to queuing for rations, but the thought of being responsible for feeding this small human made me see things in a whole new light. It was stressful enough trying to feed oneself in occupied France. Being responsible for feeding another, especially when that other was your own child, must have been horrendous.

'Well, let me make you some dinner then.'

'Thank you. I don't drink wine, though,' he said earnestly, looking at the empty wine bottle on the table.

'Very glad to hear it!' I exclaimed. 'I was actually going to use that bottle as a candlestick.'

'How do you mean?' He looked at it curiously.

I tore a piece from the bread and handed it to him. 'I'll show you.'

I fetched a candle and a book of matches from the cupboard and stuck the candle into the top of the bottle. '*Et voilà*! A candlestick,' I said as I lit the wick.

'I think that looks very nice,' he mumbled through a mouthful of bread.

'I'm glad you like it.'

I sat down opposite him and cut him a slice of cheese. *If only the peacock could see me now*, I thought to myself. *He would love it.* I was certain he'd be a natural with kids. If he'd been with us, I'm sure he'd have sung the boy a song or taught him how to dance. How on earth was I going to keep my young guest amused? Hopefully he'd be tired from all the trauma of the day and want to go to sleep straight after eating. Then, once he was asleep, I'd try to formulate some kind of plan. The only thing I could think of off the top of my head was to go to the Capoulade and ask Raymond for help. I hadn't seen him since I'd called him insufferable, but surely even he wouldn't be so hard-hearted he'd refuse to help a child.

Unfortunately, rather than make Joseph sleepy, the food only seemed to energise him. He slid down from his chair and started pacing around the room.

'When will I see Maman?' he asked, looking anxious.

'Soon.'

'Tonight?'

'No, not tonight, but tomorrow I'm going to take you to see someone who will hopefully be able to help you see your maman again.'

'Who?'

'A... a friend of mine, in a cafe, here in Paris.'

He frowned, then started inspecting the room again. 'What's in there?' he asked, pointing to the darkroom door.

'It's my darkroom,' I said, relieved for the diversion.

'Why is it dark?'

I smiled. 'It's where I make photographs, so it needs to be dark.'

'You make photographs?' Now he looked genuinely interested.

'I do.' Then I had a brainwave. 'Do you want to see how it's done?'

'Yes please!'

'OK, let me get my camera.'

I went and fetched my Kodak Six-20 from the darkroom.

'Would you like me to take a picture of you?'

Joseph nodded but looked down at the floor as if suddenly overcome with shyness.

'OK, how about you come and sit at the table by the candle.' I pulled on the clip and opened the camera.

'Wow!' he exclaimed as the camera accordioned out.

'It's a folding camera,' I explained.

He went and sat at the table, then gazed into the lens with such a solemn expression, I had to fight the urge to laugh.

'You can smile if you like,' I said, looking at him through the viewfinder on top.

He instantly pulled a ridiculous rictus grin.

'OK, maybe don't try so hard to smile.'

'What do you mean?'

'Well, how about you think about something that makes you happy?'

He frowned for a moment as he thought, then the most beautiful smile appeared, like the sun bursting through cloud.

'Oh, that's lovely,' I said, pressing the shutter release as his grin grew wider. The golden glow of the candlelight made his face look angelic. I only hoped I'd be able to capture it on film.

'Tell me, what were you thinking about to make you smile so much?' I asked as I placed the camera on the table.

'I was thinking about playing hopscotch with my maman and papa,' he replied, and it felt like a knife to my heart.

20

APRIL 1943, PARIS

'So, now I have to seesaw the film through the developing solution,' I explained to Joseph, who standing on a chair beside me in the darkroom.

'Seesaw?' He looked at me, puzzled.

'Yes. I have to move the film like it's a seesaw going up and down, like this.' I demonstrated.

He frowned at the film. 'I don't see me.'

'Not yet,' I replied. 'You have to wait for it to develop.'

'What does develop mean?'

'Appear.'

'What does appear mean?'

I peered at him in the dim red light trying to work out if he was kidding, but, as usual, he looked deadly serious.

'It means you'll see yourself soon. Look, there's your head.' I pointed to the outline appearing on the paper.

'It doesn't look like my head.' He paused for a moment, continuing to watch. 'Oh, there's my hair.' He touched his hair as he looked at the picture.

'Yes, and here come your eyes.'

'And there's my nose,' he murmured, clearly rapt.

We watched in silence as his mouth and that beautiful grin began to materialise and, once again, I wished that the peacock had been there to witness it. He would have loved this little kid for sure.

'Look at my smile!' Joseph exclaimed.

'It's a beautiful smile,' I replied.

'This is like magic!' he gasped as the full picture came into view.

'It really is.' I nodded and seeing his eyes so full of wonder took me back to the time I first used a camera. My Aunt Gina had gifted it to me on my fourteenth birthday. It was almost exactly a month after my pops had been killed and I'd retreated into an interior world, refusing to communicate with anyone other than to nod or shake my head – mostly shaking my head no to everything. No, I did not want to go back to school. No, I did not want anything to eat. No, I did not want to engage with a world where the very worst could happen at any moment and without any warning.

I don't know if Gina had hoped that giving me a camera might get me to come back out of my shell or if it was just a lucky accident. But one day, driven by boredom and frustration, I took it out onto the streets of Brooklyn, where she and my Uncle Dave lived, and I took my first street photo. It was of an old homeless man who looked as if he'd just got done hopping freight trains all the way from California. His clothes were tattered and grimy and his long hair was greasy, but there was something about him – a wildness, a sense of freedom – that instantly drew me in. I wanted to capture that essence, perhaps so that one day I'd be able to feel it too. So I grabbed my new camera and I took a shot. Of course, I hadn't yet perfected the art of street photography and the need to be as unobtrusive as possible and he heard me fiddling and fumbling with the film advance lever.

'Watcha doin'?' he hollered down the street to me.

For the first time in a month, I was able to speak. 'I... I'm sorry, sir, I just wanted to take your picture.'

'And why would you want to take a picture of me?' He came trundling up the street towards me.

One positive, if you can call it that, about seeing my daddy shot down in front of me was that I truly no longer cared if I lived or died, so this man with his ragged clothes and wild hair didn't scare me one bit.

'I liked how free you looked,' I replied matter-of-factly. 'And I wanted a picture of it.'

He stared at me for a moment and scratched his head. 'Well, I'll be darned. Thank you, young lady.' And off he went.

That night, when I got back to Aunt Gina's and she asked if I'd like any meatloaf, I said yes, instead of nodding, and she hugged me like she'd just won the state lottery. And a few days later when I got my developed photos back from the pharmacy and saw how I'd managed to capture what I saw in the man and preserve it forever, I knew that photography was going to show me how to fall in love with life again. It gave me the same sense of wonder young Joseph was clearly experiencing now.

I noticed him trying to suppress a yawn. 'You must be very tired; would you like to go to sleep?' I asked as I pinned his photograph on the line to dry.

'Are we going home?' He looked at me hopefully.

'No, you'll stay here, in my bed. I'll sleep on the floor,' I quickly added.

His worried frown returned. 'But I don't have any pyjamas.'

'Hmm, let me see if I can find you anything. Come on.'

I led him back into the living room wondering what on earth I could give him to wear. Rooting around in my chest of drawers, I found one of the peacock's vests.

'How about this as a nightshirt?' I held it up against him and it almost came down to the floor.

'It's very long,' he said, looking unsure.

'Yes, but it will keep those tired legs of yours nice and warm.'

He nodded gravely, as if that was the most logical thing he'd ever heard.

I took him through to the bathroom and helped him take off his sweater and trousers. Seeing his jutting ribcage made my breath catch in my throat. The fact that the Vichy government could go along with a scheme that was effectively starving French children made a mockery of their supposed desire to protect the family. But then, they were doing far worse than starving innocent children like Joseph.

As I helped him put the vest on over his underwear, I wished once more that the peacock was there. He'd know exactly what to do and say and wouldn't feel nearly as awkward, I was certain.

'I'll go and get the bed ready for you,' I said as Joseph perched himself on the toilet.

Thankfully, the peacock had brought his bedding over to my place before he went away so I had enough to make a bed on the floor for me. Just as I'd finished making it, Joseph appeared like a little ghost in his long white vest.

'Here you are,' I said, patting the bed.

He wriggled under the covers and as I leaned over to tuck him in the locket swung loose from my blouse.

'You have a magic necklace!' he exclaimed. 'My maman has a magic necklace too.'

'What do you mean, a magic necklace?' I asked.

'It has pictures inside it,' he replied.

'Ah, yes, it does.'

'Can I see the pictures?' he asked, sitting up.

'Of course.' I opened the locket and showed him the pictures.

'Who's that?' he asked, pointing to the photo of Lillie as a little girl.

'She's called Lillie.'

'Are you her maman?'

'No, she's... she's my friend. That's her maman.' I pointed to the picture of her parents. 'I'm trying to help Lillie just like I'm trying to help you,' I added, hoping this might comfort him.

'Why? Did the bad men take her maman and papa too?' He looked at me anxiously and I could have kicked myself for saying what I did.

'They did, but don't worry, lots of people are helping children like you and Lillie find their parents again.'

'Good.' He lay back down and I closed the locket. 'Are you going to bed now?' he asked.

'Not just yet. But I'll only be next door in the darkroom developing some more photographs.' I pointed to the door.

'OK.' He closed his eyes, then almost immediately opened them again. 'I wish we could make Maman appear like a photograph.'

His plaintive desire was one of the most beautiful yet heartbreaking things I'd ever heard. 'I wish that too.'

He closed his eyes, then opened them once more. 'Maman always sings me a lullaby to help me go to sleep.'

'Oh.' I racked my brains trying to figure out if I knew anything vaguely resembling a lullaby.

'"Au clair de la lune", do you know it?' He looked at me hopefully.

'I'm afraid I don't.'

He was so crestfallen, I was afraid he might start crying.

'I do know one called "Minnie the Moocher" though,' I said quickly.

'Could you sing it to me?'

'Of course.'

I regretted my choice almost as soon as I started singing. Not only were the lyrics slightly inappropriate for a young child, but it made me think of the peacock and how he'd been humming it the first time we met. It seemed to be doing the trick though, as his tiny eyelids had drooped closed.

I'd just finished singing the second line when Joseph opened his eyes yet again. 'What's a lowdown hoochie coocher?'

'Oh, uh, it's a funny lady.'

'Are you a hoochie coocher?' he said through a yawn.

'Um, no.'

Oh Lord, please make him fall asleep, I silently prayed.

Thankfully, he closed his eyes again and by the time I got to the end of the last verse, his breath had slackened and his eyelids were fluttering.

When I was certain he was fast asleep, I took my Leica through to the darkroom and began developing the film from earlier when Joseph's mother had been taken away. The contrast between Joseph's look of anguish in this picture and his beaming smile in the portraits drying on the line was stark.

Once I'd fixed the film and turned on the white lights, I started hatching a plan. In the morning, I would take Joseph and the photo of him being torn from his mother to Café Capoulade and tell Raymond what had happened. And, more importantly, I would ask him if he knew about the society that helped Jewish children and if we could somehow get Joseph to safety.

I heard a murmur from the other room and hurried through. Joseph was still asleep but clearly having a bad dream judging by the way he was tossing and turning. I went and knelt beside the bed and gently placed a hand on his forehead. Luckily, this seemed to soothe him and as I watched him slip into a more peaceful sleep, my eyes swam with tears. Finding out how my mom had died had left me with a morbid fear I just couldn't shake, and then I lost my pops and I'd been left with another fear – of loving someone as much as I'd loved Frankie and losing them too. But the peacock had cracked the armour I'd placed around my heart and now this tiny human in my bed appeared to be continuing the job.

But look at what happened to him and his mother today, my inner voice cautioned. *You're lucky not to be a mother in today's world.*

But as I looked at Joseph's curly hair and tiny rosebud of a mouth, I was no longer sure if my voice of caution was speaking the truth.

The next morning, I was woken by a little voice singing 'lowdown hoochie coocher' and at first I thought I was having some kind of surreal dream. Who was singing and why was my back aching so? Why was I sleeping on the floor?

I opened my eyes and saw Joseph peering down at me.

'At last!' he exclaimed.

'What do you mean, at last?' I mumbled.

'At last you've woken up.'

I couldn't help laughing. 'I'm sorry.'

'Are we going to see Maman today?' he asked hopefully.

'No, not today, I'm afraid.'

His face fell.

'Today we're going on a fun adventure,' I said quickly.

'To see Maman?'

'Not yet. But the adventure we're going on will help you see her again soon.' I hoped with all my might that what I was saying was true. 'We're going to see a very clever man who knows everything and he's going to tell us what to do.'

'OK. But can we have some breakfast first?'

'Of course.' I scrambled out of my makeshift bed, happy that this was something I could definitely do.

I helped Joseph get dressed and then we had a breakfast of the last of the cheese and the stale bread. Thankfully, he didn't complain at all. I guess by then he was used to eating next to nothing.

'Now, before we set off on our adventure, there's a little game I want us to play.'

'Is it hopscotch?' He looked expectant.

'What? Oh, no, it's not.'

'I love hopscotch.'

'Me too. But this game is about pretending to be someone you're not.'

He nodded sagely. 'I know that game.'

'You do?' I looked at him in surprise.

'Yes. Sometimes I like to pretend that I'm an elephant.'

'Oh!' I suppressed the urge to grin. 'OK, well, today's game is more about pretending to be another person.'

'What person?'

'My nephew.'

'What's a nephew?'

'It's a boy who has an aunt. Do you have an aunt?'

He shook his head.

'OK, that's fine. In our game, I'm going to pretend to be your aunt. So when we go out, you must call me Aunt Clarisse.'

'OK.' He thought for a moment. 'Will you call me nephew Joseph?'

'Oh, er, people don't usually say that.'

'Why not?'

'I don't know.' If they gave out prizes for asking questions, this kid would surely win a gold medal.

'If I have to call you Aunt Clarisse, I think you should call me nephew Joseph.'

I really didn't have the energy to argue with this, and besides, I couldn't help but see the logic to what he was saying. 'You've got yourself a deal, nephew Joseph.' I took his hand and shook it.

He tilted his head to one side and stared at me. 'Are you a good aunt or a bad aunt?'

Geez, what was with this kid and his questions? 'I'm a good aunt. A very good aunt.'

'Good. I'll be a good nephew then.'

'Thank you.' I took our plates over to the sink. 'Right, let the adventure begin!'

Fortunately, when we got to the Metro, there were no police or plain-clothes Gestapo checking people's papers. We got down to the platform just as a train was coming in and Joseph began tugging on my hand.

'We have to go in the last carriage,' he said.

'It's all right, we don't have to do that today.'

I saw a policeman making his way down the platform towards us and my heart started hammering inside my chest. What if he heard what Joseph was saying? What if he asked if we were Jewish? How would I explain it if Joseph said yes? Why hadn't I thought to warn him about this?

'We do! We do!' Joseph cried insistently and I saw the policeman look over at us.

I crouched in front of him as the breeze from the incoming train whistled around us. 'It's OK, we don't have to today because it's part of the game we're playing. Nephew Joseph doesn't have to ride in the last carriage, and neither do I.'

'Are you sure?'

'Yes.' I heard footsteps behind me and looked up to see the policeman staring down at us through close-set eyes.

'Is everything OK, madame?' he said, looking from me to Joseph.

'I'm nephew Joesph,' Joseph announced, causing my heart to plummet.

Thankfully, the rattle of the train meant the policeman didn't hear him and he frowned at me.

'What did he say?'

'He said his name is Joseph.'

'Ah, I see.'

I stood up and flashed the policeman a winning smile straight from my modelling days. He smiled back. He had one of those faces where none of the component parts seemed to quite fit together: his eyes were too small, his nose too long, his lips too pronounced for his feeble jaw.

'Pleased to meet you, Joseph,' he said, smiling at the boy. 'I hope you and your maman have a very nice day.'

'She's not my maman,' Joseph said loudly as we boarded the train.

'I'm his aunt,' I said with another smile, praying my anxiety didn't show.

'Ah.' I noticed the policeman's expression change and his glance flicked down to my now bare ring finger. Shit!

Joseph and I sat down and the train started to move. Unfortunately, the policeman stayed standing right by us.

'Very nice of you to take care of your nephew,' he called to me over the rattle of the train.

'We're having an adventure,' Joseph announced, causing my pulse to quicken.

'I have to do something to make queuing for rations more interesting,' I said to the policeman by way of explanation.

'Very enterprising.' Again, he flashed me his creepy smile. 'So, what is your name?'

'She's Aunt Clarisse and I'm nephew Joseph,' he piped up yet again.

'Very nice to meet you, Aunt Clarisse.' The train went round a curve, sending the policeman lurching towards me, his crotch barely an inch away from my face. 'Perhaps we could meet again some time, when you aren't babysitting,' he said, leaning down towards me.

'That would be great,' I lied through gritted teeth.

'Do you know where my papa is?' Joseph asked the policeman.

I prayed the driver of the train would slam on the brakes and send the officer flying to the end of the carriage.

Sadly, my prayer wasn't answered, so I stood up instead, feeling sick with anxiety. 'His father was killed in the Battle for France,' I whispered in the policeman's ear. Up this close, I could see a fuzz of dark hair growing around the rim. 'But his mother can't bring herself to tell him.'

'Ah I see,' he said. He looked down at Joseph. 'I'm afraid I don't.'

'But Maman said Papa had to go somewhere with the police,' Joseph muttered.

My heart was pounding so hard by this point I could barely think straight and I felt my face flush bright red. 'So, when would you like to meet again?' I asked the policeman, using the movement of the train as an excuse to lean into him. Bile burned in the back of my throat.

He took a notepad and pencil from his pocket. 'Here's my name and details,' he said, writing on a page and tearing it out. 'Perhaps we could go for a drink one evening?'

'I'd really like that,' I said, fighting the urge to retch.

'I want to see my papa,' Joseph muttered.

'Yes, I'd like that a lot,' I said loudly.

'Me too. Well, I'd better get back to work.' He tucked his notepad and pencil back in his pocket. 'Got to check that the Jewish swine in the last carriage are all wearing their stars.'

It took everything I had not to punch him right in the face. The muscles in my jaw ached from holding my smile in place.

As he walked off down the train and I sat back down, I

noticed the woman sitting opposite fiddling with her Metro ticket and scowling at me. *I'm not a traitor*, I wanted to cry. *I'm trying to save this kid.* She flicked her ticket at me and it landed on the floor at my feet. She'd folded it into a V-shape, the Resistance sign for victory. I wanted to tell her that we were on the same side, but I couldn't afford to blow my cover; the policeman was still within earshot. Let her think what she liked about me; all that mattered was getting Joseph to safety.

I looked down at him. He was staring blankly into space.

'Are you OK?' I whispered.

He nodded, but I noticed he was biting his bottom lip.

I put my arm around him and to my relief he didn't resist, leaning into me instead.

'Was I good at playing the game?' he said softly.

'Yes, you were excellent.' I hugged him tighter, my determination growing. What had happened with the policeman only underlined the stupidity of the government and their cruel laws. I would never again doubt my ability to make a difference. I would do whatever it took to make France safe again for children like Joseph and Lillie, even if it meant losing my own freedom in the process.

'Is Raymond here?' I asked the woman behind the bar as soon as we got to the cafe.

'He's downstairs, but I'm sorry, no children allowed.' She peered over the bar at Joseph.

'I'm nephew Joseph,' he said solemnly, giving my hand a nervous squeeze.

I squeezed it back. I had to give it to the kid for bringing so much enthusiasm to our strange game.

'We have to see him. It's *very* important,' I said, giving her a knowing look.

'Yes, we're on an adventure,' Joseph told her in his gravest voice. Why, oh why, hadn't I told him it was to be a silent adventure?

The woman looked at me, clearly confused.

I leaned over the bar. 'His life is in danger,' I whispered.

'OK, go down,' she said straight away, nodding to the stairs.

I found Raymond sitting at a table in the basement deep in conversation with two other men. When he saw me, he gave me a withering stare. Then his gaze moved to Joseph and his expression turned to one of surprise.

'Well, I wasn't expecting to see you again,' he said, coming over to greet us.

'I have an emergency,' I said, steeling myself for the helping of humble pie I was no doubt about to have to consume.

'We're having an adventure,' Joseph added, then he looked back up at me. 'Is this the very clever man who knows everything?'

'Yes, yes it is,' I replied and, to my relief, I noticed Raymond's expression soften just a little.

'That's funny,' he said, giving me a knowing grin. 'I thought I was insufferable.'

'Yes, well, you're a complex character,' I retorted and thankfully his grin grew warmer. 'Can I speak to you in private for a couple of minutes?'

Raymond beckoned one of the servers over. 'Please can you take this boy into the kitchen and give him a drink?'

'Of course,' she replied, smiling down at Joseph.

Joseph looked up at me as if for approval and I nodded. 'Don't worry, I'll be right here.'

'I have an apple in the kitchen, if you'd like it,' the woman said, and he was off like a shot.

'So, what is this emergency?' Raymond asked as soon as they'd gone.

I took the photo from my bag and handed it to him. 'I took this yesterday. The Gestapo arrested his mother and took her away. They tore the kid from her arms and left him on the pavement.'

'He's Jewish?' Raymond said.

'Yes. And I spoke to another woman after it happened, a Jewish woman, and she told me about something called the *Oeuvre de Secours aux Enfants*. She said they have safe houses for Jewish children in France. Have you heard of them?'

To my relief, Raymond nodded.

'Is there any way you can get the boy to them, through your contacts?'

He frowned. 'The safe houses are all in the previously unoccupied zone. It's incredibly dangerous to smuggle people into those areas now that the Germans occupy the whole country.'

'But surely these photographs will help you,' I said quickly, offering my one potential bargaining chip. 'Surely they'll encourage more people to join the Resistance.'

He studied the photographs again. 'They're certainly very powerful.'

'Thank you.'

He gave me an icy look as if to convey that paying me a compliment was the very last of his intentions. 'I'm sorry, but there's no way I can get the boy out of Paris. It's too risky. And, to be brutally honest, my couriers have far more important things to risk their lives over right now.'

'More important than a child's life?' I stared at him indignantly.

'Believe it or not, yes. The lives of hundreds, if not thousands, are dependent on the missions I send my people on.'

I sighed, once again feeling utterly dejected.

'But if you wanted to take him to safety, I could help you.'

'You could?' My pulse began to race at the thought of helping Joseph escape. Travelling around France was becoming increasingly difficult and dangerous, especially for someone with false papers. But there was no way I could abandon the kid, that was for certain.

Raymond nodded. 'You need to give me some time to get things organised though.'

'Of course. Thank you.' I touched his arm, overwhelmed with gratitude and relief.

He looked thoughtful for a moment. 'And perhaps there's something else you can do for me.'

'Anything.'

'I need a courier to make a very special delivery. Someone who won't arouse suspicion.'

I was elated that he finally seemed to be taking me seriously. 'I'd be happy to.' My skin prickled with nervous excitement.

'And a woman with a child isn't likely to draw much attention.'

I froze. 'You want me to deliver something with the kid in tow?'

'Yes.' He stared at me defiantly as if this was an important test of my character. I instantly felt conflicted. I wanted more than anything to do meaningful work for the Resistance, but, equally, I wanted to get Joseph to safety, and not put him in more peril. But if I said no, chances were, Raymond wouldn't help me get Joseph out of Paris. The cards I was holding were weak; I had no choice but to fold.

'OK. Tell me more.'

'Come with me.'

Raymond put the photographs in his pocket and led me out of the bar and down a dimly lit corridor into some kind of storeroom. It was freezing cold and smelled of damp and the walls were lined with crates and boxes. I watched as he carefully dismantled a tower of boxes to reveal a hidey-hole cut into the stone wall.

'Let me see your bag,' he said.

I handed him my leather satchel.

'Good, that should be big enough.'

Big enough for what? I wondered as I watched him open the secret cupboard. He took something out and turned back to face me. My mouth instantly went dry. There, nestled in his large hands, were two revolvers.

22
_____

Thankfully, I was able to maintain my composure. There was no way I wanted to give Raymond the impression that the sight of a couple of pistols would turn me into a quivering wreck. Thanks to Frankie I'd grown up around guns so they didn't faze me. It was the thought of having to courier two guns across German-occupied Paris and with a five-year-old in tow that was giving me palpitations.

'Well?' Raymond said, staring at me.

'Where do you want me to take them?' I replied coolly.

Raymond nodded. Clearly, I'd passed the test.

'I need you to take them to rue d'Alésia. To the tailor's at number 78.'

'78 rue d'Alésia,' I repeated quietly. 'When would you like me to take them?'

'Now,' he replied. 'When you get there, you're to ask for Michel. Say that your friend Monsieur Verne sent you.'

'OK.' I nodded, my mind whirring as I tried to commit the instructions to memory.

Raymond wrapped the guns in a piece of cloth, then placed

the bundle inside a brown paper bag. 'You need to keep them out of sight at the bottom of your bag,' he said.

Really? I thought I might carry them on my head, I felt like responding, but I bit my tongue. Now was definitely not the time for wisecracks.

I emptied the contents of my satchel onto one of the crates and put the guns at the bottom of the bag. I tucked my camera back in beside them and covered them with the scarf I kept for exactly that purpose, then I put the rest of the satchel's contents back on top.

'Good,' Raymond said as he watched. Praise indeed! He rebuilt the tower of boxes in front of the secret cubbyhole, and we headed back to the bar.

Just as we got there, Joseph came running back from the kitchen. 'I had an apple!' he cried with glee. 'And I saved you some.' He brought his hand out from behind his back to reveal the apple core. What little was left of the flesh was starting to brown. 'I tried to save you more, but it was too delicious!' he added sheepishly.

'This is great, thank you!' I laughed as I took the core from him and even Raymond cracked a smile.

'Give me a week to get things arranged,' he said, gesturing at Joseph. 'Then meet me back here. Bring a case with some clothes for him.'

'I will. Thank you.'

'And *bonne chance* today,' he said tersely, before heading back to his table in the corner.

'I liked that adventure,' Joseph said as soon as we were back outside. 'The apple was delicious!'

'Good,' I replied, wondering how I could frame our new gunrunning adventure to him.

'Is the clever man going to help me see Maman?'

'Yes, he is.'

'Hurray!' Joseph cheered.

'But we have to wait for just one more week.' I glanced down at him, anxious at how he would take this news.

He pursed his lips, looking thoughtful for a moment before nodding. 'That's OK. I quite like you, so I don't mind waiting.'

I couldn't help laughing at this. 'Excellent. And a week gives us plenty of time to have more adventures together.'

He took my hand and smiled up at me.

'So, let's go on our next adventure,' I said cheerily, trying not to think of what might become of us if it were to go wrong.

'Where to?' Joseph asked.

'We're going to a tailor's shop. Do you know what that is?'

'Of course. I'm not stupid.' He stared up at me indignantly.

'No, you most certainly are not!'

'Are we going to get some clothes?'

'Yes, yes we are,' I said with a grateful smile. Not only could I try to use my clothing coupons to get him something to wear, but the kid had just inadvertently come up with our cover story.

Ordinarily, I would have walked from the Latin Quarter to Alésia in order to avoid the Metro, but it was much too far for a tiny pair of five-year-old legs.

'We still have to be Aunt Clarisse and nephew Joseph for this adventure,' I told him as we headed for the station. 'And this time we have to be quiet and not talk to any strangers – or policemen.'

'OK.' He nodded studiously.

There was a queue outside the Metro and I saw a couple of plain-clothed Gestapo checking people's papers along with the police. I tried not to think about the contents of my bag, but I couldn't stop my skin from breaking out in a cold sweat.

'Remember, no talking this time,' I said to Joseph as we inched closer to the front of the queue.

He nodded, his lips pulled together as tightly as if they'd been zipped shut. If I hadn't been so nervous, I'd have laughed.

I'd been praying I'd have my papers checked by a policeman, but when we reached the entrance, one of the Gestapo looked me up and down.

'Papers!' he barked.

As I handed them to him, his colleague demanded the woman in front of me hand over her bag to be searched.

Oh no! Oh no! Oh no! I silently chanted as my pulse began to race.

'What is this?' the other German officer demanded of the woman, pulling a file of papers from her bag.

'It's just sheet music. I'm a violinist,' she said, but she looked terrified.

'Look,' the officer said to the German checking my papers, and he showed him a smaller sheet of paper that had been sandwiched in between the music.

'You need to come with us,' he said to the woman. He handed back my papers and waved Joseph and me through.

Any relief I felt at escaping further scrutiny was short-lived as I saw the abject terror on the woman's face. Was she working for the Resistance? Was the paper they'd found some kind of coded message?

'Please, I have a rehearsal to get to,' I heard her pleading as I hurried Joseph through and into the station, my heart in my mouth.

'Why is that lady upset?' Joseph asked as we made our way down onto the platform. 'Were they the bad men?' His bottom lip started to quiver.

I picked him up and stroked his hair. 'No, they just wanted to ask her a question about something she had in her bag. She was worried about being late for work, that's all.'

He studied my face for a moment, as if trying to figure out whether to believe me. Then, to my surprise, he gave a sigh and rested his head on my shoulder. I leaned my head against his and held him tighter. It was so nice to have this sweet moment of closeness in the midst of so much fear, and I wasn't sure which of us needed it most.

To my huge relief, we emerged from the Metro into Alésia without incident and made our way along the wide street to the tailor's. The sun had come out and the first of the pale pink blossom was appearing on the trees. It was lovely to feel that Mother Nature hadn't given up on us humans and was still trying to remind us of how beautiful life could be.

'Are we nearly there?' Joseph asked. 'My legs are feeling a bit tired.'

'Well, we can't have that. Would you like a piggyback?'

'Yes!' he exclaimed.

I crouched down in front of him. 'On you get.'

He clambered onto my back and I continued on my way. The sight of the blossom had put a spring in my step and I decided to resurrect Frankie's old piggyback game.

'And Joseph Lieberman races into the lead on his magnificent horse Clarisse!' I said as I broke into a run.

I heard Joseph giggling in my ear and it made my heart sing.

'He's going to win this race for sure!' I exclaimed.

'Giddy-up, horsey!' Joseph called. 'Faster!'

Oh, how I wished we really could be on a horse, racing faster and faster through the countryside, further and further away from the Germans.

By the time we reached the tailor's shop, Joseph was giggling and excited.

'That was fun!' he exclaimed as I crouched down and he slipped from my back.

I glanced into the darkened interior of the tailor's and my exhilaration subsided. But surely there was nothing to be afraid of now, I tried reassuring myself. The hardest part was over; we'd made it across Paris without the guns in my bag being discovered. Now I just had to drop them off, see if I could get a change of clothes for Joseph, and then we could get back to the relative safety of my apartment.

'Come on,' I said, taking Joseph's hand. 'And don't forget, we're Aunt Clarisse and nephew Joseph.'

'I like horse Clarisse the best,' he said as we headed to the door of the shop.

'Well, I'll be horse Clarisse as soon as we've finished this adventure, OK?'

'OK.'

I opened the door and a bell above it jangled loudly, causing me to jump.

A bespectacled older man appeared from a room at the back. He had curly grey hair and was wearing a pinstriped suit. A tape measure hung around his neck.

'Can I help you?' he said, peering at us over the top of his half-moon glasses.

For a second, fear made my mind go blank. What was it Raymond had asked me to say?

'I... I'm here to see Michel,' I stammered. 'Monsieur Verne sent me.'

The man visibly started. Clearly he understood the subtext – or at least I hoped he did.

'Monsieur Verne?' he asked.

'Yes. He gave me something to give to Michel.'

'OK, please follow me.'

We followed him behind the counter and into a room at the back of the shop. It was crowded with tailor's dummies wearing jackets and shirts, dotted with pins, in various stages of production.

The tailor opened a closet half full of rolls of fabric. 'You can leave it here,' he said, gesturing at one of the shelves.

I fumbled in the bottom of my bag, nerves turning my fingers to jelly. Finally, I found the package. But just as I was taking it from the satchel, the bell above the shop door rang out again.

'Shit!' I exclaimed, almost dropping the guns.

'That's a bad word,' Joseph said in that matter-of-fact tone of his.

'I know. I'm sorry.'

I looked at the tailor imploringly. Did he still want me to put the guns in the cupboard? He frowned and shook his head. And then I heard something that chilled me to the core.

'Hello, is anyone there?' a man called from the shop, in a thick German accent.

23

'Don't make a sound,' the tailor whispered.

I nodded and hugged Joseph to me.

'Good day!' the tailor exclaimed, hurrying into the shop. 'How can I help you?'

'I need a suit,' the German stated.

'But of course,' the tailor replied. 'I was just about to close for lunch. Is there any way you can come back in half an hour?'

'Close for lunch?' the German said derisively. 'Is that all you French can think about? Your stomachs?'

Joseph's eyes widened at the sound of his voice. I put my finger to my lips and he nodded and leaned into me.

'I'm sorry, sir, of course I can help you now. I'll need to take some measurements.'

'Good,' the German said tersely.

Joseph and I remained frozen in silence as the tailor got to work. They were just talking about the kind of fabric the man would like when the unthinkable happened and Joseph coughed. I held him tight, hoping the German might not have heard.

'What was that?' he said. 'Who is back there?'

'Oh, just my daughter and grandson,' the tailor replied, somehow managing to keep his cool. 'They came to see me for lunch.'

'I see,' the German replied.

My heart was pounding so violently, I thought it might actually burst from my chest.

'They're being very quiet out there,' the German said and I heard the sound of his boots walking across the wooden floor.

'Yes, my grandson fell asleep almost as soon as they got here. He does enjoy a morning nap.'

How the tailor was able to remain so calm under pressure was beyond me. I was in awe of his composure and I needed to take a leaf out of his book.

I silently sat down on the floor, leaning against the wall and gestured to my lap. 'Lie down and pretend to be asleep,' I whispered to Joseph.

He quickly did as he was told and with not a second to lose. There was a sound in the doorway and I looked up to see a heavy-set German soldier with cold blue eyes staring down at me.

Thankfully, Joseph kept his eyes closed. I smiled up at the man and put my finger to my lips. In a moment that seemed to drag on forever, he stood there staring at me, then finally he gave an almost imperceptible nod and returned to the shop. I sat there, heart racing as the men got on with the fitting, and I stroked Joseph's hair, as much to soothe my nerves as his.

After what felt like an eternity, the tailor had got all he needed and told the German to come back at the end of the week to collect his finished suit. When the bell above the door jingled as he left, I wanted to weep with relief. I heard the click of the door being locked and the tailor reappeared.

'My God, that was close!' he exclaimed.

'Too close,' I agreed. I gave Joseph a gentle nudge and realised that he really had fallen asleep. 'I told him to pretend to sleep and he's taken me literally,' I said and the tailor laughed. 'Please, take the package from my bag.'

He did as instructed and put the guns in the back of the fabric closet.

'I was wondering if you had anything that might fit him.' I nodded to the sleeping Joseph. 'He doesn't have anything apart from the clothes he's standing up in.'

The tailor looked concerned. 'Why, what happened to him?'

'It's a long story.'

Thankfully, this seemed to be enough of an explanation and the tailor nodded and went over to another closet.

'These might be a little on the long side, but you could take them up,' he said, producing a couple of pairs of boys' trousers. 'And he can have this too.' He took out a pale blue short-sleeved shirt.

'Thank you so much. I have some clothing coupons in my purse. I'm not sure if they'll be enough.'

The tailor shook his head. 'It's on the house. Now, you'd better get going.'

'Of course. Thank you so much.' I gently shook Joseph to wake him up.

'Can I talk yet?' he whispered sleepily.

'Yes, you can,' I replied. 'You've been such a good boy, this nice man is going to give you some new clothes.'

His eyes lit up as the tailor showed him his new trousers and shirt. 'Thank you!' he exclaimed.

'You are very welcome, sir,' the tailor replied with a smile.

As we left the shop, I felt physically wrung out. Once again, we'd evaded capture, but I couldn't help worrying that it was only a matter of time before our luck ran out.

. . .

Fortunately, the rest of the week was a lot less fraught. Once again taking inspiration from my father's school of parenting, we spent hours playing cards. Poker was a little too advanced for Joseph's five-year-old brain so we embarked upon epic snap tournaments instead. I also spent a considerable amount of time preparing him for our upcoming journey, whilst praying that Raymond had been able to put some plans in place.

'Soon we're going to be going on a really big adventure,' I told him.

'To see Maman?' The hope in his eyes broke my heart.

'It will bring you closer to seeing her,' I replied, but inside I was beset with doubt. What if it didn't? What if he and his maman never saw each other again? The fact that she'd been taken by the Gestapo meant that she'd almost certainly be sent east – if she'd survived their interrogations that was. We'd all heard rumours about the torture that went on at the Paris headquarters in the apartments they'd requisitioned on avenue Foch, and the screams that came from those buildings at all hours of day and night. What if I was putting Joseph in more danger by taking him out of Paris? But he was adamant that he had no other family in the city and he couldn't remember where he lived, so I felt as if we'd run out of options. If he stayed with me for too long, we were bound to be found out. Not that I'd ever desert him. I'd grown so fond of the kid, I knew I'd risk my own freedom to protect him.

When the day to leave came, I packed a small case with Joseph's change of clothes, a pencil and a notebook for him to draw in, and a stale stick of bread. We found Raymond in the upstairs bar at the Capoulade. To my relief, he leapt to his feet as soon as he saw us and beckoned us to follow him through to a tiny office next to the kitchen, where he gave Joseph a children's book about animals.

'Something to keep him occupied,' he said to me gruffly.

'Thank you,' I replied, both grateful and surprised that he should have been so thoughtful.

While Joseph began eagerly leafing through the pages, Raymond ushered me over to a desk in the opposite corner of the room.

'Thank you for last week,' he said quietly.

'You're welcome.' I was going to say something about the near miss we'd had but decided against it. It had been hard enough trying to earn Raymond's respect; I didn't want to blow it by appearing weak. 'Any time,' I said instead.

'In five minutes, we will be having a delivery of potatoes from a farmer in Lyon. You two are to hide in the back of his van and he will take you back with him. He's going to take you to a safe house in the country, where you are to wait until someone comes to get the boy. Then the farmer will bring you back with his next delivery here. Is that clear?'

'Oh, yes... OK.' I'd been expecting Raymond to give us false documents to travel by train. Hiding in the back of a van seemed like a slightly safer option, although it wouldn't be without risk. We were bound to encounter German checkpoints en route.

Raymond opened the desk drawer and took out something wrapped in a cloth. 'Have you ever used a pistol before?' he whispered.

I stared at the bundle in shock.

'A pistol,' he repeated. 'Do you know how to use one?'

I nodded. Learning how to be a crack shot was another key lesson in the school of Frankie Esposito. Not that it had been any help in the event of his death. And since seeing him shot dead the thought of using a gun made me feel sick. It was one thing couriering a couple of revolvers across Paris, but clearly Raymond was giving me this one for my own personal use in the expectation that I might need it.

'You sure?' He looked at me dubiously.

'Yes, I learned with a Colt .45. I've also fired a tommy gun.'

'What, like the American gangsters?'

Damn, in my desire to prove myself to him, I'd risked blowing my cover.

'I know how to handle a pistol,' I replied tersely.

'Good.' He passed me the bundle. 'Keep that on you, just in case.'

Just in case of what? I wanted to ask. I found it hard to imagine a scenario where, faced with the police or the Germans and armed only with a pistol, I'd come off better. But I didn't have time to worry about that now. I quickly slipped the pistol into the bottom of my bag beneath the scarf.

I heard a man's voice in the passageway outside.

'Raoul's here,' Raymond said. 'I'll give you a minute to explain to the boy and someone will come and get you when it's time to go.'

'OK, thank you.'

He looked me straight in the eye. 'Raoul is one of my best operatives. Don't do anything to put his life at risk.'

'Of course not.' I frowned. Was he ever going to give me any credit?

As soon as Raymond left the room, I joined Joesph sitting on the floor.

'Look, it's an elephant,' he said, showing me one of the pictures in his book.

'That's great.' I took the book from him and held his hands. 'We're about to go on our big adventure.'

'OK. Can I take my book?'

'Of course you can. And this adventure is going to be really fun because we'll be going in the back of a van.'

'A van?' he echoed, eyes wide.

'Yes. And we might have to play hide-and-seek as well. Do you know that game?'

He nodded. 'I used to play it with Maman and Papa.'

'Good, so that means you'll be really good at hiding.'

'Oh yes,' he replied solemnly and my heart contracted. If anything happened to him on the journey we were about to take, I knew I'd never forgive myself.

We both jumped at the sound of a sharp rap on the door.

'Time for the adventure to begin,' I whispered to Joseph before kissing the top of his head.

I opened the door to find a tall, wiry man with stringy brown hair, dressed in muddy overalls. 'I'm Raoul,' he said, looking from me to Joseph.

'Clarisse,' I replied.

'She has a boy's haircut because it's more fun being a boy,' Joseph explained in that comically adult manner of his. I laughed and hugged him to me.

'Is that so?' Raoul looked back at me and smiled. He seemed warmer than Raymond at least, although that wasn't difficult. 'Come,' he said. 'The van is parked out back.'

We followed him along the corridor and out of the rear exit.

Raoul glanced up and down the street, then opened the back doors of the van. 'Quick,' he whispered, ushering us inside.

The back of the van was muddy and smelled of old vegetables. It wasn't a smell I used to enjoy, but I'd been so hungry for so long it prompted my stomach to rumble.

'You're to go in here,' Raoul instructed, moving a panel to reveal a hidden cavity between the back of the truck and the driver's cab. It was a tiny space, but it would definitely fool anyone doing a cursory check. I wasn't so sure it would escape a thorough inspection, though. I thought of the gun in my purse and my stomach churned.

'OK, it's time to start playing hide-and-seek,' I said to Joseph as we climbed into the truck, trying to hide my fear and keep him calm.

'You can use these to cover yourselves too,' Raoul said,

passing me a handful of potato sacks. 'If we get stopped for an inspection, I'll knock three times on the wall.'

My mouth went dry at the mere thought of that happening and I placed a protective hand on Joseph's back. 'OK, thank you.'

'Who's hiding first?' Joseph asked.

'We both are,' I replied. 'Won't that be fun?' He looked at me sceptically and once again I felt sick to my stomach at the way the Nazis were ruining children's lives.

We scrambled into the cavity and Raoul began putting the false wall back in place. *'Bonne chance,'* he whispered before disappearing from view.

'Bonne chance,' I whispered into the sudden darkness.

'Who's going to be looking for us?' Joseph whispered.

My pulse quickened as I thought of the possibilities. I didn't want to worry Joseph, though. 'One of that man's friends, but we're going to go for a drive first.'

I heard Raoul shifting some of the crates around in the back, no doubt placing them against the false wall. *We are going to be OK*, I told myself and I instinctively felt for Lillie's mother's locket. I might not have been able to reunite Lillie with the necklace, but I was going to get Joseph to safety. I had to.

If only you could see me now, I thought to the peacock as I shifted to make more room for Joseph. *And if only I could see you...* Both of us were now living in bizarre new realities, that was for sure. I still found it hard to picture the peacock as a Resistance fighter. I couldn't imagine him wearing anything other than his brightly coloured suits for a start.

'It's very dark,' Joseph said as the van juddered into life and I could detect a waver in his voice.

'Well, that means it's perfect for telling you a story,' I replied.

'Why?'

'Because it's so much easier to imagine things in the dark.'

'Why?'

'Because you can't see anything else to distract you. Shall I tell you a story now?' I asked, eager to keep his fear at bay.

'Yes please, can it be about an elephant?'

'Of course.'

So, for the next few hours, I told Joseph a protracted saga about a family of elephants. Storytelling was definitely not my strong suit, so I ended up loosely basing the elephants on my family, and it was heart-warming to hear Frankie the Esposito elephant raise a lot of laughs from the kid.

Every time I heard the hiss of the van's brakes and felt it come to a halt, my stomach practically fell through the floor. Thankfully, there was no knock on the wall, though. But after we'd been travelling for what felt like days, the truck stopped and the engine cut out. I prayed that we'd reached our destination or Raoul was stopping for a bathroom break, but then came three sharp raps on the partition, almost causing my heart to stop.

'OK, it's time to play hide-and-seek,' I whispered, pulling the potato sacks over us.

'Is that man's friend looking for us?' Joseph said.

'Shhh, yes, so we have to be very, very quiet.'

'OK.'

I put my arm around him and pulled him close, hoping he couldn't feel me trembling.

I heard the muffled sound of Raoul saying something and then his door opening and closing.

'I am just on my way back from making a delivery in Paris,' he said loudly, probably for my benefit.

And then came a sound that made the hairs on the back of my neck stand on end. Another man's voice, speaking in German.

24

APRIL 1985, PARIS

I only worked half-days in the library on Tuesdays, and after what had happened during story-time I was relieved to be able to escape at lunchtime. I had no desire to go home, though; the last thing I needed was to be cooped up with the Pandora's box of emotions I seemed to have unwittingly unleashed, so I decided to walk into the heart of the city. Hopefully, I'd happen upon an exhibition at one of the museums or galleries that would take my mind off the strange events of the past two days.

As I made my way through the second arrondissement, Le Centre Pompidou, with its infamous 'inside out' design, loomed into view. When it had opened in 1977 many Parisians had been vociferous in their condemnation of the building, with its brightly coloured pipes and other mechanisms lining the exterior rather than interior of the building. 'It is like a human being with all of its innards on display,' was one common refrain and an article in Le Figaro declared that just as Scotland had Nessie, Paris now had its own monster. But I liked the way the ugliness of the plumbing and the wiring had been put on full display, and in dazzling primary colours too. To me, it felt like the only honest building in Paris, the only structure that didn't tuck its dark secrets beneath an elegant Haussmann facade.

A young girl of about thirteen whizzed past me on those bright blue roller skates with the canary-yellow laces that were now all the rage. A pair of headphones were clamped to her ears and a Walkman was attached to the waistband of her shorts. She looked so happy and carefree. I wondered if she knew that there was once a time when kids her age were torn from their parents on these very same streets.

I tried to shake the thought from my mind and focused instead on the Stravinsky Fountain and its vivid moving sculptures. It was hard to feel down when looking at the fountain and in the two years since it had been built, I'd spent many an hour there watching water cascade from the colourful elephant, serpent and firebird.

I walked on towards the centre. I just needed to lose myself in an exhibition, then I'd go back home, have something to eat and an early night. I decided to avoid reading any more of Madeleine Bernier's book. I felt the urgent need to get my life back onto its carefully cultivated even keel. I'd had a strange couple of days, but it was time to put my younger self and all the accompanying memories away again. Tomorrow I would return Bernier's book to the library and go back to my normal life. I didn't need to take a lover or go travelling. And I didn't need to be absolutely free. My life of routine had served me perfectly well for decades.

When I reached the entrance, I looked at the display of posters advertising the current exhibitions and my throat instantly tightened. Surely I was mistaken, surely it couldn't be. But no matter how hard I blinked, the headline on the poster remained the same: PHOTOGRAPHE ET RÉSISTANTE – PHOTOGRAPHER AND RESISTANCE FIGHTER – and so did the photograph beneath it. The photograph of my younger self.

25

APRIL 1943, FRANCE

'It's a bad man!' Joseph gasped at the sound of the German's voice. 'It's a bad man!' His tiny body began to quiver.

'It's OK,' I whispered. 'We just have to be really quiet, so he doesn't find us.'

'Is the bad man playing hide-and-seek?' Rather than getting quieter, his voice rose.

'Yes, I think so, so we have to be totally silent, OK?' I hugged him tighter to me and adjusted the potato sacks so we were completely covered.

'I don't want to play,' he said, starting to cry.

As the men's voices made their way to the back of the van, my heart was beating so fast, I could hear the blood pulsing in my ears. I had to get Joseph to be silent, but how?

'We have to play if you want to see your maman again.' It seemed like a cheap shot, using his maman as some kind of bargaining chip, but I felt I had no other option. Thankfully, it worked and he fell silent.

I listened as the back door of the van creaked open.

'And where is your farm?' the German asked.

As Raoul replied, Joseph began shifting about.

'Try to stay still,' I whispered, stroking his hair.

'Am I being still enough?' he asked, his voice raised.

My heart practically stopped as the men fell silent and, for a second, I was sure the soldiers had heard and our number was up. Very slowly and very quietly, I felt in my purse for the bundle Raymond had given me. My fingers worked their way beneath the cloth and I felt the cool metal of the pistol. It had been so long since Frankie had taken me to the firing range, would I still remember what to do? Would I be able to fire straight? Should I fire at all? There was bound to be more than one German officer present, so even if I succeeded in shooting one, surely his buddies would be right there to back him up, and I knew enough about those animals by now to know that they wouldn't think twice about shooting Joseph. I took my hand off the gun and tucked it back beneath the cloth.

I heard some movement in the back of the van and closed my eyes. This was it. The game was up. Rather than save Joseph, I'd led him straight into captivity – or worse. The German said something about potatoes and then the door slammed shut. They'd shut the door! I stayed frozen rigid as I heard them walk back round to the front of the truck.

'Did the bad man find us?' Joseph said in a scared little voice.

The truck moved slightly as Raoul got back into the cab. He called out good day and the engine choked back into life.

'No, no he didn't.' I hugged Joseph to me, overcome with relief. 'Because you're so good at playing hide-and-seek. Well done!'

'Will I see Maman now?' he asked.

'Not yet, but hopefully one day,' I answered, hugging him even tighter.

'Because I hid so well?'

'Yes, exactly. You've been a very good and brave boy, and I'm very proud of you.'

'That's what Maman says to me.' He leaned into me and my eyes filled with tears. This tiny human was going to be the death of me – if not literally, then certainly emotionally.

After what felt like another day of driving but was probably only another hour or two, the truck came to a halt and the engine cut out. I held my breath, anticipating the coded knock from the driver's cab, but mercifully it didn't come and I heard Raoul get out.

'I think we might have arrived,' I whispered to Joseph.

'Where?' he whispered back.

'Somewhere safe to stay.'

The back door of the truck creaked open and the whole thing rocked from side to side as Raoul climbed in.

'We're here,' he called as he started removing the false wall.

By this point, my legs had gone to sleep and I was barely able to move. Joseph, on the other hand, eagerly scrambled from our hiding place.

'Don't forget my book, Aunt Clarisse,' he called over his shoulder.

I felt a strange delight at him calling me this so instinctively. I knew it was probably because he took the rules of our 'adventures' so seriously, but still, part of me hoped it was because my growing affection for him was reciprocated. I fumbled around for his book and the case and forced my numb legs to move.

I stumbled from the van to discover that we were on a dirt track outside a stone cottage. We were surrounded by fields and the jagged outline of a forest was silhouetted on the horizon. Dusk was gathering and high above us ravens circled, cawing as they prepared to roost for the night. After so long confined to Paris, it felt strange to be in the countryside again. The cool, fresh air smelled of earth and trees. If only I could have relaxed enough to enjoy it.

'Is this your place?' I asked Raoul, stretching my aching limbs.

'No, this is a safe house. It's empty at the moment. You're to wait here until tomorrow, then someone will come to fetch him first thing.' He nodded to Joseph, who was busy examining some flowers growing by the side of the track. 'I'll be back to get you later in the day. There's some food in the kitchen and you should sleep in the cellar, just in case...'

In case of what? I wondered but thought better than to ask.

I looked at the cottage. The windows were all dark and blank, like sightless eyes.

'The Vichy militia are active in this area,' Raoul continued, 'so you have to make sure no one realises you're here. Only use the lamps in the cellar and obviously don't light a fire.'

'Of course.' There was no way on earth I was going to do anything to signal to the Milice that we were there.

'Come with me.' He led us through a rickety gate, hanging on by one hinge, and up the overgrown garden path. The red paint on the front door was chipped and I couldn't help noticing a dent near the bottom as if someone had kicked it.

'Are you sure it's safe here?' I whispered to Raoul. He looked over his shoulder at me and raised his eyebrows.

'Right now, nowhere is safe,' he hissed.

'I'm sorry, it was a stupid question. I'm just worried about him.' I looked at Joseph, who was following behind us clutching a handful of bright yellow flowers. It was such a beautiful sight I had to fight the urge to capture it on my camera.

'I understand,' Raoul replied with a sad smile.

He led us down a narrow passageway into the kitchen. The cottage was deathly cold, as if it hadn't been lived in for quite some time. The kitchen was bare apart from a solitary pot on the stove that looked to be about a hundred years old. One scuffed boot lay on its side by the back door. What had happened to the other, I wondered, and indeed, to the owner?

Were they currently hopping around somewhere in search of a lost boot? It must have been the release from the tension of the journey, but I found the sight strangely comical.

'Food!' Joseph exclaimed, his eyes on stalks as he stared at the table.

As I followed his gaze, my mouth dropped open. It wasn't just food on the table, it was a *cornucopia* of food. A tray had been filled with a round loaf of bread, a large golden pat of butter, what looked like a sizeable wedge of cheese wrapped in brown paper, slices of ham, four apples, six eggs and a large jug of milk.

'Is this all for us?' I asked, hardly daring to believe that it could be.

'Yes,' Raoul replied. 'Let's take it downstairs.' He went over to a small door in the corner and undid the iron latch. 'Be careful,' he said as he led us down a flight of steep stone steps.

'Why's it so dark?' Joseph asked from beside me. 'Is it so you can tell me more elephant stories?'

'Yes, that's right,' I replied cheerily but internally groaned. If I never told a story about an elephant again, it would be too soon. Thanks to Joseph, I now understood how having a child was a truly priceless gift, but, my God, mothers deserved medals for the relentless questioning they were subjected to.

I heard a match being struck and Raoul lit a lamp.

'It's OK, we have light,' I said to Joseph, giving his hand a squeeze.

'I don't mind, you can still tell me an elephant story,' he said.

'There are some blankets and pillows over there.' Raoul pointed to a pile of bedding in the corner. 'And if you need to use the bathroom...' He indicated a white porcelain chamber pot covered in a pink rose design.

I looked around the cellar. The walls were lined with bare

shelves, and aside from the bedding, a small table and a couple of rickety chairs, there was nothing else down there.

'I'd better go now, so no one sees my van,' Raoul said, placing the tray of food on the table. 'When my contact comes to get the boy in the morning, he'll knock five times on the cellar door. Don't come up until you hear the signal. And I'll do the same when I come for you later in the morning.'

'OK, thank you.'

As I watched him go back up the stairs a little of my new-found relief went with him. Now it was just Joseph and me, in a cold dark cellar in the middle of nowhere, or rather, the middle of an area where Vichy's dreaded militia, the Milice, were active. But we only had to make it through one night, I reminded myself. Then Raoul's contact would be coming to get Joseph. I needed to prepare him.

'Why is there so much food?' he exclaimed, still mesmerised by the contents of the tray.

'It's because you did so well at hide-and-seek,' I replied. 'And tomorrow you'll have to play another game.'

'Can I have an egg please?' he asked, clearly unable to concentrate on anything but the food. And who could blame him?

'Of course.' I tapped one of the boiled eggs and began peeling off the shell.

'I haven't had an egg for ten years,' he said gravely.

'Hmm, are you sure? I thought you were only five.'

'Oh yes, I am!' For some reason, he found this hilariously funny and his giggles were infectious.

'I haven't had any butter for five hundred years,' I chuckled, cutting him a slice of bread.

'How old are you?' he exclaimed.

'You're not supposed to think that I'm older than five hundred!' I replied. Although, in truth, these days I certainly felt it.

. . .

After a dinner of bread and butter and eggs and ham, all washed down with glasses of the most deliciously creamy milk, I made up a bed of sorts in the corner. It wasn't going to be the most comfortable night on the stone floor, but thanks to the combination of the stress of the day and more food than I'd been used to in a long time, I felt suddenly sleepy. Joseph clearly felt the same as he kept yawning and rubbing his eyes.

'Can you tell me a story about the elephants, Aunt Clarisse?' he said as we snuggled down together.

'Of course.' Now we'd eaten and were relatively safe, I really didn't mind. It felt so nice to be snuggled up with him. 'You don't have to keep calling me Aunt Clarisse, you know. We're not playing that game anymore.'

'I know,' he replied. 'But I want to.'

My heart glowed. 'Thank you, nephew Joseph.' And as I began telling him a tale about the Esposito elephants getting involved in a food fight with some bad foxes and pelting them with hard-boiled eggs, my eyes filled with grateful tears. If only this didn't have to be our last night together. I couldn't imagine how hard it was going to be to say goodbye.

26

We must have both fallen asleep midway through my tale because the next thing I knew I was waking with a start to the sound of footsteps walking across the kitchen floor above. I looked around frantically, trying to get my bearings. The lamp had gone out and the cellar was pitch dark. I heard a man's voice and thought – *hoped* – that it might be Raoul. Or maybe his contact had come early to fetch Joseph. But there was no coded knock on the door. I heard a scraping sound, like one of the chairs upstairs was being moved. I slowly and carefully disentangled myself from Joseph and stood up. I needed to get the pistol, but where was my bag? My head was still fuzzy from sleep. I fumbled around in the dark and finally managed to locate my bag on the table, took out the gun and crept over to the stairs.

The man laughed, then said 'Come here' in French. I breathed a sigh of relief. At least he was French, not German. Then I heard the high peal of a woman's laughter. My mind began to race as I tried to work out who they might be and why they might be here. Could they be members of the local Resistance who knew it was a safe house? Perhaps they were using it for a lovers' tryst. The thought wasn't exactly appealing, but it was certainly preferable to the alternatives.

I was about to creep back to the bed and cover us in blankets when the man exclaimed, 'What is this?' I stayed frozen to the spot and strained to hear what he was saying. 'Where did these flowers come from?'

The hairs on the back of my neck stood on end as I had a terrible flashback: Joseph clutching the bright yellow flowers he'd picked on the way into the cottage. We'd both been so excited by the food we hadn't thought of anything else. He must have left them in the kitchen.

If the man was a member of the Resistance, then surely it wouldn't matter if he found us.

But what if he isn't? my inner voice cautioned and I tightened my grip on the pistol, my hand suddenly clammy.

'We need to go,' the man said.

'But why?' the woman asked.

'Just go, quick,' he hissed, and I heard their footsteps padding across the floor above, then the sound of a door being closed.

I sat on the steps and took a shaking breath. That had been close. Too close. What if a group of police or Germans on patrol had come to the house and seen the flowers?

I waited for about ten minutes until I was sure the coast was clear, then tucked the pistol into the pocket of my culottes and crept up the steps. I opened the cellar door as slowly as I could, but it still let out a loud creak. I heard Joseph murmur in his sleep, but thankfully he didn't wake. I inched the door open wider. I just needed to retrieve the flowers and get back downstairs.

Cautiously, I stepped into the kitchen. The light from the moon was pouring in through the window, casting a silvery beam upon the table, right onto the bright yellow flowers. I took a couple of steps towards them, then heard a sound from the other end of the room which almost caused my heart to stop.

'Don't move,' the man said, stepping from the shadows by the door and pointing a gun at me, turning my blood to ice. As he approached the table, I saw from his outline that he was wearing a beret, and then as he stepped into the moonlight, I recognised the blue uniform, the brown shirt. *Milice!* 'I knew someone was here,' he said, smugly, 'the minute I saw the flowers.'

It was the man I'd heard before with the woman. He must have just pretended to leave and I'd walked straight into his trap. The realisation was sickening. I glanced around, but there was no sign of his companion.

'What are you doing here?' he asked, still pointing his gun at me. He had the kind of mean face that looked as if it had been pinched into being.

I thought of the pistol in my pocket. If I reached for it now, he'd shoot me for sure. 'I... I... I'm on my way to my sister's house, but I got lost,' I stammered. 'I found this place, so I thought it would be safe to rest for the night.'

'Oh really?' Clearly he didn't believe me one bit. 'This place is very out of the way to just stumble upon it.'

'What can I say? I was very lost.' I gave a nervous laugh, hoping he'd dismiss me as a ditzy woman, the way Raymond and Pierre did.

'Yes, very lost indeed.' He looked me up and down, but before either of us could say another word, there was the sound of a clatter from the cellar. Joseph must have woken.

'Joseph, stay down there,' I called, my heart in my mouth.

'Who's Joseph?' the man hissed. I watched in horror as he aimed his pistol at the cellar door.

'He's my nephew. He's only five; I'm bringing him back to my sister's place. Well, trying to...'

There was another clatter from the cellar. No doubt, Joseph

was having trouble finding his way in the dark. He was probably terrified at waking up in the cellar alone but I had to keep him down there.

'Joseph, go back to bed,' I called, my voice shrill.

'Why isn't he saying anything?' the man hissed, inching closer to the cellar door.

'He's probably scared. He's only five,' I said, horror filling me. Did he think there was a grown man down there?

'Joseph, are you OK?' I called. Surely if the man heard his voice, he'd relax. But there was no reply and then I heard movement on the steps. 'Go back to bed! Please!'

'Do you think I'm stupid?' the man said, glancing at me while keeping his pistol trained on the door.

Yes! I wanted to yell. *I knew you were stupid the second I saw you in that uniform, you traitor!*

'No, of course not.'

'A woman wouldn't be all the way out here on her own.' He inched closer to the door. 'There's a man here with you, isn't there?'

'No, I'll show you,' I said, moving towards the cellar door.

'Stay there!' he yelled, and before I could do anything to respond, something came flying through the air from the cellar doorway, hitting him smack in the face. 'What the hell?' he yelped and the crack of a gunshot reverberated around the room.

'No!' I cried, my ears ringing. 'No! No!' I pushed past him to find Joseph lying face down at the top of the steps. 'Joseph!' As I went to pick him up, I felt something warm and sticky. I knew what it was instantly, remembered that same feeling all those years ago when I'd hugged my dying father. 'No!' I screamed, reaching into my pocket for my pistol.

I turned back into the kitchen to see the man rubbing his cheek, the hand holding the gun hanging down at his side.

'He threw an egg at me,' he muttered.

'So you shot him?' I raised the pistol and aimed it at his chest. 'He's a child!' I cried.

He saw my weapon and raised his own. But he was too slow. I squeezed the trigger and watched him crash to the floor.

27

I looked at the body on the floor, feeling sick to my stomach. Even in the pale moonlight, I was able to see the dark stain flowering on his shirt. Was he dead? Had I killed him? But he'd shot Joseph, I reminded myself. *Joseph!*

'Joseph!' I cried, turning to the tiny body lying at the top of the steps. 'Oh, Joseph!' I collapsed on the floor beside him. How had this happened? I'd tried so hard to help keep him safe, but I'd failed him spectacularly. 'I'm so sorry,' I sobbed, gently scooping him up into my lap. 'I'm so sorry.'

'I was just like the elephant throwing eggs at the naughty foxes,' a little voice murmured, causing me to practically jump out of my skin.

I stared down at him in shock, but no, I wasn't imagining things, he was stirring. 'Joseph!'

'My arm hurts,' he moaned.

'It's all right. You're going to be OK.' Very slowly and very gently, I stood up, holding him to me. 'You're going to be OK,' I said again, as much to reassure myself as him, and I carried him back down the steps. After placing him on our nest of blankets,

I lit the lamp and carefully peeled back the sleeve of his sweater.

'Ow, it hurts,' he moaned.

'It's all right. I'll make it feel better, I promise.' I held the lamp up to examine the wound. Thankfully, it didn't appear to be too deep and there was no sign of the bullet. It must have just grazed him. As long as I could stem the bleeding and keep the wound clean, he should be OK. The relief I felt was overwhelming.

I quickly fetched a headscarf from my case and bound it around the wound. Joseph's eyes fluttered open.

'I'm just giving you a bandage,' I said, 'to make you feel better.'

He nodded. 'Was I good?' he murmured.

'What do you mean?'

'At the silent game?'

I thought back to how he hadn't replied when I'd called to him from the kitchen and it made me want to cry. He'd been trying to do the right thing by not answering me.

'I threw an egg at the bad man,' he said, 'just like Frankie the elephant did in your story.'

Once again, I had to fight the urge to weep. 'You did great,' I whispered, kissing him on the forehead. 'You were so brave. I'm just going to check on something; I'll be back in a minute.'

I covered him with a blanket and hurried back up the steps, worried that the man might have made a similarly remarkable recovery. I took my pistol from my pocket and crept back into the kitchen. He was still lying on the floor; the dark stain on his chest had grown even bigger. I crept over and placed my fingers on the side of his neck. There was no pulse and no sign that he was breathing. The relief I felt at this soon faded. I'd killed someone. It was a thought too enormous to even begin to process. But I couldn't fall apart now. Joseph needed me. In the morning, Raoul's contact would be coming to take him to safety, and hopefully he would be able to help me take care of the body. The body – of a person I had killed.

I pushed the thought away. I had to focus on Joseph. Joseph was still alive, but that meant I'd killed the man for no good reason.

Of course it was for good reason, I told myself. *He was a member of the Milice – who knew what he might have done to you if he'd realised why we were there.*

But if he'd seen that Joseph was just a child, he may have believed your cover story.

On and on my internal argument raged. Then I thought of the woman I'd heard with him earlier. The man had told her to go away, but what if she hadn't? What if she was outside? Or, even worse, what if she'd heard the shot and gone to get help?

I had to hide the body, but where? I looked around frantically and tried a door in the corner. It opened onto a pantry. That would have to do. I went back to the body and picked up the feet and started dragging it across the stone floor. He hadn't seemed all that large before, but now he seemed to weigh a ton.

Once the body was safely concealed, I went back into the kitchen, firmly shutting the pantry door behind me. There was a trail of blood on the floor, but there was no cleaning equipment anywhere to be seen. All I could do now was take care of Joseph and hope and pray that Raoul's contact arrived before anyone else did.

I picked up the yellow flowers and returned to the cellar.

'Aunt Clarisse?' Joseph called.

'It's all right, Joseph, I'm here.'

'Nephew Joseph,' he mumbled.

'*Nephew* Joseph.' I got into our makeshift bed, being careful not to bump his arm. It was only when I lay down that I realised that I was shaking like a leaf.

'Has the bad man gone?' he asked, nuzzling his head against me.

'Yes,' I replied, feeling in my pocket for the pistol. 'The bad man's gone.'

Needless to say, I didn't get a wink of sleep and poor Joseph kept waking from the pain in his arm. But somehow, we made it through the rest of the night. As soon as I heard a distant cockerel crowing, I gingerly eased my way out of bed.

'Where are you going?' Joseph asked, instantly waking.

'To get some breakfast,' I said cheerily. 'Would you like some?'

'Yes please.' He winced as he tried to sit and as I lit the lamp, I saw that the scarf around his arm was stained with blood. Raoul's contact had better show up soon or I wasn't sure what I'd do.

'I'm just going to go upstairs to get some water to wash your arm.'

When I reached the top of the stairs, I paused but all seemed deathly quiet, so I pushed the door open. The kitchen was bathed in pale dawn light and I grimaced as I saw the trail of blood on the floor leading straight to the pantry. Then a terrible thought occurred to me – what if the man wasn't dead? What if I'd been mistaken when I tried and failed to find a pulse?

I went over to the pantry and hesitated for a moment before going in. The body was exactly where I'd left it and the shaft of light coming through the door illuminated his face. His skin was paper white with a slightly blue hue.

'My God!' I slammed the door shut again, looked at the stains on the floor. What should I do? But before I had time to do anything, I heard the sound of a car approaching. Was it the woman, returning with help? I pictured the Milice swarming into the kitchen, following the bloody trail to their dead comrade, then discovering Joseph and me and exacting a bloody revenge. I hurried to the cellar door and shut it behind me, feeling for the pistol in my pocket as I raced down the steps to Joseph.

'Is it breakfast time?' he asked eagerly.

'Not quite yet, we have to hide first.'

His face fell, his chin starting to wobble.

I quickly put the food in a darkened corner, blew out the lamp and joined Joseph in the bed, hugging him to me.

'I don't like this game anymore,' he whispered.

'Just one more time,' I replied.

'If I play it once more, will I see my maman?'

'Hopefully.' I had no choice but to lie; I had to get him to be quiet. Fortunately, it did the trick.

I pulled the blanket up over us and we both lay still as statues as footsteps made their way across the kitchen floor above. I heard a man curse. Presumably he'd seen the blood. I waited, but no other voices came. Could he be on his own? I slid the pistol from my pocket as I heard more footsteps and the creak of a door opening, but it couldn't be the cellar door as the cellar remained dark.

The man cursed again. He must have followed the trail of blood and seen the body. Now what would he do? If he was alone, I might be able to deal with him, as long as I shot him first. But could I really shoot another person? Joseph shifted beside me, snuggling into my chest, and my resolve stiffened. I would do anything to save him.

I heard the footsteps make their way back across the kitchen, then stop.

Please, please, please do the coded knock, I silently begged.

But all remained deathly quiet and then, slowly, the cellar door creaked open.

28

The door creaked open further, sending a thin shaft of pale light spilling down the stairs.

'Hello?' the man called. He sounded nervous.

But I mustn't let that lull me into a false sense of security, I told myself, peering out from under the blanket and aiming the pistol in his direction.

'Hello?' he called again and I felt Joseph move. I placed my free hand on his head to try to reassure him. 'Is anyone there?'

'No!' Joseph called at the top of his voice. My throat tightened as I put my finger on the trigger and prepared to squeeze.

'Oh, thank God,' the man cried. 'I thought you were dead.'

I froze as he made his way down the stairs. As he was silhouetted against the light coming from the kitchen, I could see that he wasn't holding a weapon.

'Where are you?' he asked as he reached the bottom of the stairs.

'Shall I throw an egg at him?' Joseph whispered.

'No, it's OK, stay there,' I whispered back.

'It's all right. Raoul sent me,' the man said, making his way over to us. Now he was up close, I could see that he was young, early twenties, I'd guess, and he looked as anxious as I felt.

'Why didn't you knock?' I hissed. 'To let us know it was you.'

'I'm sorry. I saw the body upstairs and I panicked. I thought maybe you'd been shot too.'

'He has.' I pulled the blanket back to reveal Joseph. 'Thankfully, it just grazed his arm, but I'm worried about infection.'

The man nodded. 'It's OK, I can get it cleaned up once we reach our destination.'

Joseph stared up at him. 'Is he a bad man?' he whispered.

'No, no, he's good. He's come to help us.' I felt a sudden sinking feeling. In all of the drama of the night before, I hadn't thought to tell Joseph that we'd now be going our separate ways. The prospect of being parted from the kid had been bad enough before, but now it felt as if I'd be losing a part of me. It was crazy how he'd come to mean so much to me. I turned to Joseph and stroked his hair. 'This nice man is going to take you somewhere safe.'

'OK,' he said.

'But I'm not going to be able to come with you.'

'Why not?' His bottom lip started to quiver.

It took all of my resolve to hold firm. 'Because I have to go back to Paris.'

'But... but... who's going to tell me stories?'

'You have your new book,' I said, trying my hardest to remain positive for him.

'But it isn't as good as your stories.'

'We really should get going,' the man said. He glanced anxiously at the cellar door before looking back at me. 'When is Raoul coming to get you?'

'He said sometime this morning.'

'OK, good. You don't want to be here if the Milice come looking for their friend.' He looked up the stairs again.

'I don't want to leave you, Aunt Clarisse,' Joseph whimpered.

'I don't want to leave you either. But if you go with this nice man, your maman will be able to find you.' Again, I had no idea if this would actually be the case, but I had to do something to get him to go willingly.

'OK. I'll be brave for her. And for you,' he said stoically, causing my heart to splinter.

'Oh, Joseph.' I kissed the top of his head. 'I have something for you,' I said, remembering the gift I'd packed for this very moment. I went over to my bag and took out a photo. I'd taken it during the week we were holed up in my apartment together. It was of Joseph and me fooling around pretending to be elephants, using our arms as trunks. I deliberately hadn't shown it to him when I developed the film as I'd wanted it to be a surprise.

'It's too dark, I can't see it,' he said.

'I'll carry you upstairs. Can you bring the case?' I asked the man as I carefully picked Joseph up. As soon as we reached the light of the kitchen, he gave a delighted laugh.

'We're elephants!' he exclaimed.

'Yes. And now you can see me whenever you want,' I said, praying that this would be enough.

'OK.' He nodded, smiling shyly up at me.

I carried him outside. An old car was parked on the track leading up to the cottage.

'I'm afraid he'll have to go in the boot,' the man said apologetically.

I winced as I thought of Joseph stuffed in the boot all on his own. 'This is just to keep you safe,' I said as I placed him inside, wrapped in his blanket.

'I don't want to hide again,' he whimpered, and I felt anger mingle with my sorrow. The fact that an innocent child should have to be hidden like this was abhorrent. An innocent child who'd now lost both his parents and had been shot. How had the world become such an obscene place?

'It's just one more time, I promise,' I said, stroking his hair. 'And if you get scared, you can talk to me in the photograph.'

He nodded and pressed the photo to his chest. 'My arm hurts.'

'Don't worry, you're going to see someone who will make it all better.'

'Maman?' Once again, his eyes filled with hope.

'Not yet but soon.' I hoped with all my might that what I was telling him would come true: that one day he and his beloved mother would be reunited.

'We have to go,' the man said, glancing up the track. As he got into the car, I leaned down and kissed Joseph's cheek.

'I love you, Aunt Clarisse,' he murmured.

'Oh Joseph, I love you too.' I turned my face away so he wouldn't see my eyes filling with tears and carefully shut the boot.

The car choked into life and bumped off along the track. As I stood there watching them go, it felt as if I was being torn in two. *Come back!* I wanted to yell. *I don't care if you ask me endless questions about everything and want me to tell you stories about elephants forevermore. Just please don't leave.*

The car disappeared from view, and I don't think I'd ever felt so alone.

29

Raoul arrived to get me about half an hour later. He was none too pleased when I told him that a dead member of the Milice was now being stored in the pantry, but, quite frankly, by that point I didn't care. I just wanted to get out of there. Hopefully once I was back in Paris, I'd be able to forget that I'd shot and killed a man and shake off the growing feeling of horror this was causing.

You thought he'd killed Joseph, I reminded myself. *He could have been about to shoot you too.*

But a seed had been planted and its first tentative shoots were coiling their way into my mind. I'd shot and killed a man, just like the hitman who'd been sent to kill my father. And, even worse, I couldn't escape the truth that, in the moment when I'd squeezed the trigger, I was so consumed by rage, I wanted to end him.

The journey back was relatively uneventful. Raoul had to stop a couple of times to show his papers, but thankfully there was no inspection of the truck. On my own in the hiding place behind the false wall, I pined for Joseph and the feeling of his tiny body pressed into mine. I wondered where he was and if he was OK.

At least he now has a chance of being safe, I tried reassuring myself, picturing him one day being reunited with his mother and regaling her with tales of his fun adventures with his pretend aunt.

We arrived back at the cafe in the late afternoon. It was one of those beautiful spring days where the sky had never seemed bluer, and the air was warm with the promise of summer. I emerged, blinking from the back of the truck, dazzled after so long in the darkness of my hiding place.

'You need to tell Raymond what happened,' Raoul muttered as we made our way through the back door into the kitchen.

My heart sank. It had taken so long to get Raymond to even grudgingly accept me. Once he found out I'd killed a member of the Milice, he'd no doubt want no more to do with me.

I made my way down to the cellar bar and found him at his usual table, tucked away in the far corner, writing something in a notebook.

'How did it go?' he asked as soon as I reached him.

'The boy has been taken to safety,' I replied, shifting awkwardly from foot to foot.

He looked genuinely relieved at this, which was encouraging. Perhaps there was a heart beating beneath that gruff exterior of his after all.

'But he was shot,' I continued.

'The boy?' His mouth fell open in shock.

'Yes. Luckily, the bullet just grazed his arm, so I'm sure he'll be fine but...' I trailed off, unsure how to tell him what had happened next.

He raised his eyebrows questioningly.

'I killed the man who shot him.' I looked away, across the cellar bar, waiting for the inevitable dressing-down.

'*You* killed a man?' Even though I was far from proud of what had happened, the fact that Raymond sounded so incredulous irked me.

'Yes,' I said, meeting his gaze. 'He was a member of the Milice. He came to the house in the middle of the night.'

'Does Raoul know?'

'Yes, and the man who came to get the boy saw the body.'

'OK, good, so they'll know not to use that house anymore.' He frowned. 'What the hell was he doing there?'

'He'd come with a woman, presumably for a lovers' tryst. They must have been there before and known that the house was empty because he noticed that there were some flowers on the kitchen table.'

'And how the hell did they get there?' He glared at me accusingly.

'The kid picked them and brought them in. I didn't realise they'd been left there. Anyway, as soon as the man saw them, he told the woman to go. I thought he'd gone too, but he caught me when I came up from the cellar.'

Raymond scratched his head. 'I don't understand. How did the child get shot?'

'He threw an egg at the man and—'

'He did what?' Raymond interrupted. His eyes looked as if they might pop out of his head.

'It's a long story.'

'So the man shot him?'

'Yes, and I thought he'd killed him.'

'So you shot him in retaliation?'

'Yes, and in self-defence. I thought he was going to shoot me next.' I took the pistol wrapped in cloth from my bag and slid it across the table, preparing myself for Raymond's outburst, but, to my surprise, he was looking at me with what appeared to be admiration.

'Interesting.' He nodded thoughtfully as he slid the pistol

from the table and onto the chair beside his. 'Clearly I've under-estimated you.' He met my gaze and for the first time I saw no hint of hostility there. 'Those Milice bastards killed my wife last year,' he said, his voice strained.

'Oh... I'm so sorry.' So this must have been what the peacock meant when he said that Raymond had been through a lot.

'Yes, well, that's why I'm not sorry you killed one of them. As far as I'm concerned, they're even worse than the Germans, turning on their fellow countrymen and women – and even children.'

I nodded. Even though I was shocked and saddened to hear about his wife, a small part of me was grateful to have won his approval. It made the reality of what I'd done slightly easier to live with.

'I've received word from Louis – or the peacock as you call him.' He gave an amused smile.

'You have?' Hope surged through me.

'Yes.' He picked up his notebook and flicked through the pages. 'He sent you a message.'

It took all I had not to cry out with relief, but as I'd only just earned Raymond's respect, I knew I had to keep it together. I gripped the edge of the table to steady myself. 'What... what did he say?'

He stopped flicking and began to read. 'To my darling, incomparable Fire...' He raised his dark bushy eyebrows and sighed. 'All is OK here. I hope you are still using your incredible eye to capture pictures that say more than a thousand words about what the German swine are doing to our country. I miss you terribly and dream of the day we're reunited and can dance through the streets of a free Paris. All my love, your peacock.'

Hearing the peacock's loving words delivered with Raymond's gruff and slightly sarcastic tone added a slightly comical element to the message, but I didn't care. The peacock was OK!

Raymond tore the page from his pad. 'He had to dictate the message to one of my men, who dictated it to me.' He handed me the page. 'Here, take it.'

The thought of one of Raymond's men dictating the peacock's gushing message to Raymond and Raymond having to write it down seemed even funnier. I was so giddy with joy and relief that it took everything I had not to burst out laughing.

'Thank you so much!' I took the message and tucked it in the lining of my satchel, normally the hiding place for my photographs.

'Yes, well...' he muttered before clearing his throat. 'The photographs you've been giving me have been very helpful, as was the job you did for me last week. Speaking of which, I might have another job for you.'

'Really?' I looked at him expectantly, eager for a distraction from the pain of being parted from Joseph.

'Yes' – he pointed to the chair opposite him – 'why don't you sit down instead of hovering around like a gnat.'

Hmm, clearly I still had a way to go before I could refer to Raymond as a friend.

I did as instructed and sat down.

'An informant of mine in the police has told me that there's going to be a raid on a Jewish orphanage here in Paris tomorrow.'

'What?' I instantly thought of Joseph, and even though he was miles away in the country I felt sick to my stomach.

'Yes. The pressure is on the Germans here to deport more Jews – apparently they haven't been meeting their quotas.'

I stared at him in disbelief. How could they talk about deporting people in such a cold and businesslike way? 'So they're going after the children?'

'Yes.' Raymond's face was grim.

I thought again of Joseph and a shiver ran up my spine. What if the Germans extended their search for Jewish children all over France in their desperate need to meet their cruel quotas? 'What do you need me to do?'

'We don't know which orphanage they're targeting, and there could be several. If I were to give you the location of one, would you go and try to get some pictures? Obviously, it would be highly dangerous as the Germans will be carrying out the raid, so if you don't want to take the—'

'I'll do it,' I cut in. 'But isn't there some way of warning the orphanages in advance? Helping them get the children to safety?'

He shook his head. 'Unfortunately not. For a start, we're not exactly sure which one the Germans will be targeting and there are far too many parentless Jewish children in Paris now to be able to hide them all.'

My heart sank. He was right of course, but it didn't make it any easier to digest. Being warned about the possibility of this atrocity but not being able to stop it was sickening, and being sent to take pictures of innocent children being rounded up felt abhorrent. How would I be able to maintain my composure? What if I lost my cool again, the way I'd done when the Milicien had shot Joseph? But, as the peacock had urged in his message, I had to take pictures to let people know what was happening. I had to do this for Joseph. 'OK, where do you want me to go?'

Raymond stood up, clearly my cue to leave, so I followed suit. 'Come by here tomorrow morning and I'll give you the details.' And then, to my surprise, he extended his chunky hand across the table to me. 'Thank you,' he said as we shook hands, and his grip might have been tight as a vice, but his tone was warm and sincere. And as I met his warm and grateful gaze, I realised that he wasn't just thanking me for accepting this new mission, he was thanking me for avenging his wife.

. . .

It was only when I got back home that the reality of what I'd just agreed to do hit me. As I paced around the living room, two questions echoed through my mind: if the orphanage I was sent to did end up being raided, how would I be able to capture photographs without the Germans seeing me? And what would they do to me if they caught me?

Trying to counter the fear growing inside me, I went over to the fireplace and took my picture of Lillie down from the mantelpiece. Just one look at her haunted expression was enough to galvanise me. Who knew what she'd had to endure since the day our paths crossed and I'd taken the picture. I felt for the locket around my neck, or the magic necklace, as Joseph called it. This was not the time for my courage to falter. I owed it to Lillie and to Joseph and all the other children terrorised by the Germans to do everything I could to help bring about an end to the occupation, even if I ended up losing my own life in the process.

30

APRIL 1985, PARIS

'I'd like a ticket for the photography exhibition please,' I said to the girl behind the counter. I was in such a state of shock, my voice sounded muffled and disconnected from my body.

'Which one?' she asked cheerily. 'The wildlife photography or World War Two?'

'World War Two,' I replied, my mouth going dry.

'Good choice,' she said, tapping on her cash register. 'It's so powerful.'

'I can imagine.'

I momentarily contemplated telling her the truth, that I knew better than anyone how 'powerful' the photographs would be – or the one I'd seen at least – but I was still too dazed.

I fumbled in my purse for the money to pay and my clumsy fingers sent the coins spinning all over the counter. 'I'm sorry. I must have had too much coffee,' I joked lamely.

'That's OK, I don't think I've had enough,' she joked back as she tried in vain to catch them before they rolled onto the floor. 'The exhibition is on the third floor,' she said, handing me my ticket. 'I hope you enjoy it.'

I stared at her. The notion of enjoying being taken back to

that time felt so foreign to me, I wondered if I'd made a terrible mistake and ought to leave. This latest turn of events was so shocking and unexpected, yet I couldn't shake the feeling that it hadn't happened by accident. Ever since I'd seen the bird on the steps at Sacré-Coeur, I'd felt my younger self calling through time to me. And now I'd seen her – really seen her – in the photograph on the poster, I felt compelled to see more.

'Thank you,' I murmured and headed over to the lift. I pressed the call button and watched the display as it began its descent to the ground floor, my heart pounding and my head filling with questions. But in spite of my growing apprehension, one thing was for certain: if I wanted to know more, I'd have to visit the exhibition.

31

APRIL 1943, PARIS

I arrived at the cafe the following morning feeling as jittery as if I'd drunk ten cups of coffee. I'd hoped that my exhaustion from my trip with Joseph and my relief at hearing from the peacock would have ensured me a full night's sleep, and indeed I'd fallen asleep almost as soon as my head touched the pillow. But just an hour later, I had been jolted awake by a terrible nightmare. The man I'd shot had come back to life and was in my apartment, looming over my bed, his face bluey-white and chest soaked with blood. It had taken me a full minute or so to realise that he wasn't actually there, but by then the damage had been done and I couldn't stop trembling. I thought of Joseph out there somewhere on his own, and my heart broke thinking that one day the Germans might raid wherever he'd been taken to. What had become of humanity that even children were no longer safe from such barbarity? *But was I really any better*, a little voice inside my mind had whispered. I'd killed someone, and even though he was a member of the Vichy militia, he was still a human being. In the end, I had to get up and light a candle and read the peacock's message over and over. One day we would be dancing in the streets of a free Paris. I had to keep holding on to that hope to prevent myself from being overwhelmed by despair.

When I asked for Raymond that morning, I was taken to his office. I found him pacing up and down, glass of whisky in hand. It was only nine in the morning so I took this as a bad sign.

'Is everything all right?' I asked.

'One of the British networks here in France has suffered a major loss,' he replied. 'The SS have arrested two of their members here in Paris. I'm going to have to lay low for a while.' He sat down at his desk and scribbled something on a piece of paper. 'I need you to memorise this address,' he said, handing it to me.

'Of course. Is it the address of the orphanage?'

'No, it's for a safe house here in the city, for you to deliver your photographs to, and for you and I to exchange messages.'

'OK.' I read and re-read the address until I'd committed it to memory. 'Do you still want me to go to one of the orphanages?'

'Yes, absolutely. My informant tells me that it's scheduled to happen this afternoon, but the Germans have been keeping the exact location very close to their chest, so it could be that I'm sending you on a wild goose chase.'

Secretly, I couldn't help hoping that he was. My chronic exhaustion wasn't doing anything to help my nerves.

Raymond must have noticed my agitated state because he picked up the bottle of whisky and offered it to me. Normally I would have said no, wanting to keep a clear head, but I was in urgent need of some Dutch courage, and besides, it might also help to calm me down somewhat.

I nodded and he sloshed a generous shot into a glass and passed it to me.

'If you do get some pictures, take them to the safe house. When you get there, knock on the door three times quickly and three times slowly and tell them you have something for Aveline.'

'Aveline,' I echoed.

'Yes.' He went over to a filing cabinet and opened one of the drawers. 'I have a disguise for you, to help you not arouse any suspicion today.'

'OK.' I watched as he took a grey wig and a long plain dress and woollen shawl from the drawer. 'And you can hide your camera in this.' He reached under the desk and brought out a wicker shopping basket. 'It has a false bottom, so to anyone who might see you, you look like an elderly woman on her way to collect her rations.'

'Thank you.' I took the basket and clothes from him.

'Remember to walk like an older person too. With a slight stoop maybe.'

'Of course.'

'You can change in the bathroom next door.'

I gulped down my whisky and headed to the bathroom. I felt marginally better now that I had a disguise to hide behind and the warmth from the whisky was spreading through my body. I quickly transferred the contents of my bag into the concealed compartment in the bottom of the basket before getting changed.

It was incredible the difference the grey wig made. As I looked into the grimy mirror, it was like seeing my seventy-year-old self. What if this was the only time I'd get to see what I'd look like as an older woman? I couldn't help wondering. What if the Germans were going to catch me and I only had a matter of days or hours left to live?

Pushing the fear from my mind, I hunched my shoulders and practised walking with a slight stoop. *'Bonne chance,'* I whispered to my reflection before leaving the bathroom.

I returned to the office to find Raymond emptying his desk drawers. I wondered if I'd ever see him again. I really hoped so, and not just because he was my only link to the peacock and Joseph. Since he'd told me about his wife being killed, I'd viewed him in a far more sympathetic light and I felt as if he was finally warming to me too.

As I hobbled into the room, hunched over, he did a double take.

'Very good,' he muttered, nodding his approval. He picked up the whisky bottle. 'One for the road?'

'Why not.'

He topped up my glass. 'Good luck, Clarisse.' I was pretty sure that this was the first time he'd ever said my name and it felt like more proof of him warming towards me.

'Thank you. And to you. I hope our paths cross again.'

'Yes.' He chinked his glass against mine. 'To a free France.'

'A free France.' I raised my glass and gulped down the drink.

The orphanage I'd been sent to was located on a side street in the Malakoff suburb of Paris. *This might be all for nothing; the Germans might be raiding another orphanage, or, better yet, none at all,* I told myself as I shuffled down the street clutching my basket. As I thought of Lillie and Joseph, I really hoped this was true.

I saw an apartment building directly opposite the orphanage and, after checking no one was looking, I hurried over. The huge wooden door was painted dark blue and bore an iron knocker in the shape of a fox's head. I tried the handle and found, to my relief, that the door was unlocked. I peered inside to see a courtyard with a well-manicured lawn and a couple of spindly trees. I'd always loved the way that the doors to Parisian apartment buildings could open onto such magical sights, but now I had a much deeper appreciation. This doorway and the courtyard it concealed could provide the perfect cover for my mission.

As I didn't know how long I'd have to wait and didn't want to arouse any suspicion by loitering around, I shuffled a little further down the street. Thankfully, I discovered a small park about halfway down. I'd brought a book in case I needed to while away some time, so I made my way over to a bench and sat down. The sky was overcast and a thin gauzy drizzle hung in the air. I normally hated this vague excuse for rain and the way it clung to your skin, but today I was relieved. Hopefully it would stop anyone else from coming and sitting beside me.

I opened my book and pretended to read. It was a copy of the French edition of Margaret Mitchell's *Gone With the Wind*. I'd started reading it some months before, but the parallels between the hardships of the American Civil War and the German occupation had been too painfully close for comfort and I kept having to stop reading. I glanced along the street at the large, darkened windows of the orphanage. I thought of the children on the other side of those windows blissfully unaware of what might be about to befall them. I hoped against hope that Raymond's informant was wrong and that the Germans wouldn't be targeting children in their senseless desire to meet their quotas. I thought of Joseph and how quiet it had been since he'd been taken away. I hoped that someone kind was now taking care of him and his wounded arm, and he wasn't feeling as lonely as me. I couldn't bear the thought that I might have unknowingly placed him in more danger or caused him more pain. I continued pretending to read, my unseeing eyes scanning the page as fear and anticipation coursed through my veins.

An hour passed. I stood up and shuffled a little further along the street, past an old bookstore and a hairdresser's that had been boarded up. The shampoo shortage was so bad now that many hairdressers had been forced out of business. I hoped that my wig didn't look suspiciously clean. I went all the way to the end of the street, then turned and started making my way back again.

The clouds were darkening, creating a premature dusk. I could see chinks of light leaking out from cracks in the orphanage's blackout blinds. What if I had to wait long into the night? What if the Germans had decided to carry out their raid after curfew? As much as I was dreading this particular assignment, I didn't want to let Raymond down. I desperately wanted and needed to keep working for the Resistance.

Then, just as I was about to go back into the park, I heard the low rumble of an engine and saw a German lorry making its way down the road. *It might just be a coincidence; they might just drive past,* I told myself. But then I heard the hiss and sigh of brakes and the truck came to a halt.

My mouth went dry and my heart began to thud. It *was* this orphanage they were raiding and I had to take the pictures.

Take the pictures that will speak a thousand words – the words from the peacock's message rang around my head.

Yes, I urged myself. I was going to document what these animals were doing to the children and one day the whole world would see the evidence.

I fumbled in my basket, loosening the false bottom, and felt around for my camera. I sat down on the bench so that I was as inconspicuous as possible and waited as the soldiers jumped down from the lorry and marched up to the orphanage. As they began hammering on the door, I was reminded of that terrible day the previous summer when I'd witnessed the police take Lillie away. I was doing this for her too, I reminded myself and I felt her mother's locket for good luck as I prepared to move.

The door to the orphanage opened and I heard a woman cry out as the soldiers stormed inside. I thought of children as young as Joseph cowering inside, not understanding what was happening and why the 'bad men' had come for them. I took a breath, trying to suppress my growing rage, and I got to my feet. As I slowly made my way closer, I heard children crying from inside the building and the sound of soldiers barking orders.

I slipped into the doorway of the apartment building and took my Leica from the basket, my palms suddenly clammy. A couple of the soldiers came back outside, frogmarching two children each into the back of the truck. I quickly took a picture without checking the viewfinder and knew instinctively that it wouldn't be clear enough. My photographer's instincts took over and I crouched down so I could get a steadier grip and a better focus.

A scream rang out from inside the orphanage and there was a flash of light as someone pulled back the blind on one of the third-floor windows. I saw a small figure framed against the light and the windows burst open. 'Help!' the child cried, sending a chill right to the core of my being. But what could I do? If I ran over to help, I'd only end up getting arrested too.

Take the picture, I imagined the peacock urging me and I raised the viewfinder to my eye.

A figure appeared behind the child and for a moment I thought it was a member of the orphanage staff. But then I saw the peaked hat and my blood ran cold. It was a soldier.

One of the other soldiers who'd come back out to the truck went and stood beneath the window and called something in German, causing his comrade in the window above to laugh. I swallowed hard, my finger hovering over the shutter release. The soldier closed in on the child and I took a shot as he went to grab them. But instead of pulling the child back from the window, he picked them up and then, to my horror as I wound the film on, he threw them out. Without even thinking, my finger pressed the shutter button.

Time seemed to slow as the child's body spiralled through the air, limbs flailing. *Catch him!* I wanted to yell to the soldier standing below the window, but he stepped back and watched, arms folded. The child landed with a sickening thud on the ground.

No! No! No! No! I remained crouching, frozen to the spot, unable to believe what I'd just witnessed.

Another figure appeared beside the soldier, silhouetted in the window, a woman. She leaned out and gave a piercing scream. The soldier yanked her back by her hair. All of the guilt I'd been feeling about shooting the member of the Milice vanished, replaced by a murderous rage. If I'd still had the pistol Raymond had given me, I would have taken it out and shot those monsters right there and then. But I didn't have the pistol and if I stayed there any longer, I was in danger of being seen.

Shaking, I stood up, opened the door and snuck into the courtyard. I took cover in a storage cupboard filled with bicycles and gardening tools and took a few deep breaths, trying to get my racing heart to slow down. But it was impossible. How could I feel calm when I'd just witnessed a child being murdered in the most brutal way imaginable, a child as sweet and innocent as Joseph?

I looked at the camera in my basket and thought of the terrible images it now contained. Part of me wanted to tear the film out and wreck it by exposing it to the light, but another part of me, a part that was incandescent with rage, knew that I must keep it, develop it and show the world the soldiers' depravity. A depravity that couldn't be adequately described, not even in ten thousand words.

32

APRIL 1985, PARIS

As the lift began its ascent to the third floor, my head spun. Was this really happening or was I having some kind of surreal dream? The doors opened with a ping and I stepped out to see a banner bearing the headline: *CLARISSE ALARIE – PHOTOGRAPHER AND RESISTANCE FIGHTER – EXHIBITION*.

I showed my ticket to the attendant and stepped inside.

'Let me know if you have any questions,' she called after me.

'I will, thank you,' I murmured in response, not that she would ever be able to answer the questions all clamouring for attention in my head.

She said something else, but I was no longer listening; I was no longer able. All I could focus on was the first photograph in the exhibition, a much larger version of the photograph I'd seen on the poster downstairs. My knees weakened and for a moment I thought I might faint. I closed my eyes tight and took a deep breath, then looked back at the picture. The girl couldn't be me, surely. Those couldn't be my eyes, so full of anguish and fear.

I studied the photograph in more detail. It was the hair that did it – the jagged fringe. 'Oh, Lillie, what have you done?' Maman had cried when she'd seen how I'd tried to make myself look like my hero Amelia Earhart with her kitchen scissors. 'It is so uneven!' I'd completely forgotten that haircut – in the light of what was about to happen to us it had paled into insignificance. But now it all came flooding back. The hammering on the door, the men yelling, my mother's screams, our hateful neighbour, Monsieur Leblanc, hanging from his window watching with glee, and of course, the woman who'd taken the photograph.

I'd never forgotten her. How could I? She was a frequent visitor to my nightmares, popping up in various other memories that came back to haunt me, in that surreal way that dreams have of weaving random strands of our lives together. Once, she appeared when I dreamed of my arrival at Auschwitz, poised with her camera as the SS guards opened the cattle truck doors. Once, I dreamed that she was there taking photographs the day I was whipped to within an inch of my life. Another time, she appeared in a nightmare about the guard's dog that bit me, clicking away on her camera as the beast's teeth tore into my thigh.

Perhaps you're imagining it, I told myself now as I studied the picture. *Perhaps it's your mind playing tricks on you.*

I stepped closer to the photograph and found the definitive proof that I wasn't imagining things: the small scar by the side of my eye. It was the only scar on my body that had been acquired before the war, when, as a young child, I'd fallen from a wall pretending to be Humpty Dumpty and cut my head on a sharp stone. There was no doubt: the girl in the photograph was me. But how? And why?

I turned to read the sign by the door. *An exhibition of Resistance photographer Clarisse Alarie's wartime work*, it read. *The photographs featured give an incredible insight into life in Occu-*

pied Paris and were used by the Resistance at the time to encourage other people to join them in their fight.

There was a photograph of a woman beside the text. An old-fashioned camera hung around her neck on a leather strap and her expression was deadly serious. She had shorter hair than I remembered and looked a lot less glamourous, but there was something familiar about the shape of her face and her plump lips.

I re-read the text and frowned. When she'd appeared that day with her camera, I'd been completely thrown off guard. My mother was being beaten to death behind me. I was being dragged from her and my home. And then suddenly a woman who had looked as glamourous as a Hollywood movie star was on the pavement in front of me taking my picture. It didn't make any sense and only added to the horror. In the days that had followed, when I was trapped inside the hell on earth that was the velodrome, I'd tried to work out what she had been doing. The only conclusion I'd been able to come to was that, like my neighbour Monsieur Leblanc, she'd got some morbid glee from our misery. In my worst moments, I imagined her getting the photograph developed and showing it to her friends in some bar or cafe, the way one would pass around snaps from a holiday. In my mind she'd always been some kind of monster, but clearly I'd been wrong; she'd been working for the Resistance. As this new truth dawned upon me it felt as if my whole world had been turned inside out and upside down.

I looked at the text beside the photograph of me and began to read.

Paris Round-Up, 16 July 1942: *16 and 17 July 1942 saw the largest round-up of Jewish men, women and children organised by the French police. Thousands were taken to the Vel d'Hiv and other internment camps around Paris before*

being transported east to the concentration camps. Alarie
photographed this Jewish girl being taken from her home in
Montparnasse in the early morning of 16 July. The raw
emotion on display and the closeness with which Alarie was
able to get to her subject was typical of the unique and
unflinching style she became known for as a Resistance
photographer. Alarie credits this photograph as being her very
first for the Resistance. Seeing the suffering of the Jewish
people in Paris affected her deeply and made her determined to
do something to fight back.

I stared at the text until the words all blurred into one and I
began mentally correcting the story I'd been telling myself all
these years. The woman from my nightmares hadn't been some
kind of sinister voyeur; she'd wanted to help. In fact, what had
happened to Maman and me that terrible day had inspired her
to help. I re-read the text on the sign by the door. The Resistance had used Alarie's photographs to encourage other people
to join the fight against the occupiers.

Nothing would ever erase the pain or terror of that day, and
nothing would undo the terrible things it had led to, but for the
first time in forty years, my faith in humanity felt slightly
restored. This woman, Clarisse Alarie, had seen my pain and
been moved to take action. And perhaps others had seen it and
been moved to act too.

I shook my head. It seemed impossible to believe that in one
of my darkest moments I'd unwittingly been someone's inspiration, but now I knew the truth about the woman with the
camera, or some of it at least, I was eager to learn more. Who
was this person I'd inadvertently inspired, and what pictures
had she gone on to take?

With a growing curiosity I made my way into the first
section of the exhibition and was greeted with a photograph of a

young dandyish-looking man clad in a huge jacket and skinny trousers. His dark wavy hair was long and shiny and he was beaming into the camera as if he was the happiest man on earth. Then I noticed a star pinned to his chest pocket and my stomach churned. But instead of saying JUIF, it said ZAZOU. What did that mean?

The description beside the picture informed me that the zazous, with their outlandish style, love of jazz and all things British, were the original punks of Paris, paving the way for subsequent subcultures and the invention of nightclubbing. Apparently, they used their appearance as an act of resistance. Many zazous like the young man pictured wore yellow stars in solidarity with the Jewish people, which made them a target for fascists.

I looked back at the yellow star on his chest and shuddered. When we'd first been ordered to wear those wretched stars, I'd kicked up one hell of a stink, telling Maman there was no way I was going to wear it. I was approaching thirteen and developing my own unique and slightly eccentric style, inspired by my heroes Josephine Baker and Amelia Earhart. Being told that I had to wear a stupid yellow star at all times made me beside myself with indignation.

'Why don't we all just refuse to wear them?' I remembered demanding. I winced now at my naivety. Little did I know that the Germans had far worse in store when it came to their plan to dehumanise us.

I instinctively felt for the place on my arm where they'd tattooed the label that would last forever and told me that, to them, I was no more than a number. But to this man, and the other zazous who wore their own stars in solidarity, and to Clarisse Alarie, who sought to tell the story of our persecution through her pictures, I was still a human being.

I moved on and saw an image that stopped me in my tracks.

It was of the inside of the velodrome after the round-ups. As I looked at the people all crowded onto the stands, that acrid smell came back to me and I had to fight the urge to gag. Being held captive inside the arena had been one of the worst things to have happened to me, and that was saying something after my time in Auschwitz. The pandemonium inside the velodrome was bad enough but it was nothing compared to the chaos in my mind as I wondered what had become of my mother and if I'd ever see her again. But how had Alarie taken the picture? How and why had she got inside the stadium?

I read the text beside the image and couldn't help gasping out loud.

The Vel d'Hiv, July 1942: *After witnessing the round-up of the young girl in Alarie's first Resistance photograph, she tried in vain to find her in the velodrome, posing as a Red Cross worker to gain access to the stadium. Sadly, Alarie wasn't able to find the girl due to the sheer number of people being held prisoner there. What she saw was so shocking, it further inspired her work for the Resistance.*

I took a step back, barely able to breathe. Alarie had tried to find me. But why? Had she been hoping to rescue me?

My skin erupted in goosebumps. If only she'd found me. If only I'd known.

I moved on to some pictures of a food riot at rue Daguerre and then a portrait of a young man, with just his head and bare shoulders in the frame. At first, I thought it had been taken in one of the camps because his hair had been shorn until he was mostly bald aside from a few remaining clumps. I shivered as I remembered my arrival at Auschwitz and the brute of a woman who'd set about my head with a razor, not caring if she nicked my skin. Whoever had given this man his haircut clearly hadn't cared either. Jagged cuts were visible on his pale scalp, along with patches of what looked like dried blood. One of his eyes was so badly swollen and bruised it was practically closed. There was something strangely familiar about his sad smile, though. I felt a jolt of surprise as I made the connection and hurried back to the picture of the zazou. The smile was the same. The dimples etched into his cheeks were the same.

I returned to the portrait and read the description.

Zazou beaten, February 1943: *This portrait is of Alar-ie's lover following an attack by members of the fascist* Jeunesse Populaire Française. *In 1943, attacks on the zazous become more and more widespread and following the intro-duction of the* Service du travail obligatoire *in February of that year, requiring all French men between the ages of 20 and 23 to go to work in Germany, the zazou movement came to an end. This portrait by Alarie seems to perfectly symbolise that moment in history.*

I looked back at the photograph, full of compassion. What had happened to him, I wondered, after his scalping? Did he manage to avoid being sent to Germany, or did he, like so many others who were sent east, end up perishing at the hands of the Nazis? And what had it done to Alarie to see her lover beaten like this? I pictured her on the other side of the lens, the recip-ient of his sad smile, and I felt a moment of deep connection as I remembered what I'd witnessed happening to my mother. Much as I tried not to think of what had taken place that fateful day it had haunted me ever since.

The next series of photographs were from Alarie's career as a fashion photographer during the war. There were pictures of women wearing scarves wrapped turban-style around their heads and others of women clad in outlandish hats. I was a little confused as to why they'd been included in the exhibition until

I read the description, which informed me that staying glamourous despite the shampoo shortage and clothing rations had been an act of resistance amongst French women. While I was grateful for any act of resistance, I couldn't help sighing as I thought of the lice-infested rags we were made to wear at the camp. Not having any shampoo was the least of our worries. My skin began to itch from the memory.

I moved on to the next section and once again stopped dead. The first photograph showed a young child of about five being torn, screaming, from his mother's arms. I saw the star pinned to the woman's chest and was once again reminded of the fateful day I was torn from my own beloved maman. She and I had been so close, especially after my father was killed trying to defend the Maginot Line from the Germans. Being taken from her had been terrifying and having to survive life in the camps without her had caused a part of me to shut down entirely, I could see that now. For those two and half years, I'd lived mainly in my head, losing myself in the fantastical tales I'd invent – tales in which I was free to travel anywhere I wanted in my twin-engine monoplane à la Amelia Earhart.

Nothing could have prepared me for the photograph I saw next. It had clearly been taken in poor light, but I could make out a building, a large house. My eyes were drawn to the one splash of white light, coming from an upstairs window. The dark silhouette of a man standing there, looking out. Who was he? And what was the building? Then I noticed some other men gathered outside the building – three, no, four of them – and I could tell from their peaked hats that they were soldiers. Germans. My mouth went dry. Even all these years later, the sight of that uniform made me sick with terror. Two of the men outside were looking up at the window and, following their gaze, I noticed something halfway down the wall of the building, something falling through the air. No, not something, *someone*. I could see two arms flailing, and a pair of legs. But they were tiny. It was clearly an infant. I stared harder at the picture and my nausea grew. Had the child jumped or...

I looked at the description, hardly daring to read.

Orphanage Raid, April 1943: *When the round-ups in Paris first began, Vichy government policy was to only deport Jewish adults, which meant that a large number of Jewish children were sent to live in orphanages. As the round-ups intensified, these orphanages went from being safe havens to German targets and from the summer of 1943 there were an increasing number of raids upon orphanages like the one pictured. It is clear from this picture that a child has been thrown from the window of the orphanage to a certain death, making it one of Alarie's most powerful wartime photographs.*

I stared, aghast, at the falling child until he or she became no more than a blur of black and white pixels. I knew I shouldn't be shocked by this show of barbarity. How could I be, after two years in Auschwitz? I thought of the day I'd arrived at the camp and how the guards had instructed us to walk to the right or to the left, none of us realising that those going to the left were trudging towards their imminent death. So many of them had been children, all so young and innocent. And once more I was face to face with the depths of Nazi brutality.

How had Alarie managed to be at the orphanage to capture this picture? I wondered. And what had witnessing such a thing done to her? I wondered if she was still alive. At a guess, I would have said she was in her late twenties or early thirties when I saw her that day she took my photograph, which meant that she'd be in her seventies now.

A thought occurred to me. What if I was able to get in touch with her? Surely the Centre Pompidou would have her contact details if she was still alive. I could let her know that I was the girl in the photograph that first inspired her work for the Resistance. I felt a shiver of excitement at the possibility of creating a happy ending to the story that had begun so long ago on that terrible day.

But would it be a happy ending for both of us, or had Alarie's story already come to a close?

33

JANUARY 1944, PARIS

Every winter during the occupation seemed to be even worse than the one before, as if paralleling the growing savagery of the Germans. They might have been losing the upper hand globally, with Russia gaining on the eastern front and the Allies finally preparing to make their long-awaited European landings, but in Paris our occupiers were growing increasingly brutal. Like a cornered animal, the Gestapo became ever more vicious, and executions and shootings on the streets were becoming increasingly commonplace.

In January 1944, I was dropping some photographs off at the latest safe house – the locations changed regularly to keep the police and Germans from discovering them – to find Raymond sitting in one of the stiff-backed armchairs by the fireplace in the living room. I hadn't seen him since the day I'd gone to the orphanage and he'd gone into hiding.

'You're alive!' I exclaimed, unable to disguise my relief. The Germans had recently destroyed one of the major Resistance networks in Paris and I hadn't received word from him since, so I'd been living with the constant gnawing fear that he'd been among those arrested.

'So it would seem,' he replied drily. He looked thinner than before and had acquired a bushy black beard.

'Is there... is there any word from the mountains?' I hardly dared ask the question and mentally prepared myself for the worst.

'The fighting there has intensified, but don't worry, he's still alive.'

'Oh, thank God.' I sank down into the other chair and took a breath. My fervent daily prayers for the past eight months had been answered. The peacock was still alive.

The woman whose house it was, who I knew only by her codename, Starling, brought us both tin cups containing generous slugs of whisky. I drank mine eagerly, grateful for the warmth it brought.

'You've been doing some excellent work,' Raymond said, raising his cup to me. 'I used the photograph of the child being thrown from the orphanage window in a flyer that's been distributed all over Northern France. It's encouraged many people to join us, women especially.'

'I'm glad something good came from it,' I said with a shudder as I recalled that terrible day. I'd taken hundreds of photographs since but that was one image I simply couldn't unsee.

'And on that note, I have a job for you.'

My skin prickled with a mixture of fear and excitement. For Raymond to be personally giving me a job, I knew it would be important and therefore dangerous. 'Of course. What is it?'

'The internment camp at Drancy is overflowing and the Germans are sending more and more transports east. We have heard from many reliable sources that these people are being sent to death camps in Germany and Poland.'

I instinctively felt for the locket around my neck, wondering if Lillie had been sent east. I still carried her increasingly battered photograph everywhere with me for inspiration and prayed for her every night, along with Joseph and the peacock.

'Word is that the Nazis are gassing people as soon as they arrive.'

'Gassing them?' I stared at him, horrified, and clutched the locket tighter. What if Lillie had been gassed? What if I never got to find her again?

It's just a rumour, I tried telling myself. *And besides, even the Germans wouldn't gas innocent children – would they?*

'I'm afraid so.' Raymond took a swig of his drink. 'I want you to go to Drancy and take some photographs of the transports out of there so we can let people know the urgency of the situation.'

'Of course.' I thought back to my previous visit to Drancy. Hopefully enough time had passed for the guard to have forgotten about me, if indeed he was still working there. 'How should I get there, though? It's getting so hard to travel anywhere these days with the constant checks. Do you have a cover story for me?'

'Yes.' He reached into his jacket pocket and pulled out an envelope. 'You're to go tomorrow and if you're stopped and questioned, you're to say that you're delivering a letter to your neighbour who was arrested and sent to Drancy last week.' He leaned forward to hand me the letter. 'This is addressed to a genuine detainee, so the name will check out. But you're only to deliver it if you get stopped.'

'OK.' I put the envelope in my purse, praying I wouldn't have to deliver it and risk encountering the guard again. The prospect of going to Drancy felt like walking into the lions' den. If I was caught, would I be put straight on one of those trains headed east?

You have to do it for Lillie, I told myself.

'It's safer to make the last leg of the journey by bicycle, so you're to get the train to Le Bourget, then go to this address.'

Raymond passed me a scrap of paper containing the address of a corset shop. I studied it for a few seconds until I'd memorised it, then returned it to him. 'When you get there say that Dorothy sent you to collect some fabric and they will provide you with the bicycle. Once you've been to Drancy, you're to return the bike to the shop.'

'Understood.'

'And if you get stopped en route to Le Bourget your cover story is that you're taking a corset that needs to be mended to the shop.'

On cue, Starling came back into the room holding a white corset. I took it gratefully. It was becoming increasingly hard to believe that there was once a time we could move freely and without worry around Paris.

As I stood up to leave, I had to fight the urge to give Raymond a farewell hug. In spite of his prickly manner, it had been so nice to see him again.

'I don't suppose you've had any word on how the boy, Joseph, is doing?' I asked.

He shook his head. 'All I know is that he made it to the children's home in Izieu safely.'

I breathed a sigh of relief. If I had managed to help save Joseph's life, it would make all of the hardship of the war worth it. 'That's great, thank you.'

He stood up and then, to my surprise, he grabbed me in an awkward embrace. He might have thinned down a bit, but he was still strong as an ox. *'Bonne chance*, Clarisse,' he muttered in my ear before letting me go.

Nice as it was, I couldn't help wondering why the sudden display of affection. Was it because he knew exactly how dangerous my next mission was? Did he think I might not make it back?

I pushed the fears from my mind and made my way to the door.

. . .

Needless to say, the prospect of my trip to Drancy meant another sleepless night, but thankfully when I set off the following morning, I had so much adrenaline coursing through my body I didn't feel tired at all. If anything, I was a little too alert. As I left my building, the sound of the boulangerie shutters clattering open caused me to practically jump out of my skin.

It's all going to be OK, you have excellent cover stories, I told myself as I made my way down the hill to the Metro. But then I thought of my camera hidden beneath the corset in my satchel and I was instantly jittery again.

I'd thought that by leaving early I might avoid having my papers checked, but as the station came into view, my heart sank. A group of gendarmes were clustered around the station entrance and a queue had formed, waiting to go in.

You have an excellent cover story, I reminded myself, *you're simply going to Le Bourget to have a corset fixed.* I'd tucked the letter to the Drancy detainee inside my bra, so hopefully there was no chance of them finding that and my cover stories becoming confused.

As I joined the queue, I heard raised voices coming from the front.

'They're not forged!' I heard a man cry. 'They're genuine.'

The next thing I knew, a scuffle had ensued, with one of the gendarmes forcing the man into a headlock. Everyone around me remained stony-faced, an expression we'd become accomplished at these past few years, for to even grimace at the sight of a fellow Parisian being arrested or a Jew being persecuted could so easily lead to one's own arrest. But what was this doing to us? I wondered as the man was dragged past me, kicking and yelling. How could we not be damaged by constantly having to suppress our horror and fear as, around us, men, women and children were brutally attacked?

As I neared the front of the line, my skin erupted in a cold sweat. The police manning the checkpoint were clearly in a vile mood. Perhaps they, like the Germans, could sense the end approaching and were starting to fear what would become of them. *I hope you all rot in hell,* I thought, before forcing myself to smile sweetly at the officer demanding my papers. The seconds seemed to slow to hours as he studied them. The only time it had taken this long before was with the guard at Drancy. Had this officer realised that they were a forgery too? I felt a bead of sweat trickle down the side of my face and my pulse began to race.

'And where are you off to today?' he asked, looking up from the papers. His gaze was icy cold.

'I'm going to Le Bourget to get a corset fixed.' My voice sounded shrill and strained. *Relax! Take a breath! Don't give the game away.*

'A corset?' he sneered.

'Yes. It's in my bag. Do you want to see it?'

Why did you say that? I silently berated myself. *You don't want him looking in your bag; he might find the camera!*

Just as he was about to reply, I saw another officer approaching and it felt as if my heart had dropped like a stone to the floor. The last thing I wanted was two of them checking it.

'Well, hello again!' the second policeman exclaimed.

I looked at him blankly.

'How is that nephew of yours? I hope you had a fun adventure queuing for your rations.'

And then I remembered. It was the officer from the train.

'Hello!' I cried, as if greeting a long-lost friend. 'It's so lovely to see you again.'

'You never got in touch,' he said a tad dejectedly.

'I'm so sorry, I, er, lost the piece of paper with your details. I was really hoping I'd bump into you again.'

'It must be fate,' he said, placing his hand on the small of my back. 'Come, I'll walk you down to the platform and we can arrange a date.' He nodded to his colleague, who returned my papers.

'Excellent,' I replied through gritted teeth. But at least he had saved me from further interrogation.

'So, where are you off to?' he asked as we went down the steps to the platform.

'Just to Le Bourget to have a corset fixed.'

'A corset, eh?' He gave me a salacious grin that instantly reminded me of Pierre. Then his smile faded as he looked at the floor. It was littered with little V-shapes made of card. I realised that they were Metro tickets, just like the one the woman had flicked into my lap the day she'd seen me talking to him. Now there were hundreds of them all over the platform, clearly made and discarded by passengers as they got off the train, proclaiming victory to the Resistance. The policeman began kicking them off the platform onto the track.

I heard the rattle of the train approaching. 'Quick, give me your details again. I promise not to lose them this time.' I smiled at him coquettishly.

He scribbled something on his notepad and tore out the page. 'I feel like you and I meeting like this is definitely destiny,' he said as he tucked it into my hand.

'Oh absolutely!' I trilled.

The train came to a halt and he opened the door for me.

'See you soon,' he called as I got on board.

Not if I can help it, I silently muttered, while turning up the beam of my smile. 'I can't wait!' I cried gaily.

As the train began moving out of the station, I slumped into a seat, my heart thumping.

. . .

Fortunately, collecting the bicycle from the corset shop went without a hitch and even though it had been a long while since I'd cycled anywhere, I was pleasantly surprised at how quickly it came back to me, and how much I enjoyed it. Many Parisians cycled these days as no one could afford to run cars anymore and I liked how free and relatively safe it made me feel compared to the Metro.

I'd memorised the directions to Drancy the night before and after taking a couple of wrong turns, I finally arrived in the suburb at just after eleven. As I drew closer to the internment camp, I saw a row of German army trucks parked outside. I felt sick as I thought of the purpose of those trucks, and the people who were going to be herded onto them. Then I thought of Lillie again, whose photo was, as always, tucked inside my pocket. She had to still be alive. I refused to entertain the alternative.

I cycled past the camp, glancing quickly to my right. Barked orders were coming from inside in French. 'Keep in your lines. Stand still. Be quiet.' I continued on to the end of the road and dismounted and, as I did so, German soldiers began swarming from the back of the trucks. My mouth went dry. Was a transport about to take place?

I crouched beside the bike, pretending to examine the front tyre as the soldiers formed a line in front of the camp. A procession of prisoners came trudging out, shepherded by armed policemen. There were people of all ages – men, women and children, all of them haggard and thin and most of them clutching suitcases. I couldn't begin to imagine how terrified they must have felt. The police yelled and shoved at them as they got onto the back of one of the trucks.

For a moment, I remained rooted to the spot, but as the shouting intensified, I came to my senses and quickly got back on my bike. It wasn't safe to take pictures so close to the camp, but I knew the route to the station. Hopefully, if I rode on a bit further, I could find a safer spot.

I cycled until I reached a street containing a small row of shops. As usual, there were queues of people snaking out of the doorways. Trying to take a picture with so many people about ran the risk of being spotted and arousing suspicion. But, on the other hand, it would be a lot easier to blend in.

I leaned my bike against a wall and readied my camera in my bag. I would have to be quick, that was for sure. As I waited for the first of the trucks to appear, I stared into the window of a bookshop. But instead of looking at the books on display, I kept my gaze fixed on the reflection, on the lookout for any patrolling policemen or German soldiers, or indeed anyone resembling the plain-clothes Gestapo.

I was just starting to worry that I'd memorised the route to the station wrongly when I heard the faint sound of singing. I snuck a glance along the street and saw the first truck heading my way. As it approached, the singing got louder and I realised that the people on board were singing 'La Marseillaise'. It was a sound that sent a shiver down my spine. An act so bold and beautiful, it moved me to tears.

But I couldn't cry, not now. I had a job to do. I grabbed my camera and prepared to turn and take a picture. Just as the truck reached me, it juddered to a halt and I saw that it had stopped to let an old woman with a cane cross the road. The singing faded and I turned to look at the truck. It was so close that I could see eyes peering out at me from between the wooden slats. So many eyes. How many people had they crammed in there?

'Help! Please!' a young woman cried.

How could I take a picture of them? What would they think of me?

You have to take it to help bring an end to this, I reminded myself.

I took the camera from my bag, then saw a pale hand reaching through the slats towards me. It was clutching a folded piece of paper.

'Please, take it!' the woman's voice begged.

I stepped closer, reached out and took the piece of paper, then pressed the shutter release on the camera.

'Thank you!' the woman cried and for the briefest moment our eyes met between the slats.

'I'm so sorry,' I said, not caring if anyone heard me. 'I'm so sorry this is happening to you.'

The truck juddered back into motion and the woman's eyes closed. As it drove on down the street, there was no more singing, but the ensuing silence was deafening.

34

I made the journey home feeling numb with shock and despair. I couldn't get the woman's eyes or voice from my mind. Who was she? And what did it say on the piece of paper she'd thrust at me? I'd stuffed it straight inside my bra for safekeeping, so it was only once I was back in my apartment that I was able to look at it properly. I lit the lamp on the kitchen table and carefully unfolded the page.

At first, it was impossible to decipher the writing; it had clearly been written in a hurry and the letters bled into one bumpy line. I could tell from the layout, though, that it was a letter. And at the bottom, printed in slightly neater writing, there was an address. I recognised the street name straight away as it was just round the corner from Pierre's place in Montparnasse.

I held the page up to the lamp and studied it more closely and finally the bumps in the pencilled line formed coherent words.

To my darling Andreas,

I pray with all of my heart that this letter somehow finds its way to you, for I fear now that I will never see you again. After two months in Drancy, it's my turn to be shipped east and we've all heard the rumours about the terrible fate that awaits us there. But I don't want to waste my precious last words to you on such terrible things. I want to spend my words on heartfelt things. I want to tell you to always think of me when you see a pink rose or hear a violin – especially if it's playing anything by Tchaikovsky!

Oh, my darling, I wish we had had more time, there's so much I still want to say. But in the end everything I want to say to you can be condensed into this: I LOVE YOU. Now and always.

Your beloved Natalia

I stopped reading and started to cry, and I just couldn't stop. I cried for this stranger, Natalia, and her beloved Andreas, and I cried for the peacock and me. I cried for Raymond and his wife. I cried for Joseph and his parents. I cried for Lillie and her mother. I cried for all the people so cruelly torn from the ones they loved. Then I thought of the man I'd killed and the woman he'd come to the house with. Had they loved one another? Was she now mourning somewhere because of what I'd done?

'Be quiet! Be quiet! Be quiet!' I said out loud, trying to tame my errant thoughts.

I got up and went over to the cupboard for what was left of my wine ration. I'd *had* to kill the member of the Milice. I thought he'd killed Joseph. I thought he was going to kill me. I sloshed some wine into a cup and took a gulp.

Oh, what I would give to be able to go dancing with the peacock, without a care in the world. It had been almost a year since I'd last seen him and it felt as if my loneliness was gnawing into my soul.

'Don't be weak. You need to stay strong,' I muttered. But I felt far from strong, pacing up and down the room, talking to myself.

Desperate to drown out my increasingly fearful thoughts, I turned on the radio. But instead of tuning it to a station playing music, some dark force made me seek out the German-controlled Radio Paris.

'I'm certain that my neighbour is working for the Resistance.' As the presenter's voice filled the room, I felt an icy dread seep into my bones. It was *Répétez-le*, the show that encouraged listeners to write in, denouncing their neighbours. 'She has all kinds of people calling for her, day and night, and she never had that many visitors before the war.'

I thought of Starling, and the other women whose apartments I'd visited to drop off photographs for Raymond. This letter being read could be about any one of them, and they could now be about to be paid a visit by the police or, even worse, the Gestapo.

'What is wrong with you people!' I exclaimed to the radio. 'How can you live with yourselves?'

'Thank you so much for your letter, Madam X,' the show's host said.

'Huh, you're so brave, Madam X, hiding behind your pretend name with your poison pen!'

I turned the radio off and took my camera from my bag. The only thing that seemed to be keeping me sane these days was my photographs and the hope that they might help the Resistance. I needed to keep focused on this purpose.

I looked back at the letter. Tomorrow I would try to deliver it to Andreas, another small thing I could do for the good. I took the photograph of Lillie from my pocket and placed it next to the letter, then I fetched the pictures of the peacock and Joseph I kept by my bed. 'I'm doing everything I can for you all,' I whispered. 'I promise I won't give up.'

. . .

The next morning, after another night of fitful sleep, I set off for Montparnasse with Natalia's letter tucked inside my bra. It was a sunny day for the first time in what felt like forever, although it was still bitterly cold. As I reached the apartment building in the address, my apprehension grew. It felt horrible to be the bearer of such awful news. I could only hope that Andreas would gain some kind of comfort hearing from Natalia.

The camps people were being sent to might not be death camps, I told myself as I slipped through the main door and into a small foyer. *They might just be labour camps and Natalia and Andreas might one day be reunited.*

Andreas's apartment turned out to be on the fifth and top floor. As I reached the door, I heard the sound of someone playing the cello. The piece they were playing was angry and forceful, almost as if the bow was a saw trying to tear through the strings.

I took a moment to compose myself before knocking. The music came to an abrupt halt. I waited, but nothing happened, so I knocked again and finally heard the soft thud of footsteps.

'Who is it?' a man asked from the other side of the door.

'I have a message for Andreas,' I replied. 'From Natalia.'

The door opened a crack and a man peered out. He had brown hair sprinkled with grey that was so curly it sprang from his head at all angles, seeming to defy the laws of gravity. A pair of round wire glasses were perched on the end of his nose, slightly skew-whiff. 'Who are you?' he whispered.

'My name is Clarisse. I saw Natalia yesterday and she gave me something to give to you.'

He opened the door wider. A pair of baggy brown corduroy trousers and a thick, woollen shirt hung loosely from his thin frame. 'Where did you see her?'

'At Drancy,' I whispered back.

'You were at Drancy?' His eyes widened.

'Yes, I was on the street and... and she went past me.'

'She's free?' he exclaimed.

I felt full of dread at the news I was about to deliver. 'No. She was... she was in a lorry, going to the station.'

'My God!' He leaned against the door frame, clutching his head with his hand. I wondered if he'd heard the same rumours as Raymond.

'I'm really sorry. I wish this wasn't happening. I wish I had better news.'

'It's not your fault.' He ran his hand through his hair, making it even more unruly. 'Come in.' He beckoned me into a plushly carpeted hallway. The walls were lined with framed pictures, mostly black-and-white photographs of orchestral musicians and posters from concerts. I followed him into a high-ceilinged living room, decorated in an Art Nouveau style. A cello was propped against a chair by the window and sheets of music lay in a scattered semicircle on the floor all around it. 'Excuse the chaos,' he muttered.

'It's OK, this is exactly how the inside of my mind looks these days, so I feel very at home.' I instantly wanted to kick myself for the insensitivity of my wisecrack, but thankfully he smiled.

'So, how exactly did you get to see Natalia?'

'The lorry she was being transported in stopped right by me and she passed me a letter she'd written to you through a gap in the slats. I didn't really get to see her as such, just her hand, and her eyes.' Those eyes had been seared in my memory ever since.

'I see.' He looked close to tears.

'Excuse me, I just have to...' I unbuttoned my coat and turned away so that I could retrieve the letter from my bra. 'I had to keep it there for safekeeping,' I explained. I passed it to him, the paper warm from my body. 'Would you like me to leave, so you can read it in peace?' I asked, not wanting to intrude on such a personal moment.

'No, wait, please.' He unfolded the page and started to read. Clearly he was accustomed to her handwriting as he seemed to understand it straight away. 'Oh, Natalia!' he gasped, holding the letter to his chest. 'I'd been hoping for a miracle.'

'I know that feeling,' I sighed.

'You've lost a loved one to those animals too?' He peered at me over his glasses.

'Yes, but in a different way.'

He looked back at the letter. 'This is so typical of Natalia, to remain positive even as she's being carted off to God knows where.'

'Yes, I know someone like that too.' I thought of the peacock and his irrepressible spirit and felt a longing so strong, it took my breath away.

'Are you all right? Would you like a drink or something?'

'Oh, I don't want to impose, especially if you're busy.' I glanced at the cello.

'There's no way I'll be able to concentrate now,' he replied. 'I was barely able to focus before. And besides, I could do with the company.'

I gave him a grateful smile. If only he knew how much I craved company too.

He tucked the letter into his trouser pocket. 'Tea?'

'Yes please.'

He swept a sheaf of papers from the sofa and gestured at me to sit down. While he busied himself in the kitchen, I glanced around the room. The alcoves either side of the fireplace were lined with shelves, heaving with books. A painting of a woman playing the violin hung over the mantle. Was it Natalia? I wondered. Her face was a study of concentration as she played, and the artist had captured an almost ethereal glow about her.

The eyes were different though – full of life and joy rather than fear and desperation.

I turned my gaze to a polished wooden dining table at the other end of the room. A woman's fern-green cardigan had been slung over the back of one of the chairs and a violin case lay by it on the table. The lid of the case was open and the bow was protruding. A pair of dainty, gold-framed glasses sat beside the violin, the chain they were attached to coiled like a snake on the gleaming wood. There was something so poignant about this vignette, at once so personal and yet universal. I wondered how many other homes in Paris contained scenes like this – the haunting evidence of people snatched from their lives, from their loves, from their dreams. I itched to take a photograph of it.

I stood up and walked over to the table, using my hands to frame the shot, crouching slightly so that the cardigan was in the foreground and the violin perfectly centred.

'Oh, what are you doing?'

I jumped as Andreas came back into the room.

'I'm sorry, I was just... The cardigan and the violin – are they Natalia's?'

'Yes.' He looked at me strangely.

'I'm a photographer,' I said, my face flushing. 'I've been taking pictures for... for the Resistance.' I would never normally be this forthcoming, but I felt I had to explain, and given the circumstances, I was sure I could trust him. 'Pictures that tell the story of what is happening here in France.'

He looked completely bewildered.

'I'm so sorry, it just seemed like such a powerful image of how a person can be snatched from their life. One minute, they're placing their cardigan on the back of the chair, about to play the violin, and the next, they're gone.' I returned to the sofa and picked up my bag. 'I really didn't mean to upset you. I should leave.'

He shook his head. 'No, no, not at all. What you're saying, it interests me.'

'It does?' I felt a surge of relief.

'Yes. I like the idea of using our art as a way of fighting back.'

'Yes! That's exactly what I'm trying to do.' I put my bag down, elated that he understood. 'And I never would have taken a picture of your table without your permission; I was just imagining what it would look like.'

He nodded and looked over to the table. 'I think it would make a very powerful shot.'

'You do?'

'Yes. Natalia, she is so full of life. One of those people who fills the entire room with her energy – even when she's gone. Everywhere I look there are traces of her.' He went over to the table and picked up a scrap of paper. 'Here's a list she was writing before she was taken away. It's a list of all the places she wanted us to visit once the war was over.'

I went over and looked at the piece of paper. Her writing was more legible and my eyes scanned the list of places, wincing when I saw my home city – New York. Not that it really felt like home anymore. I'd been gone so long it felt like an old friend I'd fallen out of touch with.

'And now, where will she get to see?' he asked, his eyes glassy with tears. 'Have you heard what those animals are doing to them, once they're sent east?'

'I've heard they're being sent to labour camps,' I replied, not wanting to add to his agony.

'Huh, labouring them to their deaths!' he exclaimed. He put the list back on the table. 'I want you to take a picture of this. I want people to know how they are stealing people's lives and dreams.' There was a real urgency to his tone.

'Are you sure?'

'Yes. You're welcome to come back with your camera any time.'

'I actually... I have a camera in my bag.'

'Oh.' He looked at me, surprised.

'I'm a street photographer. I like to carry it wherever I go.'

'Well, in that case, feel free.' He stepped away from the table. 'I've been trying to compose a musical piece about what's been happening, but I'm afraid I'm so angry I might break my bow.'

'Yes, I know that feeling too.' I took my camera from my bag and went back to the table. Compared to most of my shots these days, having to be taken undercover and at breakneck speed, it felt like such a privilege to be able to take more time, and I was determined to do the picture justice. I desperately wanted to capture the poignancy of the setting to show people the personal toll of the incessant round-ups and transports east.

I placed the list at the edge of the table by the glasses and positioned myself so that it was in the front of the shot with the cardigan to the left and the violin case framing the back. Then I noticed the pen that Natalia must have been using lying on the table, so I placed it right by the list to show that she'd just finished writing.

While I snapped away, Andreas started playing his cello. This time, the music wasn't angry, it was beautiful, and as it built to a crescendo, my skin erupted in goosebumps. The piece he was playing was familiar, but I couldn't quite place it. I stopped taking pictures and turned to watch. Andreas had his eyes closed and it was as if he had become one with his cello, every inch of his body moving in perfect synchronicity. As I had my camera in my hand, I couldn't resist taking a quick shot. Then the music faded to silence and he sat still, head bowed.

'That was so beautiful,' I said and, to my embarrassment, a sob burst out. 'I'm sorry,' I gasped, but I seemed unable to stop.

'It was the "Enchanted Lake" from *Swan Lake*,' he

murmured. 'By Tchaikovsky. It was... *is* Natalia's favourite piece.'

'She will come back to you. You can't give up hope,' I said, wiping the tears from my eyes.

He nodded, but I could tell he was unconvinced. 'Did you get the picture you wanted?'

'Yes. Thank you so much for allowing me to take it.'

'You're welcome,' he replied. 'You can take a picture of her letter too, if you think that would help.'

'Are you sure?'

'Yes. I want people to know what she was like, not just that she's gone.'

'Of course.'

He stood up and handed me the letter and I placed it on the table and took a shot.

'Thank you.'

He shook his head. 'No, thank *you*, for being kind and brave enough to care.'

35

APRIL 1985, PARIS

I hovered in the background as the exhibition attendant helped another patron with their query. The attendant was a young woman, in her twenties I'd say, and her eyelids were plastered with the bright blue eyeshadow that was currently all the rage. Against her olive skin and brown eyes, the effect was quite startling. I looked down at my hands, tightly clasped in front of me, and the loosening, parchment-like texture of my skin. Oh, to be in my twenties again, ripe with possibility. But, of course, my twenties hadn't felt ripe with anything. Looking back now, that chapter of my life could definitely be titled 'The Numb Years'.

After leaving Auschwitz and being repatriated to France at the age of sixteen and finally learning that my mother had been killed that terrible day we were wrenched apart, I fell into a deep pit of depression. The one thing that had kept me going at Auschwitz was the hope that Maman was still alive and we'd one day be reunited. Every time a new transport arrived at the camp, I'd be hit by conflicting emotions, desperately hoping she'd be among the women who arrived and equally hoping she'd somehow escaped the horror and was safe in hiding somewhere. When I learned from my Great-Aunt Sofia that I was an orphan, my last hope was taken from me.

Sofia welcomed me into her home in Lyon and tried her best to love some life back into me. But it was a hollowed-out version of myself that returned to Paris at the age of nineteen, numbly going through the motions of my new life in the city as a trainee librarian.

The attendant finally finished with the other exhibition-goer and turned to me. 'Hello, can I help you?' she asked pleasantly.

'Yes, I was wondering, what happened to the photographer, Alarie?' *Please, please, please, still be alive,* I silently chanted.

The attendant's smile faded. 'Oh, it's very sad.'

My heart sank. I'd been so hoping for some kind of happy ending but of course that had been naïve for I knew only too well that happy endings only happened in fairytales.

'Yes, it's very sad indeed,' the attendant said, lowering her voice and stepping closer, as if about to impart some terrible secret.

36

APRIL 1944, PARIS

I visited Andreas regularly over the next couple of months. After taking him the photographs I'd captured of the table scene and him playing the cello so beautifully, he suggested that I come by every week. 'Perhaps we can encourage each other in our artistic acts of resistance?' he'd suggested, and I'd practically bitten his hand off in my haste to accept the invitation. I so desperately craved company by that point, it didn't bother me that Andreas wasn't exactly the cheeriest of souls and had the slightly disconcerting habit of racing to his cello whenever musical inspiration struck and without any warning. It was just so nice to have someone to talk to, especially as our main topics of conversation were Natalia and the peacock. I guess it was our way of keeping them alive and with us, and in my most optimistic moments I allowed myself to dream that one day the four of us would be in that living room together, Andreas and Natalia playing music while the peacock and I danced.

By April, the weather finally warmed, but I'd never seen Paris so desolate. We were all so hungry and tired by then – apart from the collaborators, of course, who received extra rations in exchange for their betrayals. One day, when I was out walking, I took two pictures that I felt perfectly captured the great divide between the two sides. The first was of a woman who'd been walking in front of me along rue Norvins. As she hurried to join a queue for potatoes, her culottes fell from her thin frame onto the ground, pooling around her ankles. I got my viewfinder out just in time to capture a shot of her hauling them back up. I'd had to raid the peacock's closet for one of his belts to keep my own culottes in place, so her predicament was painfully relatable to me.

But then, just a few minutes later, I came across a woman I couldn't relate to at all. She was sashaying out of a dance hall, arm in arm with a German soldier. Not only did she still have a curvy hourglass figure with no need for a belt, but she was wearing stockings. And not an ancient pair of stockings full of holes, but sheer, immaculate stockings that caused her legs to shimmer in the spring sunshine. As she cooed and flirted with the German officer, I could tell she was French and it made me sick to my stomach. Surely, as a French woman, she would have lost male friends and family members to the Germans in the fighting before the occupation. How could she so easily switch allegiances? Was she that desperate for stockings?

I stepped back into a boarded-up shop doorway and took a picture of her planting a kiss on the soldier's cheek. I wondered what would become of collaborators like her if the Allies finally did invade. After yet another long hard winter it was hard to summon the hope for an Allied victory, but they did seem to be tightening the screws on the Germans. There'd recently been a lot more bombing raids on the French railway lines to try to thwart the movement of weapons and troops.

Recently, I'd taken to spending most nights at the peacock's apartment as a way of feeling close to him, but that night I decided to stay at my own place as I had a roll of film to develop. It was shortly after midnight and I'd just hung the last of the pictures on the line to dry when I heard a low rumbling sound.

At first I thought it was thunder, but then the air-raid siren began to wail. I hurried into the living room and peered outside. In the event of an air raid, my neighbours and I were supposed to take shelter in the Metro station at the bottom of the hill, but I had no desire to spend the night crammed like sardines with hundreds of strangers, and besides, the planes would be bombing the railway lines, not here.

My thoughts were interrupted by an almighty boom and the entire building tremored. 'What the...!' I gasped and looked back outside. There was another boom and another, reverberating right through me. The sky lit up with dazzling trails of anti-aircraft fire. Blinding flashes illuminated the horizon. And then came a sound like hail, rattling against the windowpanes and onto the ground. What was happening? Were the Allies bombing all of Paris?

I raced through to the dark room to fetch my camera. Just as I got there, the red lamp went out, plunging the room into total darkness. The electricity must have gone out. I felt simultaneously scared and excited. Could this raid be the Allies paving the way for their invasion? Paris was so beautiful that even Hitler had been reluctant to bomb it, but the Germans had subsequently brought so much horror to the city, and inflicted so much pain and misery, part of me didn't care if it was now razed to the ground. Anything to bring about an end to the occupation.

I returned to the living room, opened the window and set up my camera. The noise outside was deafening. A discordant symphony formed by the wail of the siren, the incessant rattle of anti-aircraft fire, the roar of planes swooping by overhead, and the thud and boom of the bombs. Adrenaline coursed through my body as I watched the display. I knew my camera wouldn't be able to capture the terrible magnificence of what I was witnessing, but I kept taking pictures regardless. If this raid did signal the beginning of the end for the Germans, I was sure as hell going to capture it.

The raid lasted for two hours and there came a point when I seriously started to wonder if I would survive the night. From the sounds of things, Montmartre had sustained a heavy bombardment. As the ground shook yet again, I curled up on the bed clasping my photos of the peacock, Lillie, Joseph and Natalia to my chest. Perhaps it was the years of hunger, exhaustion and loneliness, but I no longer cared if I died, especially if I died in a bombing raid that led to a free France. As far as I was concerned then, *c'est la vie*. But, finally, the bombing stopped and the sirens fell silent. I tucked my photos beneath the pillow and crept back over to the window. People were trickling back up the hill from the shelters and I could hear others calling out for help. I quickly put on my coat and shoes and went downstairs.

'I can't find my wife!' a man shouted from the end of the street. 'People are trapped.'

I hurried in the direction of his voice and couldn't help gasping as I turned the corner. There was a huge crater where the butcher's shop used to be. All that remained was the blackboard sign that, until today, had hung by the door; the word *sausages* was written on it in chalk. Then I thought of the peacock's building and began running in the direction of his street. *Please, please, please*, I silently implored as I raced around the corner. *Please still be there!*

'Oh no!' I cried as I took in the smouldering heap of rubble where the milliner's used to be.

'Did you live there?' a woman asked.

'No, but someone I know did.' A straw hat came rolling along the pavement towards me on the breeze, coming to rest by my feet. I looked around and saw hats everywhere, giving the scene an even more surreal feel.

'Do you know if they were home or had they gone to the shelter?' the woman asked.

'No, it's OK, they weren't there,' I replied.

But it wasn't OK. All of the peacock's possessions had been in that apartment – his beloved records and maracas and, of course, his colourful clothes. Spending time amongst those possessions had been the only remaining connection I had with him. Some nights I'd even worn one of his jackets while I listened to his music just to feel closer to him. I thought of how I'd been planning to stay the night there and how I'd only gone to my own place to develop the film. If I hadn't done that, I'd be dead. The realisation sent shock waves right through me, as if another bomb had gone off, but this time inside of me. I bent over double and hugged myself tightly.

'Are you all right?' The woman gripped my elbow.

'Yes, it's just... it's all such a shock.'

'It certainly is. Did your home survive? Do you have some-where to go?'

I nodded and slowly came back to my senses. 'Yes, thank you. I'd better get back there now.'

I turned and hurried back along the street, trying to process the night's events. The peacock's apartment had been destroyed. I could have died.

I could have, but I didn't, I told myself, trying to calm myself. I turned onto my street, walking past the people returning from the shelters, all looking shell-shocked as they took in the scenes of devastation. *I didn't die tonight, and neither did the peacock; it was only his apartment that was destroyed. Only possessions.*

As I fumbled in my pocket for my key, I saw a sight that made me freeze. A man was lurking in the doorway to my apart-ment. He was wearing a long dark coat and a flat cap pulled down low. Had the Germans found out about my Resistance work? Was he Gestapo? I was about to do a U-turn when he stepped out of the darkness in front of me.

'Looks like I picked a fine night to come back to Paris!' he said softly.

My breath caught in my throat. *Is it... Could it be...?* Perhaps I was hallucinating after the trauma of the evening.

I stared at the man as he took off his cap. His dark hair was cropped short and his chin was covered in stubble, but there was no mistaking those eyes and that smile. By some kind of miracle, the peacock was standing right in front of me.

37

'Is it really you?' I gasped as the peacock took a step closer. 'Or am I hallucinating? Please tell me I'm not hallucinating.'

'You're not hallucinating, Fire,' he said with a grin. 'Your beloved soulmate really is standing before you, although he sadly no longer bears any resemblance to his former self and his beautifully coiffed moustache has been reduced to stubble.'

I burst out laughing. 'Now I know for sure that I'm not hallucinating. Only you would come out with something so melodramatic!'

His smile faded. 'Oh, Fire, I have missed you more than... more than life itself.'

'Hmm, I'm not sure that even makes sense, perhaps you ought to just—'

'Shut up and kiss you?' he interrupted. He pulled me close and whispered in his British voice, 'It would be my absolute pleasure, my dear!' And with that, he kissed me passionately on the lips.

'I can't believe you're here,' I cried. 'I've missed you so much. I was so scared I was never going to see you again. I was so scared you'd be killed or arrested or sent to Germany.' I heard the rumble of a vehicle approaching and quickly unlocked the door. 'Come in quick.'

'I was beginning to think you'd never ask.' He followed me into the darkened hallway and as I shut the door behind him, he pulled me into another embrace. 'I never want to let you go again,' he said breathlessly.

'I'm not going to let you,' I replied. And then I remembered what I'd seen right before returning home. 'Do you... uh, do you know what's happened to your apartment?'

'No. I came straight here.'

'I'm so sorry, it was bombed tonight. I just got back from seeing it. The whole building was destroyed.' I thought he'd be heartbroken at the thought of his beloved clothes and records going up in dust, but if he was, he didn't appear to show it.

'All I care about is that you're OK,' he whispered before kissing me again.

I held his hand tightly as we went up the stairs. The electricity still wasn't back on, so I lit a candle, then looked at him nervously. It had been so long since we'd seen each other, over a year; would things be different between us? Would things feel awkward or stilted?

He seemed to be experiencing a similar fear as he looked at me shyly. 'I was worried that... that you might have met someone else,' he said softly.

'Are you insane?' I cried. 'I think about you all the time. I *talk* about you all the time, to the one and only friend I see these days.'

He looked at me so hopefully, it made me want to laugh and cry and sing and wail from the mixture of joy and sorrow coursing through me. I wasn't sure if it was the candlelight and the stubble, but he looked a lot older, more rugged, less boyish. If anything, this only made him more attractive. 'I think about you all the time too,' he said. 'I even talk to you.'

'What do you mean?'

He took something from his jacket pocket and passed it to me. It was the photograph of us that I'd given him as a parting gift.

'I talk to a picture of you too!' I exclaimed. I went over to the bed and took his photo out from under the pillow.

'What a crazy world this is,' he said, shaking his head.

'But you're here now.' I grabbed his hand and squeezed it tight. '*How* are you here now? *Why* are you here? Are you back for good? Please say you're back for good.'

He laughed. 'I am back for good, to fight for the freedom of Paris.'

My pulse quickened. 'Are the Allies about to invade? Is that what all the bombing was about tonight?'

'It's getting closer. The Resistance are starting to send men back to Paris in preparation.'

I shivered as I thought of the full implications of what he was saying. The Germans were highly unlikely to give up Paris without a fight. The peacock and I might be reunited for now, but there was still no guarantee we'd both make it out of this alive.

He raised my hand to his lips and kissed my fingers. 'For so long I have dreamed of this, of us being together again.'

'Me too.'

'And for so long I've dreamed of making love to you again.'

'Well, maybe it's time you stopped dreaming.'

'What do you mean?' He looked at me anxiously.

'And start doing!' I exclaimed.

In an instant, we were tearing at each other's clothes. As I helped him lift his shirt over his head, I noticed a scar on his side.

'What's this?' I whispered, gently tracing my fingertips over it.

'It is nothing,' he whispered, unbuttoning my blouse.

'It doesn't look like nothing; it looks like a bullet wound.'

'It was just a graze.' He pulled me over to the bed.

But as I lay down beside him, an unwelcome memory popped into my head. It was of the man I'd shot, lying bleeding on the stone floor. Would the peacock think less of me if he knew I'd killed someone?

I pushed the fear from my mind and melted into his embrace.

I woke the next morning feeling momentarily disorientated. Something was different, but I wasn't sure what. And then it dawned on me; I could hear the peacock breathing. The peacock was in bed beside me!

I lay still, not wanting to wake him. I needed to take a moment to process everything that had happened the night before. Our lovemaking had been passionate and intense and afterwards he'd held me so tight, I'd thought my heart might actually burst from the joy and relief. But as soon as he'd fallen asleep, memories of that terrible night in the country with Joseph came back to haunt me. I'd lain awake for ages deliberating over whether I should tell the peacock what had happened.

'What are you thinking?' His voice made me jump.

I turned onto my side to face him. 'How did you know I was awake?'

'I could hear you sighing.'

'Oh.' I rested my head against his chest. I had to tell him. It felt physically impossible to keep a secret from him.

'What is it? What's wrong?'

'Something happened, while you were away.'

I felt his body tense. 'What?'

'I did something.'

He wrapped his arm around me. He felt stronger than

before. More muscular. 'It's OK,' he said softly, 'you can tell me.'

'I was taking a Jewish child to safety – in the country – and we had to spend the night in a cellar.'

'Oh!' he said, clearly surprised. 'Go on...'

'A member of the Milice turned up in the middle of the night and discovered us and... and I shot him.' I felt sick as I heard myself say the words.

'You shot him?' He shifted slightly and I risked looking up to meet his gaze. He was staring at me, eyes wide.

'Yes. He'd shot at the boy and I was so angry and I was afraid he was going to shoot me next so... I killed him.' I waited with bated breath.

'My God. I don't believe it. I—'

'I feel terrible about it,' I interrupted, my voice shaking, terrified he would think the worst of me. 'I keep having nightmares. I keep reliving it. I never thought I'd be able to kill someone. I don't know what happened to me. I wouldn't blame you if you think I'm a monster, if you never want to see me again.'

'Fire!' He cupped my face in his hands. 'What are you talking about? You're not a monster! The Milice are the monsters. You said he shot the child. Did he kill the child?'

'No, thankfully.' I thought of Joseph and my eyes misted over. 'He was – is – such a lovely kid. Look...' I felt under the pillow and pulled out my photo of Joseph.

'He looks so sweet,' the peacock said, studying the photograph. 'How can you feel badly for saving his life? And saving your own. I'm glad you killed him.' He kissed me on the tip of my nose. 'And, to be honest, I'm a little relieved.'

'You're relieved that I killed someone?' I stared at him in shock.

'Yes. I thought you were about to confess to having met someone new.' He gave me a sheepish grin.

'What do I have to do to convince you that I love you and

only you!' I cried, hugging him to me. The peacock knew my darkest, most shameful secret and he didn't think any worse of me.

'Hmm, I'm sure I could think of something, my dear,' he quipped in his ridiculous British voice.

'I know, I shall make you a nice cup of tea,' I said, slipping from his arms and out of bed.

'No! Don't leave me!' he cried.

'But I thought you Brits loved tea,' I giggled, practically giddy with gratitude and relief.

Once we'd had a quick breakfast of watery tea and dry bread topped with the thinnest slivers of cheese, the peacock and I went out to help with the rescue mission following the bombings. It turned out that I wasn't the only one to have shunned taking shelter in the station, and many people were now trapped beneath the wreckage. I shuddered at the thought of how close I'd come to death – and on the day of the peacock's return to Paris. I should never have been so reckless.

We worked long and hard helping pull them to safety and by the end of the day our clothes were covered in grime and dust and our hands were red raw and cut. I made sure to take a few photographs too, hoping that one day they would come to symbolise the night the tide turned and the liberation of Paris was set in motion. How else would we be able to justify such loss of life and devastation?

The following day, the peacock had to meet with Raymond at a safe house and he told me that I was to go with him too. This news delighted me and demonstrated how far my relationship with Raymond had come since those early days when he barely acknowledged my existence. Our destination was an apartment in Pigalle. The peacock had false papers claiming to be a farmer from Bordeaux and, thanks to over a year living in the country, he certainly looked far more like a farmer than he did before. Nevertheless, it was a nerve-wracking journey. Thankfully, we arrived without incident and an older woman let us into the apartment and showed us through to a small kitchen.

Raymond was sitting at the table, his head in his hands. As soon as he saw me, he sighed and my heart sank. Had he reverted to his old unfriendly ways now the peacock was back? He gestured at me to take a seat.

'Clarisse, I'm afraid I have some bad news.'

'What is it?' I stared at him, dumbfounded. How could he have bad news for me; the peacock was standing right beside me. Perhaps he was about to tell me that the peacock had to go away again, but wouldn't he have told him first?

'The boy you rescued.'

'Yes?' My voice quavered. *Please, please don't let something have happened to Joseph.*

'An informant in Lyon told the Gestapo about the children's home at Izieu. They raided it earlier this month.'

'The Gestapo?' My throat tightened.

'Yes. They took all the staff and children.'

'Oh no,' the peacock murmured behind me.

'Took them where?'

'To the prison in Lyon at first.'

'At first?' I stared at him in horror.

'Then they were sent to Drancy.'

'To Drancy?' I leapt to my feet. 'I have to go there, to get Joseph.'

'There's no point.'

'What do you mean, there's no point? He must be terrified.'

'They've already left.'

'Left Drancy?' For the briefest of moments, I felt a spark of hope. Could the authorities have come to their senses and released him?

'On the transports.'

I collapsed back down on the chair, sobbing, my breath coming in short sharp gasps.

'Fire, I'm so sorry.' The peacock stood behind me and placed his hands on my shoulders.

'I told him he'd be safe. I told him he'd see his mother again.' I thought of Joseph and all he'd been through and how brave and stoic he'd remained. How he'd tried to save me by throwing an egg at the Milicien. I could hardly breathe for the sorrow and rage engulfing me. 'What is wrong with these people?' I cried, slamming my hand on the table. 'How can they do this to children?' I thought of Lillie being dragged from her mother. I thought of the child I'd seen pushed from the orphanage window and my vision blurred. It was too much. Too horrific to comprehend.

'You did everything you could, Clarisse,' Raymond said. 'You even killed a man to keep that boy safe.'

'But for what?' I asked, staring at him. 'For what? Maybe it would have been better if that bastard had killed him; at least he wouldn't have had to endure the terror that he must be going through now.'

The peacock squeezed my shoulders, but I shrugged his hands off. I didn't want anyone's sympathy. I was so tired of this godforsaken war and the way any sign of progress, any small victory, was almost instantly snuffed out by the evil of the Nazis.

As the men started talking in hushed tones about Resistance preparations for an Allied invasion, I felt something hardening inside of me. I'd felt so guilty about taking a life, so ashamed to tell the peacock what I'd done, but I no longer felt any remorse. If someone had given me a pistol in that moment and taken me to the bastard who'd informed on those innocent children, I'd have felt no compunction in pulling the trigger.

38

APRIL 1985, PARIS

I arrived home from Le Centre Pompidou feeling utterly discombobulated. It was a little like discovering that a book or movie has an unreliable narrator and everything you've read or seen must now be reinterpreted through the lens of truth. But in this case it wasn't a book or a movie that had misled me, it was my life. Or the part featuring Clarisse Alarie, anyhow.

Even though our paths had only crossed for a matter of moments, the ramifications had rippled down through the years for both of us. I had inadvertently become her inspiration as a Resistance photographer and, due to my wrongful belief that she was somehow revelling in our misfortune, she had convinced me that there was no hope for humanity. How different might I have felt if she'd been able to whisper to me that she was trying to help? How different might things have been if I'd seen her when she snuck into the velodrome to try to find me? If only she had found me, I felt like things could have turned out so differently for both of us. I shivered as I thought of what the attendant at the exhibition had told me about what had happened to Clarisse.

I went into the living room and looked at Madeleine

Bernier's book lying on the arm of the sofa. I'd vowed that I wouldn't read any more of it, but that was before. Discovering what I had about myself and Clarisse had caused a thread in my life to come loose and I felt the overwhelming urge to keep tugging on it, especially now I'd learned the horrible truth about Alarie's fate.

I kicked off my shoes and picked up the book, turning straight to the section on travel. I wanted to re-read the opening page, where Bernier talked about her first ever solo trip. As I read her description of the nervous excitement she felt as she sat waiting for her plane to India to take off, I felt butterflies in the pit of my stomach too. I'd never flown anywhere before, never felt the desire to, in spite of the dreamlike quality of the Air France commercials. Surely it was too late in my life to start.

Pfft! I heard my younger self say and I pictured her plonking herself down beside me. She looked to be about eight this time and it sparked a sudden memory. It was my eighth birthday and my parents had bought me one of those spinnable globes on a stand.

'Now you can map out all the places you're going to sail to,' my father had said with a chuckle as I gazed at it in awe. I'd been going through a phase of wanting to be a pirate and played for hours in my pretend galleon, *The Black Heart*, constructed from an old crate. That globe instantly became my most trea-sured possession. Every night when it was time for my bedtime story, I'd spin the globe and stop it randomly with my finger and get my maman or papa to tell me a swashbuckling tale set in that place. Once they'd gone, I'd lie gazing into the darkness, dreaming of all the adventures I was going to have in exotically named places like Ceylon and Yugoslavia. One of the reasons I'd resisted travelling after returning from Auschwitz was a sense of guilt that I should get to experience things that had been robbed from my parents. But my parents had bought me that globe, filled my head with tales of adventures sailing the

seven seas. They'd wanted me to live my life to the fullest, not
shrink it down to the confines of a city.

I looked back at the book. *Travelling solo, especially as a
woman, can be a scary prospect,* Bernier wrote. *But, my God, if
you can find the courage to embark upon a solo adventure, the
freedom you'll experience is truly life-changing.*

I stood up. Sat back down. Stood up again.

You need to change your life, I pictured my eight-year-old
self saying before spinning her globe. And, for once, I found
myself agreeing with her.

I put my shoes back on and headed to the door.

I'd walked past the Bon Voyage Travel Agency numerous times
over the years and never, ever felt the desire to go in. So, as I
stepped inside, it was a little like entering a completely different
universe.

'Ooh, you're just in time,' a woman said, smiling up at me
from behind one of four desks.

'I'm sorry?' I stared at her, confused. How did she know I'd
left it so late in life to travel?

She looked at a row of clocks on the wall, showing the time
in London, New York, Paris and Sydney. 'We close in fifteen
minutes,' she explained.

'Ah, I see. I can come back tomorrow,' the fearful part of me
chimed up, eager to head straight back outside.

'No, no, it's fine. Please, take a seat.' She gestured at a chair
on my side of her desk.

'Thank you.'

As soon as I sat down, my heart started thumping. I had no
idea how one went about booking a trip. I was bound to look so
stupid and naïve. But I thought back to what the attendant had
told me in the exhibition and felt a seed of determination plant
itself deep inside of me.

'Are you looking to book a holiday?' she asked, moving a pile of brochures closer.

'Yes... no, not exactly,' I stammered.

She rested her elbows on the desk, putting her hands together in a kind of prayer position. Her nails were painted bright scarlet to match her uniform.

'What I mean to say is,' I continued, trying to regain some kind of composure, 'I need to book a flight, and if possible a hotel for the first night of my stay.'

'Of course,' she replied. 'And where is it you would like to go?'

I took a breath. *Go on!* I heard my younger self urge.

'To America,' I said, my voice trembling slightly.

39

JUNE 1944, PARIS

It was as if the news about Joseph broke something inside of me. My spirit, which had been stretched so taut over the previous few years, finally seemed to snap and even the peacock and his relentless enthusiasm couldn't put it back together again. I'd had enough. Enough of the Germans and their cruelty. Enough of the French government and the traitorous collaborators and the cowardly denouncers. Enough of being starved to distraction. I'd tried so hard to put my photography to good use, but it hadn't stopped people being taken and terrorised, tortured and killed, children being torn from their parents and sent to their deaths. The only thing that would stop those monsters wreaking their havoc upon the world was to meet their violence with violence, I could see that now, in blinding clarity. And I vowed that if and when the time came for the Resistance to rise up and take to the streets, I was going to be there with them, and not just taking photographs.

Then, on Tuesday 6 June, the day we had all been waiting and praying for finally arrived – the Allies launched their invasion of France.

'Let's go out!' I said to the peacock, feeling a sudden burst of energy. 'I want to see how other people are reacting to the news.'

'If only I hadn't lost all of my clothes in the bombing,' he replied. 'Today is a day for bright colours, not dressing in shades of mud!' He looked down at his brown shirt and trousers and huffed.

I kissed him on the cheek. 'I think mud is a very fetching shade on you, and anyway, you don't want to draw attention to yourself. The Allies might have landed in France, but those animals are still in charge of Paris – for the time being.' I looked at him and grinned. 'I have an idea – for a photo shoot.'

'Not of me in these clothes!' He looked horrified.

'Yes, but it will be our way of getting one up on the Germans.'

He smiled. 'Now that I like the sound of. Tell me more.'

Fittingly for a day of such good news, the weather was beautiful, the sky bright cornflower blue and the temperature just right, the warmth fresh rather than humid. The city was full of German troops on leave, sitting and walking around in the sunshine but there was no sign of their customary ease and arrogance today. It was satisfying to see the smugness wiped from their faces as they huddled together, talking in hushed tones. In sharp contrast, the cafes and terraces we walked past were abuzz as news of the Allied landings spread amongst Parisians like wildfire. Even though they were still a long way from the city, the fact that Allied troops were now on our shores made everything seem brighter somehow.

As we drew close to the Eiffel Tower, I saw a group of German soldiers standing talking and smoking beneath their hated 'Germany is victorious on all fronts' sign. *Not for much longer!* I wanted to yell, but it was time for my cunning plan.

'Go and stand over there, in front of those soldiers,' I said to the peacock.

'What? Why?' he asked, looking bemused.

'Because they'll have no idea that you're a Resistance fighter, ready and waiting to fight to free Paris right under their noses.'

He laughed with delight. 'Raymond's going to love this one.'

He went and stood between me and the soldiers and I lined up the shot so that the Germans and their sign were visible in the background. The peacock grinned from ear to ear as I took the picture.

Later that week, when I developed the photograph, I hoped that my optimism hadn't been premature. The Germans had had us in such a vice-like grip for so long that it felt impossible to imagine we might one day regain the upper hand. And Raymond was becoming increasingly annoyed at the Allies' reluctance to airdrop weapons to the Resistance. 'They're scared of too many guns falling into the hands of the communists,' he grumbled, 'but if they don't do something soon, we'll have to take the Germans on with nothing more than peashooters!'

But at the end of the month, the Resistance pulled off a major coup, assassinating the hateful Vichy Minister of Information, Philippe Henriot. All through the occupation, Henriot had broadcast his hateful anti-Semitic poison twice a day on Radio Paris, so to see one of the chief puppets for the Germans silenced forever felt like a major victory.

The next day, the peacock and I were coming back from a walk when we saw a man with a bucket of paste putting up some posters. It was a portrait of Henriot along with the slogan, *He told the truth – they killed him!*

I thought of the times Pierre had insisted on listening to his terrible show and the bile he'd spouted about the Jewish people. I thought of Joseph and Lillie and it took everything I had not to run over and deface the poster.

'Do you think we'll ever return to a time when bare-faced lies aren't paraded as the truth?' I asked the peacock as we walked on by.

'I hope so,' he replied. 'Surely the world will return to sanity once this insanity is over.'

'Hmm,' was all I was able to utter. The Germans and the Vichy government had spun such a tangled web of hatred and deceit it was hard to imagine ever being free from it.

As the fighting in Normandy and the bombing raids on the railway lines intensified, food supplies became even more sparse. With nothing to sell, most grocery stores remained closed with their shutters down and any store that did receive a supply soon had its shelves stripped bare. One day I queued for hours only to find a solitary sprig of parsley remaining. There was something so pitiful and symbolic about it, I felt compelled to take a photo of it.

'Do you really think the Parisians will be able to defeat the Germans in Paris?' I asked the peacock as I made us a parsley soup that evening – or maybe parsley tea would have been a more accurate description. 'How can we beat them with no weapons and no food? We're not even getting supplies of wine anymore.'

The peacock laughed. 'I'd say that will ensure our victory. There's no way Parisians will accept a life with no wine without a fight. They will fight the enemy to the death for that right.'

I laughed. 'True.'

'Raymond says that the Parisian Liberation Committee are organising protests about the food shortages on Bastille Day.'

'Really?' I felt a shiver of excitement at the thought of

people taking to the streets.

'Yes.' The peacock went and fetched something from his jacket. *'Voilà!'* He produced two small brown glass bottles from the pocket.

'Is it alcohol?' I asked hopefully.

'No, it's dye!' he chuckled. He put the bottles down and took hold of my hands. 'We're going to make some flags. For the protest.'

'The Tricolore?' I grinned. Ever since the Germans had occupied France, the French flag had been banned.

'Yes indeed. All we need is a white sheet.'

And so we spent the rest of the evening cutting a sheet into strips and dying one third red and one third blue.

'How are you feeling now?' the peacock asked as I took one of the blue strips from the basin. 'About what happened to Joseph?'

After Raymond had delivered the terrible news about Joseph, I'd told the peacock that I didn't want to talk about it. It was too horrible and heartbreaking to bear and the only way I'd been able to deal with it was by burying it deep inside of me. The peacock had honoured my wishes, but, as always, he seemed to know exactly what to say and when, and now I felt ready to talk.

'I'm terrified,' I sighed. 'I'm scared of what will become of him.'

'He must be a really special child, to have made such an impression on you.'

'He is. You would love him. He's so funny. I kept wishing you could have been here to meet him. I feel like you would have been so good with him.'

The peacock gave one of his warm smiles. 'It sounds as if you did just fine with him on your own.'

I nodded. 'I was so nervous at first, though. I've never had to take care of a kid before, let alone in such terrible circumstances. I didn't have the first clue what to do, but, somehow, I figured it out.'

He looked down into his bowl of red strips. 'I think you'd make a wonderful mother.'

For once I didn't wince at the thought of being a parent. 'Really? That's funny, because all the time I was with Joseph, I kept thinking about what a great father you'd make.'

He looked at me, clearly surprised. 'You thought that about me?'

'Yes. You're so full of love and joy. How could you not be a wonderful parent?'

'I really hope I get the chance one day.'

We held each other's gaze and I felt a fluttering deep inside at the implication of what was being said. But it wasn't my old fear about what had happened to my mother come back to haunt me. It was a feeling of excitement at what could be.

'I hope that for you too.'

'Do you think that maybe...' He broke off.

'What?' I asked softly, willing him to have the courage to say it.

'Maybe one day you and I might be parents together?'

A lump formed in the back of my throat. In that moment, I couldn't think of anything more magical or life-affirming than having a child with the peacock. Unable to speak, I nodded.

His eyes lit up.

'I... I can't think of anything I'd rather do,' I said.

He flung his arms around me and hugged me tight.

'It would be so beautiful,' I sobbed into his shoulder. 'I'm so tired of all the fighting.'

'We're so near the end now,' he whispered. 'The Allies are getting closer to Paris every day. Just another month and this could all be over, and we'll finally get to dance in the streets of a free Paris. And maybe one day we'll dance in those streets with our children – Cab, Django and Count.'

'I'm sorry, who?' I exclaimed, wiping my tears away.

'Well, we'd have to name them after the jazz greats.' He grinned. 'Would you prefer Duke to Count?'

'I'd prefer it if I got to name them!' I exclaimed. 'It is a family we're talking about starting, not a band!'

'What about their middle names then?' He looked at me hopefully. 'Can I at least choose them?'

'Maybe.' I laughed and leaned into his embrace, trying to imprint the image of our dancing family onto my mind, like a photograph of happier times to come. Happier times to strive for.

The morning of Bastille Day dawned bright and sunny. As soon as the Germans had occupied France, they'd banned the national Bastille Day celebrations, which had always been a fiesta of dancing and fireworks. It felt great to wake up on 14 July and feel excitement again, although my excitement was tinged with nerves as it was still illegal to protest.

I snuggled up to the peacock and held him tightly. As he murmured in his sleep, I prayed that we'd both make it through the day in one piece. Since our conversation about having children, I'd felt closer to him than ever. Once again, he'd managed to infuse me with his endless hope, but this made the thought of losing him all the more terrifying.

'Good morning, my love,' he murmured.

'Good morning.'

'Happy Bastille Day!' He kissed me on the end of my nose.

'And to you too.'

I sat up and peered out of the window. Everything looked relatively calm. It was impossible to imagine that hundreds of people could be taking to the streets later. Indeed, some sections of the Resistance had been predicting that the whole thing would be a disaster, and that hardly anyone would turn up. Others had been saying that even if people did take to the streets, the reprisals from the authorities would be devastating. I was determined not to let my nerves show, though. The people of Paris had to rise up at some point. We couldn't be starved into submission forever.

Once we'd had a meagre breakfast of tea and boiled potatoes, I packed my bag with my camera and our home-made flags. Protests had been planned all over the city and we were going to the one in the Latin Quarter.

'I've got a very good feeling about today,' the peacock said as we prepared to leave.

'Do you ever have anything but a good feeling?' I joked, but, as always, I was grateful and fortified by his optimism.

As soon as we neared the Latin Quarter, I heard the chants of 'Bread! Bread! Bread!'

'It sounds as if there's been a good turnout!' I exclaimed and the peacock nodded excitedly.

Nothing could have prepared me for the scenes that greeted us, however. Hundreds and hundreds of people filled the cobbled streets dressed in red, white and blue or draped in Tricolore flags. I quickly took our own flags from my bag and we put them round our shoulders like cloaks. Then people began singing 'La Marseillaise' and it was a sight and sound so beautiful, I stopped for a moment and soaked it in like a sponge. Even the police who were present appeared to be moved, some of them joining in with the singing.

'It's happening, isn't it?' I said to the peacock, my heart aglow. 'The tide is finally turning.'

'Yes, my dear, it certainly is!' he replied in English, before taking my hand and spinning me around. 'We are dancing on the streets of a soon-to-be free Paris!'

'I need to take some pictures,' I exclaimed, fetching my viewfinder from my bag.

I took a picture of the peacock holding his home-made flag aloft, and one of a woman chanting 'Bread! Bread! Bread!' as she waved her empty shopping basket. Then I spied an elderly man in a shabby suit holding a flag with the words *Free France* painted across it.

'I'm just going to get a picture of that man,' I said to the peacock, pointing up ahead.

'Of course,' he replied, taking a handful of leaflets from one of the organisers. 'I'll start giving these out.'

I wove through the crowd to the man and managed to get a shot of him holding his flag aloft with a beaming grin. A row of medals on his chest glistened in the sunshine.

'La Marseillaise' grew louder and louder. 'To arms, citizens!' we sang. 'Form your battalions, let's march, let's march.' My heart swelled with every word. We were going to do it; we were going to beat the Germans. We hadn't been starved into submission despite their best efforts.

As the anthem finished, I heard a cry ring out and saw a policeman waving his arms.

'The Milice! The Milice!' he yelled.

My throat tightened as I caught a glimpse of the dreaded blue uniform as a group of Milice suddenly appeared from a side street. I should have known that protest would bring them out, but surely they would be outnumbered, especially as it seemed that even the police no longer supported them.

The crowd scattered as the Milice ran down the street and then I saw a sight that made my blood turn to ice. They'd grabbed a man draped in a flag – but who?

I pushed my way back through the crowd, my heart pounding, just in time to see them dragging the peacock down the side street and into the back of a van.

40

JULY 1944, PARIS

'Well, there's good news and there's bad news,' Raymond said as we walked together beside the Seine. I'd received a message to meet with him the day after the protests, which I was hugely grateful for as I think I might have gone out of my mind with worry otherwise. Clearly, I wasn't the only one wrought with anxiety; his bushy hair was more dishevelled than ever and there were dark shadows beneath his eyes.

'What's the good news?' I asked, feeling sick with nerves. After I'd seen the peacock bundled into the back of the van I'd ended up wandering aimlessly for miles. Trying to walk off my fear. Trying to walk some hope back into me. It hadn't worked and I'd returned to my apartment exhausted but far too anxious to sleep.

'The good news is, he's still alive.'

'Oh, thank God.' I stopped walking and grabbed the wall running alongside the river to steady myself. 'And the bad news?' I hardly dared ask.

'The bad news is that the Milice delivered him to the Germans.'

'Oh no!' My mind immediately went to the stories I'd heard

about how the Germans would torture Resistance members at avenue Foch.

'And they've sent him to Fresnes.'

'The prison?'

Raymond nodded before glancing up and down the path. 'Come, let's keep walking.'

I ran to keep up with his stride, 'But that's good, isn't it? Surely the prisoners will all be liberated as soon as the Allies reach Paris.'

'Yes, that's the hope.' There was a hesitation in his voice.

'Why do I feel like there's a but coming?'

'*But* there's always the risk of the Germans taking reprisals in the face of defeat.'

'You mean killing prisoners?'

'Yes. They carry out reprisals every time even one of them is killed here in Paris. Who knows what they might do once the fighting properly begins.'

I gazed out across the river. The sky was leaden and, after the joyful protests of yesterday, the city felt strangely subdued. It was hard to imagine that there could soon be full-scale fighting on these streets. For so long I'd prayed for the Allies to arrive and help liberate Paris, but now this could mean the death of the peacock. It was a twist of fate so cruel, I could hardly bear to think about it.

'Is there anything we can do? Any way of getting him out of there?'

Raymond shook his head. 'We just have to do all we can to get those vermin out of our city.'

'I'll do anything, just tell me what you need. And I don't mean just taking photographs,' I added.

He stopped and looked at me, his expression deadly serious. 'Would you be prepared to fight for Paris's freedom' – he leaned closer and lowered his voice – 'if I were to get you a weapon?'

'Yes!' I replied without hesitation.

'OK. I'll be in touch. Stay safe, Clarisse.' He turned on his heel and walked away.

I stood motionless for a moment, my mind reeling. The peacock was in Fresnes prison, which was definitely preferable to the terrible scenarios that had kept me up all night. And hadn't he come back to me before? I had to keep believing in miracles. We were so close now to our dreams of a free Paris, of dancing on the streets, of having a family. I had to adopt some of the peacock's relentless positivity. I had to keep believing.

For the next couple of weeks, I maintained my sanity in my tried and true way, seeking solace in viewing the world through my camera. Once again, forcing myself to see things with the objectivity of a photographer helped save me from being overrun by sorrow and fear. And this was helped by increasingly good news from the Allies. By the end of July, there were rumoured to be one million Allied soldiers on French soil, and they'd made it halfway to Paris from Normandy. It was a good job too, as we were facing increasingly punitive restrictions. Gas was only available for half an hour at lunchtime and an hour in the evening and the Metro was no longer running between eleven in the morning and three in the afternoon. There was the strangest sensation of living in some kind of end of days, and I prayed and prayed that we would soon see the end of the German tyranny and the peacock would be free.

The radio became my main source of information and inspiration, and it was never more inspiring than on the evening of 7 August when the leader of the Free French, Charles de Gaulle, broadcast to the nation from Algiers. It had been a strange day as the city had been shrouded in a blanket of orange-grey cloud from a bombing raid on the petrol depots in Saint-Ouen. As I sat at the table listening, his words restored my faith and sent shivers running up and down my spine.

'Everyone can fight. Everyone must fight,' his voice crackled from the speaker. 'Those who are able should join the FFI.'

'I will,' I whispered in response.

'In the countryside, in the factory, in the workshop, in the office, at home, in the street... you can always weaken the enemy or prepare that which will weaken him.'

I stood up and walked over to the tiny mantelpiece, where I'd propped my photos of the peacock, Lillie, Joseph and Natalia. I'd last seen Andreas the week before and it had been apparent from the grey shadows beneath his eyes and the frown lines etched above his nose that he was finding her deportation increasingly hard to take.

'Please, please, please stay safe until we win,' I whispered.

A few days later, I saw a sight that further filled my heart with hope. I'd been out walking for hours with my camera when I heard the rumble of engines and turned to see a convoy of German lorries making their way towards me. Instinctively feeling fearful, I stepped back into the shadows. But as the lorries drew closer, I realised that they weren't loaded with troops or weapons; they were laden with mattresses and furniture and crates of wine and champagne. One even contained a piano. Could it be that they were leaving Paris? I was so transfixed that for a moment I forgot to reach for my camera. I only managed to get one shot of the back of the last lorry and its teetering pile of bedding.

'It's happening,' I whispered. 'It's really happening. They're starting to leave!'

Then I heard another rumbling sound, but this time from far away. There were a series of faint booms and my spirits soared as I realised it was the Allies fighting to the west of the city. They were so close now, I could hear them!

I carried on walking and looked up at the sky. It was

streaked with brilliant shades of orange and pink from the setting sun, as if it too were celebrating this turn of events.

But over the next few days, the weather seemed to mirror the growing tensions in the city, and it became increasingly hot and oppressively humid. We now had no gas at all, which meant that the bakers couldn't bake bread, and water pressure had been reduced to such a level that people started collecting it in bottles and bowls for fear that we might run out altogether. I ran as much as I could in my small bathtub and added a few drops of potassium permanganate to sterilise it, although this hardly made drinking it appealing as it turned the water purple.

When I stalked the streets with my camera, I couldn't help but be infected by the growing feeling of apprehension in the air. People were still out and about, but there was an eerie silence hanging over the pavements and cafe terraces and the beautifully made-up women in their summer dresses reminded me of shop mannequins, made quiet and still by worry as they listened to the distant rattle of gunfire coming from the west.

Every day I prayed with increasing fervour that the peacock and his fellow prisoners would be released, but day after day passed with no news. Then, early one morning in the middle of August, I was woken from a fitful sleep by a loud knocking on my door. My first thought was that it was the police or the Germans come to arrest me for my Resistance activity, but I opened the door to find Raymond standing there. His face was ashen and his brow creased.

'I have news,' he said, walking past me into the studio. 'The prisoners are being moved.'

'What? Where?' I wrapped my robe tighter round me.

'To Pantin station.'

'The goods station? But why?' As I stared at him, the terrible truth dawned on me. 'They're being deported.'

He nodded. 'I knew those bastards would be ruthless to the bitter end.'

'But the Germans have already started leaving Paris; I've seen them. Why are they bothering to do this now? They know they're beaten.'

'Because they're pure evil.'

'But there must be something we can do. Some way to stop them from being deported,' I cried in desperation.

'We can't. We just don't have the weapons yet to take on the battalions still stationed here; there are still so many of them. But the day is fast approaching.' Raymond reached inside his jacket pocket and brought out something wrapped in a scarf. I knew instantly that it was a pistol. 'We have to do whatever it takes to get rid of them once and for all.' He handed the gun to me and my skin prickled with goosebumps. 'We still have a severe shortage of ammunition, but here's some to start with.' He took a small box from his pocket and handed it to me. 'I'll be in touch when it's time to begin the fight; until then, I suggest you get to Pantin as quickly as possible.'

'Do you think I might be able to see him?' I looked at him hopefully.

He shrugged his broad shoulders. 'It's worth a try.' He took a step towards me and gave me a slightly awkward hug. 'I'm so sorry, Clarisse, but don't lose faith. It isn't over yet.'

I nodded, biting on my lip to stop myself from crying.

As soon as Raymond left, I got dressed, my heart pounding. It was about six miles to Pantin from Montmartre and as the Metro was no longer running, I'd have to go on foot.

The sun was already beating down outside and as I strode along the pavement I felt increasingly light-headed from the shock and the fear and the heat. Everyone was saying that the Allies were just days away from reaching Paris; why did the Germans have to deport the prisoners now? It seemed so cruel. But then everything they'd done since arriving here had been an exercise in cruelty. Why should I expect any better of them now?

'Brooch, miss?' I jumped as a young man appeared from an alleyway just in front of me.

'Pardon?' I replied, flustered.

'Would you like to buy a brooch, to celebrate the liberation of Paris?' He opened his jacket to reveal a row of brooches pinned inside, made up of three overlapping flags – French, American and British. Ordinarily, I would have admired his enterprising spirit, but in the light of what was happening at Pantin, it seemed crass and premature.

'We're not free yet,' I hissed, marching past him.

'You traitors are going to get what's coming to you,' he called after me and I realised that he must have misinterpreted my anger for me being a collaborator. Not that I cared. In that moment, all I cared about was the peacock and the chance that I might get to see him.

When I finally got within a mile of the station, a truck drove past full of men in the back, heads bowed. My stomach lurched. Could the peacock be among them? The bell-like tinkle of a woman's laughter rang out from a nearby cafe and I had to stop myself from crying out in sorrow. The BBC had announced the success of Operation Dragoon – the Allied invasion of the Mediterranean coast of France – the day before, and since then the city had been abuzz. There was something so heartbreaking about seeing Parisians sitting in the sunshine, dreaming of a freedom that was surely just around the corner and yet, at the same time, other Parisians were being taken to their deportation and possible death.

He's not going to die! I told myself as I carried on walking, faster and faster. *He can't, not now, not so close to our happy ending, or rather our happy beginning, in a free France.*

As I neared the station, I saw a stream of people all headed the same way – mostly women, some with young children. I felt certain that we wouldn't be allowed in to see our loved ones, that the authorities would show us no compassion, but to my surprise, I was able to follow the other women into the station and onto the platform.

A train made up of cattle trucks was waiting there. German guards were patrolling up and down the platform, but they made no attempt to stop us approaching the train. The air was filled with the sound of women calling men's names and children crying. I saw hands pushing pieces of paper through the cracks in the side of the trucks and I was instantly reminded of Natalia.

Was the peacock there? One thing was for certain, I was going to do my damnedest to find him. I made my way to the first truck and cleared my throat.

'Peacock!' I yelled at the top of my voice.

A couple of children turned and looked at me and started to smile. Some of the women looked at me as if I was deranged. But I knew that if he was there, calling 'peacock' would definitely get his attention.

'Peacock!' I yelled again.

'Why are you saying "peacock"?' a little girl in a faded summer dress asked with a shy smile.

'It's my nickname for my friend,' I explained. 'I'm trying to find him.' Then I had an idea. 'I don't suppose you could help me, could you?' I looked at the woman beside her, who I assumed was her mother. She was deep in conversation with one of the men crowded around the open door of the truck. 'Could you call "peacock" with me?'

The girl smiled and nodded.

'One, two, three,' I counted.

'Peacock!' we both cried. But there was no response.

'Why do you call him Peacock?' the girl asked.

'Because he's as beautiful as a peacock,' I replied.

'Men aren't beautiful, silly,' she said with a giggle.

'This man is,' I said, and it was as if I could feel my heart splintering in two. What if I couldn't find him? What if I never saw him again?

I moved down the platform to the next truck and saw that the girl had come with me.

'One, two, three,' she said, unprompted.

'Peacock!' we cried again. And again I thought it was to no avail, but then I saw a flurry of movement in the truck as a man jostled his way to the open door.

'Fire?' I heard him cry and it almost floored me. 'Fire!' the peacock exclaimed as he came into view. His face was bruised and he was now sporting a bushy beard.

'Is that him?' the little girl asked.

'Yes!'

'He doesn't look very beautiful,' she said matter-of-factly. 'I'm going back to my maman now.'

'OK, thank you,' I said without even looking at her. I couldn't take my gaze from the peacock's.

'Fire, how did you find me?' he asked.

'Raymond told me they'd brought the prisoners here. Oh, Peacock, I'm so sorry.'

'It's OK. The Allies are so close now, hopefully they'll be able to catch up with our train before we get too far east.'

For the first time since Raymond had delivered his terrible news, I felt a glimmer of hope. Trust the peacock to be able to find hope in even this most dire of situations.

'We're still going to dance on the streets of a free Paris,' he said. 'And with our children Cab, Django, Count and Duke too,' he added with a grin.

'We're having four now?' I smiled back, willing my eyes not to betray me and fill with tears.

'Yes, that way we can have a family band. One on drums, one singer, one on bass and one on trumpet – and me on guitar.'

'You have it all figured out.'

'Yes, well, I've had a lot of thinking time this past month.' He leaned forward. 'I've thought of nothing but you, Fire.'

'I've thought of nothing but you too. And I always will. I'll even agree to our children being named after the jazz greats if it keeps you happy!'

'You will?' His face lit up.

'Yes, as long as you come back to me.'

'Of course I'll come back to you!'

Try as I might, I couldn't stop my eyes from filling with tears.

'It's going to be all right, Fire, I promise.'

Further along the platform, I heard a yell from one of the guards and saw them slamming the door shut on the first truck.

'I'm going to do everything I can to defeat those bastards and get them out of France,' I said quietly. Out of the corner of my eye, I saw the guards approaching. Oh, if only I could touch the peacock, hug him goodbye. 'I love you so much,' I cried instead.

He laughed, but I saw that his eyes were now shiny too. 'Meeting you has been the best thing that's ever happened to me.'

'Same. The best thing ever.'

The guards arrived at the truck and started yelling at us women to move back, their eyes cold and their faces stony.

'I love you, Peacock,' I said again.

'I love you, Fire.'

And in that moment, the love that passed between us felt like the strongest force on earth. I felt that the peacock and I could never, ever be defeated. But then the guards slammed the door shut and slid the bolt into place.

'Move! Move!' they bellowed, brandishing their rifles at us and the love I'd been feeling was replaced by an icy hate.

I hope you burn in hell for your cruelty, I wanted to yell, as all along the platform, the voices fell silent, and we women and children filed away, ashen-faced. Some of the children began to sob and call for their fathers and it was a sound that made me ache as I thought of Joseph and Lillie. I felt for the locket around my neck, trying to draw some strength from it, but it was impossible. I felt completely defeated.

We all congregated at the end of the platform and watched as one by one the doors were shut. Then the whistle blew, piercing the silence and piercing my heart as the train slowly began pulling out from the station.

41

AUGUST 1944, PARIS

The morning after the peacock was deported, I woke with a steely sense of determination. I wasn't going to sit around crying; I couldn't afford to – my very sanity depended upon me staying strong. I had to take action and do whatever I could to hasten the German defeat so that the prisoners could be saved.

I got out of bed and put on the radio, but there was no electricity again, so the room remained silent. Humming 'Minnie the Moocher' to try to lift my spirits, I had a quick wash with the cold water I'd stored in the basin and got dressed, choosing culottes, a short-sleeved blouse and flat shoes, my 'ready for anything' outfit. Perhaps once this was all over, I could ask my contacts at *Vogue* to commission me to do a Resistance-style photo shoot, I mused as I looked in the mirror. It was hard to imagine my former life as a fashion photographer now. It all seemed so frivolous.

I tucked the pistol Raymond had given me into the lining of my satchel and loaded my camera with a new roll of film.

'We're going to save you,' I said to my friends in their photographs on the mantelpiece. 'Please stay strong.'

My gaze fell upon the battered picture of Lillie. It had been almost two years since I'd taken it; the chances of her still being alive were slim at best if the rumours about the camps were true.

But they might not be true, I told myself, trying to remain hopeful. *And one day they might all be back in Paris.*

I decided to go and visit Andreas and tell him what had happened to the peacock. Now he and I really were in the same boat, and I knew we'd be able to offer each other some vital moral support as the tensions in Paris built.

As soon as I got outside, I saw new posters plastered all around. But for once they weren't Vichy or German propaganda; they were from the Resistance. *Avenge your martyred sons and brothers,* the poster read. *Avenge the heroes who have fallen for the independence and freedom of the fatherland. Your action will hasten the end of the war. Have as your slogan:* 'Everyone get a Hun!'

In the distance, I could hear the crackle of gunfire from the battle raging to the west of the city. It was louder than ever, which meant the Allies were closer than ever. My skin erupted in goosebumps as I thought of taking up arms to avenge all those who had been captured or killed. I still found it so hard to imagine fighting on the streets of Paris, but I knew without a shadow of a doubt that I'd be there the second Raymond asked for me.

I made my way down the hill with a spring in my step. My action would hasten the end of the war and freedom for the peacock and everyone else whose liberty had been stolen by the Nazis.

By the time I reached the Jardin du Luxembourg, my spirits soared even higher as I saw Germans removing their anti-aircraft artillery from the roofs of the surrounding buildings.

'The vermin are fleeing,' an older man said to me as we both stopped to watch.

'What a sight to behold!' I exclaimed before taking a couple of pictures of the guns being lowered onto the street.

Down by the river, I was greeted with a truly bizarre scene. German troops were wandering around looking shell-shocked and dishevelled, while just behind them a group of girls bathed in the Seine, giggling and splashing without a care in the world. More German trucks trundled past loaded with cases of food and wine and filing cabinets.

Oh, Peacock, please don't give up, I silently implored. *Freedom is so close, I can practically taste it!*

As I cut down a side street, I heard a cry of 'Champagne!' and saw a woman crouching by a crate that must have fallen off one of the trucks. As I approached, she looked up at me and grinned.

'Please tell me my hunger isn't causing me to hallucinate,' she said, pointing at the contents of the crate. It was full of bottles of champagne and whole rounds of cheese.

'Well, if you are, then I am too,' I gasped.

'Here,' she said, handing me one of the bottles and a cheese.

'Thank you.' I quickly stuffed them in my satchel and carried on my way. Now Andreas really would be pleased to see me!

When I got to his apartment, I knocked on the door and held the bottle and cheese aloft.

'Hello, Clarisse,' he said softly as he opened the door a crack. Then he opened it wider, and his eyes became big as saucers. 'Hello, cheese!' he exclaimed, his mouth gaping. His chin was covered in a grey sheen of stubble and his hair was lank and dark with grease at the roots.

'I'll try not to be offended that you seem happier to see a cheese than you do to see me,' I retorted as I stepped inside.

While Andreas busied himself getting plates and glasses, I told him what had happened to the peacock. He was as supportive and understanding as I'd predicted.

'We have to keep the faith that they'll come back to us,' he said, glancing at the portrait of Natalia on the wall. 'We owe it to them to not give up.'

'Absolutely,' I agreed. 'I'm so glad we met – although I'd much rather it be under different circumstances,' I quickly added. 'Your strength and faith are an inspiration to me.'

'And your courage is an inspiration to me,' he replied with a sad smile.

We feasted on champagne and cheese and he played me his new composition, 'The Storm', inspired by the occupation, which moved me to tears. Everything felt so fragile in that moment, and so heightened. The fear of imminent loss mixed with the jubilation of imminent victory, magnified by the effects of the champagne, made for a potent cocktail.

As the evening drew in, I felt no desire to return to my apartment. The truth was, I was a little afraid to be on my own, worried that my fears about the peacock might creep back and overwhelm me. Andreas must have been feeling the same as he told me I was welcome to stay the night in his spare room.

As darkness fell over the city, I noticed a stream of lights snaking through the streets below. After years of nightly black-outs, it was a surreal sight.

'What do you think it is?' I asked as we watched from the window.

'More Germans leaving,' Andreas replied. 'I suppose they see no point in the blackout anymore.'

As he spoke, the light on the ceiling suddenly came on and the radio crackled into life, filling the room with the sound of static and interference.

'My God!' I exclaimed, jumping in shock.

Andreas laughed. 'The power's come back on.' He looked at the radio and frowned. 'That's funny. I had it tuned to Radio Paris before – not for pleasure, you understand, just to find out what the enemy were saying.' He fiddled with the dial but still got nothing but static and interference.

'Do you think...' I didn't dare finish the sentence in case I was wrong.

'That they've stopped broadcasting?' he said.

I nodded.

'It certainly sounds like it.'

'Oh, happy day!' I exclaimed. For so long, Radio Paris had polluted the airwaves with German propaganda and hate, the thought that it might be gone for good was truly wonderful and another indication that our longed-for freedom was just around the corner.

Andreas tuned the radio to the BBC, where the Free French spokesman André Gillois was urging the people of Paris to use strikes as a weapon of war. The rail and postal workers were already on strike; could a general strike be next? The feeling of living in some kind of end times intensified.

Before I went to sleep that night, I got down on my knees at the end of the spare bed and I properly prayed for the first time since I was a kid. 'Please, please, keep him alive,' I whispered over and over into the darkness. 'Please let us dance together on the streets of a free Paris.'

The following morning, I set off early, eager to return home in case Raymond had left a message for me. More new posters had been put up in the night, urging Parisians to chop down trees to make barricades to block the main roads. Nervous excitement coursed through me. The battle for Paris was inching ever closer.

I arrived back at my apartment to find a note pushed under the door with the words *Wishing well* written on it. It was the code for one of the safe houses I'd used as a drop-off for my photographs. I quickly hurried back out again. There was no sign of any German soldiers on the streets. There appeared to be no sign of any food either; every grocery store I passed had its shutters down.

When I got to the safe house, I saw a sight that made me almost cry out for joy. The German street sign on the corner had been taken down!

Oh Peacock, I wish you could see this, I thought to myself.

I climbed the stairs to the apartment with a new zest and knocked on the door in the designated code.

One of the peacock's Resistance friends who I'd met in the Capoulade opened the door.

'I'm so sorry,' he said as soon as he saw me. Clearly Raymond had told him about the peacock's deportation.

'Thank you, but I'm sure it will be all right,' I replied, determined to remain optimistic. 'We're so close to achieving freedom in Paris, surely it won't be long before the prisoners are freed too.'

A look of confusion flickered across his face as I stepped past him and went into the living room. Raymond was pacing up and down as he talked to another man who was standing by the fireplace. The man looked thin and worn and his clothes were dirty. A stale smell hung in the air.

'Clarisse,' Raymond said with a soft smile. 'Thank you for coming.'

He never normally thanked me for coming. He never normally gave me such a welcoming smile either.

It must be because the peacock's been deported, I reasoned. *Because he knows I'm worried.*

'I'm afraid I have some news,' he said, coming over to me.

Afraid? Why did he say 'afraid'? Part of me wanted to turn on my heel and hotfoot it out of there. I didn't want to hear whatever he was afraid to tell me. I couldn't. I had to stay strong. I had to stay positive.

He cleared his throat and looked down at his scuffed boots.

'The train your peacock was on was forced to stop before Nanteuil-Saâcy station due to an Allied bombing raid.'

The hairs on the back of my neck stood on end. 'Was the train bombed?'

'No, they bombed the bridge over the Marne, which meant that the train couldn't go any further.'

'Oh, thank God!' I allowed myself to exhale.

'The prisoners were made to march to meet a new train at Nanteuil-Saâcy,' Raymond continued.

Was this why he'd said he was afraid? Was his news that the peacock had almost been saved by the Allies but not quite?

The other man, who was still standing by the fireplace, shifted awkwardly from one foot to the other. Why did they all look so grim-faced?

'He and another Resistance member tried to escape,' Raymond continued.

'Tried?' My throat tightened and I felt sick.

'Yes. But only Luc here made it to safety.' He gestured to the man by the fireplace.

I stared at him. 'You were with him, on that train?'

He nodded.

'So what happened to the peacock? Was he recaptured?' I said, my voice barely more than a squeak.

Raymond shook his head, looking more serious than ever. 'I'm afraid he was shot.'

The room seemed to tilt slightly and I reached out to grip the back of an armchair. 'But not killed,' I said, my voice shrill. 'Please tell me he wasn't killed!'

He placed his hand on my shoulder. It felt heavy as lead. 'I'm so sorry.'

'No!' I bent over double, hugging my arms to my waist. 'But we're so close. The Germans are leaving. Paris is going to be free within days.'

'It's terrible timing,' Raymond said. 'But if he'd stayed on that train, he would have faced certain death.'

'How can you be sure?' I looked up at him through tear-filled eyes.

'All of our intelligence is telling us that they're death camps, especially for Resistance fighters. He would have been executed one way or another and he knew that.'

'He just wanted to get back to you,' Luc said, his voice cracking. 'The whole time we were on that train he talked about you and how much he loved you.'

'Don't say it!' I cried. 'I can't bear it!'

I felt Raymond's arm around me, gently guiding me into an armchair.

'Get her a drink,' he said to someone and the next thing I knew a tin cup was being thrust into my hands. 'He died a hero, a true patriot of France,' Raymond said, crouching in front of me.

But all I could think was that he died to be with me – *because* of me. I took a sip of my drink. And another and another.

Raymond was talking about what an invaluable contribution the peacock had made to the Resistance and how his death would be avenged through our victory over the Germans, but I couldn't get over the sheer cruelty of this turn of events. The fact that the peacock should survive so much only to be murdered at the very last minute was unbearable. We'd had so much to look forward to. A life to share together. A family to build. The agony was crippling as I realised that it wasn't just the peacock's life the Germans had taken – they'd stolen the lives of our future children too.

'The insurrection begins tomorrow,' Raymond said. He placed his hands on my arms. 'Did you hear what I said?'

'The insurrection,' I repeated numbly.

'Yes, beginning with the takeover of the Prefecture de Police.'

'The Prefecture is being taken over?' The thought of the police headquarters falling to the Resistance jolted me from my shock and I blinked away my tears.

'Yes, and it will be your chance to avenge his murder.'

What's the point? I felt like yelling. *What good is a free Paris if I don't have the peacock to enjoy it with?* But then I thought of Joseph and Natalia and Lillie. What if, by some miracle, one or all of them were still alive? I owed it to them to see this thing through to the end, to do everything I could to help beat the Germans.

'I'm in,' I said tersely and as Raymond patted me on the back, it dawned on me that this terrible twist of fate might actually make me an invaluable member of the Resistance. For without the peacock, I no longer cared if I died, and surely this would make me the most fearless of fighters.

42

JUNE 1985, PARIS

As I sat in the plane, waiting to take off from Charles de Gaulle Airport, I couldn't help noting the marked difference between how I was feeling about my maiden flight and how Madeleine Bernier had felt. In her book, she'd described 'fireworks of delight exploding inside of her' as she waited for take-off, whereas I felt more like a damp squib, paralysed by my fear. As the air became fogged with the cigarette smoke drifting through from the back of the cabin, I couldn't help wishing I was a smoker. I was willing to try just about anything at that point to help ease my nerves. My anxiety certainly wasn't helped any by the glamourous air hostess at the front of the plane waxing lyrical about what to do in the event of a catastrophe.

You've been through far worse than this, my inner voice reminded me, and I instantly thought of Auschwitz and the *Blockalteste* in our hut brandishing her whip.

It had been almost two months since I'd gone to the travel agency to book my trip. I'd had to wait six weeks for my passport to be issued – and in that time I'd experienced a powerful shift in the way I viewed the world, and indeed myself. It was as if my younger self, who had felt like a separate entity the day she had first reappeared on the steps at Sacré-Coeur, had been absorbed back into me. It was a slightly surreal but not unpleasant feeling becoming reacquainted with her grit and positivity, although she seemed to have abandoned me without trace as soon as I boarded the aircraft.

As the pilot instructed the air hostesses to prepare for take-off, I gripped the arms of my seat so tightly my knuckles went white. *You can do this*, I told myself. *You've got to do this*. As my thoughts flitted back to Clarisse Alarie, I smiled at the fact that Paris's airport had been named after Charles de Gaulle, the wartime leader of the Free France movement. I thought back to the exhibition of Alarie's photographs, which I'd returned to many times over the past few weeks, and the pictures she'd taken towards the end of the war. There was one in particular that had moved me so much I'd bought a postcard of it, which I'd kept inside my bag ever since.

The plane picked up speed and the engine started to roar. If Clarisse was brave enough to do what she did, I could definitely find the courage to make this flight, I told myself as I looked out of the window at the landscape racing by. I didn't just owe it to myself, I owed it to Clarisse.

The nose of the plane began tilting upwards and my heart raced. *Please don't let us die. Please don't let us die. Please don't let us die*, I chanted over and over in my head. The land disappeared and we rose higher and higher through a bank of thick cloud, magically defying gravity. Then, suddenly, the clouds were below us, a fantastical, cotton-like landscape, and the sky above was sunny and blue.

I leaned back in my seat and took a breath. I'd done it! I'd made my very first flight – or first take-off at least. I was on my way to America, to pay tribute to the woman who'd done so much to try to help me without me ever knowing.

43

AUGUST 1944, PARIS

I spent the rest of the day at the safe house. I guess Raymond realised that it wouldn't be wise for me to be on my own, so he insisted I stay the night too. Once the initial horror faded enough for me to regain the power of speech, I felt the overwhelming need to interrogate Luc about the peacock and their escape bid.

'Please, can you tell me what happened? How he died?' I asked as we sat hunched in a pair of fraying armchairs in front of the fireplace.

'Are you sure?' he said softly.

'Yes. I want – I *need* to know.' I clasped my hands tightly in my lap as I waited for his response.

For a moment, the only sound was the ticking of the clock on the mantel and the low hum of Raymond and the other Resistance man talking in the kitchen. Then Luc cleared his throat.

'After the line was bombed, the Germans ordered us off the train, to march us to the next station.'

I nodded.

'We were being marched through a village when some of

the prisoners spotted a water fountain and broke free to try to quench their thirst.'

'Is that what you and the peacock – Louis – did?'

He shook his head. 'No, we stayed in the march. But when the soldiers guarding us ran after the others to the water fountain, we saw our chance to escape. We ran back to a farmyard we'd recently passed. Louis thought we'd be able to hide there.'

I let out a sigh. Damn the peacock and his endless optimism.

'He ran into a barn, but I thought it might be safer to separate, so I hid in some haystacks on the back of a truck instead.' Luc glanced at me anxiously, clearly hesitant to continue.

'Go on.'

'After about ten minutes or so, the soldiers arrived and they headed straight to the barn.' His voice wavered and he wiped his eyes. 'He... he died a hero.'

'Of course he did; he was trying to escape the Germans.'

'Yes, but he did more than that. When they brought him out of the barn, they were demanding to know where I was and he refused to tell them, even when they put a gun to his head.'

'You saw what happened?'

'Yes, through a crack in the back of the truck. He knew I was in there, but he didn't let on. He told them I'd carried on running.'

My heart burst with pride as I thought of the peacock, so brave and selfless to the very end.

'And then what happened?' I whispered, hardly bearing to ask.

'Then they shot him.' Luc leaned forward in his chair, head bowed. 'I'm so sorry.'

'It's not your fault!' I exclaimed.

'I wish I could have done something.' He began to cry, his thin shoulders quivering. 'I wish I could have stopped them.'

'They would have killed you too if you'd tried anything.' I

went and crouched in front of him and placed my hands on his knees. 'I'm glad you survived. I'm glad you're alive.'

He looked at me and wiped his eyes. I wasn't sure I'd ever seen a face so full of anguish. 'Really?'

'Of course. Please, I don't want you to feel guilty.'

He let out another sob. 'He was right about you – you're a very special person.' And then we were both crying.

'So, how did you escape?' I asked once I was able to compose myself and returned to my chair.

'I stayed in the truck until they'd gone. Thankfully, they must have believed Louis as they didn't look anywhere else in the farm for me.'

'Did they... did they take him with them?'

'Yes.' Luc grimaced. 'They probably wanted to show the others what would happen to them if they tried to escape.'

'And you're sure he was dead?' I asked, grasping for any final straw of hope.

'Absolutely certain,' he replied grimly.

I decided against asking him why he was certain. Those were details I didn't want or need to know.

I didn't sleep a wink that night on my makeshift bed on the sofa. I couldn't stop going over and over what had happened. I'd been so hopeful that the peacock would return to me. Knowing that he wouldn't was utterly devastating. Once again, I was reminded of my father's death. After losing Frankie, I thought I'd figured out a way to survive in a world where tragedy could strike at any minute. As my new French persona, Clarisse Alarie, I'd created a barrier to hide behind and I'd been able to keep that vulnerable part of me protected. Damn the peacock and the way he'd disarmed me with his zest for life and his relentless optimism. Damn him for loving me into lowering my guard. Damn him for dying. Damn him for leaving me.

'Why did you have to try to escape?' I sobbed over and over into my pillow. 'Why did they have to kill you?'

It felt as if morning would never arrive and I'd be trapped forever in the darkest depths of night, but finally the first of the stark dawn light began edging its way beneath the blind. I dragged myself off the sofa and joined the men in the kitchen. Like some kind of magician, Raymond produced a tin of corned beef and a stick of bread and divided it between the four of us, along with a pot of watery tea. Then he gave us all some ammunition. I put mine beside the pistol in the pocket of my culottes for easy access. There was no need to hide our weapons now. According to Raymond, the order had gone out for Resistance members across the capital to gather on Île Saint-Louis to await further instruction. The battle for Paris was about to begin.

I can't remember a thing about our walk there, I was still so numb from shock and sorrow. We arrived to find people wearing FFI armbands swarming around like bees in a hive, abuzz with excitement.

'The Prefecture has been occupied already!' a man told us. 'We need to get there right away.'

'Already?' Raymond said, clearly surprised.

'Yes, our Resistance comrades in the police took possession of the building at dawn.'

As if on cue, the rattle of gunfire echoed through the air.

'This is it!' Raymond exclaimed. 'The insurrection has begun!'

I nodded and forced a smile, but inside I felt strangely disconnected.

Hordes of us streamed down the road and I could hear 'La Marseillaise' being sung.

'Look!' someone cried, pointing to the Ministry of Education. The Tricolore had been raised over the building. It was a sight that should have filled me with joy, but all I could think was that the peacock would never get to see it. We'd never get to dance on these streets once they were free again.

When we reached the Prefecture, we were divided into small groups and given instructions. The German troops remaining in the city were bound to not accept the fall of the police headquarters without a fight and would undoubtedly launch some kind of counterattack. We needed to make sure they didn't succeed in retaking the building. Raymond, Luc and I were positioned behind the winged dragon sculptures in front of the Fontaine Saint-Michel, with the order to fire on any German soldier who might appear.

As I crouched behind the stone plinth, pistol in hand, I felt a steely determination take hold of me. I itched for the opportunity to avenge the peacock's death. And, with any luck, the Germans would kill me too and my nightmare would be over. I simply couldn't imagine a life beyond the war without the peacock in it.

All remained eerily quiet at first, but then a German armoured car appeared around the corner, accompanied by lorries full of German troops. As the car opened fire on the Prefecture, a volley of shots rang out from the Resistance fighters stationed behind the parapets on the Quai Saint-Michel. The battle for Paris really had begun.

Another German car appeared, slowly purring towards us. I placed my pistol in the gap between the top of the plinth and the bottom of the dragon's belly. It was utterly surreal to think that when I'd first come to Paris I'd stopped by this fountain several times, gazing in awe at the statue of the Archangel Michael wrestling with the devil. If someone had told me then that one day I'd be crouching beneath Michael about to open fire on some German soldiers, I would have thought them insane.

As the car drew closer, I resisted the rage-fuelled desire to fire a volley of shots. It wasn't just my life at risk after all. I needed to make sure that I didn't miss. My lessons from the firing range with Frankie came flooding back to me. I straightened my arms and gazed along the barrel of the gun, waiting for the car to daw level, then I unleashed a shot, straight through the driver's side window. The car instantly veered off course and Raymond and Luc peppered it with shots.

'Good work,' Raymond whispered across to me as the car crashed into a wall and came to a halt.

I waited with bated breath, but no one emerged.

I expected to feel some kind of satisfaction at having avenged the peacock, but, if anything, I only felt more disconnected.

All day long, the Resistance defended the Prefecture. At one point, a German tank arrived, positioning itself in front of Notre-Dame and firing straight at the entrance to the police headquarters. We watched, frozen, to see if the tank would storm the building, but after what felt like forever, it trundled off. In the early evening, a convoy of German lorries approached and the Resistance opened fire, causing one of the vehicles to crash into the Hotel Notre Dame and burst into flames. The other lorries soon retreated. I saw a few injured Resistance fighters being carried off on makeshift stretchers, but the occupation of the Prefecture held and by the end of the day, we received word that the Resistance now controlled over half of the eighty Parisian neighbourhoods.

Once again, the weather perfectly mirrored the events unfolding on the ground and the humidity of the day erupted into a violent thunderstorm.

'Would you like to come back to the safe house with us?' Raymond asked as we prepared to leave for the night.

I shook my head. 'I need to go back to my place.'

'Are you sure you'll be OK?' He looked at me, concerned.

'Absolutely,' I replied firmly. I was overwhelmed by the need to be alone.

As I made my way back to Montmartre, lightning crackled and thunder roared. It was so loud, it felt as if the sky itself was going to break in two. Unable to take another step due to the sorrow now consuming me, I sat at the bottom of the steps leading to Sacré-Coeur and allowed my tears to come, mingling with the rain upon my face. Then, seemingly out of nowhere, a German soldier appeared, weaving his way along the street towards me. He'd probably been drinking in one of the local clubs or musical halls the soldiers so liked to frequent.

Well, they won't be able to use the city as their playground for much longer, I thought to myself bitterly. Then I realised that it was way past the curfew. Surely, he would have more important things to do than bother a woman sitting alone on the steps in the rain, but then I thought about what the Germans had done to the peacock. And the way they'd rounded up innocent children like Joseph in their desperate desire to meet their depraved quotas. These people would be relentlessly cruel until the very end, so the soldier would have no compunction in arresting me.

I glanced left and right. It was as if the storm had washed the streets clean and there wasn't a soul to be seen. It was just the soldier and me. And my pistol. I slipped my hand inside my pocket, wrapped my fingers around the grip. The soldier wove his way closer, wiping the rain from his face. Finally, he noticed me and came to a halt. He looked to be in his early thirties. His uniform jacket was buttoned up incorrectly and his hat was slightly skew-whiff. The Germans were usually so immaculately presented, it was strange to see one of them in such a state of disarray. It struck me as being kind of symbolic, given what was happening in the city.

He said something to me in German which I didn't understand. I stood up, placing my forefinger on the trigger of the pistol in my pocket.

'Are you all right?' he asked in French. His tone was soft, concerned almost, which caught me a little off guard.

'I'm fine,' I replied curtly.

'You shouldn't be out here on your own,' he said, stepping closer. His eyes were bloodshot and his chin was covered in a sandy stubble.

'I'm fine,' I said again, my heart thudding. There was still no one to be seen. I could shoot him right there and probably escape back to my apartment without being caught. I could take his life as needlessly as they'd taken the peacock's. Perhaps then I'd feel some kind of justice.

'Would you like it if... Shall I walk you home?' he said in broken French.

Why was he offering to walk me home rather than arrest me? This was not at all what I'd expected. A terrible thought occurred to me. Was he hoping to have one last liaison with a French woman? A final fling before fleeing the country. And if I said no, would he force himself upon me? An image of Pierre came back to haunt me. His huge body looming down upon me in the hallway, his fat fingers around my throat.

'No! I would not like you to walk me home,' I snapped, taking the gun from my pocket and aiming it at his chest.

The solider gasped and took a step back. 'What? No!' he cried. I thought he might have reached for the gun on his belt, but he raised his arms in surrender instead. '*Bitte!* Please!'

I stared at him, the rain obscuring my vision. Why was he begging with me? For the entire occupation, I'd never seen a German solider behave like this. They'd always lorded their power over us, enjoying every bit of it. It was very disconcerting.

He's probably trying to trick you, my inner voice warned, *lull you into lowering your guard. Don't fall for it!*

'Please,' he said again, bowing his head. 'I'm sorry.' He

murmured the words so softly, I barely heard them over the rain. 'I don't want to be here,' he continued, looking back at me. There was a loud crack in the sky above and a sheet of lightning illuminated the street. 'I don't want to be in your country.'

But you are, I wanted to reply. *And you've decimated it.*

However, I felt my gun arm begin to waver and brought my other hand up to steady it. 'Why are you here then?' I asked. The rain grew heavier, streaming down my face.

'I had no choice,' he yelled above it. 'I had no choice.' And then, much to my bewilderment, he began to cry.

There was something about this sight and his vulnerability that instantly lanced the bitterness that had been growing, tumour-like, inside of me. I knew in that moment that I was physically incapable of killing him, but if I lowered my weapon, surely he'd revert to type and arrest me, or worse. The truth was, I was so tired, I no longer cared.

I put the pistol back in my pocket and the soldier let out a gasp of relief. I waited for him to draw his own gun, but then I heard the hiss of tyres approaching on the wet street.

The soldier grabbed my arm and I waited for him to take my gun from me. But he pulled me across the street and into a shop doorway.

'What are you doing?' I yelled.

'Shhh!' he replied, putting his finger to his lips.

The sound of the car grew louder and the soldier and I stared at each other. He looked nervous, which didn't make sense. Unless of course he thought the car belonged to the Resistance. I felt a glimmer of hope. But then the car drew level and I saw that dreaded red flag bearing a swastika on the end of the bonnet. I waited for it to drive by, my pulse racing, but to my horror, the car came to a halt right beside us. I looked back at the soldier, expecting him to frogmarch me out onto the street. But he put his arms around me instead and hugged me close. I stood, frozen rigid in his embrace, as the car door opened and someone stepped out.

I heard a man call something in German and the soldier replied over my shoulder. There was a beat of silence that seemed to drag on forever, and then the other man laughed. I heard him get back into the car and shut the door. Was he going? I hardly dared believe it could be so. But, sure enough, the engine rumbled back into life and the car drove off along the road.

As soon as it had gone, the soldier released me from his embrace.

'You need to go. Home, yes?' he said in broken French.

I nodded.

He looked both ways up the street. 'It is OK.'

I nodded again, too shocked to speak.

As I stepped out into the rain, he took hold of my arm.

'I'm sorry,' he whispered before letting me go and hurrying off in the opposite direction.

All the way back to my apartment, his words rang in my ears. *I'm sorry. I'm sorry. I'm sorry.* As soon as I got inside, I slid down the wall and onto the floor and began to wail.

44

I spent the next couple of days in bed, where I stayed buried beneath the covers until I finally, mercifully, got some sleep. I re-emerged to find new posters plastered everywhere, this time urging Parisians to build barricades and attack German soldiers and seize their weapons. All of my desire to kill as a way of avenging the peacock's death had gone. My interaction with the German soldier had shifted something in me and I returned to my trusty friend, the camera, to try to make sense of things.

As I roamed the streets, there were signs of the previous days' fighting everywhere. Buildings pockmarked by bullet holes, the ground stained with blood and covered with broken glass, makeshift barricades erected at junctions. I took pictures of people building them from everything they could get their hands on – trees, furniture, paving stones, scrap metal. The atmosphere was akin to a street party as neighbours came together to help.

But then, as I ventured into Pigalle, I heard a commotion. A small crowd had gathered outside an apartment building, shouting and jeering.

'Shave it off!' I heard a woman cry and I instantly had a flashback to the day the peacock was attacked by the fascists.

I slowly made my way towards the crowd and saw, to my surprise, that the object of their taunts was a woman. She was dressed in a beautiful summer dress and smart shoes and her auburn hair was styled into neat rolls. Two men were holding her arms and about ten women had congregated behind them. They didn't show any signs of belonging to the Milice, so I ventured closer.

'What's going on?' I asked a woman at the back of the group.

'She's my neighbour and a collaborator *horizontale*,' the woman hissed. 'She's been having an affair with a German soldier all through the occupation.' She turned back to the woman. 'Where's your soldier lover now, eh? Fleeing like a coward.'

'Shave her head,' someone else called.

I moved closer and looked at the woman. Her face was full and round and her skin glowed with health. There were no signs of the malnutrition that had plagued the rest of us for so long.

'Please!' she begged. 'Please, not my hair.'

I thought of how the peacock had been scalped on the steps of Sacré-Coeur and I had to fight the urge to retch. I couldn't stand here and watch them do the same to this woman, no matter what she'd done and who she'd slept with. It felt wrong to be a part of this baying mob.

One of the men produced a razor and while the other man held the woman's arms, he began hacking at her hair.

What is happening to you? I wanted to cry. *Don't become monsters too.*

'No, please,' the woman begged, but to no avail. Her thick auburn locks began littering the pavement.

Another woman came forward holding a kohl eyeliner. 'We

need to brand her so that everyone can see she's a traitor,' she said, before drawing a swastika on the woman's forehead.

The other women laughed and I saw with dazzling clarity how hatred is like the very worst infectious disease. For there to be any hope for the world, we had to live like the peacock had and remain loving – even in the worst of circumstances.

The photographer in me took over and I took my camera from my bag and quickly captured a shot of the mob surrounding the crying woman. The glee on their faces a stark contrast to the pain on hers. *This is what happens if you let hate win*, I imagined telling people as I showed them the photograph as some kind of cautionary tale. *We all become monsters.*

After countless and increasingly feverish rumours sweeping through the city streets, the Allies finally arrived in Paris two days later. I, along with hundreds of others, had gone to the Hôtel de Ville, which, like the Prefecture, had been taken over by the Resistance. As darkness was starting to fall, a cheer rang out in the distance and we heard the rumble of engines. Unable to quite believe that the rumours could finally be true, I prepared myself for the sight of German tanks and lorries.

'They're here!' the cry reverberated, again and again, as the vehicles slowly made their way towards us. As I caught my first glimpse of them, my eyes filled with tears. A motorcycle leading a procession of tanks, all covered in French flags! Some of the women in the crowd clambered onto the tanks, raising their arms in delight. I started to sob and I couldn't stop, it was such a bittersweet moment.

As some of the tanks stationed themselves in front of the building, I wished with all my might that the peacock could have seen this sight too. I managed to compose myself enough to take a few pictures before setting off back to Montmartre. The church bells that had been silent for so long began to peal, causing more cheers of excitement to erupt.

'They're here! They're here!' people sang.

All I could think was that the peacock wasn't here, and he'd never be here again.

But Lillie and Joseph and Natalia might return, I reminded myself, feeling for the locket around my neck. I still might one day get the opportunity to return the necklace to Lillie, even if the chance was paper slim.

As I reached the bottom of the steps leading to Sacré-Coeur, I saw that the basilica had been lit up for the first time in years and was glowing white against the night sky. I thought back to the day on those same steps when the peacock and his band had tried to bring joy back to the city. I thought of the little girl I'd photographed so happy in that moment. Then I thought of all the other pictures I'd taken over the previous two years. Hundreds of prints and negatives hidden beneath the floorboards in my bathroom. And I thought of how the peacock had urged me to take them so that one day people would learn exactly what had happened in Paris during the occupation. I might have lost the peacock physically, but I knew for certain that he'd always be with me in spirit, guiding me.

Take pictures that will say more than a thousand words, I imagined him whispering in my ear. I'd taken those pictures; now, finally, I might be free to share them.

That's the spirit, Fire, I heard him encourage as I started making my way up the steps, the bells of Paris urging me on.

45

JUNE 1985, NEW YORK

As the plane touched down in New York, I was reminded of the line from *The Wizard of Oz* when a stunned Dorothy says to Toto, 'I've a feeling we're not in Kansas anymore.' The differences between America and France were immediately apparent. The airport trucks were squarer, with bonnets like snub noses, and the men working on the ground looked like characters from a Hollywood movie with their baseball caps and muscular physiques. It was clearly a lot hotter in New York too. The heat coming from the tarmac was causing the air to bend and swirl.

I'd been so concerned with the plane making it across the Atlantic in one piece, I hadn't given much thought to what would happen once we landed. As I undid my seat belt, anxiety began to bubble away inside of me.

It's OK, you have a hotel booked for the night, I reassured myself. *All you have to do is find a taxi and it'll take you there. And if you can't find a taxi at an airport, there truly is no hope for you!*

The plane came to a standstill and the pilot thanked us all for flying with Air France. I took a quick look at my postcard for luck, before tucking it back in my bag, and we began filing off. There weren't many other passengers travelling on their own, and those who were looked like seasoned solo travellers – brief-case-holding businessmen who strode with great purpose towards airport security.

As we all got in line to have our passports checked, I experienced a flashback so unpleasant, I broke out in a cold sweat. I was back at the internment camp in Drancy being made to queue for the transports that would take us to Auschwitz. The horror of the memory and the humidity in the airport made me feel dizzy.

You're not in Drancy, you're in America, I reminded myself. *You're a free citizen, you're allowed to move freely.*

I fumbled with the zip on my bag as I took another quick look at the postcard. *Remember why you're doing this,* I reminded myself, *take inspiration from Clarisse and her bravery.*

Finally, I reached the front of the queue. I handed my passport over to the burly, shaven-headed guard and hoped he didn't notice how my hands were trembling.

'Welcome to the USA,' he boomed. 'Is this your first visit?'

Thankfully I was able to understand him as I'd taken English lessons in my thirties so I could read the original editions of my favourite UK and US authors.

'Er, yes.'

'You here on vacation?' He looked up from my passport and gave me a piercing stare. Images of Nazi guards began flickering in my mind, like an old Pathé newsreel, staring at me and screaming obscenities.

'Y-yes,' I stammered, although I wasn't entirely sure that my reason for coming to America could be described as a holiday. There was no way I'd be able to explain the real purpose of my visit though, so I forced a tense smile.

'Awesome.' He stamped my passport and handed it back. 'You have a nice day.'

'Thank you – thank you very much.'

I was so relieved to have made it through that I felt almost drunk as I waited for my luggage to arrive. Luckily, my suitcase survived the journey and I had no issues locating the taxis either as they were so well sign-posted. As I got into the back of one of those famous yellow cabs, I felt as if I was stepping into my very own Hollywood movie and had to pinch myself to make sure I wasn't dreaming.

My Hispanic driver wasn't the talkative type – apart from when he was yelling expletives at other drivers, which only seemed to add to the experience, and I was grateful for the opportunity to sit back in my seat and drink in the view. As we drew closer to the heart of the city, my pulse quickened. The sight of the skyscrapers was truly breathtaking.

The travel agency had booked me into a hotel close to Broadway, which was a thrill in itself, even though I wouldn't have time to take in a show. As I gazed out of the window at the flashing neon signs and the sparkling lights and the swarms of people on the pavements, tears filled my eyes. For so long, I'd truly believed that I'd be safer and happier never leaving France. And now here I was, in my fifties, acutely aware of all that I'd missed.

The driver pulled up outside a grand-looking hotel.

'Here you go, lady,' he said.

I looked at the meter and fumbled in my wallet for the correct amount of dollars plus a generous tip.

I stepped out into the heat and took a look around. I was in New York, birthplace of Clarisse Alarie, who, it had turned out, hadn't been French at all. And hopefully tomorrow I'd be able to bring some closure to the chain of events that had begun that awful day I was rounded up and my mother was killed.

46

SEPTEMBER 1945, PARIS

Every day for months after the war in Europe ended, I returned to the side street in Montparnasse where it all began – for me at least – with the photograph of Lillie and her mother's locket. Auschwitz and the other death camps had been liberated earlier in the year and the surviving prisoners had been returning to Paris. The first time I saw some of them arriving by train into Gare d'Orsay, my breath caught in my throat. It was one thing to hear the rumours of what had happened in the camps but quite another to see the results, as the skeletal figures proceeded, clearly dazed, along the platform, many still in their raggedy striped uniforms.

Ever since the liberation of Paris the previous August, I'd held on to the hope that at least one of the people in the photographs I prayed to and for every day would make it back alive. But a year after the liberation Raymond informed me that all the children taken from the safe house in Izieu had perished in Auschwitz. The thought of Joseph's life being snuffed out so cruelly and needlessly utterly devastated me.

'I should have kept him with me,' I wept into Raymond's chest as he held me tight. 'He might have survived.'

'You did what you thought was best for him,' Raymond replied. 'And it worked. You got him to safety. It's not your fault someone told the Gestapo about the safe house.'

But there was no consoling me and I felt my future closing in like a dark tunnel with no light at the end.

Natalia had never returned either, which could only mean that she too had been murdered in the gas chambers or on the death marches the prisoners had been sent on. Lillie was my one remaining hope and every night when my heart broke for Joseph, Natalia and the peacock, I consoled myself with the dream that she'd one day return to Paris and I'd be able to reunite her with her mother's locket. It was almost as if it had become an obsession, as I made those daily pilgrimages. But each time I found the house empty, the windows still darkened by blackout blinds.

But then, one day in September, I arrived to find a van parked outside and a pile of furniture on the pavement. A man in overalls was sitting on one of the dining-room chairs, smoking a cigarette.

'Excuse me,' I called, hurrying over. 'Do you know the family who used to live here, during the war?'

To my disappointment, he shook his head. 'No, sorry, I'm just here to clear it out.'

'You're clearing it? But why?'

'It's another one where they won't be coming back,' he said. 'Jewish,' he added in a hushed tone, as if this explained everything, and sadly it did. To have been Jewish during the war meant there was every likelihood you would have disappeared, just like Joseph and Natalia and so many countless others. But, please, not Lillie too.

'So... so none of the family survived?' I stammered, my mouth suddenly dry.

'I guess not.'

A desperate rage began to consume me and I had to fight

the urge to take it out on him. He wasn't responsible for the fate of people like Lillie and her mother; he was simply being paid to complete the final stage of their disappearance, removing all trace of them from their former home.

'I'd better get on,' he said, standing up and flicking the end of his cigarette into the gutter.

'Yes. Me too.'

I stumbled down the road in a haze of grief so powerful I could barely breathe. They were all dead. All the people I'd prayed so hard for and tried to save. I was overcome by a crippling sense of futility.

I reached the end of the road and the grey stone wall of Montparnasse Cemetery came into view. I'd heard on the grapevine a while ago that Pierre had relocated to Italy, so at least there was no danger of running into him. Like so many other traitorous collaborators, he'd fled Paris the second it was liberated, afraid of being on the receiving end of some rough justice now that the tables were turned.

I made my way along to the cemetery entrance and gazed at the rows and rows of graves. It was hard to imagine that when I used to come to the cemetery before the war, it made me grateful to be alive. Now all I wanted to do was join the dead – after all, that was where everyone I loved was, everyone who'd given me a sense of purpose. I thought of the peacock and Joseph and Lillie and Natalia and I knelt on the grassy verge beside one of the graves, clasping the locket. For so long I'd seen it as a lucky talisman that would one day bring me back to Lillie. I'd clung to that hope in order to stay strong, but now there was no need for hope or strength. There was no need for anything. It was time for me to give up and let go and to join them.

47

JUNE 1985, AMERICA

I woke after my first night in New York fully understanding why it was known as the city that never sleeps. Despite being seven hours ahead of the local time, it had taken me till about three in the morning to drop off, when the constant soundtrack of revellers and traffic and sirens had finally dimmed to an acceptable level, only to be rudely awoken an hour later by the clatter and rumble of the refuse trucks doing their rounds. Not that I minded. I was so full of nervous energy at the mission I was about to embark upon, I didn't really feel tired at all.

After a refreshing shower in my en-suite bathroom, I dressed and went down to the hotel restaurant for breakfast. Any nervousness I was feeling was soon soothed by the smiling waitress named Sherry-Lynne who greeted me. She took me to a table by the window and instantly provided me with a large white mug of coffee from the pot she was carrying.

'Just let me know when you need a refill,' she said.

The mug she'd given me was about four times the size of the tiny coffee cups we had in France, but after a sleepless night, I guessed I'd be in need of more caffeine than usual. Without any need for deliberation, I ordered pancakes, bacon and syrup, revelling in the opportunity to experience an authentic American breakfast. When the pancakes arrived, I did a double take. They were stacked so high, I thought maybe there'd been a mistake. But no, it seemed that in America everything was bigger, not just the buildings. I still couldn't bear the thought of letting any food go to waste after years of near starvation, so I kept going until I'd devoured every single morsel of the sweet, fluffy pancakes.

After another mug of coffee, I went back upstairs to pack and then down to the lobby, where I checked out and ordered a taxi to the station. I couldn't help feeling a burst of pride as I got into the taxi. At this rate, I was going to be a seasoned traveller like Madeleine Bernier in no time. But, of course, the real challenge was yet to come. This next leg of my adventure hadn't been expertly planned and booked by a travel agent, and I had no way of knowing how it might turn out. It was a thought that filled me with excitement and fear in equal measure.

48

After my harrowing experience on the train journey to Auschwitz, it had taken a very long time for me to feel comfortable travelling by rail again. Just the sound of the rattle on the tracks and the sway of the carriage would trigger any number of traumatic memories – being crammed so tightly against complete strangers, the fear that we'd run out of air to breathe, grown adults sobbing and wailing. But travelling by train in America turned out to be a delightful experience. The seats were bigger and the carriages more spacious than in France, and as for the conductor, well, he should have been on the stage, he was so theatrical. Every time we approached a new station, he announced it with all the flamboyance of a circus ringmaster welcoming a tantalising new act. It was hugely entertaining and really helped to ease my nerves. Until, of course, he announced my destination.

'And next up, ladies and gentlemen, we will be arriving in Serendipity, New York!' he cried, his rich drawl emphasising every last syllable.

As I opened the train door and lifted my case down onto the platform, my heart began to race. I'd managed to find a description of Serendipity in a book on New York in the library, which had informed me that it was a charming small town in the Catskill Mountains with a population of four and a half thousand, but other than that, I had no idea what to expect. I hoped it lived up to its whimsical name.

I made my way along the platform and into the station house, which was miniscule compared to Grand Central Station where I'd boarded. I quickly checked the timetable on the wall to see when the last train back to the city left. I was hoping to find a room for the night, but as there was no guarantee I would, I needed to keep my bases covered.

'Can I help you, ma'am?'

I turned to see a smiling middle-aged man in a navy-blue uniform and peaked cap. The badge on his chest informed me that he was the station manager and named Bert. His sunny demeanour couldn't have been more different to that of the menacing guards who'd manned the stations in Paris during the war.

'Oh, yes please,' I replied. 'Could you tell me if there's a hotel in town? I'm hoping to stay the night.'

'Of course. There's the Woodstock Inn and Pine Lodge. And Nelly's guesthouse – although I'm not sure she's taking guests right now due to her varicose veins,' he muttered. 'Let me write them down for you.'

He disappeared into the ticket office and reappeared a couple of minutes later holding a piece of paper.

'Here you go. Both the hotels are on Main Street so you shouldn't have any problem finding them. Just take a left out of the station and follow the road down the hill until you reach the end where it joins Main Street. It's about a five-minute walk.'

I took the paper from him and tucked it into my pocket. 'Thank you so much.'

'You're welcome. Have a great day!'

I left the station with a spring in my step. The people were so friendly here. It certainly helped ease my anxiety.

Thankfully, even though it was just as sunny here, it was a lot cooler than in the city, and the fresh air was perfumed with the sweet scent from the pine trees lining the street. Every so often, I caught a glimpse of the craggy grey mountains on the horizon, surrounding the town like a protective granite bowl. High above me, eagles circled in the bright blue sky, drifting lazily on the breeze. It was the complete opposite of New York City with its bustling streets and looming skyscrapers and never-ending soundtrack of sirens. All I could hear in Serendipity was the rustle of the breeze through the trees and the sweet sound of birdsong.

I thought back to the little bird that had landed on my lap a couple of months ago on the steps at Sacré-Coeur. It was incredible to think that she'd sparked a chain of events that had led to me flying all the way across the Atlantic. It was incredible to think that after so many years of living my life in such a rigid routine, I was now meandering through the Catskill Mountains without even having a place to stay!

I followed the road round a bend and saw a sign for Main Street. A pick-up truck drove by, carrying with it the strains of a rock song. I turned onto Main Street to be greeted by the most delightful sight. Wooden-fronted stores painted in bright shades of blue, yellow, red and green lined either side. It was reminiscent of the streets you'd see in a Western movie, only more colourful.

A man in denim overalls and a plaid shirt walked past, greeting me with a cheery 'Hey!' which helped ease my racing pulse a little.

I'd only walked a few yards when I came across the Woodstock Inn. It was a charming Victorian-style house, complete with a wrap-around porch. *FREE SPIRITS WELCOME*

HERE! a cheery, hand-painted sign by the door proclaimed, instantly making me smile.

I went up the steps and opened the door, causing a bell above to jangle. I walked into a cool, dark hallway. The wooden floor gleamed and a grandfather clock ticked loudly in the corner.

A woman with long auburn hair hurried out from a room behind the reception desk.

'Well, hello!' she said warmly. 'How can I help you?'

'I was looking for a room for the night,' I said, praying my luck would be in.

'You haven't booked?'

I shook my head, still unable to believe that I'd become the kind of person who didn't rigorously plan every detail of my life.

She opened a huge leather-bound ledger. 'That's OK, I think we still have a couple of rooms free.' She looked up and smiled. 'Is it just for one night?'

'I think so.'

'No worries. If you need to stay longer, you can just let me know. I'm Carrie by the way.'

'Thank you. I'm Lillie.' I smiled at her gratefully.

After she wrote down my details and I made the payment, she took a couple of keys from a row of hooks on the wall behind the desk. 'I'm going to put you in the yellow room. Come.'

I followed her up the wide wooden staircase to the third floor. The yellow room certainly lived up to its name. Everything in there, from the bedspread to the rug on the floor and the frilly curtains, was bright as sunshine.

'This is perfect,' I said. And it was. It felt somehow symbolic of this new chapter in my life I was embarking upon.

'Great, well I'll let you get settled in and if you have any questions just come find me downstairs.' She turned to go.

'Actually, I do have a question you might be able to help me with.' My heart began to thud.

'Yes?' She looked back at me from the doorway.

'Do you know of a woman named Clarisse Alarie? She was a photographer in France during the Second World War.'

She frowned. 'I'm sorry, history isn't my strongest suit. You might want to ask in the library. They might have a book about her?'

'No, I'm not looking for a book about her.'

'Oh.' She looked at me questioningly.

'I'm looking for *her*. I understand that she lives here now, in Serendipity.'

49

'Clarisse, you say?' Carrie looked thoughtful for a moment.

'Yes.'

'I'm sorry, it's not ringing any bells. And I'm sure I'd remember if I had come across her. It's a real pretty name.'

I smiled, trying to mask my disappointment. 'Not to worry.'

'You should still try the library, though. And Rainbow Street Cafe. It's the most popular place to eat in town, so if she is here, I'm sure those guys would know her.'

'Thank you, that's really helpful.'

Carrie went back downstairs and I put my suitcase next to the bed, trying to ignore the gnawing doubt I now felt. Serendipity wasn't that small a town. I couldn't expect everyone to know everyone, but still... I couldn't help feeling a little dejected. What if I'd come all this way for nothing?

When the museum attendant had told me that Clarisse had suffered a breakdown after the war, it had really tugged on my heartstrings. Once I knew the truth about her, I couldn't bear the thought of her suffering. I'd instinctively come up with the hare-brained scheme of travelling to America to try to find her in the hope that she might gain some kind of comfort from seeing me again after all these years, just as I'd gained comfort from learning her story.

'Apparently she lives as a recluse,' the museum attendant had told me in dramatically hushed tones, 'with only her cats for company.' She knew that Clarisse lived in Serendipity because the Centre Pompidou had tracked her down to ask her permission to put on an exhibition of her work. I'd taken the fact that Clarisse had agreed for her work to be shown as an encouraging sign, but now I was here the potential flaws in my plan were beginning to appear. Clarisse had clearly been living as a recluse for a reason. Maybe she didn't want to be reminded of such a painful time in her life. What if I did find her and my appearance triggered some kind of traumatic relapse?

But the thought of being able to thank her for what she'd done still outweighed my fears. And I'd felt so much better since discovering the truth about her. Hopefully, she'd feel the same, learning the truth about me.

A wave of tiredness rolled through me, but however tempting the bed with its bank of fluffy pillows looked, I had to press on with my mission – first stop, Rainbow Street Cafe. Hopefully they'd be serving the same bottomless mugs of coffee as my hotel had at breakfast and I'd be able to recharge and find out about Clarisse too.

After a quick freshen-up in the primrose-yellow bathroom, I set off for the cafe, which according to Carrie was on a side road at the other end of Main Street. I walked past a store selling fudge in just about every flavour and another selling a wide range of outdoor gear, from hiking boots to fishing tackle. The window of a vintage clothes store also caught my eye. The mannequins on display were wearing brightly coloured Sixties-style attire and shaped into comical poses. Perhaps on my way back from the cafe, I'd pop in and buy myself something. One thing that hadn't changed these past few weeks was my sensible attire and my wardrobe was still in desperate need of brightening up.

It turned out that Rainbow Street Cafe was impossible to miss due to its brightly coloured awning. As I walked in, all of the customers sitting at the bar on the right-hand side of the narrow room turned to look at me, or at least it felt as if they did, and instantly my face flushed.

It's OK, you can do this, I told myself. *You're a global traveller now, the type who doesn't even make reservations!*

'Hey!' a waitress called, hurrying over. She was young, early twenties, I'd say, with frothy blonde hair and a beaming smile. Her lips shimmered with pale pink lip-gloss. 'How can I help you today?'

'I was hoping to get something to eat,' I replied, trying my hardest to appear like a nonchalant woman of the world.

'Sure thing.' She whipped a laminated menu from a stack on the bar and beckoned at me to follow her to an area at the back. 'Is this OK?' she asked, pointing to a table in the far corner.

'It's perfect,' I replied.

'Cool!' She waited for me to sit down, then filled my glass from a jug of iced water. 'Where are you from?' she asked. 'I can't place your accent.'

'France. Paris, to be precise.'

'Oh my!' She clapped her hands to her heart. 'I'd so love to go to Paris! It looks so romantic.'

I stifled a laugh. If only she knew what a romance-free zone my life in Paris had been. 'It is a very beautiful city,' I replied, and as I uttered the words, I realised that I no longer thought them to be a lie. Learning about Clarisse and her work for the Resistance had made me see that the streets of Paris had their share of beautiful as well as shameful secrets. And perhaps this was true of every place.

'What brings you to Serendipity?' the waitress asked, laying out some cutlery.

'I'm looking for someone who lives here – or at least I think they do. A woman named Clarisse Alarie.' I looked up at her hopefully, but she frowned and shook her head.

'I've never heard of her, but I'm fairly new to town. I'll go ask the owner, Joe, while you decide what you'd like to eat.' She handed me the menu and disappeared off through a door at the back.

I stared at the menu with unseeing eyes. All I could think was that I might be about to discover where Clarisse was. And if I did, then what?

The waitress reappeared with a man wearing a tie-dyed T-shirt, faded jeans and sandals. 'This is Joe,' she said as they reached my table.

'Welcome to Rainbow Street,' he said with a smile. 'I understand you're trying to find someone?'

'Yes. A woman by the name of Clarisse Alarie.'

To my disappointment, he shook his head. 'I'm sorry, I haven't heard of anyone with that name. Are you sure she lives in Serendipity?'

'Yes, that's what I was told. I was told that she keeps to herself, so maybe she doesn't come into town often.' I couldn't help feeling I was clutching at straws.

'Hmm.' He scratched his head. 'She might live in the forest. There's a few folks living in cabins out there. Hippies mainly, from the 1960s.'

'OK, I'll try there,' I replied, although the thought of wandering aimlessly through a forest felt daunting, to say the least, even for my new intrepid explorer persona.

'Good luck,' he said, 'and nice meeting you.'

'Thank you, and you.'

I looked back at my menu and ordered the first thing I saw – a cheese and ham omelette.

The food was delicious, but as soon as I'd finished, I was hit with a wave of exhaustion, which in turn affected me mentally. What had I been thinking, coming halfway round the world on a wild goose chase? If Clarisse didn't want to be found, she'd probably lied to the Centre Pompidou about where she lived. For all I knew she could be living in Sydney, Australia.

I paid the waitress and set off back along Main Street with a heavy heart.

Don't give up now, I heard my younger self urge me from somewhere deep inside. *Not now you've come so far.*

And I had come a long way, emotionally as well as physically. My spirits lifted a little. I needed to get a good night's sleep and then in the morning I'd book another night in the hotel and head off for the forest to see if I could find Clarisse there. I couldn't leave until I'd exhausted every option.

As I drew level with the vintage clothes store, I noticed a turquoise scarf covered in little silver songbirds draped around a mannequin's neck. It was a beautiful reminder of how this crazy adventure had all begun, and it would help brighten up my wardrobe, so I decided to buy it. As I stepped inside the dimly lit store, it took a moment for my eyes to adjust after the bright sunshine outside. Every nook and cranny was crammed with rails of vintage clothes and shelves of vintage hats. A 1970s disco number was crackling away on what sounded like a record player and the air smelled of patchouli incense. I went over to the counter, where a woman with short, dyed blue hair was sitting, head bowed, writing something in a notebook.

'Hello, I was wondering if I could buy the scarf in the window,' I said. 'The one with the silver birds.'

'Of course!' she said, looking up and I was surprised to see she was older than I'd assumed, around seventy at a guess. I wondered if I'd ever have the courage to dye my hair blue at that age. Probably not. Buying a turquoise scarf was about as avant-garde as I'd get. The woman put her notebook down and came out from behind the counter. 'It's a beautiful scarf. I'm so pleased it's found a home.'

'Well, I'm very happy to provide it with a home,' I replied. 'I'm trying to brighten up my wardrobe, so I thought it would make a good start.'

I watched as the woman went over to the window and took the scarf from the mannequin. She was wearing a long, sky-blue kaftan that perfectly matched her hair. It dawned on me that she might be one of the old hippies who lived in the forest that the cafe owner had talked about.

'Where is your accent from?' she asked as she returned to the counter.

'France,' I replied, smiling.

'I thought so.' She took a carrier bag from beneath the counter and folded the scarf and put it inside. Then she grabbed a jar of tiny gold heart-shaped confetti from a shelf behind her and sprinkled a handful inside the bag. 'I like to add fun little extras,' she said with a sheepish grin. 'I hope you don't mind.'

'Of course not.' I looked at the store logo printed on the side of the bag. It was the outline of a peacock with the words LOUIS & LILLIE'S emblazoned across the top of its open feathers.

'Oh, how funny,' I said, pointing at the logo. 'My name's Lillie.'

'It is?' She smiled. 'Well, then clearly you and that scarf were meant to be.'

'Absolutely.' I laughed.

'So, what brings you to the Catskills?' she asked, picking up the jar of hearts.

'I'm trying to find someone.'

'Oh really? Who?'

'Someone named Clarisse. Clarisse Alarie.' I looked at her,

prepared for her to frown and shake her head like everyone else had done, but instead there was an almighty crash as she dropped the jar and tiny gold hearts cascaded all over the counter.

'No!' she gasped, staring at me as if she'd seen a ghost.

50

'Are you all right?' I asked as the woman leaned on the counter to steady herself.

'Are you... are you Lillie Kramer?' she whispered.

Now I was gaping in shock too. 'How do you know my name? Are you... are you Clarisse?'

'No,' she replied, and I instantly felt awash with disappointment and confusion. 'But I was.'

'I don't understand.'

She came out from behind the counter and took hold of my arms. Her grip was surprisingly strong. 'Lillie Kramer?' she asked again.

'Yes.'

'I thought you were dead,' she cried. 'He told me you were dead.'

'Who did?'

'The man who was clearing out your house. I went there after the war, to see if you'd returned, and he told me your family had all died.' She let go of my arms and clapped her hands to her chest.

My mind raced as it tried to catch up with these latest

developments. The woman *was* Clarisse and she'd continued trying to find me even after the war. 'I went to live in Lyon with my great-aunt after I came back from Auschwitz,' I replied. 'My parents had both been killed.'

'I'm sorry,' she said softly, then shook her head, clearly still deeply shocked. 'How did you know about me, though? And how did you know where to find me?'

'I saw the photograph you took – the photograph of me – in the exhibition at the Centre Pompidou in Paris. One of the attendants there told me that you lived in Serendipity.'

'My God!' She clapped her hand to her mouth.

'What did you mean, you *used* to be Clarisse?'

'Clarisse was the new identity I gave myself when I moved to Paris before the war. Afterwards, I couldn't bear to be reminded of that life, so I changed back to my birth name when I returned to America – Nancy Esposito.' She patted my arm, gently this time, as if making sure I was real and not some kind of apparition. 'You're Lillie,' she said. 'You're alive!'

'And... and you're not living in the forest as a recluse,' I stammered.

'No, I live in the apartment upstairs.' She frowned. 'Why did you think I lived as a recluse?'

'Oh, something the attendant at the Centre Pompidou said,' I muttered. 'I read about how the photograph you took of me inspired you to join the Resistance,' I added to change the subject.

'Oh, it did more than that.' She smiled. 'So much more.' She hurried back behind the counter and pulled out a purse. 'You have been my inspiration to keep going for over forty years.' She opened the purse and took out a photograph and passed it to me. It was faded and the edges were frayed and worn, but I saw straight away that it was the picture of me. 'Even after the war, when I thought you were dead, I kept it with me.'

I gave a little laugh of disbelief and opened my own purse.

'This is the strangest thing.' I took out the postcard I'd bought at the Centre Pompidou. It was a self-portrait of Alarie that she'd taken just before she was about go and join the fight to liberate Paris. She was staring grim-faced into the camera, holding a revolver to her chest. Her hair was cropped short and she looked exhausted, yet there was a steely determination in her gaze. I knew from the exhibition that when she took the picture she'd just learned that her lover had been murdered by the Nazis. 'I bought this at the exhibition of your work and I've kept it with me ever since, to inspire me to be courageous – like you.'

'No!' she cried as she looked at the postcard. 'This is... this is unbelievable.'

'I know.' I almost laughed.

'That was such a terrible time for me,' she said, nodding to the postcard. 'I'd just learned that my beloved peacock had been killed.'

'Peacock?'

'Yes, that's what I called him; his real name was Louis.'

My gaze instantly went to the logo on the bag. 'Louis and Lillie's,' I said softly.

'Yes.' She gestured around the shop. 'I dedicated this place to both your memories. But you're not dead!' she exclaimed. 'You're alive!'

'I am.' I laughed. 'At least I hope I am. I'm starting to think I might be hallucinating.'

'You and me both.' Then she let out a gasp. 'Oh my goodness, I have something for you.' She came out from behind the counter and gripped my arms again. 'Don't go anywhere!' she ordered. 'I'll be right back.'

'Don't worry, I won't!'

She disappeared off through a curtained doorway and I heard her footsteps going up some stairs. I looked back at the old photograph of myself, at one of the very worst moments of my life frozen forever. But now that image had come to symbolise something different, something so much better.

I was jolted from my thoughts by the sound of the shop door opening and turned to see an elderly man walk in. His cropped hair was white as snow against his tanned skin and although he looked to be about eighty, his shoulders were broad and he walked tall.

'*Bonsoir!*' he called as soon as he saw me.

'*Bonsoir!*' I replied automatically, before remembering that I wasn't in Paris anymore. 'Wait a minute, are you French?' I asked in French.

'*Mais oui,*' he replied with a beaming grin. 'And I take it you must be too?'

'I am!'

But before we could say any more, Nancy reappeared, clutching something in her hand. As soon as she saw the man, her face lit up.

'You will never guess who this is,' she said to him, pointing at me.

'Well, I know she's from France,' he replied in English with a slight American accent.

'It's Lillie!' she cried. 'She's alive!'

'Lillie. What, *the* Lillie?' His smile faded and he stared at me.

'Yes! She saw the exhibition of my photographs at the Pompidou in Paris and she tracked me down.'

'I told you you had to do that exhibition!' he exclaimed.

'Yeah, yeah, you were right, as always,' she laughed, then she came over to me. 'I have this for you. I found it on the ground that day – after they took you and your mother away.'

She opened her hand and I saw a silver oval locket on a chain that instantly triggered a cascade of memories.

'Oh my!' I gasped.

'I think it belonged to your mother.'

'It did. Oh my God. Can I?' I reached for the necklace.

'Of course. It belongs to you.'

I picked up the locket and undid the clasp. And there, inside, just as I remembered them, were the pictures of me and of my parents on their wedding day. It was the first time I'd seen this photograph of them in all these years. The emotion I felt was overwhelming and I burst into tears.

'It's OK,' Nancy said softly, putting her arms around me.

'I never thought I'd see it again,' I sobbed into her shoulder. 'I never thought I'd have anything from that time, anything of my mother's.'

'I'm so sorry,' she said, holding me tightly.

'So many things were stolen during that time,' the man said softly.

'Yes.' I pulled away and wiped my tears, looking at Nancy. 'Thank you. Thank you so much for keeping it all this time. I can't tell you how grateful I am. This is the best gift I think I've ever been given.'

'I tried to get it to you a couple of days after the round-up, in the Vel d'Hiv,' she said sadly, 'but it was impossible to find you in there. There were so many people. And then I went to Drancy to try to find you, but I almost got arrested.'

'You did?' I stared at her, stunned that she'd risked so much to try and find me.

She looked at me and shook her head. 'I still can't believe you're here. That I found you at last. Or, rather, you found me.'

'It's incredible,' the man said, his voice cracking with emotion.

'Oh, I'm sorry, where are my manners.' Nancy took hold of the man's arm. 'This is my husband, Raymond. He was in the French Resistance too. He ran the network I was a part of.'

'Wow.' I looked at him through teary eyes. Another person who had risked everything to try to help people like me.

Another reason to have faith in humanity. 'I'd love to hear more about that.'

He nodded and smiled. 'I'm sure you will.'

'Raymond saved my sanity after the war,' Nancy said. 'When I felt like I had nothing, or no one left to live for.' She leaned her head on his shoulder.

'Yes, well, someone had to talk some sense into you,' he said gruffly.

'He told me in no uncertain terms that I owed it to you and the peacock and others that I'd lost to keep going.'

'And aren't you glad you listened to me now?' Raymond said with a chuckle.

'Yes, honey! It annoys the hell out of me sometimes, but you do have a tendency to be right about almost everything.' She looked at me and laughed. 'I have so many questions, but how about, are you hungry? We could go to our son Joseph's place, Rainbow Street Cafe, and get some dinner.'

'I was just looking for you in there!' I exclaimed. 'And I met your son, but he said he didn't know a Clarisse Alarie.'

Nancy nodded. 'No one here knows the name I used back then. I had to let that part of my life go in order to be able to carry on.' She smiled at Raymond. 'When we got married and moved here we vowed we'd put all of the pain behind us and start again.'

'Best decision we ever made,' Raymond said, planting a kiss on top of her head.

The love between them was palpable and it warmed my heart. 'When did you move here?' I asked.

'1946,' Nancy replied. 'I opened the store and Raymond started a landscaping business, and then we had Joseph and Natalia – our daughter.' She smiled at me and I saw that her eyes were shiny with tears. 'There was a time, after the war, when I really didn't want to live anymore. I honestly couldn't see a future worth having after losing so much.' A tear rolled down her cheek.

'I understand,' I said quietly.

'Of course you do.' She took my hand and clasped it tightly. 'But I've learned that if you can just find the grit to hold on and wait, life might just gift you with a future so incredible it makes you believe in magic and wonder again.'

My eyes filled with tears but I didn't do anything to fight them. They felt cleansing, as if they were washing away a grimy film of pain, so that I too might see a future filled with magic and wonder and possibility.

'I'm so happy you're here. I'm so happy you're alive,' she said, wiping her eyes.

'So am I,' I replied. '*So* happy.'

'I think a celebration is in order,' Raymond said with a beaming smile.

'Yes!' Nancy exclaimed. She looked at me hopefully. 'Shall we go get some dinner?'

'I'd love that,' I replied, not caring one bit that I'd just eaten a huge omelette.

Nancy put the cash from the till into the safe and then the three of us headed out the door. As I stepped into the golden light of the setting sun, I felt overwhelmed with gratitude that my life should have taken such a delightful and unexpected twist.

'How long are you staying for?' Nancy asked, linking her arm through mine. 'Please don't say you're leaving tomorrow. I need to know everything about you. *Everything*,' she repeated dramatically.

'No, I most definitely won't be leaving tomorrow.' I laughed, feeling high on joy and new-found possibilities. 'I can stay for as long as I want.'

A LETTER FROM SIOBHAN

Dear reader,

Thank you so much for choosing to read *The Secret Photograph*, I hope you enjoyed it. If you want to be kept up to date with all my latest releases, just sign up at the following link. Your email address will never be shared and you can unsubscribe at any time.

www.bookouture.com/siobhan-curham

The inspiration for this book began when I came across the story of Lee Miller, an American woman who'd been a fashion photographer before the war. Miller came to Paris as soon as it was liberated and became one of just a handful of female photojournalists to cover the aftermath of the war, travelling with Allied troops to document the German defeat and the liberation of the concentration camps. I was intrigued by what it must have been like to be a photographer at that time, especially as a woman, and the toll it must have taken to document the horrors of war at such close quarters. I wanted my novel to be set during the German occupation of France and about a member of the French Resistance in Paris, which got me thinking – what if my main character was a fashion photographer in Paris who ended up using her talents to help the Resistance?

As I like my historical novels to be rooted in fact, I needed to know if any such woman had existed, and after some extensive digging, I discovered the story of Julia Pirotte, a young

Polish woman who fled to France in 1940 and settled in Marseille, where she was hired as a photojournalist for several local publications. Pirotte joined the Resistance early on and photographed the Jewish women and children interned in the Bompard camp, as well as the operations of the Maquis in the area. In August 1944, she took part in the liberation of Marseille and documented the event with her camera. And so the idea for Clarisse Alarie was born – a photographer in Paris who joins the Resistance.

Although *The Secret Photograph* is a work of fiction, most of the events that Clarisse documents on her camera really did happen. The velodrome round-up, the internment camp at Drancy, the Jewish families torn apart in the street and even, tragically, the incident at the orphanage where the child is thrown from the window. The safe house that Joseph was sent to in Izieu also existed and the forty-four children and seven staff were rounded up on the order of Klaus Barbie and sent to Auschwitz, where all the children were killed. I also used real-life accounts of the liberation of Paris for the scenes at the end of the novel, such as the takeover and defence of the Prefecture.

Another thing I wanted to explore in this novel is the ethical dilemma facing photographers when trying to document the horrors of war. On the one hand, the world needs to know about atrocities when they take place, but what must it feel like for the victims to have their pictures taken in moments of such acute pain? It was fascinating to explore this through the characters of Clarisse and Lillie. And in a strange and sad case of life imitating art, while I was writing this novel, my son moved to Ukraine to work for an aid organisation, helping victims of the war there. The photographs he's sent me of the devastation caused by the invasion have shown me first-hand how powerful and moving such photography can be.

KEEP IN TOUCH WITH SIOBHAN

siobhancurham.com

 facebook.com/Siobhan-Curham-Author

twitter.com/SiobhanCurham

instagram.com/siobhancurhamauthor

ACKNOWLEDGMENTS

Thank you, thank you, thank you to Kelsie Marsden, my wonderful editor, for your expert insights and guidance. I'm so grateful to get to work on these books with you. And I'm so grateful to Richard King, Foreign Rights King, for making my wildest international writing dreams come true – thank you! And, as always, huge thanks to the whole team at Bookouture, Sarah Hardy, Kim Nash, Noelle Holten, Ruth Tross, Alex Crow, Alba Proko and Sinead O'Connor, to name but a few. Much love and thanks as always to Jane Willis at United Agents for all your support.

I'm also hugely indebted to all the people who take the time to review my historical novels on their blogs, Goodreads, NetGalley and Amazon. There are way too many of you to mention here, and I'd hate to accidentally miss someone out, but please know that I read and deeply appreciate every review, and all the work you do to support authors and the book industry.

I'm extremely grateful to the friends and family members who have been so supportive of my historical fiction. Special thanks to Michael Curham, Anne Cumming, Alice Curham, Bea Curham, Luke Curham, Katie Bird, Steve O'Toole, Lacey Jennen, Gina Ervin, Amy Fawcett, Rachel Kelley, Charles Delaney, Carolyn Miller, Thea Bennett, Linda Lloyd, Sara Starbuck, Pearl Bates, Marie Hermet, Gillian Holland, Caz McDonagh, Sass Pankhurst, Linda Newman, Lesley Strick, Diane Sack Pulsone, Jan Silverman, Patricia Jacobs, Mavis

Pachter, Mike Davidson, Liz Brooks, Fil Carson, Jackie Stanbridge, Pete Haynes and Abe Gibson.

And thank you to my lovely new writer friends, Ruth Mitchell and Wendy Taylor Carlisle, in Eureka Springs, Arkansas, where I was based when I began writing this novel. Your positive response to the first draft of the first chapter was so encouraging, thank you!

And last but by no means least, MASSIVE thanks to all the readers who've taken the time to send me such lovely messages about my World War Two novels. I really appreciate you taking the time to reach out to me.

Made in the USA
Las Vegas, NV
28 October 2023

79841392R00208